SEABREEZE

MICHAEL ENEARU

SeaBreeze marks the gripping beginning of a planned trilogy, setting the stage for an unforgettable journey.

First edition

ISBN: 978-1-3999-8394-5

To Paula, Will, and Stephen, for believing in me even
when I found it difficult to believe in myself.

CONTENTS

1. MEMORIES

'I don't understand, Mam,' said Amen, a worried expression forming on her face. 'Why do the other kids always stare?'

'Because you're weird,' Iska replied from her bed as she flipped through the pages of a textbook.

Aré lingered in the doorway. 'You're not weird, my baby.' She smiled sadly. 'And you need to learn to ignore the kids who stare at you; they lack manners.'

'I do ignore them,' said Amen. 'But there are others who call me names or say there's something wrong with my eyes.'

'Amen, haven't I told you there's nothing wrong with your eyes? Would you rather listen to other people than your own mother?'

Never. Amen would not dare dispute Aré's words. However, Aré couldn't deny it was strange for anyone to have ghost-white eyes. Yes, multiple optometrists in the country had confirmed Amen's vision as "normal" after conducting a series of tests to understand the unusual nature of her eyes. Nonetheless, the kids and teachers at school and just about anyone who interacted with her, made it clear it was far from normal.

'People will always react awkwardly to things they don't understand,' said Aré. 'It's best to pay them no attention.'

'But—'

'That's enough, Amen. You two need to get some sleep.'

'Mam, *I've* been ready for bed,' said Iska, dropping her textbook to the floor. 'But Amen keeps asking silly questions.'

Too exhausted to give a lecture on the benefits of sisterly affection, Aré kissed Amen and Iska goodnight and turned off their bedroom light.

Oh God, thought Iska, pointing at something perched

atop the window ledge just outside their room. *That annoying nightjar is back again.*

Amen, who heard her thoughts as clearly as if she'd spoken aloud, looked over at the nightjar. *I don't think he's annoying. I think he's cute.*

And how do you know it's a he? wondered Iska.

I don't know, it just feels like a boy.

Well, whatever it is, I wish it'd stop coming here. It creeps me out. Iska shivered in disgust. *Also, you really should stop asking Mam those questions.*

Why? Amen furrowed her eyebrows. *You're not the one who's made fun of or called different.*

Because you should know by now that she doesn't have the answers, Iska replied. *Plus, I get made fun of, too. Whatever names they call you affect me, too—we look exactly the same. If it bothers you so much, next time you get picked on, I'll protect you as the older twin.*

You wish *you were older,* thought Amen while Iska rolled her eyes. *I don't want you getting in trouble or hurt because of me.*

I won't get hurt. Iska waved her arms in the air. *I've been practising my tai chi.*

As if! Mam would kill us if we ever got into a fight—or if she finds out we're still up. Goodnight, Iska. I love you.

Come on, there's no way she can find out. Iska turned over in her bed. *You know she can't hear our thoughts.* But despite everything, she *was* still tired. She pulled her covers up tighter. *Goodnight, Amen. Love you, too.*

St. Margaret's Boys and Girls, located at the top of Church Street, was an old Catholic school established in 1877. Regrettably, its buildings had been destroyed during the Irish War of Independence and had only been rebuilt a few years after the end of the Second World War. Despite the countless times Amen and Iska had heard about the history of their secondary school, they neither liked it nor had any interest in sitting in its classrooms.

Today's classes were even more tedious than usual. The biology teacher droned on about various types of bacteria and their functions, but nobody bothered paying attention.

I really don't understand why we need this information, thought Amen, as she doodled on her notebook.

Neither do I, Iska replied. *I really can't wait for summer to be here.*

It's going to be so much fun at the shop. I want Mam to teach us how to do a catch stitch.

I know right, thought Iska. *And how to skim stones in Bray—*

'Anyone want to have a go at what the two main functions of the Escherichia coli bacteria are?' The teacher's question jerked everyone upright in their seats even though it was quite evident that no one knew the answer.

'Yes,' said Iska, drawing a few puzzled stares to her desk. 'The E. coli bacteria has the ability to digest undigested food in the human stomach and reverse the process of nitrification.'

'That—that's correct,' said the biology teacher, taken aback that Iska had somehow answered the question correctly.

Show off, thought Amen as she gazed at Iska from across the classroom. *How do you always know these things?*

No idea. The answers just seem to be right there in front of me.

To Amen and Iska, the only redeeming aspect of St. Margaret's was its backyard. Although it was old and slightly dilapidated due to a lack of recent renovations, this didn't bother the students much. They had access to an outdoor basketball court, a football pitch, and several wooden benches and tables for lunch. Just beyond the eating area lay a lush green field with half a dozen rows of hawthorn trees that served as Amen's sanctuary, providing her with an escape from the other kids during lunch breaks.

As usual, Amen was sitting under one of these trees, engrossed in her book when she was startled by the sound of rustling leaves.

'There she is, girls,' said a chubby girl with a mouth full of braces. 'What've you got there, freak eyes?'

'My name's Amen,' she grumbled, 'and it's a book.'

'She reads! Who knew?' said the girl, provoking snickers from her friends. 'Give it here, I'd like to see what it's about.'

Ignoring the girl, Amen returned the book to her satchel.

'Did you hear what I said, or are you deaf as well?'

'This is my personal copy,' Amen said coolly. 'I can give you the name of the book; I think there are copies in the library if you really want one so bad.'

'Being cheeky, aren't you?' The girl responded through clenched teeth. 'You either give me the book, or I beat it out of you.'

Amen, now on her feet, contemplated whether to hand over the book and avoid a fight or be brave and resist being bullied. She could take on the chubby girl by herself, but things might go badly if the girl's two friends decided to get involved.

Just as she was calculating how to escape this situation, Amen heard a voice that slowed the pounding in her chest.

'What's going on here?' said Iska, walking around the three girls to join Amen at her side.

'Oh, look, it's the freak's twin,' said one of the chubby girl's friends.

'Says the one with the lisp,' Iska shot back.

In the heat of the moment, all five girls didn't notice that the blue skies had turned dark grey and were letting out a drizzle.

Already upset, Amen decided she'd had enough of the goading from the girls. 'Come on, Iska,' she said. 'Let's get back to class. It's not worth it.'

Iska, still locked in a stare-down with all three girls, considered Amen's suggestion and concluded that it was indeed best to back down. But as they started to walk away from the confrontation, the chubby girl, perhaps feeling embarrassed at not getting the reaction she had hoped for, decided to taunt the twins one last time. 'Yeah, walk away—just like how your dad walked away from your whore of a mam.'

This certainly did the trick. Iska abruptly stopped in her tracks and spun around with a scream of rage. She flashed toward the girl. 'I'm going to kill you!'

But just as quickly as Iska reached the chubby girl, she found herself on the ground in a heap. In her fit of rage, Iska hadn't exactly planned out what she was going to do when she confronted the girl. Now, she was half-conscious and being pelted by heavy rain.

'Iska, are you okay?' said Amen, trying to stop the blood flowing from her sister's nose. She glared up at the chubby girl, who blinked as if confused. 'Are you crazy? Why did you hit her?'

'She came at me,' the chubby girl replied, equally surprised by her actions. 'What else was I supposed to do?'

Just as Iska was regaining her composure, a teacher wearing an oversized raincoat approached them. The chubby girl and her friends scrambled to retreat, but their escape was in vain.

'Susan, Maeve, Cara! You three, escort yourselves to your classrooms immediately!' Ms O'Sullivan shouted over the howling winds. 'What in God's name happened here?'

'It was those girls who started it,' Amen sobbed. 'I was minding my own business, reading my book, and they tried to bully me—Iska came to help me—and—'

'That's enough. We need to get inside and get your sister to the sickbay. There's a storm coming.'

The storm cleared just as quickly as it had arrived, leaving behind a silvery, overcast sky. It was now three-thirty in the afternoon, and the school bell had just rung to signal the end of the day. Yet instead of heading home, Amen, Iska, and the three girls from earlier found themselves in the principal's office. According to Ms O'Sullivan, if Iska hadn't retaliated to Maeve's provocation and "initiated a fight", she could have made a case for only Maeve and her cronies to face detention and a week of school community service. Unfortunately for Amen and Iska, the principal decided that all five girls would have to serve two Saturdays' worth of detention—a punishment the twins desperately tried to beg their way out of, fully aware of how Aré would react when she heard the news. But their pleas fell on deaf ears. Right before their eyes, the principal made a phone call to Aré and informed her of the incident.

Back in their classroom, Amen and Iska sat silently at their desks, eyes fixed on the second hand of the red clock behind Ms O'Sullivan as it ticked along. They hoped (and prayed) that the moment Aré would walk through the door would never come.

It's all my fault, thought Amen as she eyed the classroom doorknob, willing it not to turn. *I should have just given her the book.*

No, I messed up—ouch! Iska winced, gently touching the rolled-up tissue in her right nostril. *I should have kept walking with you. I let that donkey get to me, and now we've landed in trouble with Mam. I'm sorry.*

Don't be sorry. You were only looking out— Amen was mid-thought when the classroom door swung open and Aré's imposing six-foot frame bounded in.

'How could you?' she began, not even noticing Ms O'Sullivan standing behind her with an outstretched arm. 'I'm so disappointed in both of you. You promised! Look at you, Iska—you're all bloodied up. And you, Amen; I expected better. You're usually more level-headed.'

Just as the twins had anticipated, Aré was livid, scolding them so intensely that it took Ms O'Sullivan stepping in and reminding her to compose herself on school grounds to bring her back to calm.

As they exited the school, Iska and Amen silently counted their blessings that Ms O'Sullivan had reassured Aré the incident hadn't been entirely their fault. Neither had the courage to explain what had really happened, though they felt deeply sorry all the same. The walk home seemed to give Aré enough time to process Ms O'Sullivan's words; by the time they reached the house, she was in a noticeably better mood.

'Girls, go change out of your uniforms,' she called from the kitchen, her voice raspy but calm. 'Do your homework and shower when you're done. I'll make us some dinner.'

Iska and Amen nodded in agreement, careful not to say or do anything that might upset their mother again. They followed Aré's instructions like clockwork: changing out of their blood-stained uniforms, tackling their homework, mostly completed by Iska, and then washing each other's hair under the shower. Since the bathroom was located directly above the kitchen, Iska and Amen could hear Aré moving around with grace and efficiency, her cheery hum filling the house.

Among the many things that impressed the twins, their mother's exceptional sewing skills sat right at the top. Her culinary abilities were a close second—a talent that Aré herself said she had developed and perfected in Nigeria when she'd been around the same age that Amen and Iska were now. According to Aré, a few people had suggested that she open a restaurant when she moved to Ireland, but she'd declined. As she explained it, doing so would have stolen her passion for the craft.

Amen and Iska couldn't have been more thankful she'd made that decision because the aroma finding its way into the bathroom reminded them how hungry they were. They quickly showered, changed into their pyjamas, and hurried down to the kitchen.

'Mam,' said Iska, sniffing the air. 'What are we having for dinner?'

'Girls, please set up the table,' said Aré as she stirred a bowl of salad. 'We're having mixed-veg fried rice with salad, fried plantains, and chicken wings. The hot chocolate fudge is for dessert.'

Living in a two-bedroom house, their kitchen was not particularly fancy or spacious. In fact, it was so cramped in the corners that if any more than a few full-grown adults had tried to fit in, they would have been packed in so tight, like pieces of a Jenga tower. Nonetheless, this was Amen and Iska's home, and they loved everything about it, including the tiny kitchen and its minuscule dining table Aré had readied for their dinner.

'Iska,' said Amen, as she hurried through her meal. 'Can you pass me the bowl of salad, please?'

Aré frowned at her. 'Slow down, love. You don't want to choke or get the hiccups from eating too fast.'

'I know Mam, I'm just so hungry. We forgot to get lunch today after what—' Amen stopped herself mid-sentence, remembering how irritated Aré had been about the school incident.

But the expression on Aré's face showed anything but annoyance. 'Hey, I'm sorry,' she said, reaching out her hands to touch them, 'for my outburst earlier today, it's just... I was really worried, and I panicked. I'd be heartbroken if anything happened to either of you... Do you forgive Mummy for being an angry troll today?'

Iska and Amen chuckled, feeling both amused and relieved. 'We're really sorry,' they said in unison. 'We promise to stay out of trouble.'

'Thank you,' Aré replied, a reassuring smile growing on her face. 'So, what actually happened between you two and the girls?'

'Oh, nothing really.' Amen replied, feeling embarrassed.

'Oh, come on; I'm not angry anymore. You can tell me. You two always tell me everything.'

As tempting as it was to tell Aré what really happened, Amen was determined to stay tight-lipped. But Iska had other ideas. 'They tried to bully Amen,' she said. 'They wanted to take her book, nasty girls. But I joined her; we didn't even want trouble or anything; we were about to leave when Jabba the Hutt said something really rude—'

'Go on then, what did she say?' said Aré, her curiosity piqued.

Amen glanced at Iska, silently pleading with her not to say anything, but Iska's mind was already made up.

'She…she said you were a whore and that's why Dad left you.'

Kilcock was a small town with a population of about three thousand six hundred people. It was a tightly knit community where most residents knew each other. However, the downside of this closeness was that gossip spread easily, and for those who were not well-informed, creating rumours became a popular pastime. But for Iska and Amen, the talk of their father's disappearance was more than just a rumour. Ever since they'd first heard about it, he had failed to return home. In fact, throughout their entire lives, the twins had only lived with Aré; it wasn't until a parent-teacher meeting a few years ago that they realised most of their classmates had two parents.

'You're right, Iska,' said Aré, after what felt like eternity. 'That's rude and untrue, and I'll have to bring this up with your principal and those girls' parents.'

'But, Mam, what really happened?' said Iska, her face a mixture of curiosity and reflection. 'You never talk about him; did he really abandon us?'

'I know I don't talk much about your father,' said Aré, after another long pause. 'But for good reasons. I promise I'll tell both of you all about him when the time is right. But I want to make something crystal clear: don't believe anything anyone in this town or your school says about me or your father, ever.'

Amen and Iska nodded in agreement, but they couldn't hide their disappointment. For once, they had hoped to learn more than just the fact—thanks in no small part to eavesdropping on Aré's conversations through the years—that their father was Irish, and that his name was Patrick.

Following their familiar routine, the twins helped Aré with the dishes and cleaned up the kitchen before calling it a day. Despite its small size, Amen and Iska's room was always tidy, with each side of the room reflecting the personality of the twin who owned it. For as long as they could remember, Amen's bed had always been by the window, offering a view of the front yard, while Iska's bed was across the room by the wall—a setup she had never been particularly fond of.

Right before bed, Aré had a ritual of reciting a poem to Iska and Amen. Each night brought a different poem, some completely made up, while others the twins already knew from school. Though she hadn't told them about their father, Aré knew she couldn't escape to her room without treating Iska and Amen to clever wordplay.

'Mam, what will it be tonight?' said Amen expectantly.

'Believe it or not, I can't think—'

'Please Maaaam, pleeease!'

'All right, all right,' Aré conceded. 'But one really short poem, and that's it.'

Amen and Iska giggled in excitement as they huddled around Aré, who wrapped her arms around them and began:

Some may come and some may go,
do not fret and do not feel low.
For what is important is right here, you see,
I'll give you a hint, it is neither riches nor fame, it's family.
You may travel far and wide and still feel alone;
ultimately, what brings us happiness is a sound mind, a just
heart, and a loving home.

Aré said her goodnight to Amen and Iska and turned off the lights, plunging them into a silent darkness that was only made more ghostly by the wind whipping against the trees outside. In her bed, Iska was smoothing the bridge of her nose when Amen whispered into her head.

Guess what.

What? Iska replied, still feeling her nose for a broken bone.

Our friend is here. Amen tapped her finger gently against

the window.

That bloody bird again, what does it want? thought Iska. *We need to trap it and find it a new nest or something.*

First of all, that's a stupid idea—Amen was saying before something caught and held her attention. *Hey, can birds have the same type of eyes as humans?*

What do you mean? Iska was sitting upright in her bed now.

I swear, this bird has green eyes, just like—the bird was gone before Amen could finish her sentence.

Thankfully for Iska, that was the last she and Amen saw of the bird in the weeks that led up to their summer holidays. By now, the bullying incident was a distant memory; the only thing that mattered was what sort of activities they could squeeze into two months away from school. Top of the list was learning to stitch clothes, and for the twins to achieve this, they had to accompany Aré to the tailoring shop where she worked.

Despite its small size, *Aunt Pamela and Dutters Tailoring* had a striking presence with its beautifully designed glass walls. Inside the shop, six white eclipse sewing tables were arranged in pairs on either side of the main room. Aré occupied the innermost sewing table on the left, positioned next to mannequins and dummies dressed in elegant suits and lace gowns.

'All right, girls, come here,' said Aré, as she prepared a table with fabric pieces, threads, needles, a pincushion, and two pairs of scissors. 'Today, you're going to learn to catch stitch.'

Iska and Amen stood by the table, feeling a mix of excitement and nervousness for their first stitching lesson.

'First, I want you to thread the needle double and knot it at the end,' Aré continued. 'Then, I need you to push the needle into the fold of the hem, so that the knot is enclosed and not visible... Next, take a small stitch from the right to left. Remember, the smaller the stitches, the more invisible your inside hem will be.'

'That's good,' said Aré encouragingly, pleased Iska and Amen were following her instructions. 'And then—'

'You come give me a big hug.' A voice from behind startled them.

'Aunt Nikki!' The twins screamed as they ran into the lady's outstretched arms.

'You two have gotten so big,' said Aunt Nikki, her icy blue eyes flicking between Iska and Amen, taking them in. 'Not much longer and I won't be able to pick you up like this—Iska, your finger is bleeding!'

'Oh, it's fine, Aunt Nikki,' said Iska, sucking on her bleeding finger. 'I pricked it when you startled us; we didn't see you come in.'

'How could you?' Aunt Nikki said with a laugh. 'You were all so engrossed in your sewing, you didn't notice me walk in.'

'But the bell—'

'Nice to see you, Nicoleta,' said Aré, cutting off Iska.

'How many times have I told you not to call me that?' said Aunt Nikki, her face contorting with displeasure. 'It irks me.'

Aré chuckled. 'Exactly why I do it. It's fun getting on your nerves.'

'Remind me why we're friends again,' said Aunt Nikki, breaking into laughter. 'You look good!'

'Not looking too bad yourself,' said Aré, eyeing Aunt Nikki up and down. 'How much time do you spend in the gym, eh?'

Anyone could guess it was a lot, judging by Aunt Nikki's athletic build. In fact, Amen and Iska had a running theory that their fierce-looking aunt might be a Russian spy. It made sense; her uncanny ability to sneak up on people, her sleek dark-brown hair always pulled into a tight ponytail, and her habit of dressing entirely in black. How could she not be a KGB agent?

'Ha! look who's talking,' said Aunt Nikki, gently setting Iska and Amen back on the floor. 'I swear you don't look a day over twenty.'

'Now, you're taking the piss.' Aré motioned for Aunt Nikki to take a seat. 'Come, get comfortable. Girls, keep practising what you just learnt. I'll teach you the final step of the stitch later.'

Amen and Iska tried to do as they were told and continue with their lesson but found Aré and Aunt Nikki's conversation distracting.

'So, tell me Nikki, what have you been up to? How's the home? And the children? Are you seeing anyone?'

Aunt Nikki laughed at the flurry of questions. 'Well, I'm up to my ears with work, so there's no time for dates. It's a miracle I was able to come see you and the girls today. Since I only get Sundays off, I figured I'd stop by.'

'I completely understand,' Aré replied.

'Running the home,' Aunt Nikki continued. 'Well, that hasn't been easy, but thankfully, with the grant from the government, we'll be able to get more help. The children are doing really well; some of them struggle when they first move in, but soon enough, they get used to the environment—you remember the little boy I brought in from Japan about three years ago? He *really* struggled in the beginning, but now he's so popular and gets along great with the other children.'

'Oh, bless him,' said Aré. 'I can only imagine the trauma some of those kids have experienced.'

'Speaking of kids…'

Amen and Iska could feel Aunt Nikki's gaze slowly fall on them as they pretended to work on their stitching technique, 'yours are growing fast. Do they know? Have you spoken to them about it?'

From the corner of her eye, Iska noticed Aré tense up in her seat, then subtly glance over to see if she and Amen had caught the question.

'Could you have said that any louder?' Aré whispered a few seconds later, satisfied with the thought that they hadn't heard anything.

I don't know why Mam won't just tell us about Dad, thought Iska. *Even Aunt Nikki wants her to.*

Aunt Nikki chuckled at Aré's slight panic. 'I'm sorry, I didn't realise you were keeping it a secret… And *why* are you keeping it a secret, if I may ask?'

'It's not—' Aré stammered. 'I'm not trying to be secretive. They're just kids. I feel like now's not the right time to tell them. Maybe when they are a bit older?'

'I hear you,' Aunt Nikki whispered. 'But you have to keep in mind that they're growing every day. Need I remind you? They usually start showing signs around this age.'

The conversation seemed to make Aré uneasy. She kept glancing over at Iska and Amen with concern. 'I know, I know. I'll tell them soon enough, I promise… Since we're on the subject, can I ask you for a favour?'

'Sure, what is it?'

'Please stop doing *this*.' Aré snapped her fingers loudly. 'Besides nearly giving me a heart attack, those two are a lot smarter than you think.'

Instead of feeling remorse or apologising for whatever she had done to upset Aré, Aunt Nikki simply burst into laughter.

The holidays had been kind to Amen and Iska so far. Along with all the sewing techniques they had learnt from Aré, the weather had been consistently sunny, allowing for a few adventurous hikes along Bray Head, visits to Dublin City Centre, and plenty of swims in the town lake.

Today, like the days before, the air was warm and pleasant and teeming with vibrant insects. Puffy white clouds filled the sky, though darker grey ones had begun gathering cautiously at the fringes, threatening to spill in later. The lake buzzed with laughter and splashes from neighbourhood children, while a few adults lounged along the grassy banks.

Amidst the other swimmers, Iska and Amen were competing to see who could hold their breath underwater the longest when, suddenly, a sharp pain shot through Amen's head.

Iska, where are you? she whispered, her vision blurring up. *I can't see you; I can't see anything.*

Haha! Stop making excuses and just give up.

Iska! Amen screamed this time, her head bobbing in the water. *I'm hurt; I'm hurt really bad.*

What's the matter? thought Iska, swimming over to Amen as quickly as she could.

'I don't know,' Amen gasped. 'But I feel like my head might crack open; please help me out of the water.'

Iska had only just grasped Amen's arm when she recoiled from the intense heat radiating from her sister's limb. It was then that Iska noticed the water around Amen appeared to be evaporating. Taking care not to get burnt, Iska gently nestled her voice within Amen's mind and, with painstaking focus, guided her first to the lake's edge, then out of the water. Anxious that more curious eyes might turn their way, she quickly gathered Amen and their belongings and hurried away from the lake.

But the walk home proved to be just as challenging as helping Amen out of the water. Though she had regained her vision and leaned on Iska for support, Amen's head throbbed with pain, and the pelting rain only worsened the tremors rippling through her body.

'Just a little farther,' said an exhausted Iska as they trudged along a lonely, murky road. 'We're nearly home.'

'I don't know if I can—' Amen was saying when she suddenly lost her footing and fell hard into a deep puddle, causing her to wince in pain. 'Iska, please help me up,' she said at last, wiping muddy water from her face.

But Iska's hands were pressed tightly over her mouth, as though she were deliberately holding back a scream.

'Jesus, am I hurt really bad?' Amen asked. She was about to inspect her body for gashes when she caught sight of the transparency of her own skin and let out a bloodcurdling scream that was muffled only by the thunderous pouring rain.

Still kneeling in the puddle, Amen eyed her arms warily. Although she could feel them, they were as clear as water. She tried to use them, but only ended up thrashing and splashing helplessly. Refusing to give up, Amen focused even harder at getting to her feet. After several painful attempts, her form slowly began to solidify.

'What was that?' said Iska, her face pale with fear.

'I—I don't know, but we need to get home quickly,' replied Amen, her now-congealed heart pounding against her ribcage.

But when Iska extended her hand to help, Amen was afraid to grasp it. She was terrified her trembling hands might jerk unexpectedly and snap her sister's wrist, or that she might vomit the burning acid rising in her throat and accidentally scald her.

'You'll be okay,' said Iska, as though reading Amen's mind. 'Everything's going to be fine. Come on; we're nearly home.'

Despite the lingering feeling of suddenly melting into liquid again, Amen felt a lot better as they neared the house. Bursting through the front door into the hallway, she was certain of one thing: if anyone could explain what had just happened to her—if anyone could make her feel safe and whip up a remedy for her sudden affliction—it was Aré.

'Mam! Mammy!' screamed Amen, tears and rain streaming down her face as she searched the empty kitchen before heading towards the living room. 'Where are you? The scariest thing—'

Amen and Iska couldn't help but rub their eyes. They needed to be sure, perfectly sure, that the scene in front of them was not a trick of the mind induced by everything that had just happened. But the harder they rubbed, the clearer they saw that Aré—or rather, what looked like a pale, grotesquely shrivelled version of her—was sitting comatose in one of the chairs in the living room. Aré's eyes were wide open, but they were devoid of life, just like the rest of her body.

Amen, who was still at the foot of the door, was already crying, but Iska staggered towards the body. 'Mam,' she whispered, feeling the hardened wrist for a pulse. 'Can—can you hear me?'

But the only response she received was silence.

As Amen lay on her bed, reflecting on a life that seemed like an eternity ago, she couldn't help but let the tears stream down her face. She couldn't stop wishing that these memories didn't belong to her.

2. UNIX

A lot had changed for Amen and Iska since Aré was found dead nearly six years ago. For one, they no longer lived in Kilcock. As minors and orphans, they had to be under the custody of a designated guardian. The only person they ever considered family (and truthfully, their only option) was Aunt Nikki—who graciously took them in.

Another change in Amen and Iska's lives was their sleeping arrangement. Whereas they had once shared a room between themselves, now they occupied a bunk bed in a room alongside two other girls. After moving in with Aunt Nikki, they found themselves in Digglefield Park, a castle-like house that served as a home to numerous homeless and orphaned children from around the world. Initially, it was difficult for Amen and Iska to adjust to sharing their room with unfamiliar girls and living in a mansion filled with strangers. But as time went on, they recognised the practicality of their situation and began to feel thankful for what they had. Moreover, having Aunt Nikki watch over them gave the twins a sense of ease they couldn't trust any other soul in the world to provide.

Perhaps the most significant change in the twins was how much they had physically grown in the five and half years since they moved to the vibrant fishing village of Howth. The plump, childish cheeks they once had had given way to beautiful, angular faces, complemented by their tall, lean stature. Even their complexion, once a Navajo white all those years ago, had darkened to a smooth café au lait.

Yet, despite all these changes, one thing had remained constant: Iska and Amen missed Aré every waking moment.

On the day Aré died, there had been no sign of forced entry into their home, at least according to the Gardaí. Iska and Amen had also been interrogated about their activities prior to discovering Aré's corpse, and they earnestly explained themselves, withholding only the details of the puddle incident.

A few months after Aré's death, an autopsy report was released, stating that she had died of "unknown natural causes" and that "further investigation would be carried out". But Amen and Iska expressed their distrust of the report to Aunt Nikki, who promised to conduct her own investigation.

Initially, this promise gave the twins hope, but as weeks turned into months and then years, hope gradually turned into disappointment, which eventually transformed into understanding. They came to understand that it was nearly impossible for Aunt Nikki to play detective while managing Digglefield.

As time marched on, Amen and Iska's desire to uncover the true cause of Aré's death diminished into sporadic, amateurish detective work that yielded no results. They had fully settled in at Digglefield park and, somewhat ironically, built bonds with children who, like them, had no other person or place to call home.

With their priorities shifted, Iska and Amen's focus now revolved around performing well in their Leaving Certificate Examinations; a mission Iska was determined to take seriously.

'Wake up, you; we need to get ready for school,' she said.

'Mmm, give me five more minutes.' Amen groaned and turned her head away from Iska.

'I'll give you three. You know what happens when we don't use the bathroom early; I'm not in the mood for a cold shower this morning.'

Not finished with her duties as a human alarm clock, Iska headed towards another bunk bed where two girls were still fast asleep. 'Wake up, Senait. Stop sleeping, Rima,' she said, shaking their bed. 'I honestly don't know how yous are still asleep. Especially at a time like this, wake *uuup*!'

'Just because the exams are easy for you,' said Rima, failing to keep her eyes open, 'doesn't mean they're easy for all of us, Iska.'

'How am I the only one who's excited that exams end today?' said Iska, still shaking the girls' bed. 'All that time spent studying, and in a couple of hours it'll all be over; I'm so gassed!'

'Yeah, yeah, whatever,' said the other girl in the bottom bunk.

The feeling of completing the last exams of their secondary school lives would have been one of excitement if the girls didn't have to say goodbye to their classmates almost immediately. For many, this was the last time they would see each other for a while, or possibly forever. Some of the boys, who had been occupied with their studies during the exam season, recognised that this was their final opportunity to ask the girls they were interested in to accompany them to the school's Debs. As a result, Amen, Senait, and Rima had to wait for Iska outside the school.

'Sorry for making yous wait.' Iska bounced up to them with a smile plastered across her face. 'Brady asked if I'd like to go to the Debs with him.'

'And?' said Senait curiously.

'Well, I said yes.'

'I really hoped you would say no,' said Rima, rolling her eyes in disappointment. 'He gives off weird vibes and can be a rude arsehole if you ask me.'

'I know he is, but he can be sweet. Plus, he was the only one brave enough to ask. Anyways, what about yous—who are you going with?'

'Tom asked me,' said Rima, her tone unrepentant. 'But I told him I'd let him know if I could make it. Spoiler alert: I'm not going to the Debs, let alone going with him.'

Senait shrugged her shoulders. 'I thought Cillian was gonna ask me, but he didn't, so I guess I'm not going either.'

Feeling a little unimpressed with their decisions, all

three girls were now staring at Amen who had been quiet for most of the conversation.

'Oh, um,' she stuttered, not realising she was supposed to give an answer as well. 'No one asked me, but I don't mind going with you, Senait. And Rima, I think you should come along, just for the craic.'

Just as the girls were mulling over Amen's suggestion, four boys came running out of nowhere, nearly knocking Rima and Iska to the ground.

'Eejits!' yelled Rima. 'You nearly knocked us over.'

'SORRY!' one of the boys yelled back while still running.

'Numbskulls,' Rima muttered. 'Who were they anyway? Did anyone get a good look?'

'Yeah,' said Senait, speaking quietly. 'The tallest one was Luke McDermott, and the chap running like he just shit himself was Colm Neeson. The other two I only recognise because they live in Digglefield, but I don't know their names.'

Rima snapped her fingers sharply. 'Grand! I'm reporting them to Nikki; that should teach them a lesson. As for Luke and Colm...they're lucky they might never see me again.'

Just as the four girls resumed their walk, a thought crossed Amen's mind. 'I still find it weird that we hardly ever get to see the boys from Digglefield,' she said. 'Except maybe in school. That's why we couldn't recognise the two lads from earlier.'

'It *is* weird,' said Senait. 'I've practically lived in Digglefield all my life, and I can count on one hand how many times I've interacted with the boys. I figured it was one of Nikki's many rules—never really thought to ask.'

'If they all behave like those two did, then I'm more than happy not to spend time with any of them,' said Rima.

The girls burst out in laughter.

The Digglefield household was bustling with activity, especially now that the summer holidays were in full swing. With over five hundred children officially on break, the potential for anarchy was ever-present. However, Aunt Nikki and her team had effective methods of managing the chaos. Children between the ages of three to eleven years were assigned minders whose primary responsibility was to plan engaging activities within the castle. Pre-teens and teenagers aged twelve to sixteen were supervised by house leaders who were allowed to organise a maximum of two excursions per week. The seventeen and eighteen-year-olds were granted more freedom to do as they pleased, as long as they adhered to the 8 p.m. curfew—a simple rule that Aunt Nikki put in place a few years ago after catching a group of boys trying to sneak off to a party in the middle of the night.

Fortunately for Aunt Nikki, breaking house rules or sneaking off to parties were the furthest things from Amen and Iska's minds. They were too busy worrying about receiving offers from the colleges they wanted to get into and were, at the moment, sitting in Digglefield's lush back garden, reviewing their options for the billionth time.

'What were your top choices in your CAO application again?' said Amen, scrolling through a website on the house laptop.

'TCD, UCD, and DCU,' Iska replied. 'But what does it matter if you're going off to Dingle? I'll never get to see you. Are you sure there aren't any colleges in Dublin offering fashion courses?'

'I already checked. The only college with a fashion programme in Dublin is the McNair Institute of Design.'

'You could go there,' said Iska, quickly typing on the laptop.

'I can't. It's a private college that costs fifteen thousand euro…per year.'

This piece of information made Iska pause. 'That's a lot of money.'

'I know,' Amen replied. 'There's no way I can afford it. That's why SHU is the best alternative for me.'

'It's not fair, though. We always said we'd be close to

each other, remember? We made that promise after Mam passed away. Now you want to go all the way to Dingle. *Dingle*!'

'I remember the promise,' said Amen as she wrapped her arm around Iska and kissed on her forehead. 'I don't plan on moving to Dingle just for the sake of it; you know I would never do that. But you also know what fashion means to me... If it makes you feel any better, I'll—keep searching for fashion colleges within Dublin or any nearby county.'

'That's all I ask,' said Iska, her lips slowly curving into a smile. 'That you exhaust all your options before abandoning me.'

'All right, all right. But don't—' Amen was interrupted by the sight of two boys fighting across the back garden. 'Is it me, or are those lads...having a go at each other?'

'Where?' Iska squinted her eyes. 'Oh yeah, I see them. I think they are.'

'Should we do something?' said Amen, now on her feet. 'It looks rough.'

'I don't think we should—' Iska was beginning to say, but one of the boys had put the other in a tight chokehold which he was tightening by the second.

'Let go of him,' screamed Amen as she ran over to where the boys were violently tussling with each other. 'You're going to kill him.'

Iska joined Amen, and both of them tried their hardest to pull the boys away from each other.

'For goodness' sake! Will—you—stop!' said Iska, still trying to separate the jet-black-haired boy from his opponent.

'Um, will you let go of me?' said the other boy, panting heavily but managing to speak calmly, which surprised Amen.

'I know, right? What in God's name is wrong with both of you?' said the boy Iska was holding on to.

'What's wrong with us?' Iska responded, annoyed by the

boy's question. 'What's wrong with yous? You two are try-ing to kill each other over God-knows-what. And you,' Iska pointed at the dark-haired boy. 'You should talk; that ding-bat over there nearly put you to sleep! Amen, I tried to tell you—we should have minded our own business.'

Nodding in agreement, Amen started to back away from the boys when they burst into laughter, further irritat-ing the twins.

'Gobshites,' said Amen. 'What's so funny?'

'Come on, Amen, let's leave,' said Iska.

'No, please wait,' said the red-haired boy in a Los An-geles-meets-Mayo accent. 'We're sorry; we don't mean to be rude at all. We're laughing because you thought we wanted to *kill* each other.'

The other boy joined in on the conversation. 'Thank you for trying to save us, but Lake and I weren't hurting each other. We were...sparring.'

'Spar...ring?' Iska's eyebrow raised.

'Yes,' the black-haired boy replied with a laugh. 'Believe it or not, we do that from time to time. And no offence, but I would have taken him if you... Hold on a second. I know you; you're the girl from school with *the* eyes!'

'Yeah, do you have a problem with that?' Iska retorted.

'No, not at all,' said the black-haired boy. 'It's actually really cool.'

Amen would have been embarrassed by the boy's com-ment if she herself hadn't noticed something interesting about him and the other boy. 'I remember yous from some-where,' she said. 'Weren't you two a part of the group of boys who nearly knocked us over on Friday? Remember Iska? On our way back home from school.'

Before Iska could jog her memory to confirm if Amen was right, the boy with black hair spoke. 'Yeah, that was us,' he said in a remorseful tone. 'We're really sorry about that day. Myself and the lads made a bet—the loser of the race had to buy us food from the chipper. I hope we didn't hurt yous.'

'We're grand,' said Amen, 'but our friend was pissed; she promised to tell Aunt Nikki what yous did.'

'Fair enough,' said the red-haired boy. 'Well, we're sorry again. By the way, I'm Lake, Lake Fitzgerald. Nice to meet you.' He extended his hand to Iska and Amen.

'Aito Takanashi, at your service,' said the black-haired boy.

Aito and Lake stood tall, easily towering over the twins, with Lake having a slight height advantage over Aito. Judging by their physiques, it was clear that both boys were into sports. Despite Lake's poorly cropped hair, his green eyes seemed to hold countless stories. Aito, on the other hand, sported long hair that cascaded over his broad shoulders.

As the group returned to the spot where Amen and Iska had left their computer, a question arose in Amen's mind. 'Do yous know which college you want to go to?' she asked.

'Not really,' said Aito as he readjusted his hair into a neat bun. 'I'm actually thinking of taking a gap year and getting an apprenticeship with a construction firm. I figured I might as well make some money and travel.'

'What about you?' said Iska, tilting her head in Lake's direction.

'Maynooth University has offered me a football scholarship,' Lake said quickly, as if not wanting to go into details. 'So has Rollins College in the United States, but I haven't made up my mind yet.'

At this point, Iska decided to ask something she'd been curious about. 'Lake, your accent's interesting. Whereabouts are you from?'

'Well, I'm originally from Contra Costa County, California,' Lake replied, allowing a brief pause for the information to sink in. 'I lived in a foster home over there. I never knew my parents; the caregivers were my family. I moved here about five years ago, and that's when I met this moron.'

'Moron? Chap, I'm practically your only friend, and that's only because you bribed me,' Aito shot back, which made all four of them chuckle.

'But why did you move here?' said Amen.

'It wasn't really my choice,' Lake replied. 'Apparently, the home I lived in was starting to take in a lot more children, and space needed to be made. Most of the older children, including myself, had to be relocated. Next thing I know, I'm being told I'm moving to Ireland. I didn't want to move, but then Nikki came for me and that was that.'

'I'm so sorry,' said Amen. 'Being forced to move away from your friends and family without your consent couldn't have been easy.'

'Ah, no worries at all. If I'm being completely honest, I like it here—'

'You're very welcome!' Aito interjected.

'What about you, Aito,' said Amen. 'What's your story?'

'It hurts to talk about,' said Aito, his eyes instantly teary, as if the question had triggered a painful memory. 'I was kidnapped from Japan and brought here. Forced to learn English and abandon my heritage, my people.'

There was an awkward silence amongst the four of them.

Lake patted Aito's back while Amen and Iska hung their heads, searching for words of consolation.

'I'm messing with yous!'

'Jesus; why would you say stuff like that?' said Iska, clutching her hands to her chest in relief.

'Come on, it was funny, you should have seen your faces,' said Aito. 'I'm just trying to lighten the mood.

'Unlike Lake here, I actually knew my parents; sorry, Lake. I mean, my memories of them aren't as vivid as they used to be, but I had an older brother and a little sister. Our family lived in a small town called Narai-juku, where my parents ran a tea shop from the ground floor of our house. My brother and I always got into fights, constantly trying to outdo each other. He wanted to become an architect, meh! I wanted to run the family business; I always enjoyed helping out anyways. My sister, on the other hand, was a character: cunning and mischievous, but honestly the sweetest person you could meet.

'On a random winter night, I woke up to our house burning from every corner. It took a second for me to realise I was downstairs in the shop; I honestly don't remember how I got there. I could hear my family's screams coming from above, but I didn't know how to reach them; the stairs leading up to the first floor were completely burnt, and I couldn't see anything through the smoke. I kid you not, I was about to pass out when some neighbours broke through the shop's entrance and pulled me out. I told them my family was still trapped inside; the neighbours did their best to rescue them, but...it was too late.'

Now there was an uncomfortable silence in the air.

'I'm really sorry, Aito,' said Amen, embarrassed by the slight tremble in her voice.

Aito waved his hand dismissively. 'Ah, don't worry about it,' he said. 'This was ages ago. I was six at the time. After the incident, the neighbours who saved me took me in, but only for a short while; they were already struggling as a family, and adding another child, especially one who wasn't even theirs, made things even more challenging. Eventually, they brought me to an orphanage in Kyoto— godawful place, that home. I hated it there. Thankfully, I was there only a few years before Nikki and Marius came for me; they said that I would be taken care of in much better conditions. Packed my bags in minutes; I didn't even protest.'

'You *poor* thing,' said Lake, a hint sarcasm in his voice. 'I reckon it must have been difficult when you first moved here. The food, language...'

Aito chuckled at Lake's comment. 'Oh, believe me, I really struggled a lot at first. I didn't understand a bloody word of English, and the weather... Don't even get me started; it was always cold. But eventually I settled in. Digglefield's been my gaff for the past nine years.'

Aito and Lake's stories stirred something within Iska and Amen. It reminded the twins that they were not the only ones who had faced hardships in life. It had always been so easy for them to get caught up in their own pain, constantly feeling like victims of their circumstances. But these boys served as a timely reminder that they didn't have to look too far to see that others also struggled with loss and grief.

'Now you know a bit more about Lake and me,' said Aito, bringing Iska and Amen back to the conversation. 'How did yous end up here?'

'You don't want to know,' Iska replied almost immediately. 'It's a long story, really. Right, Amen?'

'Come on, don't be shy,' said Aito. 'You can give us a summarised version.'

Iska was still reluctant to speak, but Amen started. 'We lived with our Mam in a small town about two and a half hours from here,' she said. 'Everything was fine, we were good. But during one of the holidays…'

Reliving that day was harder than Amen thought, and Iska could see that. So, she picked up where her sister left off. 'We came home and…and saw our Mam was dead. She was sitting in a chair, lifeless. I—I felt her hand, and I'd never felt anything colder… I'm sorry, I really can't—'

'Hey, hey,' said Lake. 'It's fine, you don't have to speak about your past if you don't want to.'

Aito joined in. 'Yeah, I'm sorry about your Mam. Sometimes health problems—'

'She was murdered,' Iska and Amen interjected in unison, the last word hanging in the cold summer air.

A few more seconds passed before Amen spoke. 'She never had any underlying health issues; she would have told us, she told us everything. Someone, or something, killed her.'

'Did yous find out who?' said Aito, his deep voice lowering to a whisper, 'or *what* did it?'

'Never,' said Iska, finding her voice again. 'We searched, even with the help of Aunt Nikki, but found nothing.'

Engrossed in the memories of each other's pasts, Iska, Amen, and the boys failed to notice how dark the day had become. Realising it was getting late and not wanting to break curfew, they said their goodbyes and promised to meet again.

Back in the girls' dormitory, the twins ran into Rima and Senait, who were on their way to the dining hall for dinner. 'Where have yous been?' asked Rima.

'In the back garden,' Iska replied, 'with the lads who nearly knocked us over on Friday.'

'Wait, what?' said Rima, not believing her ears. 'What were they doing on our side of the garden? Did you report them to Nikki?'

'Oh, no,' Amen responded. 'We were with them for an entirely different reason; we sort of…ran into them.'

Rima glanced curiously at each of the twins. 'Riiight. Well, I need to see Nikki tomorrow anyways. I'll tell her what they did myself.'

'Oh, Rima, just let it go,' said Iska. 'They apologised for what happened. Truth is, they're not as bad as you think. You might actually like them if you meet them.'

Rima scoffed and continued down the stairs, clearly uninterested in continuing the conversation.

On Tuesday, just a few minutes before noon, a house-wide announcement was made, requesting the presence of all the teenagers who had just completed their Leaving Cert exams in Digglefield's west garden at four in the afternoon. It seemed that Aunt Nikki had some important information to share.

It was now 3:45 p.m., and Iska, Amen, Rima, Senait, and a group of other girls were making their way to the garden.

'Does anyone have any idea what Nikki wants to talk to us about?' asked Senait. 'The announcement this morning sounded urgent.'

The girls remained silent, but Iska had a thought. 'Rima, two days ago you said you needed to see Aunt Nikki,' she said. 'Please tell me you didn't tell on those lads. Is that why the announcement was made?'

'I didn't,' Rima quickly responded. 'I went to see Nikki concerning some skin care products I need.'

'It doesn't matter,' said Amen. 'Clearly, none of us knows what's happening; we'll just have to wait and find out.'

Digglefield's gardens always put on a beautiful show during summertime, but today, the Bog-Rosemaries, Easter Lilies, and Buttercups were all displaying an extra level of beauty. Amen noticed their bloom only because she and the girls were looking around the crowded garden for a place to sit while a group of boys chattered away about why the meeting had been called.

'—I think some people snuck out of Digglefield last night—' one of the boys suggested.

'—Nah, I think we're going on an excursion—' another chimed in.

A few more colourful theories were still circulating around the garden when Aunt Nikki suddenly appeared before everyone.

'You're not a kid anymore, Christian; stop hoping for excursions,' said Aunt Nikki, amusing the crowd.

Meanwhile, a few people asked how she had managed to make her way to the front of the garden without being seen.

Aunt Nikki heard them. 'I will answer that question shortly,' she said. 'But before I do, I want you all to understand why I called this meeting... What I'm about to tell you is very important, and it has taken me and my team a significant amount of time and preparation to gather you all here. Therefore, I urge you to listen attentively and let every word I speak sink in. And most importantly, be brave.'

Be brave. These two words somehow managed to silence the crowd. Cheery faces that had only minutes ago been glad to see Aunt Nikki were gone, replaced now by curious ones eagerly awaiting her next words.

'Some of you were wondering how I was able to reach the front of this gathering so quickly. Well, the answer is simple: I am a Unix.' said Aunt Nikki, pausing to let the weight of her words settle. 'Now, I know you are all curious about what this means. To put it delicately, a Unix has...abilities, powers, supernatural talents; whatever you want to call it. But the main takeaway is that Unix can do what humans can only dream of.'

Except for her team members, whose expressions remained as solid as rocks, it was clear that no one in the crowd had any idea what Aunt Nikki was talking about. Nevertheless, she pressed on with her speech.

'I can see the confusion on your faces. You're probably wondering, "What does this have to do with me?"' she said to the perplexed audience. 'Well, young ladies and gentlemen, I am here to inform you that each and every one of you is a Unix. Yes, you heard that right. From the little children currently playing indoors to every minder patrolling the grounds of Digglefield, we are all Unix...'

Aunt Nikki was still speaking when a girl in the crowd raised her hand. She was the only one brave enough to make a move while the rest of the group worked hard to process the information they were receiving.

'Yes, Saoirse, what is it you want to know?' said Aunt Nikki before facing the group. 'You all can ask me any question. That is why this meeting is being held.'

'You say you're a Unix,' said Saoirse, her voice filled with curiosity. 'So, what's your ability?'

'That's a good question,' Aunt Nikki replied with a smile. 'Well, I am fast. Very, very fast.'

'How fast?' someone in the crowd asked.

'Let's just say that if Usain Bolt and I were in a hundred-metre race, by the time he got out of the starting blocks, I would already be at the finish line, cheering him on.'

Chatter erupted among the crowd.

'That's impossible,' said another person, struggling to believe Aunt Nikki's claim. 'No one can be that fast.'

Aunt Nikki shook her head, disappointed by the group's scepticism. 'Well, I am,' she said, 'but let's save the exhibition for another time. There are more pressing matters to discuss—'

'How,' one of the boys stuttered, his voice filled with doubt, 'how do you expect us to believe any of this if there's no proof?'

Aunt Nikki, though appearing slightly impatient, had an expression that suggested she anticipated questions like this. 'Marius?' she called out to her second in command.

'Yes, boss,' Marius responded almost immediately.

'Please show our friends here a quick snapshot of your ability.'

'No problem,' Marius replied as everyone huddled closely together to see what he was going to do. Marius took off his shoes and socks, but just as he was unbuttoning his shirt one of the boys at the back of the huddle sniggered loudly.

'Oh wow; Marius's ability is stripping naked.' he added sarcastically.

Perhaps egged on by the laughter that followed his joke, the boy began to catcall Marius. But the whistling abruptly stopped. When everyone turned around to see what had happened, Aunt Nikki was standing right beside the boy, firmly pinching his lips together—in reaction to this, another boy immediately fainted.

The idea that Aunt Nikki had somehow managed to make her way to the back of the crowd in a matter of seconds was still settling in everyone's mind when the sound of bones cracking, clicking, and rearranging themselves came from where Marius stood. Instead of the familiar four-foot-tall figure, Amen and Iska were stunned to see a six-foot-tall Marius who continued to grow. Many in the crowd wanted to scream as they watched Marius gradually transform into a hulking man, but Aunt Nikki quickly shushed them.

'You don't want to alarm people in the castle,' she said.

'Now, I understand that you're all scared, but this is why my team and I are here—to answer your questions and explain everything you need to know about this strange revelation. There are no silly questions.'

Aito raised his hand.

'Very brave, Aito. Go ahead.' Aunt Nikki smiled encouragingly at him.

'Are we going to be super-heroes?'

'Yes, Aito, because we are the Avengers,' Aunt Nikki responded sarcastically.

'But you just said—'

'How do you know we're all Unix?' Senait interrupted Aito.

'Good question,' said Aunt Nikki, still sizing up Aito. 'We have a group of individuals. You can call them extraordinary sleuths, for lack of a better word, who help us search for Unix all over the world. No, you can't identify them; yes, they're always there, but they are incredibly discreet. They could be shop-clerks, CEOs of Fortune Five-Hundred companies, barbers, hairstylists, or whatever they need to be to blend in. They search for young, abandoned, homeless, or orphaned Unix who need a home and a family.'

'How come we haven't seen or been able to use our abilities?' said another girl with a high-pitched voice.

'Another excellent question,' replied Aunt Nikki. 'You see, a Unix's ability is like a muscle, a very well-hidden muscle, I might add. And, to the best of my knowledge, most children, whether human or Unix, don't really care about building their muscles until they reach your age or older. It may not be the best analogy, but I think it conveys the message appropriately. Your abilities have always been within you; you just never knew they were there or bothered to use them. That being said, Unix often show what we call a *spike* during their earlier years, typically between the ages of ten to thirteen. A spike is a momentary display of a Unix's ability; it occurs swiftly, but it is also very unpredictable and not every Unix experiences one…'

Aunt Nikki continued to explain the concept of a spike, but Amen's heart was racing. It was as though she had just fallen into that puddle from all those years ago, suddenly feeling cold, confused, and very afraid. She instantly understood that what she had experienced on the day Aré died was a spike, and this epiphany made her feel even more queasy.

'Get a grip,' Iska whispered, noticing Amen rock back and forth on her feet, 'I know what you're thinking, and I know you're scared; I am too. But please, don't pass out like that lad did. Take deep breaths and try to calm down. We'll talk about it later.'

Taking Iska's advice, Amen took in lungful breaths, steadied herself, and focused on listening attentively to Aunt Nikki, who was still speaking '…In fact, there's someone among us who experienced a spike at the age of eleven, although they didn't know it at the time. Or did you, Aito?'

Gasps reverberated through the crowd as everyone's attention shifted towards Aito, who appeared equally stunned. 'Jesus; no, I didn't. When did this happen?'

'Do you remember a couple of years back when you woke up screaming from a nightmare?' said Aunt Nikki. 'Your bed was soaked, and people wondered how you could sweat so much.'

'Yeah,' Aito replied. 'I had dreamt that I was outside a lighthouse during a crazy storm in the middle of the night. I was nearly struck by lightning when I woke up screaming, and then you came to get me.'

'Correct,' said Aunt Nikki, 'except for the fact that it *wasn't* just a dream. That was real life. You were blood, flesh, and bone at a lighthouse—in England, to be precise. You must have experienced a spike while you were asleep, teleported to the lighthouse, and then returned to Digglefield within a matter of minutes.'

Everyone's mouth hung open in awe except for Aito's. 'Jaysus, I can teleport,' he said, astonished. 'But Nikki, how did you know the lighthouse I teleported to was in England?'

Aunt Nikki smiled in response to the question. 'That required a bit of investigation,' she said. 'You see, when I came to get you that night, apart from the soaked sheets, I noticed some rocks on your bed, which I took with me. Through further research, I discovered that the rocks were gneiss, a type of rock unique to beaches of Cornwall. Coincidentally, one of the minders had found a book titled *The Earth from The Air* under your bed. Beautiful book with loads of photographs of Earth's remarkable landscapes.

'One day, as I was flipping through the book, I stumbled upon it. Right there, on one of the pages, was the lighthouse. The photo's description read: *Eddystone lighthouse, Cornwall, England; situated on the dangerous Eddystone seawater and known for its Precambrian gneiss rocks.* It was at that moment I was convinced that you possessed the ability to teleport.'

'Jesus, Mary, and Joseph,' said Aito, putting his hands on his head in disbelief.

'Very well,' said Aunt Nikki firmly. 'One more question, and then we'll call it a day. We'll reconvene here at twelve tomorrow. I'll provide more information on what it means to be a Unix and conduct tests to discover each of your abilities.'

As soon as Aunt Nikki finished speaking, a boy familiar to Amen and Iska raised his hand to ask a question.

'I guess Lake has the final question for the day,' said Aunt Nikki.

'Why now? Why have you chosen this time to tell us we're...different?' said Lake.

Aunt Nikki took a moment to reflect on the question before responding. 'The simplest way to put it is that there has never been a more perfect time to let you all know that you're...unique,' she said. 'Most of you will be going off to college in the fall, some of you might get jobs, travel, make new friends, attend gatherings, and there are countless ways your abilities may manifest themselves, which you or those around you may not be prepared for. That's why you need to know who you are, what you can do, and most importantly, learn to control it.

'All right then, that's enough for today. As I said earlier, we will be meeting here tomorrow; don't be late. Enjoy the rest of your evening, everyone.'

In a matter of minutes, Aunt Nikki, Marius (who had returned to his original height), and the rest of her team vacated the garden, leaving shell-shocked teenagers to figure out what this revelation meant for them. Unsurprisingly, a good number of people were rattled by the fact that their lives were not what they seemed. Meanwhile, a few others—excited at the prospect of having special abilities—cornered Aito to interrogate him about the night he spiked.

As for Amen, Iska, and the girls, they were making their way back to the main building when Rima broke the silence. 'I can't believe we can do these things,' she blurted out. 'To be fair, I always knew there was something different about me, like there was another dimension to my being that I wasn't aware of.'

'For the record,' said Senait, her calm, melodic voice a much-needed presence at a time like this, 'this is completely miles away from what I was expecting to hear today.'

The discussion about what happened in the garden carried on well into the evening until it was time for dinner. But while the other girls made their way to the dining hall, Iska and Amen stayed in their room—they weren't particularly hungry, and they wanted to have an uninterrupted conversation.

'I guess today explains why we can talk to each other in our heads,' said Iska. 'I just always assumed it was something every twin could do.'

'Do you think my spike had anything to do with Mam's death?' Amen asked dryly.

'What do you mean?'

'Well, it's obvious that I spiked the day I fell into that puddle, but do you think it hurt Mam?'

'I, I honestly don't know, but it's highly unlikely. Aunt Nikki didn't say anything about spikes causing harm to family members.'

'What if she doesn't know all the facts?' Amen retorted.

'Then we have no way of knowing either. We literally found out a few hours ago that we're not even regular humans. Don't work yourself up, Amen. You loved Mam, and there's no way you could have done anything to hurt her.'

'You really think so?' said Amen, staring blankly at the ceiling. 'When I get the chance, I'm going to ask Aunt Nikki.'

'If it will make you feel better, go ahead. But I'm confident you did nothing wrong,' said Iska with hope rather than conviction.

The meeting kicked off precisely at twelve o'clock, although several teenagers seemed to have arrived hours earlier, no doubt armed with all manner of questions for Aunt Nikki. Unlike the gloom of the previous day, the sun hung high and bright in the sky today, though it wasn't hot enough to dispel the bitter chill in the air.

'First things first,' said Aunt Nikki, after taking a roll call to confirm everyone's presence. 'Many of you, after our brief meeting yesterday, may have wondered about the origins of Unix or how they came to be. I can say with some certainty that no one knows specifically the origins of Unix. We could be aliens who came to Earth hundreds of thousands of years ago and formed a coexistence with humans, or it could be that a genetic mutation enhanced our abilities. More different theories than I care to know have been thrown around, but there has never been a consensus on how we came to be, and I strongly doubt there ever will be.

'However, what *is* known is that the first display of a Unix's ability was reported in mid-seventeen hundreds Europe. A lady by the name of Celestine Niépce was spotted moving seamlessly through solid objects by her lover and his friends. Convinced that she was a "witch", Celestine's lover plotted to her death and successfully poisoned her.

'He was subsequently arrested and tried for murder, with Celestine's family in attendance at the trial. During the hearing, he explained his motive, describing what Celestine was able to do; but the public deemed his story a lie, and he was sentenced to death by hanging. The story goes that, as the noose was being tightened around his neck, he was heard screaming, "Ask my friends! Ask them! They know the truth!"'

'So, it's safe to say that humans still don't know of our existence,' suggested one girl.

'Correct,' replied Aunt Nikki. 'And the plan is to keep it that way.'

'Why?' asked Rima.

'Some of you enjoy reading comics, while others sneak out of Digglefield to go to the cinema and watch the latest superhero movies; I know you do,' said Aunt Nikki. 'My hope is that while you're munching on popcorn and sipping your drinks, enjoying the spectacle, you also recognise that these films often carry underlying messages. To put it plainly, there are certain things that are better left unsaid and information that is better left unknown—the world already has enough problems as it is, and humans don't need to know the extent of what we can do.'

Aunt Nikki's explanation seemed to leave the group more puzzled than enlightened, but she showed little inclination to provide more clarity. 'In line with what I've just told you,' she continued, 'to maintain our inconspicuousness, our abilities have names. For instance, I am Slinker due to my ability to move at great speed; Marius is Legar, and Aito is a Blinker. As the day goes on and we discover your abilities, you'll come to know what you're called.'

It was now clear to Amen and Iska why Aunt Nikki had chosen Digglefield's west garden as the venue for their meetings. It was the most secluded of all the gardens on the grounds and had enough space to accommodate various types of activities.

Aunt Nikki instructed everyone to form a circle around her, while her team members formed an even larger circle around them, ready to assist in case anyone felt unwell or overwhelmed. Tension filled the garden as Aunt Nikki stood at the centre of the circle, calmly scanning each person's face. She had clearly conducted this exercise many times before and remained unfazed by the occasional whimpers of nervousness.

'Who would like to go first?' Aunt Nikki asked, clearly hoping one brave person would volunteer, but everyone seemed to be paralysed by fear. 'Oh, for goodness' sake, we don't have all day. Sunail, come out here and show us what you can do.'

All eyes turned to a rangy boy as he slowly made his way to the centre of the circle, his friends whispering words of encouragement.

'—Come on, Sunny, you've got this—'

'—Do your best, Sunny—'

'Sunail, there's nothing to be worried about,' Aunt Nikki reassured the boy. 'Take a deep breath. Try not to psych yourself out. Feel all the muscles in your body, and then search for that extra muscle within. Flex it as hard as you can.'

For a moment, Sunail looked like he was going to empty the contents of his stomach on the lawn; but, perhaps even more afraid of getting an earful from Aunt Nikki, he decided to close his eyes and tense the imaginary muscle within him. Seconds later, his forehead glistening with sweat, Sunail opened his eyes.

'I can't do it, Nikki,' he admitted, his voice filled with disappointment. 'I'm sorry, but I just don't think I have it in me…'

'That's because you're *thinking* too much about the muscle,' Aunt Nikki replied, stepping closer to Sunail and gently placing her hand on his chest. 'Focus less on thinking and more on feeling. Sunail, trust me, you can do it. You're braver than anyone here for trying first.'

Somehow encouraged by Aunt Nikki's words, Sunail closed his eyes once again. He was about to tense his muscles, but he heard Aunt Nikki say, 'Feel, don't think,' so he let out a long breath and relaxed his body—only for nothing to still happen moments later.

Although Aunt Nikki had explained earlier that it was often difficult for some Unix to demonstrate their abilities for the first time, she clearly didn't have the patience to wait for those who struggled. 'Sunail,' she said, 'It's fine if you can't—'

'I can feel—I can feel it!' Sunail screamed, his eyes still closed. 'I can hear the birds talking; they are having actual conversations about where to find food and build their nests.'

'Surros,' said Aunt Nikki. 'Sunail is a Surros, an animal whisperer—he has the ability to communicate with animals, and they can communicate with him. Pretty impressive.'

Tentative claps filled the garden, while the more curious teenagers asked Sunail to communicate with the birds.

'May I, Nikki?' said Sunail.

'Please, go ahead.' Aunt Nikki responded.

Sunail took a deep breath and closed his eyes once again. After a few moments, he opened them and locked his gaze on two rooks perched on the rooftop of Digglefield. When he opened his mouth to speak, the sounds that came out of him were unlike anything Amen or Iska had ever heard. Surprisingly, Sunail's eyes had also transformed to resemble those of the birds he was communicating with. The two birds squawked and flapped their wings aggressively, and in an instant, one of the birds flew away as fast as its wings would allow, while the other gracefully glided down, landing on Sunail's outstretched arm.

'Allow me to introduce you to Vrela,' said Sunail, his eyes returning to normal. 'That was her brother that flew off. He was...terrified.'

Another guttural sound emanated from Sunail, and suddenly the rook lowered its head in a bow, leaving the crowd stunned.

With Sunail now playing the role of convivial host to Vrela, everyone felt less uneasy. Excitement replaced apprehension, and a few people were eager to showcase their own abilities. Aunt Nikki had different plans, though.

'No, no. You all had your chance to volunteer,' she said smugly. '*I* will decide who comes out next. But before I do, there's something else you all need to know. There's another trait that sets Unix apart from humans; it is a lot more subtle compared to your actual abilities, but it is still noticeable, and that is your physical appearance.

'Unix have distinguishable physical features that humans don't possess. I rarely work out, but my physique says otherwise. Aito's hair probably grows by an inch every day, Amen's eyes aren't white for no reason, and believe it or not, Iska, your eyes are special as well. You probably never noticed, but the irises of your eyes are completely black. No one else that I know, or have heard of, has eyes like yours. I presume the doctors were too fascinated by Amen's to notice yours.

'Anyway, please step forward and grace us with your ability.'

Uncertain about what had triggered her, Iska caught herself scowling at Aunt Nikki as she made her way towards the centre of the circle, a mixture of nervousness, irritation, and excitement bubbling up inside her. Like Sunail, Iska stood in the centre of the circle, wishing everyone's gaze wasn't fixed on her, eagerly waiting to see what she would conjure up. Like Sunail, she closed her eyes and focused on reaching deep within herself to find her hidden muscle. But a minute passed, and Iska couldn't sense anything; two minutes elapsed, and still, nothing. After a few more minutes with no results, Aunt Nikki decided Iska had given her best effort for the day.

'Let me reiterate,' Aunt Nikki announced. 'Some of you

aren't going to be able to display your abilities today. This is not uncommon; it may take days or even weeks for some of you to discover your abilities. That's why we will have these meetings three times a week, to give you the opportunity to explore and refine your abilities.

'If I may add one more thing: it is not a hard and fast rule that every Unix has to have a gift. There *are* cases, again not uncommon, where a Unix doesn't possess any abilities; nonetheless, they still have physical features that distinguish them from humans. Unix with this predisposition are known as Reegs.'

This latest revelation seemed to unsettle some people. It was already challenging enough to accept that they were not human; now, they had to come to terms with the possibility that they might not possess any abilities—that they might somehow be incomplete.

'Shall we continue?' Aunt Nikki's voice brought their wandering thoughts back to the present. 'Amen, it's your turn.'

It took Amen being in the circle to realise that, no matter how many people had gone before her or would go after her, being called up would always be nerve-wracking. Thankfully, she had Iska's reassuring voice in her head for support. Uncertain of what to do, Amen followed the example of those before her and closed her eyes. Almost immediately, a surge of intense heat began to course through her body. Without thinking, she began moving her right hand in a circular motion, and slowly, tiny droplets of water started to form in the palm of her hand. Ignoring her pounding heart, Amen raised her left hand above the water droplets, and to her amazement, they began to coalesce.

'You're a Telemin,' said Aunt Nikki, as the orb of water in Amen's hand fell to the ground with a splash.

Perhaps it was her natural dexterity, but there was something about the way Amen had displayed her ability that left everyone astounded. This, in turn, made her feel even more self-conscious as she returned to her spot beside Iska.

After a midday break, during which the boys and girls were informed that they could use Digglefield's atrium for lunch breaks throughout the rest of the summer, the evaluations resumed.

'—Megan is a Meridy—' Aunt Nikki announced.

'—Rodrygo, you're a Tinan—' She continued.

Abilities were identified and announced for each person who stepped forward, although there were instances where some teenagers displayed abilities that Aunt Nikki had never seen before. This process continued well into the evening, until only one person remained to showcase his ability.

'Aito, I guess you're the last,' said Aunt Nikki. 'Well, we already know you're a Blinker, so I want you to try something out. See that room on the far left of the castle, on the second floor?'

'Yeah,' replied Aito. 'That's the boys' study.'

'Brilliant,' said Aunt Nikki, motioning for everyone to give Aito space. 'Do you think you can blink there?'

'Lord,' Aito whispered nervously. 'Well, I'll give it a go.'

'You can do it,' said Aunt Nikki. 'All you need to do is visualise where you're going.'

Aito took a few quick breaths. 'Easier said than done, isn't it?'

'Remember,' Aunt Nikki continued. 'You know the room; you know the space. Keep that image in your head as you blink.'

Aito forced down a painful gulp, making Iska hide her face to stifle a chuckle. However, in the fraction of a second it took for her to look back up, Aito had already blinked into the study and was waving at them through the window.

Like Amen, Aito seemed adept at using his ability, effortlessly blinking himself back to the garden, drawing cheers from everyone.

'Very good, Aito,' said Aunt Nikki, her hands clapping together for the first time. 'You're a natural. But I wonder, would you be willing to do one more test? Nothing serious.'

'Em, sure. Why not?' Aito replied.

Aunt Nikki walked about fifty metres to an alder tree deep in the garden, tied something to one of its branches, and then returned to the group. 'You all may not be able to see it from here, but there's a little bell hanging from that alder. Do you remember my Usain Bolt analogy? Well, there are rumours that Blinkers are faster than slinkers, and I want to find out if it's true.'

'You want me to race you?' said Aito, barely containing his laugh.

'Yes, if you don't mind?'

'Of course not; let's do this.'

'All right, everyone,' said Aunt Nikki. 'Give us some space. Form a semi-circle behind us so you can see clearly. Marius, could you help us with the countdown?'

'No worries, boss,' Marius responded.

'The rule is simple,' said Aunt Nikki. 'Marius will count-down from three, and whoever rings the bell first is the winner. Got it?'

'Crystal clear,' Aito replied cheekily.

Looking unimpressed as usual, Marius positioned himself between Aunt Nikki and Aito and cleared his throat. 'Three. Two. One… Go!'

Three things happened simultaneously at the end of Marius's countdown: Iska noticed a small card fall to the ground at her feet, Aito and Aunt Nikki vanished into thin air, and Aito let out a triumphant whoop from across the garden, causing the crowd to erupt in cheers for his victory.

'Congratulations, Aito,' Aunt Nikki said, patting him on the back as they walked back to the group. 'The rumours are true, after all; I have finally lost a race. Well, everyone, that's enough for today. I want to thank you all for doing this. I know it wasn't easy for some of you, but it was necessary nonetheless.'

Before anyone could even think of leaving the garden, Aunt Nikki clicked her tongue as though a piece of infor-mation that had slipped through the cracks of her mind suddenly resurfaced. 'That reminds me,' she said. 'I will be leaving for Romania tonight on official business and will return just before the end of the holidays. During this time, Marius and our capable team will be in charge of the meetings; I advise you to adhere to their instructions—after all, this is for your own good. Thank you everyone, enjoy the rest of your evening.'

Just as Aunt Nikki was leaving the gathering, Amen and Iska broke away from the group to catch up with her.

'What's up, girls?' said Aunt Nikki, stealing a glance at her watch. 'By the way, both of you did great today.'

'Great?' Iska scoffed. 'I wasn't even able to show my ability.'

'The important thing is to not put pressure on yourself. Abilities or not, you're special in every way. Both of you.'

'Aunt Nikki,' said Amen, 'I have a question.'

'All right, honey, but make it quick. I'm in a hurry.'

'I'm sorry it's taken so long for me to tell you,' said Amen, her eyes unable to focus on anything but Aunt Nikki's collarbone. 'I spiked the day our mam died—'

'*That* explains why you're as comfortable with your ability as Aito is with his,' Aunt Nikki interrupted.

'But do you think me spiking was what killed her?'

Aunt Nikki glanced at her watch again, a second too long this time. 'It's absurd for you to even think Aré's passing was your fault,' she said finally. 'No Unix's spike has ever harmed a loved one.'

'But—'

'I'm sorry, girls, that's all the time I have right now. But I promise we can talk about this some more when I get back from my trip.'

In a flash, Aunt Nikki was gone, leaving Iska and Amen to make their way back to their dormitory.

'Well, that's that,' said Iska, as she and Amen walked along a slippery, cobblestoned path that led away from the west garden and towards the girls' half of Digglefield. 'I told you; it wasn't your fault.'

Amen let out a pitiful laugh. 'You can't tell me you were convinced by Aunt Nikki's answer,' she said.

'Well, she's sort of an expert on this matter,' said Iska, removing stray strands of her hair from her face. 'So, yeah, I *am* convinced.'

'It's just—whenever I think about it—it kills me that we might never know what really happened to Mam.'

Iska was just about to agree with Amen on this when she remembered something that halted her in her tracks. 'I have something to show you.'

3. THE PLAN

The walls and ceiling of the girls' common room were painted a bland shade of grey, with only a few pieces of candy-coloured furniture providing any sort of contrast. Apart from the room's massive window, which offered a view of Digglefield's east garden, the only other notable features were a floor-to-ceiling bookshelf that occupied the space where a home entertainment system would have been and a state-of-the art ping-pong table where two girls were currently battling it out in an eleven-point game.

A few metres away from the girls, Amen and Iska were seated on one of the sofas discussing the contents of a business card Iska had stumbled upon the day before.

'It still doesn't add up,' said Amen impatiently. 'Anyone could have that surname.'

'I get you,' Iska replied. 'But didn't Mam mention once that she had a brother named Oshu?'

'More like we overheard her saying it to someone. And that was a long time ago; it could have been a different name we heard. How did you come across the card again?'

'I'm pretty sure it's the same name,' said Iska. 'I told you; I saw it on the ground just as Aito and Aunt Nikki finished their race.'

Amen absent-mindedly watched the girls playing table tennis, trying to understand the coincidence. 'To be honest, this is all a bit strange,' she said. 'Maybe it fell out of one of the minders' pockets, or it belongs to one of the lads?'

'Maybe. But you hold on to it, I'll be right back,' said Iska.

'Where are you going?' asked Amen.

'To the study to get a laptop. I want to do a quick search.'

Still uncertain about the little matt black card, Amen

held it up and read its golden inscriptions again:

Oshu Tella
Chief Executive Officer
Quillitel
oshutella@quillitel.com

Amen wondered if this person held any significance to her and Iska. What were the chances? They had never known of any relatives besides Aunt Nikki, but Aunt Nikki wasn't exactly a relative; she was Mam's best friend. In fact, it only just occurred to Amen that Mam never told them how she met Aunt Nikki. Why had she been so secretive? What was she hiding? All these questions lingered, but Mam wasn't even here to provide any answers. She was gone, without warning, leaving them to search for clues in a suspicious-looking card found in Digglefield's garden.

'Here,' whispered Iska, 'where were you? You looked lost in your thoughts.'

'I'm always lost in my thoughts,' said Amen. 'So, what's the plan?'

'There's none, really. I just want to look up the name and see what I find.'

'Grand. It's not like this will all come back to bite us in the arse.'

'Oh, would you stop being so pessimistic,' said Iska as she turned on the computer and waited for it to boot.

As soon as the laptop's screen lit up, Iska loaded up a web browser and typed in the name from the business card. Without wasting any time, she clicked on the first article the browser returned and scanned a few lines before looking at Amen in disbelief.

'What? What is it?' said Amen, curious.

'Here, read for yourself.'

Amen took the laptop from Iska, adjusted the screen, and read the contents of the article:

Oshu Tella (born 6 March 1976) is a British-Nigerian internet entrepreneur and investor. He is best known as the founder and current chairman of Quillitel—an online classifieds company that connects independent creators of arts and crafts with buyers worldwide. Tella stepped down as CEO of Quillitel in 2014 to focus on his philanthropic work in Nigeria. Tella's net worth is said to be around the region of $750 million, largely owing to his 51% stake in Quillitel.

'Okay, he's rich,' said Amen, still scrolling through the article. 'But I don't see what this has to do with us. It still doesn't mean anything.'

'True,' Iska replied. 'But imagine if he were our uncle. Wouldn't that be crazy?'

'It would, but there's no way we can find that out—oh no bloody way.'

Iska had a mischievous grin on her face. 'I mean, what do we have to lose?' she said.

'What if we get caught and reported for pranking,' said Amen, waving her arms in the air, 'or spamming him?'

'Amen, you do know cold emailing is perfectly legal… I think.'

'You think?' said Amen. 'Well, since we're sharing our thoughts, I *think* you've lost your mind, and I *think* we should hand the card over to Marius. Someone probably lost it and could be looking for it right now.'

'Come on, how naïve can you be?' Iska shot back. 'Who in this home could possibly be acquainted with a multimillionaire?'

'That's exactly my point,' Amen's voice grew louder. 'We—don't—know. But for some odd reason, you feel perfectly comfortable contacting this "multimillionaire".'

'He could be our uncle; he has Mam's last name—'

'He's not our uncle,' Amen replied.

'But if you really—'

'He's *not*,' screamed Amen, causing the girls playing table tennis to flinch in fear. 'Look,' Amen continued, standing up from the sofa, 'I don't know why you want to do this but count me out.'

Iska watched Amen leave the common room, her mind swirling with conflicting thoughts. Amen had raised some valid points: this person was likely just a stranger who happened to share their mother's last name. What was the point in reaching out to him and hoping for some connection? Wouldn't it be better to focus their time and energy on understanding the world of Unix instead? But then again, just a couple of weeks ago, she and Amen had no idea they were anything other than regular humans. Now Aunt Nikki had shown them the world was filled with endless possibilities.

Iska placed the laptop in front of her, took one last look at the card, and then began typing.

Upon returning to the room, Iska was greeted by an enveloping darkness with the gentle moonlight streaming in through the skylight, the only source of illumination. It seemed everyone else was already fast asleep, so she quietly changed into her pyjamas and climbed into bed, trying not to disturb the silence. Just as Iska was getting comfortable, she was startled by a voice in her head.

You all right? Amen asked.

Sure, Iska replied. *Why are you still awake?*

I couldn't sleep.

Hey, Iska's inner voice grew soft. *I'm sorry I upset you earlier. That wasn't my intention.*

I know. I should be the one apologising for lashing out like that. I'm just—

Just what? thought Iska.

I'm just really scared.

I told you, it's not a crime to cold email anyone.

That's not why I'm scared. Amen turned over in her bed. *I'm worried that the man might actually be our uncle.*

There was a brief pause as both girls considered the possibility.

I guess there's only one way to find out, Amen continued. *We have to send him an email. What do you think?*

I already did, thought Iska.

You eejit! Amen struggled to contain her laugh. *You went ahead with it anyway.*

I mean, I did think about it, for about a minute. Iska defended herself.

You're so stubborn, said Amen flatly. *But that's one of the many reasons why I love you. I'm sorry for today.*

Water under the bridge. Iska replied.

So, what did you say in the email?

Amen chuckled as Iska described the contents of the email she had sent; both girls were grateful that they could have an animated conversation without disturbing their roommates.

With Aunt Nikki away, Marius, a man known throughout Digglefield for having a temper that matched his height, was given the responsibility of overseeing weekly meetings. Today, his first order of business was dividing Amen, Iska, and the rest of the teenagers into two smaller groups: those who had discovered their abilities, and those who hadn't.

'This what will happen,' said Marius, deciding to lead the latter group of teens himself, 'you all try hardest to show abilities. If you not show before the end of today, is safe to say that you Reegs… Questions?'

'I don't think that's fair,' Senait objected. 'It's a bit difficult for some of us; giving us just one day doesn't seem ideal.'

Marius shrugged dismissively. 'You see, I am practical man,' he said in his thick Moldovan accent. 'In my head, you *already* Reegs. If you no show abilities today, tiny chance of showing in the future. It best to get a move on, so you focus on other strengths. Any more questions?'

No one in the group uttered a word. In all honesty, most of the teenagers seemed to have accepted their fate. Not Iska, though. She, along with Lake and a few others, worked hard all morning to prove to Marius that they had something special. Yet, despite their best efforts, each person's attempt amounted to nothing, and at the stroke of noon, Marius ordered them to take a break.

'No need be hard on yourself,' Marius said dryly. 'Is not all bad being Reegs. Maybe you not have special abilities, but Reegs still have exceptional talents compare to weak humans.'

'How do you mean?' asked Lake.

'Why you think you so athletic, Lake? And you, Ronan, where you think you get your knack for music? Same for you, Iska. You exceptional intelligence not just coincidence. All of you have…special something; is who you are as Unix… All right, go relax, we meet in one hour.'

Since the west garden was crowded with clusters of teenagers exchanging their experiences of the day so far, Iska, Amen, Aito, and Lake decided to have lunch together in the atrium instead. Today, the cafeteria was serving burritos, carrot and coriander soup, chicken cordon bleu sandwiches, and white rice with curry sauce. After waiting in line for what felt like a lifetime—thanks to a group of indecisive girls struggling to choose their meals—Lake and Aito were finally served their sandwiches, while Amen opted for a burrito bowl and Iska chose the soup. Although there were plenty of free tables, Iska suggested they sit at the one farthest from the entrance to the west garden, away from all the chatter about abilities.

'So, how did it go?' Amen slid her empty burrito bowl towards the middle of the table where she, Iska, and the boys were sitting.

'Well, we're more or less Reegs,' Iska replied matter-of-factly. 'Right, Lake?'

'I guess,' said Lake, shoving the last bit of his chicken sandwich into his mouth. 'It's not all doom and gloom, though. Apparently, we have watered-down versions of your abilities.'

'What does that even mean?' Aito asked, glancing around the nearly empty atrium for no apparent reason.

'It means that most Reegs are more talented than humans, but not as gifted as other Unix,' Lake explained.

'In other words,' Iska added, 'Lake might be the next Lionel Messi, and I'm just really good at math.'

'I really don't mind,' said Lake. 'Couldn't be arsed either way.'

'Speak for yourself,' Iska retorted. 'Aito can teleport at will, Amen can manipulate elements, and what can I do? Solve unsolvable problems?'

'Don't let it get you down,' said Amen. 'Having these abilities isn't all that it seems. It's not like we're using them for anything important. We just need to learn to control it, that's all.'

'Easy for you to say,' said Iska. 'You know what? It doesn't even matter. Break's nearly over, and we need to get back to the others soon.'

Back in the garden, Marius was discussing with his assistants while waiting for the entire group to gather. He began to speak just as the latecomers were arriving.

'Good job to everyone today,' he said, rocking on the balls of his feet. 'I know some of you disappointed that you don't have abilities, so I make clear one thing. The character of a Unix not measured by their ability; it measured by their principles and sense of judgement. Personally, I seen Unix with strong abilities but rotten characters, and I seen Reegs with integrity that make you wonder. For few here who Reegs, you sulk all you want, I not really care. Or you can lean into what make you special and be best person you can.

'We done here. Next session in two days; more details will follow. Enjoy rest of the day.'

As soon as Marius finished addressing the crowd, everyone dispersed in different directions. Ignoring everyone and walking as fast as she could, Iska was already halfway through the back garden when Amen caught up to her.

'A couple of us are going to the beach, are you down?'

'Yous can go without me,' said Iska, still walking towards their dormitory. 'I'm not in the mood.'

'What's wrong with you? Is this because of the Reeg thing? I'm surprised this is doing your head in. I've told you; it really isn't a big deal. Did you even listen to anything Marius said?'

'Oh, I'm sorry,' said Iska, embarrassed by the unsteadiness in her voice. 'I'm sorry that I don't magically feel better just because you and Marius say so. I'm sorry that I feel bad because this is the one thing that might have made me feel connected to Mam, somehow.'

'Do you hear yourself?' said Amen, trying to close the gap between herself and Iska. 'Do you think Mam would care if you had abilities or not?'

'I guess we'll never know, will we?'

This question slowed Amen to a halt while Iska continued around a corner and out of sight.

Except for a few elderly beachgoers soaking in the sun, Claremont Beach was mostly empty. Today, the tide was lower than usual, perfect for a nice, long walk along the beach's shimmering sandbar. But in typical fashion, most of the teenagers headed east of the beach to try and spot some travelling seals, leaving Amen, Lake, and Aito to walk in the opposite direction by themselves.

'What's wrong with your sister?' said Aito, finally breaking the awkward silence that had slowly built since they began their walk.

'She seems to be very upset about not having any special abilities,' said Amen, her voice slightly muted by the crashing waves.

'No offence,' said Aito. 'But she needs to get over herself—'

'—Aito,' Lake interrupted.

'Chap what? You know it's true. I mean, you don't have

54

any abilities either, but you're not moaning about it.'

'Fair enough,' said Lake. 'But people are different. It's obviously tough on her if she's acting this way.'

'Yous are both right,' Amen chimed in. 'I've never seen her like this before. But at the same time, she really needs to move on. It's not the end of the world…'

Although she tried not to show it, Amen regretted her last words almost immediately; she might have believed everything she said, but speaking about Iska made her feel awful for not being more understanding in the first place. *Iska, if you can hear me, I hope you're okay,* she thought in a bid to salvage the situation.

Iska heard Amen but chose to ignore her. All she wanted was to fall asleep, to forget the disappointment of the day, but different thoughts clouded her mind: she had no abilities, Amen was stronger than her, and what would Mam think? She would be so disappointed. The thoughts continued to nag at her until one of them jolted her upright in her bed.

Hurrying into the girls' study, Iska found a vacant chair and grabbed a laptop. After a brief moment of clicking and typing, Iska couldn't believe her eyes. The stranger had replied to her email. Taking a deep breath, she began to read:

Dear Iska,

I am delighted that you reached out to me. Your theory was right—I am indeed your uncle. Aré was my older sister.

I would be more than happy to meet you and your sister. You are welcome to Nigeria at any time. Please let me know when you plan to visit so that I can make the necessary arrangements to welcome you. I eagerly await your response.

Cheers,
Oshu Tella

Iska fought back the tears welling in her eyes; she didn't want to have to explain to other girls in the study why she was staring at a computer screen and crying. Iska also realised that Amen would want to know the news, but then she immediately remembered that Amen was at the beach, which was about thirteen minutes away from Digglefield.

Still trying to figure out her next move, Iska was just about to log out of her email inbox when she noticed something unsettling: the email from the man claiming to be her uncle had come in three days ago. It dawned on Iska that three days was more than enough time for her to have sent a reply back, and she began to panic. She stared at the computer screen for a few minutes, trying to conceive a sensible plan. Finally, she made a decision. She would tell Amen everything when she got back home; but for now, she needed to act fast.

Good afternoon, Mr Tella,

You have no idea how much your reply means to us. We're elated. Thank you so much.

We're currently on school break, and will be for the next two months. If it is not inconvenient for you, my sister and I can make the necessary arrangements to visit you in Nigeria by next weekend. Would this be suitable for you?

Kind regards,
Iska Lyons

Iska returned the laptop to its locker and made her way back to her room. She lay in bed, staring up at Amen's mattress, wondering what Nigeria was like. She had seen photos and movies from when they lived with Mam, but that was a long time ago—those memories obviously couldn't compare to the real thing. She imagined the look on Amen's face after breaking the news to her: the multimillionaire stranger they had found on the internet was, lo and behold, their uncle. The thoughts swirled around in Iska's head like trapped houseflies; but unlike before when they had kept her awake, this time she slowly drifted into unconsciousness with a smile on her face.

All the chatter from the girls awoke Iska, and her eyes flickered open to see Amen sitting at the end of her bed.

'How long have you been asleep?' said Amen as she took off her shoes.

'I don't know, an hour. Maybe two. How was the beach?'

'Grand. You didn't miss much, though,' Amen replied, rubbing the soles of her feet. 'Look, I want to talk to you.'

Iska pushed herself up against her headboard until she was sitting upright. 'So do I, but you go first,' she said.

'Well, it's about what happened earlier today. I know you're upset, but I hope you can find a way to move past this Reeg thing. I'm here to help you, and I promise everything will be fine.'

'I know you want to help,' said Iska. 'It's hard to process; just give me some time to get used to it, okay?'

'Take as long as you need. I just want you to know I'm here for you... What did you want to tell me?'

Iska discreetly glanced around the room and motioned for Amen to come closer. 'You won't believe it,' she whispered. 'I got a reply from Mr Tella.'

'And?'

'He's our uncle!'

Amen clasped one hand over her mouth to stop herself from screaming. 'You're taking the piss.'

'No, I'm not. And, you can try to act cool.'

'Sorry, sorry. I just wasn't expecting this. Wow.'

'Wow's an understatement,' said Iska.

'I don't even know what question to ask first... What did he say? How are you certain he's our uncle?'

'Amen, I don't think someone as busy and important as this man would have the time to play games. He's the real deal. He says we're more than welcome to visit him in Nigeria at any time.'

'Wow,' Amen murmured quietly. 'That's very—forward of him.'

'I told him we could make arrangements to visit by next weekend.'

'You did what?' said Amen.

Iska gave Amen a gentle kick. 'Keep your voice down, will ye?'

'How can I?' said Amen, her nostrils flared, as they usually were whenever she was angry. 'When you've made plans for us to go see a complete stranger on another continent.'

'Well, as you've just rightly said, it's only a plan—nothing's set in stone. I'm not going to lie; your lack of belief in me is very disappointing. I've obviously thought things through.'

'I've *obviously* thought things through,' said Amen mockingly. 'Okay, genius, tell me how we're going to get to Nigeria without money or passports.'

Iska scanned the room once again to make sure no one was eavesdropping on their conversation. Satisfied that Rima, Senait, and a few other girls were chattering about their day, Iska refocused her attention on Amen. *It's better if we speak in private,* she thought, *I don't want to take any chances... Look, I wanted to run things by you, but you weren't home, so I had to think fast. It was only after I replied to his email that I remembered our passports had expired. But before I fell asleep, I had an idea.*

You had an idea, Amen replied sarcastically. *Well, go on.*

Iska paused for a few seconds as though turning the idea over in her head once more. *Aito.*

Aito? What about him? Amen asked.

Ugh; do I have to spell it out? He can take us to Nigeria, he can blink us there.

Oh my God, Amen gasped. *Oh my days.*

I know, right? thought Iska, the smugness in her voice unmistakable.

My sister is a lunatic! Iska, you're insane. I mean, I knew you had a wild imagination, but this is next level, even for you.

Iska looked over at Amen's stunned face. *I don't understand. Do you like the idea or not?*

Is that even a rational question? Of course, I don't like the idea. I think this is the craziest thing I've ever heard from you, and now more than ever, I wish you'd never found that card.

You need to calm down, thought Iska. *What part of the plan bothers you?*

Everything! screamed Amen. *The fact that you had this idea in the first place. Let me ask you some questions: Do you know if Aito can blink as far as Nigeria? Do you know if he can blink with another person, let alone two people? Have you even considered that trying such a thing could hurt him and us? Where would we tell Marius we're going? And why would he allow us?*

I understand your concerns, but— Iska was beginning to say, but Rima interrupted.

'Yous are doing that creepy thing where you stare at each other for ages without speaking,' she said. 'Senait and I are going to get dinner. Are yous coming?'

Without even giving it a thought, the twins decided that dinner could wait.

'You can go without us,' said Amen. 'We'll meet yous in the dining hall in a bit.'

As soon as the girls left the room, Amen and Iska resumed their conversation.

'I'll give it to you, those are valid questions,' said Iska. 'But I told you, I've already thought things through. I'm fairly certain Aito can blink to Nigeria; after all, he blinked to England when he was only eleven. As for him being able to blink with other people, we'll just have to try and see. With Marius, it's a bit tricky, but I'm sure we can find a way around it.'

Amen stood up and paced the room. 'I can't believe you've built your plan on an isolated event that happened years ago,' she said. '*And* you have no concrete excuse to give our guardian. Have you considered that Aito might not agree to this?'

'All right, maybe it isn't the best plan,' Iska admitted. 'It's still better than nothing, and I'm willing to give it a shot. But I can't do this without you—I need you to be onboard.'

'I don't know if I want to be a part of this, it's too dangerous—'

'Come on, Amen,' Iska interrupted. 'Have faith in something for once. We never knew our father, lost Mam, and have been living here for nearly six years doing the same things over and over again. If you aren't exhausted, I am.

'Don't you want more than just the occasional trip to Phoenix Park or the mundane excursions to the Guinness factory? Don't you want to know Mam's country, or meet our uncle—our only living relative, as far as we know?'

'I would like to, but—'

'But what?' Iska interrupted. 'The plan isn't child-proof enough for you? Well, guess what! We aren't kids anymore. I know I said I need you on this, but I'll find a way to Nigeria with or without you. So, I'll ask you one last time. Are you coming with me or not?'

It felt like an eternity to Iska, but the silence lasted only a few seconds before Amen's lips parted. 'When do we speak to Aito?'

'Yes!' said Iska, punching the air. 'I thought you were going to say no for a second there.'

'So did I,' said Amen, a smile forming at both corners of her mouth. 'But I figured you're incredibly reckless and you *do* need guidance.'

'Give me a hug, you,' said Iska, making an open-armed gesture. 'You're the best.'

'Yeah, yeah, and you're a pain in the arse.'

Today's meeting arrangement was similar to the previous

one: two groups, the first consisting of Reegs and the other of Unix. Since it had already been established at the last meeting that members of the former group possessed no supernatural abilities, Marius decided to skip training and lecture Iska and her teammates on the documented history of Unix instead. He spoke about how names were assigned to abilities, famous Unix in different industries, and past battles between Unix belonging to prominent clans. Surprisingly, the information-packed session went by quickly and soon came to an end. When the two groups reconvened, Marius delivered a brief speech, reminding them that they had one more session left for the week.

As soon as they were dismissed, Iska and Amen caught up with Aito and Lake, who were on their way to the atrium to get lunch. Although each of them wanted something different, the limited menu at the cafeteria forced Iska and Amen to order sweet chilli rice, chips, and chicken tenders before settling into an empty table with the boys.

'Iska, you seem to be in a better mood today,' Lake said as he cut into the grilled sea bass on his plate.

'Yeah, I guess so, but let's not say anything that might change that, okay?' said Iska, causing Lake and Aito to raise their hands in surrender.

'So, Aito,' Iska continued. 'How've you found the training sessions?'

'Grand; I'm getting better at blinking every day,' Aito replied. 'Apparently the name "blink" comes from the fact that when I teleport, it sounds like a blink. How cool is that?'

'Very cool,' Iska replied a little too enthusiastically. 'I'm curious. How does it feel when you blink?'

'It's hard to explain. It's almost like there's a slight pinch in my body just before I teleport, and then it's over. There's a bit of queasiness after, but that doesn't last long.'

'Deadly,' Amen chimed in. 'What's the farthest you reckon you could go?'

'Anywhere in the world, I suppose,' Aito replied, 'Marius says I just need to work on my stamina.'

'Do you think you could blink with another person?' Iska asked.

'I don't know,' said Aito. 'Jaysus, what's with all these questions? Lake, am I missing something?'

Lake shrugged his shoulders.

'Well then,' said Aito, now focusing his gaze on Iska and Amen. 'What's with the questions?'

Iska and Amen exchanged a nervous glance between themselves before Amen finally spoke. 'Lake, if you don't mind, we would like to borrow Aito for a moment.'

Surprisingly, Lake nodded in approval and continued with his meal.

'Aito, shall we go to the rooftop terrace?' Amen's voice was raspy with nervousness.

'Em, sure,' Aito replied. 'I won't lie, I'm scared. Lake, come look for me if I'm not back in ten minutes.'

Making their way to the terrace, Amen and Iska had nearly forgotten how easy it was to get queasy climbing up Digglefield's one and only spiral staircase. Upon reaching the roof, a gust of cold air forced Iska, Amen, and Aito to hide their hands in their pockets and huddle closely together.

'Of all the places to have a chat,' Aito said through clenched teeth.

'Sorry,' said Iska. 'We thought it'd be private up here.'

'So, what do you want to talk to me about?'

Leaving no details out, Iska and Amen explained their plans to Aito and expressed how desperately they needed his help.

'Let me get this straight,' said Aito as soon as the twins were done talking. 'You want me to teleport you guys to Nigeria, and then when you're done with your business there, you want me to come get you?'

'Exactly,' Amen and Iska replied in unison.

'Christ on a bike, you two are insane. I didn't even know you had it in you.'

'So, will you help us?' said Iska.

'Are you joking?' Aito said with a laugh. 'Of course; but on one condition.'

'Oh God, what is it?' Amen asked.

'Lake and I come with yous, and we stay the whole trip.'

Iska and Amen shook their heads in disagreement. 'Nope, that's not happening,' said Iska.

'You can't come along,' Amen added.

'Why not?' said Aito.

'Did you listen to anything we just said?' said Iska. 'We've never met this man before, plus he expects just me and Amen.'

'That's exactly why I'm coming along. I'm not just going to teleport you to a stranger and leave. What if something bad happens to yous? I can't have that on my conscience.'

'So, what? Are we just supposed to tell him we have two friends tagging along?' said Iska.

Aito kissed his teeth. 'I guess so.'

'No way.' Iska was shaking her head again. 'There's no way—'

'—Iska, he has a point,' said Amen. 'The man could be an imposter. I'd rather we had Aito with us just in case anything funny happens.'

'What if he doesn't agree to let us bring friends?' Iska asked.

'We have to find a way to convince him then,' Amen replied.

While the twins were mulling over Aito's suggestion, Aito was failing miserably at hiding his excitement. 'So, is this thing happening?' he asked again.

'Yeah, I guess,' Iska finally conceded. 'But why do you want Lake to come along?'

'Because he's my best mate?' Aito replied with a shrug, clearly confused as to why Iska would even ask such a question. 'There's no way I'm going to Nigeria without him.'

Upon agreeing to his terms, Iska and Amen shook hands with Aito. They had only just begun their descent back to the atrium when they ran into Lake on the staircase.

'I was just about to come get you,' said Lake. 'It's been over ten minutes since you all left. What's the craic?'

With a big smile plastered on his face, Aito slung his arm around Lake's shoulders. 'Chap, we're going to Nigeria.'

4. A VISIT

Hi Iska,

I am perfectly fine with the timing. I'd suggest flying in on Friday so that I can receive you and your sister at the airport. Do you need any form of supervision, an invitation letter, or proof of address from me to purchase your flight ticket? In any case, please let me know if you need anything. Hope to see you soon.

Cheers,
Oshu

Iska and Amen read and reread the new email in the girls' common room before taking turns trying to compose a response.

'This is really frustrating,' said Iska as she deleted her latest email draft. 'How am I supposed to make this request?'

'You're over-thinking it,' said Amen. 'Just say we have two friends coming along, and ask if he's okay with that.'

'What if he isn't okay with them coming along? Will I say Aito and Lake are our boyfriends—to sound more convincing?'

Amen chuckled. 'No, you won't,' she said. 'Look, reply to him as I told you. If he really looks forward to seeing us, he won't refuse. And if he does refuse, then I guess he's an uncle not worth meeting. Now, type up the reply; the session's going to start soon.'

Marius was not impressed; about a third of the group decided not to turn up for training today. Nevertheless, he ran over the training agenda with his colleagues at the head of the garden while Amen, Iska, and the others who were present waited awkwardly.

'Seem a few of your peers lose hope because they Reeg,' Marius said when he finally addressed the group. 'They think because they got no abilities, training is waste of time. No matter, we still hold meeting. But we keep short this time, and we focus on facts and history of our kind, instead of exercise.'

Without hesitation, Marius sat in the grass and made himself comfortable, with everyone following suit.

'Well, I know how people in my group is doing,' said Marius as he uprooted tiny blades of grass from the earth, 'But I learn from my colleagues, some of you in other group is learning your abilities pretty fast. Aito, they say you prodigy.'

'Really?' said Aito with a smile. 'I try my best, but I think I could be better.'

'You keep practising,' said Marius. 'You could be good as Kwame Acheampong.'

'Who's that?' asked Rima.

Marius seemed taken aback by this question. 'Aito, you know why you called Blinker?' he said.

'Because of the sound my teleportation makes.'

'That just trivial reason,' Marius scoffed. 'The real reason you called Blinker is 'cause how fast you teleport—you move through space at same speed as blink of eye: three hundred and fifty thousand microseconds, to be precise. That's why you win race against Nikki.'

'That's amazing,' said Senait, her voice barely matching her impressed demeanour. 'But what does this have to do with the person you mentioned?'

'Kwame was Blinker just like Aito, but similarity end there. Kwame most remarkable Blinker in Unix history. There are stories of his exploits, but by far, most famous achievement is Kwame being able to blink through space *and* time. It said that he blinked to past on different occasions to help his people in the Cape Coast Castle avoid being sold into slavery.'

'Jaysus,' said Aito. 'That kinda sounds too good to be true.'

'Shame you not believe,' Marius replied dryly. 'I guess you'll not be good as Kwame, after all.'

More facts and history lessons about Unix followed, to the extent that the session lasted longer than Marius had intended. Finally, an hour before noon, the second-in-command ended the meeting by informing Amen, Iska, and the others about the rendezvous and agenda for the following week.

While everyone else vacated the garden, Iska, Amen, Lake, and Aito hung back until they were the only ones left.

'What's the plan?' said Iska. 'Do you want us to practise here?'

'Are you taking the piss?' said Aito. 'There's no way we're practising in Digglefield. Lake and I thought it'd be better to go to Claremont Beach.'

'Why Claremont?' Iska asked.

'Well, for one, we don't have to explain ourselves to Marius; two, there's a lot more space.' Aito explained.

'What about people?' said Amen.

'It's a weekday. Barely anyone is at the beach on a weekday, plus we'll be as discreet as possible. Any objections?'

Amen and Iska's silence indicated a consensus, and in a matter of minutes, all four of them were out of Digglefield and on their way to the seaside.

As Aito had predicted, a flock of hungry seagulls were the only visible visitors. However, out of caution, Iska, Amen, and the boys scanned the entire area, starting from the west end of the beach and continuing along its coastline until they reached the opposite end.

Satisfied that they were mostly alone, Aito, who for some odd reason had been smirking at the twins for the past few minutes, pointed to a solitary island across the sea. 'Has anyone ever been to Ireland's Eye?' he said.

No one gave a response.

'I guess that makes all of us,' he continued. 'Well, that's grand because I'm blinking us there—'

'What?' said Iska in bewilderment.

'Ah, come on, don't do that,' said Aito, doing his best to suppress his laughter. 'This was your idea, after all. So, this is what's going to happen: since I've never blinked with anyone, I have to go with yous one at a time, to be extra careful. Who wants to go first?'

Lake, Amen, and Iska glanced at each other repeatedly, each of them wondering who would volunteer, until Lake finally stepped forward.

'What did you say the feeling was like again?' Lake asked.

'You'll be fine, bro,' said Aito, 'If you want, you can close your eyes.'

'And you're sure you can *see* where you're going?' said Lake, sounding really worried.

'More or less,' Aito replied, squinting his eyes in the direction of the island.

'Jesus,' said Lake, putting his hands on his head.

'Chap, there are ladies behind you. Stop embarrassing us.'

Trying to save face, Lake drew in a deep breath and closed his eyes. 'All right,' he said, 'I'm ready.'

'As soon as I drop him off,' said Aito, who had his arm wrapped around Lake's quivering shoulders. 'I'll come back for yous, okay?'

But before Amen and Iska could nod their heads in agreement, Aito and Lake had vanished, leaving the space they had been standing in completely empty. Filled with awe, Iska went over to examine the boys' footprints, while Amen watched intently until she was startled by someone behind her.

It was Aito, his hair and face damp. 'There's a bit of drizzle over there,' he said.

'How was it?' Amen asked.

'Grand; it wasn't that bad.'

'It wasn't *that bad*?' said Amen, worriedly.

'Please don't make me lie,' Aito replied. 'This time I'm going with both of you.'

'Why? You said you'd take us one at a time,' said Iska.

'Yeah, but that was because I wasn't so sure what would happen.'

'Now you are?' asked Iska, her voice tinged with concern.

'Yes. And I don't see any point coming for yous one after the other. It'll save us time and me energy.'

'Are you sure about this, Aito?' said Amen.

'Yes,' Aito replied, taking hold of each twin's hand. 'I'll do a short countdown, so yous can get ready.'

Amen and Iska let out long breaths and steadied themselves as they held onto Aito as firmly as they could.

'Ready, girls,' said Aito. 'Here we go: three, two—'

Iska and Amen felt their lungs and just about every other organ in their bodies instantly collapse, and they would have lost consciousness if it weren't for the harrowing sound drilling into their heads. Hurtling through what looked like outer space, both girls were sure they were about to be ripped to shreds when all the twisting and turning suddenly stopped. Cold, wet air whipped against Amen and Iska's faces as they scrambled to regain their vision and make sense of their surroundings. Gradually, the wild shrubs, the algae-coated rocks, and even the flock of seabirds quietly nesting began to come into focus. The twins also noticed blood trickling down Aito's nose.

'Aito, what's wrong?' said Amen, still gasping for air.

'Ah, it's nothing,' Aito replied, wiping his face on the sleeve of his shirt. 'How do yous feel?'

'You eejit!' screamed Iska. 'You didn't count to zero! We weren't ready.'

'And you never would have been. It was for your own good.'

'I'm going to make you bleed again,' Iska shot back. 'Just as soon as I can feel my arms.'

'But it was worth it right?' said Aito, pointing to a beach in the distance.

'Is that—Is that Claremont?' said Iska. The water wavered between them like a gulf, making the shore look a thousand kilometres away.

'Yep,' Aito replied, a proud smile on his face.

'We actually made it to the island,' Amen muttered. 'Aito, you're amazing.'

'I know!'

'Where's Lake?'

'Here,' said Lake, breathing unevenly. 'Yous need to come see this.'

The tower stood about ten metres tall, with its thick walls adorned in an array of colourful flowers that emitted a natural, sweet fragrance.

'What is it?' said Amen, brushing her hand against the structure's plant-coated walls.

'It's a Martello,' Lake replied.

'A what?'

'A Martello tower,' Lake repeated. 'You know, the ones used by soldiers during past wars. They are now antiquated, like this big boy right here.'

Iska sized up the tower. 'How was something this beautiful used for war?'

'It's only beautiful now because it has been dormant for so many years,' Lake replied. 'Back in the days, many soldiers dreaded being stationed at a Martello due to the severe consequences they entailed.'

'Where do these lead?' said Aito, pointing to concrete stairs that curved their way up and around the tower.

'To the best part,' Lake answered, heading up the stairs. 'Come, I'll show you.'

Upon reaching the top of the Martello, Iska and Amen's mouths fell open. They had never seen the sun this close before, or the sky, dotted with soft, lone clouds, stretching into infinity as it did now. Despite Lake's claims that it had been built for war, the tower seemed designed to remind anyone who stood atop it to never take the lounging grey seals or the wailing razorbills, or any of nature's precious little gifts for granted.

'This place is magical,' said Amen, oblivious to the tears welling up in her eyes.

'Woo-hoo!' screamed Aito. 'Now, that's something you don't see every day.'

Without even thinking, Iska, Amen, and the boys each settled into comfortable positions to admire the sun. They only realised they had been on the island for far too long when the giant orange orb was already halfway down the horizon.

'So, who's going first?' Iska asked miserably.

'Guys,' said Aito, rising to his feet. 'I was thinking, I want to take us back together.'

'No, Aito!' Amen shot back. 'You're pushing yourself too hard.'

'She's right, chap,' Lake added. 'You need to take it easy.'

'I'm fine,' said Aito. 'It was just a nosebleed. Besides, I need to practise for Nigeria.'

After a few minutes of debating Aito—and questioning his sanity—Amen, Iska, and Lake finally gave in to his suggestion and flanked him on either side.

'You're one crazy fella,' said Iska as she locked hands with Aito.

'I know,' Aito replied, an unusual determination on his face. 'Yous ready?'

'Ready!'

With a sibilant whisper, they teleported off the island.

On the way back to Digglefield, Amen, Iska, and the boys discussed the logistics of their plan, trying to uncover any weaknesses.

'What will be your excuse for missing future meetings?' Aito asked.

'We think there's someone who can help us,' Iska replied. 'What about yous?'

'Don't know yet, to be honest. But I reckon Lake and I will come up with something,' said Aito.

Amen kissed her teeth. 'Guys, we really need to be smart about this,' she said. 'Under no circumstance can Marius ever find out we're not in Digglefield. I don't want to imagine what he or Aunt Nikki would do if they did.'

'Don't fret yourself,' said Aito reassuringly. 'It won't come to that. By the way, why do yous call Nikki your aunt?'

Iska and Amen chuckled at the question, realising how strange the words "Aunt Nikki" must have sounded to other people. 'Well, she used to be our mam's best friend,' Iska explained, 'and since we can remember, we've always called her that.'

'Ah, that makes sense,' said Aito before turning to Lake. 'Chap, we were both wrong.'

'About what?' said Amen.

'Lake and I took wild guesses at what Nikki might be to yous. *I* said she's probably your aunt, but he said she's your godmother.'

Amen laughed. 'Okay, I get the aunt angle,' she said. 'But godmother?'

'Hey, you can't blame a lad for trying,' Lake replied with a shrug.

It was just about time for dinner when they arrived home, so Iska and Amen said their goodbyes to Aito and Lake, promising to be in touch with more feedback.

In the dining hall, girls belonging to different cliques and age groups sat and ate together while they jabbered on about their day. Amen and Iska, who usually shared a table with Senait, Rima, and a few younger girls, slowly worked away at their plates of mashed potato, roasted chicken, veggies, and chilli gravy while reflecting on all that they'd accomplished so far.

The twins were grateful that Aito and Lake were in full support of their plan to visit Nigeria and relieved that Aito was able to blink long distances with them. Now, all Iska and Amen needed to do was come up with a plan to conceal their absence while they were away.

At the end of dinner, the twins and a few other girls stayed back to clear the plates and wipe down the tables while everyone exited the hall. Of all the chores Iska and Amen had to do in Digglefield, cleaning the dining hall was the one they hated most. There was something about getting rid of leftover food that never quite sat right with the twins, but they did it all the same because, as Aunt Nikki had sternly reminded them when they once asked to be given another chore, favouritism wasn't condoned at Digglefield.

While cleaning the floors and loading up the dishwashers, Iska and Amen brainstormed all kinds of ways to keep their trip to Nigeria under the radar. They were just about to take out the trash when Iska suddenly remembered they'd sent an important email earlier in the day. Uncertain if they had received a response, let alone a positive one, the twins rushed through the rest of their chores and made for the study.

Even though the study wasn't as busy as it usually was during daytime, Iska and Amen managed to find a quiet corner to set up their laptop.

'What's your email address again?' Amen asked, taking charge of the computer this time since Iska's nerves were all over the place.

'Iska Lyons at gmail dot com,' Iska replied.

Seconds after Amen entered Iska's login details, the computer chimed.

'He replied,' said Amen, and Iska—her curiosity overpowering her apprehension—leaned closer to the computer screen to read the email.

Good afternoon, Iska,

By all means, you can bring friends with you; I have no qualms about that. Just a reminder, I live in Lagos, so you'll be flying into Murtala

Muhammed International Airport. When you arrive, please give me a call on this number: 08033408476.

Cheers,
Oshu
PS: please let me know what time you will be arriving.

'This is perfect,' said Amen, 'He's basically given us the go-ahead to bring the lads, and he's also given us the name of the airport we'll be flying into.'

Iska looked at Amen, her mind racing with ideas. 'With this information, we can search for high-quality photos of the airport online. Photos that Aito can work with,' she said.

Amen, already one step ahead, had opened an internet browser and was meticulously examining tiles of "Murtala Muhammed Airport" images.

'That one looks good,' Iska chimed in, doing her best to assist. 'And that one too. But skip that one; it's too pixelated.'

Since they weren't certain which part of the airport would be the most suitable for Aito to blink to, Iska and Amen dedicated half an hour to gathering detailed pictures of various areas of the airport, including the arrival and departure terminals, a good number of waiting gates, ticketing halls, and designated hangars.

While Amen and Iska were eager to update Aito and Lake on their progress, they realised meeting with them would have to wait until the next training session. Keeping this in mind, the twins finished up in the study and returned to their room, where Rima was waiting for them.

'You two have been spending a lot of time with those boys lately,' she teased.

'It's not what you think.' the twins replied, half-embarrassed, half amused.

'Hey, I'm not judging yous. I don't mind getting a smooch or two myself.'

'Rima!' said Iska with a laugh. 'We weren't doing whatever it is you think we were.'

'If you say so,' said Rima sarcastically. 'So, what have yous been up to that's more interesting than smooching?'

'All you had to do was be patient for two more seconds,' said Amen as she hopped onto her bed. 'We already planned to tell you everything.'

Before her death, Aré had always promised Amen and Iska that she would take them abroad, even though these promises always seemed to be made whenever she couldn't afford to pay for a school trip the twins desperately wanted to go on. "These excursions don't know what fun is," Aré would say, or "When I have enough free time, we'll go to a nice island, just the three of us." Naturally, the twins believed her—but unfortunately, the promises never materialised.

This was all about to change.

Although it was under different circumstances and not at all how they had imagined it would be, Amen and Iska were taking their very first trip abroad. To Amen, this was more exciting than whatever Marius and the minders were currently droning on about in today's meeting.

At the end of the meeting, Marius announced that he was giving everyone a two-week break from training, effective immediately. He explained that they had earned it for working as hard as they had in the previous weeks. But Iska and Amen were unsure whether this new information worked to their advantage or if it put them in a more precarious position.

'I say we stick to the plan,' said Aito, as people exited the west garden in different directions. 'As long as we have solid alibis, we'll be fine.'

'Well, in that case,' Iska replied. 'We have some news. We have the name of the airport we'll be flying into, and we also have photos. I think we should go somewhere private so Aito can check out the photos to see if they're good enough.'

'How about Ireland's Eye?' Amen suggested. 'It seems private enough.'

'We can't go there,' objected Lake.

'Why not?'

'I assume you have the photos saved on a laptop,' Lake replied. 'If we go to the island, we won't have any power outlets or an internet connection.'

'Fair enough. So where do we go?' Iska asked.

'I know a place,' said Aito, a smile growing on his face. 'Lake, which room in Digglefield do the lads hardly ever use?'

'I—I don't know. The study?'

'Exactly,' said Aito, before turning to Amen and Iska. 'I guess yous get the rare opportunity of seeing our gaff.'

'Oh, shut it,' Iska shot back. 'It's only the study.'

'You're welcome,' said Aito, opening up his hands for the twins to hold on to.

To Iska and Amen's surprise *and* disappointment, the boys' study was an exact replica of the girls' study in everything but the colour of the walls; the navy-blue walls in here were in direct contrast to the pink walls in their study—but even so, both walls shared a similarity in being equally hideous. This was all Iska and Amen had the time to notice as they frantically searched for a place to settle down. Despite Lake and Aito's assurance that the study was rarely used, the noise from outside the room made them feel uneasy. Finally, they found a desk to wait at while Lake retrieved a laptop from one of the lockers. Within minutes, all four of them were sifting through photographs of the airport in Nigeria.

'I can't use that one,' said Aito, pointing to one of the photos. 'That's a hangar; I can't risk getting caught in there.'

'What about this one?' said Amen.

'That looks like the main entrance to the arrival terminal,' Aito replied. 'Again, not safe. There could be too many people.'

'Are you saying that none of these photos are good enough?' Iska, visibly frustrated, couldn't keep the exasperation out of her voice.

Lake frowned. 'Maybe we should search for more pictures.'

'Hold on a second,' said Aito as he zoomed into a photo. 'This one might work. See over there, it says "arrivals". There's a little nook just to the side of that hallway; I think I can blink there.'

'Do you think you might be seen?' asked Amen.

Aito tilted his head at the laptop, considering. 'Yes, but not by a lot of people, which is fair.'

'Right,' said Lake, looking at everyone. 'Let's come up with a plan, and maybe tonight—'

Aito interrupted. '—I'm going right now.'

Amen, Lake, and Iska weren't sure if they'd heard Aito correctly, but he repeated himself, and it didn't look like anyone could change his mind.

'Aito, I'm scared for you,' Amen whispered.

'Trust me, I'm scared for myself,' Aito replied with a nervous laugh.

'Lad, be careful,' said Lake. 'If anything goes wrong, blink back here as fast as you can. Don't be foolish.'

Aito took one last look at the photograph, and then he vanished. Among the Unix with impressive abilities at Digglefield, Aito and his powers never ceased to amaze Amen and Iska. He appeared to be the only one who fully trusted his gift, which, in turn, allowed him to use it to its full potential.

With Aito gone, Iska, Amen, and Lake had nothing to do but sit and wait. At first, the game of Five-Card Draw that Lake suggested served as a welcome distraction. But as time wore on, the twins grew more and more restless—not even browsing the bookshelves to see what titles the boys had could calm their nerves. Aito had been gone for over thirty minutes now, and to make matters worse, voices and footsteps occasionally came uncomfortably close to the study. Seconds after deciding they would leave if Aito didn't return soon, Amen and Iska's worst nightmare began to unfold before their eyes. The door handle jiggled and the shadows of two, maybe three, boys darkened the space between the floor and the bottom of the door.

Lake surged to his feet, crossed the room in a flash, and slammed his body against the door as it began to open, shutting them out.

Hearts pounding in their ears, Amen and Iska slipped under a desk, trying to listen in on the conversation between Lake and the boys.

'—Come on lads, you can do that in the common room—' Lake muttered to the boys.

'—Okay, which of the lockers? I'll get it for yous—' Was he struggling to convince them to leave?

He was! Iska could hear one of the boys asking Lake to move aside.

'—Christ, go in then—' Lake screamed.

Still cowering under the desk, and with the boys' footsteps edging closer, Amen and Iska couldn't help but feel sorry that their only chance to see their uncle was about to go up in smoke. Suddenly, they found themselves on a familiar yet uncomfortable rollercoaster ride that deposited them on the lawn of Digglefield's back garden.

'That was close,' Aito said through shallow pants, while Iska and Amen ran to the nearest hedge to throw up—fear and teleportation made for a terrible combination.

'Aito, you bastard; you had us worried,' said Amen, as she wiped slimy spit off her mouth. 'Why are you sweating?'

'It's very humid in Nigeria,' Aito replied.

'You made it to the airport?' Iska asked.

'Em, I think my earlier response made that clear,' Aito said with a chuckle.

Amen enfolded Aito in a hug. 'You sarcastic wanker.' Iska joined in the hug almost immediately.

'Thank Christ,' said Lake, sprinting in from the west garden. 'You made it back in one piece.'

'Chap, you had one job,' said Aito.

'Hey, you know Conor's a handful,' Lake countered. 'Girls, I'm sorry. There wasn't much I could do.'

'You stalled long enough, thank you,' said Iska before returning her attention to Aito. 'So, how did it go? What took you so long?'

Aito took off his jacket and t-shirt, exposing his sweaty torso. Then he undid his bun and ran his fingers through his damp hair. 'First things first,' he said, 'don't even bother bringing jackets; I thought I was going to melt! Other than that, the timing was perfect because when I arrived at the airport, there weren't many people in the terminal; only two kids saw me. Afterwards, I joined a queue and soon enough found myself heading towards immigration control—that's where things got really tricky.'

'How?' said Amen.

'Well, it's obvious, isn't it?' Aito replied. 'I didn't have any form of identification. So, I did the next best thing by blinking from one queue to another until I managed to get out of there without getting caught, thank God!'

'So, what did you do next?' Amen asked curiously.

'Well, I found myself in the baggage claim area, but I had no baggage to claim. Plus, people were staring at me funny; so I tried to make my way to the main lobby. But surprise, surprise, there were more immigration officers checking baggage tags and all that shite.'

'Why didn't you just come back?' said Lake.

Aito looked like he was going to slap Lake across the face for asking such a silly question but somehow managed to restrain himself. 'Because I wasn't done,' he said. 'I had to make sure I found a suitable location for all of us. One person blinking into an airport is risky, but four people blinking at once? You're just begging to get caught.

'I did my best to scan the lobby from where I was and was able to spot a couple of shops. The one that stood out was a SIM card shop; it was just the right size, and there was no one in there, except for the person at the till.'

'So you blinked there?' Lake asked, astounded.

'No, I went to the officer to arrest me,' said Aito sarcastically. 'Of course, I did. After that, I wandered around for a bit, went to the men's restroom, and blinked back just in time to see yous nearly get caught.'

'Again, thank you for that,' Amen said earnestly.

'Always here to help,' said Aito. 'All of this brings me to my next question: will it be the shop or the gents?'

'Eww, Aito!' said Iska. 'You aren't taking us to the bloody jacks.'

'Just making sure,' Aito said with a laugh. 'The shop it is.'

Amen and Iska were sure they had checked off most items on their to-do list in the frenetic days leading up to this moment, yet something felt amiss. On Tuesday, they had visited the pharmacy to purchase a week's worth of toiletries. Then they had spent the whole of Wednesday sorting, laundering, and packing clothes that would be appropriate for the Nigerian weather. The day after that, they had taken a trip to the salon because they figured it was worth making a good first impression on Mr Tella.

Earlier in the day, the twins had met up with Lake and Aito to go over their itinerary one last time. The plan was simple: they were each entitled to just one backpack, they would blink from the terrace, and since Mr Tella was expecting them at 6:30 p.m. they would leave Howth no later than 6 p.m. Everything had been accounted for, so why then did Amen and Iska feel so unprepared?

'I'm telling yous, it's just nerves,' said Rima, making sure the coast was clear in the hallway. 'Come on, let's get yous to the roof.'

Upon reaching the terrace, Iska and Amen were relieved to find only Aito and Lake up there. Although Rima had promised to cause a distraction if there was a crowd, it was much better knowing she didn't have to risk getting into potentially more trouble for them.

'Do yous feel like you're forgetting something?' said Aito, as the twins joined him and Lake at the centre of the terrace.

'Yes,' Amen replied. 'But Rima says it's just nerves.'

'It really is,' said Rima firmly. 'By the way, I have to say that I'm jealous I wasn't included in this…expedition. But not to worry, I have other trips planned when yous get back.'

Everyone laughed at Rima's comment, but beneath the cackles, Amen and Iska knew they were all terrified. With nothing left to be said, Iska and Amen hugged Rima goodbye before clasping hands with Lake and Aito and disappearing.

Lake crashed into a SIM card stand, which toppled over and emitted a loud bang. Meanwhile, Amen and Iska were on their backsides, struggling to find their feet. Aito was the only one who managed to stay upright, but he was being berated by a very angry store clerk. The commotion was starting to attract unwanted attention, so Iska, Amen, and the boys gathered themselves up and politely exited the shop.

Aito hadn't exaggerated how hot Nigeria was. Even with all the air conditioners on, the arrival terminal felt like a sauna set to maximum heat. Making their way through the massive hall, Amen and Iska noticed how alert Lake and Aito were and tried to mimic them, but they couldn't keep their eyes off the crowds of people dashing around in all directions, trying to accomplish one objective or the other.

'Do yous still have the phone number you were supposed to ring Mr Tella on?' said Aito, his eyes darting from side to side as though he was expecting the unexpected.

'Yeah, I have it on me,' Iska replied.

'Well, get it out and let's give him a ring,' said Aito.

Iska rummaged through the smallest compartment of

her backpack until she produced a small piece of paper. 'Right. All we need now is a phone.'

'I say we go in twos and ask someone to lend us theirs,' said Lake. 'Amen, how about you go with Aito while Iska and I start here.'

Amen and Aito nodded their heads in agreement and split up from the group to seek help. But shortly after they began their search, the stares Amen received reminded her painfully of her time at St. Margaret's. Her eyes were startling strangers, which was doing more harm than good in their efforts to find a phone. Thankfully, Iska and Lake didn't have the same experience because they were back with one shortly afterwards.

Reading from the paper in one hand, Iska tapped at the phone's buttons with her other hand and then placed the phone to her ear, while Amen and the boys silently prayed someone would answer on the other end of the line.

'Hel—hello,' Iska stuttered. 'This is Iska Lyons. Yes, we are. We're currently in the arrival hall. Out the entrance? All right then, see you soon.' She hung up the phone and looked at the rest of the group. 'That was him. He says he's just right outside the hall and that we should make our way out.'

Lake returned the phone to its owner and rejoined the group. Together, they waded through the crowded terminal into a foyer and finally broke through the main exit.

Amen and Iska's eyes had barely adjusted to the blinding sunlight when one of several heavily armed men standing in front of a black Mercedes G-Wagen took a step towards them. Fearing that this was some sort of setup, Aito was about to intervene when the back door of the G-Wagen swung open, and from behind it emerged a man wearing a black, short-sleeved cotton shirt with a matching pair of trousers and black leather sandals.

'Iska?' said the man. 'Iska Lyons?'

5. SHOW YOU

He was lean and tall, easily six foot three, Iska and Amen noticed. With light brown eyes and caramel skin free of wrinkles, he looked a lot younger than they had imagined. As the man walked towards Iska and Amen, the uniformed men right behind him mimicked his footsteps so accurately that they might as well have been his shadow.

'Iska…and Amen?' The man finally stopped right in front of the twins, a nervous smile on his face.

He even smiles like Mam, thought Amen.

'*I'm* Iska,' Iska replied, clearing up the man's confusion. 'She's Amen. And these are our friends, Aito and Lake.'

'Nice to meet you.' Aito extended his hand, which the man grabbed firmly.

'Likewise,' the man replied as he shifted his hand to Lake. 'I'm Oshu; apologies if my bodyguard startled you…'

Oshu was still introducing himself when some passersby suddenly became animated.

'—Na Tella be that!—' one shouted.

'—Ah, Baba Tella! Kileni fun boys!—' another added.

'—Oga Tella, E sanu wa!—' a few other people chanted.

In a matter of seconds, the crowd had grown to a size that forced the uniformed men to come together and form a human barricade around Amen, Iska, and the boys.

'We have to leave now,' said Oshu, gesturing Amen and Iska towards a convoy of SUVs. 'Aito and Lake, you two can ride in that Land Cruiser. Girls, you can ride with me, if you don't mind.'

With the crowd closing in, Iska and Amen agreed to the arrangement and made their way into Oshu's G-Wagen. As soon as they settled into their seats, one of the guards still occupied in keeping the crowd at bay whistled to the chauffeur; the car's engine purred to life, and the convoy crawled away from the airport.

Iska and Amen watched through tinted windows as people chased after their car, cheering and jubilating. They were certain none of this would ever have happened to them in Howth.

Finally, with the excited crowd out of sight, Amen and Iska returned their attention to Oshu and his car, which smelt of tropical fruits, lavender, and fresh leather—a stark contrast to the musty Dublin buses back home.

'I'm sorry,' said Oshu, looking at Iska and Amen through the rear-view mirror. 'It can be quite embarrassing when that happens.'

'Who were they?' said Iska aloofly, trying to mask her shyness.

'Just everyday people,' Oshu replied casually, 'seeking alms or opportunities. The increasing Lagos population far outpaces the economic support the state can feasibly provide. But that's by the way; how was your trip? Trust it wasn't too stressful.'

The lie came easily to Iska's lips. 'Not at all. The flight was grand the whole way.'

'Very good,' said Oshu. 'Which of the airlines did you fly with?'

Amen swallowed hard. *What are you going to say?* she thought.

'Lufthansa,' Iska replied confidently.

'Brilliant,' said Oshu, his gaze alternating between the rear-view mirror and the road ahead. 'And that was a direct flight to Lagos?'

Say no.

'Yes,' Iska replied.

'That must have been an expensive trip. How much did that set you back?' Oshu enquired further.

He knows we're lying. Amen was beginning to panic. *Say the ticket was six hundred euro per person.*

'It cost about one thousand two hundred and fifty euro for all four us,' said Iska.

This time Oshu twisted his body around to face Iska and Amen, his cologne even more arresting than the scent of the car. 'That's far too much money to spend,' he said earnestly. 'Look, your expenses for the trip will be reimbursed, and I'll see to it that your return flight is covered.'

Iska's mouth dropped open. 'Mr Tella, you really don't have to.'

'Please, you don't have to call me that,' said Oshu, a shy smile fixing itself on his face. 'Oshu is perfectly fine. And I insist, it's the least I could do… Amen, you've barely said a word, are you all right?'

'You look just like our mam—' Amen blurted out, surprising everyone in the car, including herself. 'I'm sorry, I don't mean to be rude.'

'No, no, you're fine,' Oshu replied with a nervous laugh as he turned back around and faced the road ahead.

For goodness' sake, Amen! Iska chuckled.

Although the silence following Amen's comment was deafening, she and Iska were thankful Oshu's inquisition was over. It gave them time to prepare for more questions to come and to take in their surroundings. The twins hadn't known what to expect coming to Lagos, especially because Aré had barely ever spoken about Nigeria while she was alive. Everything—from the buildings to the billboards, to even the ways the cars drove—was different in ways they couldn't have dreamt up.

After what felt like a twenty-minute drive, the car exited the motorway onto a smaller road lined on either side by buildings of different shapes, sizes, and colours. At one point, Iska and Amen noticed a bank stationed directly beside a supermarket that leaned against a church—it was organised chaos.

The convoy continued to snake through a mix of winding and angular roads until it stopped right in front of an estate, shielded away from the public by long rows of tall masquerade trees.

'What's going on?' said Iska, as the fleet of cars edged

slowly through the gates of the estate.

'It's protocol,' Oshu replied. 'The estate security has to confirm the identity of each and every individual coming in or going out of the estate at any given time.'

Two guards now circled their car with long inspection mirrors and LEDs.

'Why is that?' Iska asked.

Oshu gave them a tight-lipped smile. 'This estate is home to some very important people in the country: politicians, corporate titans, celebrities... If there's anything Nigeria's elite cherish above all, it's their privacy.'

As they drove further into the estate, Oshu's explanation of its residents' need for seclusion began to make a lot more sense to Amen and Iska. The houses here looked like something straight out of an *Architectural Digest* magazine; each house seemed to have a personality of its own, each one equally as captivating as the next. It wasn't far-fetched that Nigeria's elite and their homes would be gawked at by a horde of strangers if they somehow managed to get into the estate.

After minutes touring the massive estate, their convoy finally stopped in front of a magnificent white house at the end of a cul-de-sac.

'This is us,' said Oshu, as the house's electric gates slid open, welcoming the SUVs into its beautiful ring-like driveway.

Compared to the other houses Iska and Amen had just seen, this one whispered class; its blend of beams, curved walls, and big windows gave the structure a sort of angelic aura. Mr and Mrs Tella clearly had taste.

'I hope you girls don't mind pets?' said Oshu, as he unbuckled his seat belt.

'We're good with dogs,' said Iska. 'Not so much cats.'

'The irony,' Oshu murmured.

'Why do you ask?' said Iska, also unbuckling her seatbelt, albeit nervously.

'Because we have a Great Dane, Roxie. She's a good

dog, very needy, though…and incredibly slow. But my wife adores her, so she's family. Speaking of, Ada's been expecting you all.'

Just like that, Amen and Iska were rocked by a fresh wave of anxiety; they hadn't even gotten the opportunity to know Oshu, and now they had to meet his wife. Thankfully, seeing Lake and Aito alight from the other car gave the twins a bit of relief—at least they weren't alone in this.

While Iska, Amen, and the boys gathered their belongings, Oshu promptly issued some orders to his head of security before guiding them through the front door of the house. Oshu and Ada clearly had a preference for monochromatic design, because the walls on the inside of the house were just as white and pristine as the ones on the outside. From where they stood, Amen and Iska could see a large cylindrical lift made of glass and stainless steel extending from the ground floor up. It had never occurred to either of the twins that lifts could be fixtures in people's homes; they had only ever seen them in malls and big corporate buildings.

Next to the lift stood a woman wearing a sleeveless, teal-coloured jumpsuit. 'Finally. We've been expecting you.'

'Everyone, meet my lovely wife, Ada.' Oshu winked at the woman. 'Ada, these are the twins: Iska—'

'—Good to see you,' said Iska, grinning from ear to ear.

'—And Amen; she's a little shy.'

'Nice to meet you,' said Amen as she shook Ada's hand.

'Your eyes,' Ada responded with a smile. 'I could stare at them all day and still wouldn't be able to take it all in.'

Ada didn't need to say much more to dispel Amen and Iska's fears; she seemed genuinely pleasant and inviting—and a little quirky.

'These are Lake and Aito,' said Oshu, advancing the pleasantries.

'Welcome to Nigeria,' Ada said to Lake before turning to Aito and bowing her head. 'Nihongo o hanasu to omou no wa machigai kamo shiremasen. Demo, watashitachi no ie e yōkoso.'

'Anata wa machigatte imasen,' Aito stuttered; whatever Ada said seemed to make him lose his composure. 'I mean, I haven't spoken it in a while, so I'm a little rusty… Thank you.'

'What just happened?' said Iska, utterly dumbfounded.

Oshu laughed. 'You just witnessed Ada showing off. She's a polyglot. Ada, you speak what? three, four—'

'Seven languages,' Ada interrupted. 'I studied life sciences with languages in college. Rubbish, if you ask me. Really, I've just always had a flair for languages since I can remember.'

Iska was about to ask a follow-up question when a strange sound began approaching them from somewhere within the house.

'Rox! Heel!' a voice called out, just as a huge brindle-coated dog came prancing into view. Amen and Iska had completely forgotten about the pet.

'She never listens,' said the boy who had been calling after Roxie.

'Last but not least,' said Oshu, looking slightly exhausted from making introductions. 'This is Walé, Ada's godson and our other guest for the summer.'

'Pleasure to meet you all,' said Walé, in the same polished English accent Oshu and Ada both had.

Walé, like Oshu, had a buzz cut, although his hair was dyed blonde. Unlike Oshu, he had a darker skin tone, much more similar to Ada's.

'You must be exhausted from your flight,' said Ada, noticing they all had been standing in the foyer for a moment too long. 'We prepared extra rooms since Oshu said we were expecting more than just the twins. Walé, do you mind showing our guests to their rooms?'

'Not at all,' Walé responded placidly.

'Brilliant,' said Ada. 'Dinner will be ready in twenty-five minutes, max. That should give everyone enough time to freshen up and meet back downstairs.'

Trailing closely behind Walé as he showed them around the house, it was hard for Amen and Iska not to marvel at whatever caught their eyes: peculiar art pieces here, expensive furniture there, rare musical instruments scattered all over. But by far the most interesting thing they had seen so far was the matryoshka-shaped swimming pool in the backyard.

Stopping in the middle of a hallway that featured some fancy-looking sculptures, Walé opened a door to his left, revealing a space that could easily pass as an expensive suite in a five-star hotel. 'This is the first room,' he said invitingly. 'Who's going to take it?'

'Me!' said Aito before anyone could even draw a breath. 'I think it's fair to say I've earned the right to some beauty sleep tonight.'

Neither the twins nor Lake could—or even wanted to—argue Aito's point; he was the reason they made it to Nigeria after all. They continued further down the hallway where there was another room. This one was less spacious but equally as luxurious as the first room, so Lake agreed to take it.

With the only available rooms on the ground floor now occupied, Walé, Amen, and Iska took the lift to the first floor.

Perhaps she had been too distracted by the Tellas, their house, and just about everything in it, but for the first time, Iska noticed how gracefully Walé carried himself. He moved like someone who had all the time in the world but was aware enough to make sure each stride he took was efficient and purposeful.

'Here we are,' said Walé, after leading the twins through a living room and into a hallway identical to the one on the ground floor. 'Easily one of the best rooms in the house,' he said, pointing to the door on his right. 'You can see Ikoyi's impressive skyline from the balcony. Whose will this be?'

'We'll share it, thank you,' said Iska. She and Amen had

always slept in the same room, and that wasn't going to change now.

'Suit yourselves,' Walé responded with disappointment. 'Dinner is in fifteen, don't be late,' he added as he made for the lift.

Wanker; what's his problem? asked Amen.

I don't know, Iska replied, setting her backpack on the bed. *But he's…cute.*

Having opted to share a room, Amen and Iska were at least grateful they didn't have to share their bathroom with ten other girls. After their shower, they each changed into fresh clothes before heading out. Not knowing how to work the lift, they used the stairs to get back to the foyer, where Ada was waiting for them. Still too shy to strike up a conversation with Ada, Iska and Amen awkwardly followed her as she guided them through another living room and into the dining area, where everyone—including Roxie—was already seated.

'Just in time,' said Oshu as three smartly dressed men burst through a false door, carrying trays of food and drinks in their hands.

Up until then, neither Amen nor Iska had had any inkling there were other people in the house besides the Tellas, their godson, and, of course, Roxie. But they should have at least suspected; with all they'd seen since arriving at Casa Tella, it would have been more unnatural if Oshu and Ada hadn't had a few butlers in their employ.

'We hope you enjoy the meal.' Oshu unfolded his napkin with precision and set it on his lap. 'We had no idea what you might like, so Ada suggested we make something…simple.'

Iska and Amen appreciated the gesture, even though there was nothing "simple" about a platter of jollof rice with hints of bay leaf in it, stir-fried noodles, roasted plantains, a huge bowl of veggie salad with condiments on the side for flavour, and a tin-foil tray of spring rolls, samosas, fried beef, and puff-puff.

'Have you ever tried jollof?' said Ada, pointing to the platter of rice the same golden colour as her hair.

Iska grinned at the familiar food. 'Yes, we have.'

'Our mam used to make it every Sunday,' Amen added, feeling a little more comfortable now.

'That's brilliant,' said Ada. 'I hope this tastes nearly as good as hers. What about you boys? Have you eaten anything like this before?'

Aito's mouth was crammed with food, so Lake did the talking. 'Nothing like this, but everything is delicious, thank you,' he said while Aito gave a thumbs up and nodded in agreement.

Looking at them side by side, it was eerie how much younger Oshu looked compared to Ada, even though multiple articles on the internet had stated he was two years older than her. Except for his mannerisms, absolutely nothing indicated Oshu was forty-three years of age.

'Iska, correct me if I'm wrong,' said the youthful-looking man. 'I take it that you all have just finished secondary school.'

'That's correct,' said Iska, not too thrilled with being the unofficial spokesperson for the group.

'Very good,' said Oshu. 'Apologies if I'm being too forward, but do you have any intentions of going to college?'

'Oh, yes we do,' Iska replied immediately. 'Amen and I sort-of know which college we want to get into, but nothing is confirmed yet. Plus, we're still expecting our Leaving Cert results.'

'Interesting,' said Oshu, dabbing at his lips with his napkin. 'I wonder what the process would be like, if you wanted to switch to universities in the U.K.'

'I'd say it's pretty straightforward,' said Walé—his first contribution to their conversation since dinner started.

'You in college?' said Aito, finally allowing himself a brief respite from eating.

'Yeah, Durham University,' Walé replied. 'I just completed my first year.'

'What are you studying?' Iska asked.

'Contemporary Human History—'

'—Enough of the academic chatter,' Ada interrupted. 'Save it for another time. I noticed you each came with just one backpack. How long will you be staying with us?'

'A week,' Amen replied.

'Really?' said Ada, smiling. 'That's not nearly enough time to get to know my nieces and their friends.'

Though unintended, Amen and Iska both cringed at being referred to as family by someone they had met just over an hour ago. For most of their lives, it had been just them and Aré, and then for the past couple of years, it had been just them. As much as they'd longed for this moment, they'd never thought it would be real. Many years ago, Iska and Amen had resigned themselves to navigating the world untethered to any loved ones. Now that they were finally someone's nieces, it just didn't feel real.

'That aside,' Ada continued, 'I'm fairly certain the bags you brought with you are too small for dresses to fit in. So, what will you wear to the event?'

Amen nearly choked on her orange juice. 'What event?'

'I didn't get a chance to mention it,' said Oshu, nervously. 'We are hosting a fundraiser here this Sunday; a couple of dignitaries and their families will be in attendance. I apologise for the inconvenience; I should have included this information in my email.'

'Em, I don't mind a gala,' said Aito, now helping himself to some finger foods. 'But I didn't bring any slacks.'

'Neither did I,' Lake added.

'That shouldn't be a problem,' said Ada. 'There are some nice retail outlets in Lagos. ATAFO is a brilliant brand, and I'm sure Oshu is willing to atone for his mistakes by taking you there tomorrow. Right, Oshu?'

'Absolutely,' Oshu replied, clearly under Ada's spell.

'As for myself and the girls,' Ada continued. 'If they don't mind, I know a few places we can go shopping.'

'We've never been in fancy dresses before.' Amen's

voice was barely more than a whisper.

'Well, there's a first time for everything. What do you say? It would double as an opportunity for us to get to know each other.'

With the whole table watching intently, Amen and Iska had no choice but to agree to Ada's proposal.

Iska and Amen woke up wondering where they were until memories of the past day's events came flooding back. They hadn't been kidnapped; this *was* their room, it just wasn't the one they had slept in for years. Feeling the fatigue of international travel, the twins sat on the edge of their bed, reflecting on the previous night. Then, as one, they straightened and stared at each other with astonishment. They'd forgotten! Together, they bolted for the bathroom door with Amen coming out on top.

As they hurriedly got dressed, Iska and Amen kicked themselves for nearly forgetting their date with Ada—so much for making a good first impression. Even though Walé finally showed them how to work the lift last night, Amen and Iska skipped the mechanical capsule and bolted down the stairs. But when they reached the ground floor, it seemed as though they were the only ones in the house until the clink of cutlery coming from the backyard caught their attention.

'I was beginning to worry you two were going to sleep all day,' said Ada as she fed Roxie some sandwiches by the pool. 'What would you like for breakfast?'

'Where is everyone?' said Iska, trying her best not to get distracted by the magnificence of the backyard.

'The boys have already left. Oshu's taken them to get some shopping done. And we'll do the same as soon as you two eat something.'

Even though Amen and Iska insisted they weren't hungry, Ada made sure they were served scrambled eggs and toast for breakfast. Fortunately for the twins, Roxie was on hand to gobble up whatever was put down—the dog's hunger was insatiable.

Out in the driveway, a chauffeur—different from the one who had driven Iska and Amen the previous day—was waiting beside a white G-Wagen, but Ada requested the car keys. 'I want it to be just the three of us.'

Ironically, driving through Lagos city was a lot calmer without Oshu's security guards blaring their sirens at every car on the road, demanding they get out of the way. It gave Iska and Amen a chance to ask Ada their most pressing questions, ranging from why there were so many motorcycles on the roads to whether street foods in the city were safe to eat. To Ada's credit, she graciously responded to every question thrown at her, up until they pulled into the driveway of a fancy-looking boutique.

'Ada, I didn't know you were coming in today!' said a slender, light-skinned lady, just as Iska, Amen, and Ada walked through the front doors of the boutique. 'And I see you brought guests with you; what's the occasion?'

While Ada spoke with the lady, Amen and Iska browsed through the boutique. Fashion in Lagos was vastly different from what was considered in vogue in Dublin. People here opted for lighter, more colourful clothing; even Ada was wearing an intricately patterned sundress coupled with expensive-looking sandals.

'Eku is one of the leading stylists in Africa,' said Ada, as soon as the lady disappeared into a room hidden behind beaded curtains. 'If there's anyone I trust to dress you two up, it's her. What are your favourite colours, if you don't mind me asking?'

'Blue.' Amen said the word slowly, and only then realised that she'd broadcasted her suspicion for everyone to hear.

'It's white for me,' Iska replied.

'Ladies, we're ready for you.' Eku was back, this time with a wide grin on her face.

Not knowing what to expect, Amen and Iska nervously followed Eku as she led them through the beaded curtains into a room filled with the most beautiful dresses either of them had ever set their eyes on. The last time they had been in a room remotely similar to this one was in Kilcock at Aunt Pamela's, and it still did not compare.

'Stand right there,' said Eku, gesturing for Amen and Iska to stand in the middle of the room while she and Ada took their seats. Then Eku snapped her fingers twice, and suddenly, two young ladies, each with measuring tapes, walked into the room.

'What did you have in mind?' Eku asked Ada while the seamstresses took Iska and Amen's measurements.

'Well, her favourite colour is white, while hers is blue,' said Ada, sending a wink Iska and Amen's way. 'So, I think we want dresses in those colours. Dresses that scream arrogance—that command attention.'

'We can definitely make that happen,' said Eku delightedly. 'And the shoes?'

Ada sized Amen and Iska up. 'Girls, have you ever worn heels?' she asked.

The twins shook their heads.

'Let's break them in with two-inch stilettos.'

After thanking them for their patronage, Eku reassured Ada the dresses would be ready and delivered by noon the next day. How that was going to happen, Iska and Amen could only imagine.

Outside the boutique, the twins noticed that the boot of Ada's SUV was being loaded up with about a dozen shopping bags.

'Forgive me,' said Ada, trying hard to hide her smile. 'But I *had* to stock you two up with new clothes… Come on, it's been a long day; we need to get something to eat.'

Between enjoying lunch at a luxurious five-star restaurant and taking an impromptu tour of Victoria Island, Iska, Amen, and Ada had completely lost track of time, and they returned home only a few hours shy of midnight.

Exhausted from a long day of being treated like golden eggs—too precious to crack, lest the world fall apart—Amen and Iska skipped taking their showers and changed straight into their new pyjamas. While Iska brushed her teeth, Amen tightened the drawstrings on her pyjama bottoms, then collapsed backward onto the bed with a long, heavy sigh.

'I can't believe the restaurant we ate at belongs to Ada's friend,' she said, unable to contain her smile. Though her head was foggy, she tried to count the little crystals adorning the dragonfly-shaped chandelier hovering above her. 'Did you notice everyone kept calling us "madam"? I don't think I've ever been called that word in my life—let alone a hundred times in one day. None of it feels real. Like, why us?'

'I've been asking myself the same question all day,' Iska replied as she settled into her side of the bed. 'And I have a theory. What if this is all Mam's doing—her way of watching over us?'

Amen switched off the bedroom light and joined Iska under the blankets. The smile that had lit her face moments before was gone. 'If your theory is correct, it would be so typical of her—always putting us first, even in the afterlife.'

'Remember how she always said she wanted to try lobster rolls?' Iska whispered, hoping that the steady hum of the air conditioner would muffle her sobs. 'We had them for the first time today, and we couldn't even share them with her. You—you know what's even more painful?' She was crying openly now, and Amen slid across the bed to wrap her arms around Iska's trembling shoulders. 'They were so *fecking* good; she would have loved them. She—she would've loved them so much!'

'I know,' Amen whispered, fighting back the tears of her own. 'I know.'

Amen and Iska wouldn't have minded watching as teams of people belonging to various event and catering companies scrambled around the house trying to get things sorted out;

however, Ada confined them to a room to have their hair and makeup done. Although sitting still for over an hour had left them with dead legs and rigid joints, Amen, with her sleek up-do, and Iska, who'd opted for box braids, couldn't deny how beautiful they looked as they slipped into their new dresses.

But as guests began to arrive, the twins weren't feeling so confident anymore. On their outing the previous day, Ada had told them what the fundraiser was for; she had explained that it was to help provide aid to rural communities in Nigeria. The dignitaries who were at the moment flocking into the house for free food and booze were the same people who had sworn an oath to look after these communities, but they'd defaulted on their vows to enrich themselves instead.

'Then why have you invited them to your home?' Amen had asked in confusion.

'Because you have to fight politics with politics,' Ada had said. 'They know Oshu and I are invaluable assets and need our help to increase foreign direct investment into the country, and we need them to pledge more money to help the people. It's the ultimate catch twenty-two situation.'

As greedy as these government ministers seemed to be, they still were very powerful and educated people. In a word: intimidating. Iska and Amen knew nothing about high society or the ruling class, yet they were being made to mingle with members of the Nigerian bourgeoisie.

'Well, we can't back out now,' said Iska, as she adjusted the strap of her off-shoulder A-line organza dress. 'We're doing this for Oshu and Ada.'

'Christ, I hope this doesn't end badly,' said Amen as she struggled to stand upright in her heels.

'It won't. You know why? Because we're the Lyons sisters and we have each other.'

Descending to the ground floor, Amen and Iska watched as a group of ushers showed people to different parts of the house, while cacophonies of conversations and laughter rang out from multiple directions. Upon exiting the lift, the twins desperately wanted to be confident and own the moment, but somehow, they ended up standing awkwardly in the middle of the foyer with no one to talk to. Just as they were contemplating retreating to their room, someone called out to them from across the hallway—it was Oshu.

'You two look unbelievable,' Oshu whispered to Amen and Iska before introducing them to the guests in their midst. Right in the middle of the introductions the twins noticed some of the other guests peering at them, but weren't sure if this was a good or bad thing.

'I'm sorry,' said Oshu, noticing that Iska and Amen felt out of place. 'This is *my* crowd—chatting about old people stuff and whatnot. Come with me.'

Doing as he said, Amen and Iska followed Oshu through the kitchen and out into the backyard, where they immediately felt the pulse of music coming from afar. With each step the twins took across the lawn, the music grew louder until they finally reached its source: an opulent white marquee that was being manned by two security guards.

'The younger folks are in there,' said Oshu. 'Including Aito, Lake, and Walé, I'm sure. Good luck, and please have fun.'

In seconds Oshu was gone, leaving Iska and Amen alone in the garden. With nothing else to do, the twins let out tense breaths and walked into the marquee.

Stepping on to the main floor, Amen and Iska quickly realised why the people in the house had stared at them strangely; Oshu and Ada's guests were Nigeria's elite, which meant their egos would never let them praise anyone who directly diminished their own importance, and Iska and Amen were no exception to the rule. Although the guests in this tent shared the same sense of self-aggrandisement as their parents, they could not help but gawk at Iska and Amen. Eku and Ada had hit their mark.

'Don't you two look lovely!' yelled a familiar voice.

'Lake!' screamed Iska and Amen in excitement and relief—they were starting to feel uncomfortable with all those
eyes on them.

'Ladies, you look fit!' said Aito, twirling Amen in his
hand to get a better look at her charmeuse halter dress.

Aito and Lake looked dashing as well; Lake had gotten
a haircut—a massive upgrade compared to his old hairstyle.
Meanwhile, Aito had let his long hair down for the occasion.
The boys explained that they had been one of the firsts to
arrive in the marquee, giving them the bad fortune of meeting Nigeria's most pompous crowd.

Except for the infrequent stares from a group of girls,
Amen and Iska were having a good time at their first party.
Although not participating, they watched from the bar as
Aito and Lake managed to dance out of rhythm to practi-
cally every song the DJ played, while insisting they were hav-
ing a dance-off.

With her money on Aito to win the dance battle, Iska
was trying to cheer him on when a boy walked up to her,
blocking her view of the dance floor. 'I've been watching
you since you came in here,' said the boy, his breath reeking
of alcohol. 'Can I just say you're gorgeous… Would you like
to dance?'

'You're too kind,' Iska responded, slowly backing away
from the boy. 'But I'm grand, thank you.'

'What accent is that?' said the boy, staggering closer to
Iska.

'An Irish one,' Iska replied firmly.

'Ah, the Emerald Isle. My mum owns a couple of prop-
erties there.'

'Good for you,' said Iska, starting to lose her patience.
'If you don't mind, my sister and I are trying to have a good
time.'

'So am I; why're you being such a rude bitch?' the boy
retorted.

Iska had had enough. 'Listen, you gobshite—'

'Hey,' a voice interrupted Iska before she could finish

her sentence. 'Oshu wants you.'

'Right now?' said Iska, her blood already boiling.

'Yes,' said Walé. 'He says it's urgent.'

Iska sized up the boy one last time before mustering up the willpower to turn away from him. Just as Iska and Walé were leaving the bar, Amen—still watching Aito and Lake on the dance floor—casually flicked two of her fingers, causing the water in the intoxicated boy's cup to splash on his face.

'Oshu doesn't want me, does he?' said Iska as she and Walé neared the swimming pool. 'You made it up just to stop me from giving out to that thickhead.'

'Yes, and no,' said Walé, flashing a sly smile.

'Encouraging poor manners, aren't you?' said Iska.

'Honestly, he deserved whatever you were going to dish out. But I couldn't let you lose your cool in there.'

'Why not?' said Iska, helping herself to a seat in one of the sun loungers.

'Partly because Oshu instructed me to look after you and Amen tonight, but mostly because I couldn't stand there and watch your pretty face get agitated.'

Iska felt ashamed of herself for letting Walé's words get to her head, especially after the incident in the marquee mere moments ago. But she was even more thankful it was too dark for him to notice her cheeks flush. Determined not to excuse Walé's charm, Iska was about to lecture him on how capable she was of looking after herself when he began singing along to a song wafting out from the marquee.

'—*If you send me the location, then I'll be right there*—'

'Who sings this?' Iska asked, feeling a little embarrassed that she had to ask such a silly question in the first place.

'I'll be honest, I'm surprised you don't know this,' said Walé, the pool lights illuminating his handsome profile. 'It's Santan Dave and Burna Boy; their music is unreal.'

'Is this what you and your girlfriend listen to regularly?' Iska asked.

Walé smiled at the question. 'I don't have a girl-friend…yet.'

Now Iska was sure Walé could see her blush.

In the days following the fundraiser, there was no let-up of activities. Amen, Iska, and the boys engaged in everything from going to a theatre to watch a live play to taking a tour of a newly commissioned megacity built on land reclaimed from the Atlantic Ocean. At one point, they even dined with the governor of Lagos State at his residence. In between all of this, Iska and Amen had been persuaded to stay in Nigeria a little longer than they had planned. Although they eventually agreed to extend their trip by a few more days, Amen wasn't comfortable being away from home for so long, nor was she thrilled with how close Iska and Walé were getting.

'Sorry, I let myself in,' said Lake, joining Amen on the balcony as she watched Iska kiss Walé in the swimming pool. 'No one's seen you all day. We were a bit worried.'

'It's weird, isn't it?' said Amen absentmindedly. 'How nice they've been to us.'

'Who? Oshu and Ada?' Lake asked. 'Yeah, I guess so. But I assume it's because we're their guests, and they can afford to be nice.'

Amen let out a sardonic laugh. 'Since we've been here, not once has Oshu said anything about our mam; who does that?'

'Is that what's eating you up?'

'Yes,' said Amen in frustration. 'And the fact that Iska, who planned all of this, by the way, hasn't noticed…or just doesn't seem to care.'

'Look, it's not my place,' said Lake, now watching Walé and Iska as well. 'But that's your sister. I'm sure if you talk to her and let her know what's on your mind, she'll listen.'

A moment of silence passed following Lake's words.

'Lake,' Amen said with a laugh. 'How old are you again?'

'Old enough to know that she's probably thinking the same thing as you,' Lake replied, also laughing. 'Even though it doesn't seem like it right now.'

Lake didn't linger around after talking to Amen. He asked her to cheer up and come downstairs for lunch, but she remained in the room until she was ready to speak to anyone. Then, all at once, she closed her eyes, and within minutes, Iska came running into the room.

'What's the matter?' said Iska breathlessly. 'You said it was urgent.'

'How's your boyfriend?' said Amen, failing miserably to hide the bitterness in her voice.

'Is this what you called me for?' Iska replied. 'I nearly slipped on my way here.'

'Oh, I'm sorry. Do you want to be pampered?'

Iska's eyes widened. 'Amen, what's wrong with you?'

'I should ask you.' Amen's voice was louder now. 'I'm not the one who's had their tongue shoved down a boy's throat over the past couple of days.'

Amen's words left Iska dumbfounded. 'Are you acting this way because of Walé?' she managed to say. 'You don't like him?'

'I'm indifferent about him. It's you that's doing my head in. You seem to have completely forgotten why we came here in the first place. If I recall correctly, the whole point was to connect with our uncle and hopefully know more about Mam.'

Amen, knowing how combative her sister could be, was expecting a retaliation, but Iska remained silent.

'The outings, the events; they're all fun,' Amen continued. 'But I'd much rather know why our uncle never bothered to look for us all these years. Why Mam never spoke of him, or why he wasn't present at her funeral.'

Iska tightened her bathrobe at the collar. 'I want to know these things as well,' she said, 'but there's been too many things going on. We've not exactly had the time.'

'Exactly,' said Amen. 'A part of me believes Oshu's trying to avoid having a conversation with us by deliberately distracting us with different activities.'

'Why would he do that? He practically begged us to stay a bit longer.'

Amen raised an eyebrow. 'Ada made that request, not Oshu.'

Iska scanned the space in front of her as she sank to the floor; as twisted as it all sounded, Amen was making a lot of sense. 'What do we do?' she finally said.

'I think we should talk to him tonight,' said Amen, pacing the room. 'Find a window when he's free and engage him.'

'But about what though? What would we say to him?'

Amen squatted in front of Iska and looked up into her face. 'I don't have any specifics, but I know there'll be something to say.'

The mood at the dinner table was pensive. Everyone was somewhat aware that something was off, but no one was brave enough to say anything, opting to eat their meal in silence instead. Half an hour later, just as the butlers were clearing out the table, Oshu stood up from his chair and tried to leave, but the twins quickly blocked him off.

'If you don't mind, Oshu, we would like to speak to you,' said Amen.

'In private,' Iska added, trying not to meet Walé's eyes, or anyone else's for that matter.

As the twins followed Oshu down the hallway, they realised that this was their first time in the eastern wing of the house; it had a secluded feel to it, almost as if there was an unspoken rule that no one except the owners of the house were allowed here.

Oshu led Amen and Iska into a large room that looked part office, part gym. When he turned the lights on, they noticed the walls on either side of the room were padded with grey soundproof panels while the rear-facing wall was just one giant window. On the left side of the room, a golden shelf displayed books, awards, souvenirs, and framed photographs. Right next to the shelf was a black sofa with an antique finish. More interestingly, on the opposite side of the room, two massive treadmills (bigger than the ones Amen and Iska had personally seen) sat alongside neatly arranged workout equipment.

'Girls, is there a problem?' said Oshu, as he sauntered towards the back of the office where an elegantly designed work desk stood. Expensive-looking computers, a stack of unopened folders, and two bottles of water left the surface of the desk looking tidy but not pristine.

Amen and Iska looked their uncle in the eyes and felt their courage drain away. Nothing either of them had been through in the past few weeks compared to bringing up the topic of Aré to her estranged brother. But, as if he could read their minds, Oshu gave the twins an opening.

'I presume this is about Aré.' His voice was calm.

'Yes,' said Amen, swallowing hard. 'She never…spoke about you.'

'Really?' said Oshu, a resigned expression forming on his face. 'I guess I can see why.'

'What happened between the two of you?' Iska asked.

Oshu stood up from the desk and walked over to the window; something was clearly eating at him. 'You won't understand,' he said, as he stared into the early night. 'It's not worth it…'

'Why didn't you come to her funeral?' Amen's voice was weak and small.

Oshu ignored the question. 'I told Ada I wasn't ready to do this,' he murmured more to himself than to them.

Amen and Iska understood that having this conversation was tough, but Oshu's indifference was starting to irritate them.

I think you should do it. Iska whispered into Amen's mind.

I don't know—

Look, it's now or never, thought Iska. *We have nothing to lose.*

Despite her nerves, Amen acknowledged that Iska was

right. She understood that regardless of the outcome of their conversation in this room tonight, she and Iska owed it to themselves to lay bare their hearts, to release their inhibitions, and speak their truth without fear of appearing weak. Tears welled up in her eyes already, Amen smoothed her forehead with her hands and let out a deep breath. 'We know this is hard for you,' she said. 'But try to imagine how it is for us… You have no idea what we've been through.'

Amen glanced at Iska, who nodded in approval. 'I want to show you something,' she continued. 'But please, try not to freak out.'

The sloshing sound caught Oshu's attention. He turned around and noticed the bottles on his desk were vibrating. He moved closer to inspect them but flinched backwards when he realised that the water in the bottles was swirling rapidly.

'We're not…normal,' said Iska, shifting her eyes from the bottles to Oshu. 'We're these things called—'

'Unix,' Oshu interrupted.

6. REGRET

Amen and Iska stared at Oshu in astonishment. 'How do you know that?' said Iska.

As if things couldn't get any stranger, two tawny lines appeared on Oshu's face, running from the caruncle of his eyes down to the sides of his mouth. Then there was a sharp tear of fabric, and suddenly a long, slender tail snaked from side to side behind him.

'Because I'm a Cruther,' said Oshu, his gaze alternating between Amen and Iska.

'Cruther,' said Iska, visibly scanning her memory. 'You're a shapeshifter!'

'Yes,' said Oshu, edging closer to them. 'And I should have known you two were—'

Oshu was interrupted by a gentle knock on his office door. He and the twins glanced in that direction to see Ada casually walk in and close the door behind her.

'Oshu, what's going on?' she asked in a cryptic tone.

'You seem to have been right,' said Oshu, his physical features back to normal. 'About Amen and Iska.'

Ada smiled in relief. 'I knew you two were one of us.'

'One of us?' said Amen. 'You're a Unix as well?'

'My hair isn't a fashion statement,' Ada replied. 'It's golden for a reason.'

Golden for a reason. Iska was in the middle of figuring out what Ada's last words meant when she overheard Amen's thoughts.

'I hate you,' said Amen again, this time aloud so that they could all hear her. 'I hate you, Oshu, because you're trying really hard to make up for being a failure as an uncle. As if any of it will work.'

Breathe, thought Iska, trying to get Amen to measure her words.

'It's much more complicated than you think—' said Oshu.

'No, I see exactly how it is,' Amen interrupted him. 'You were never there for Mam, never there for us. And now you expect us to just accept you, arms wide open.'

'I agree with you,' said Ada, which surprised Iska and Amen. 'Your uncle messed up big time.' She stepped forward, hands open and welcoming. 'And believe me, he knows it. But there are two sides to every story, and I sincerely believe you two need to know his. Please, hear him out.'

Although Ada had created an opening for him to speak up, Oshu seemed unable to form any words with his mouth. He began retreating to his desk, but Ada pinned him with a stern look. 'Oshu, darling, it's time. You need to tell the girls everything as it is. You owe it to them; you have to make it right.'

'But I don't know where to begin,' said Oshu, nervously drumming his fingers on his head.

Iska took a breath to recruit her courage. 'Start from anywhere.'

Ada gestured for the twins to sit on the sofa while she helped herself to an exercise ball in the corner.

'I don't want to blab,' said Oshu, his eyes red and teary. 'So, it'll have to be the timeline closest to your birth and onward.

'The year was nineteen ninety-four, and things were hard for our family financially. I was about the same age as you two; I had worked very hard in college, so I knew my A-level results were going to be good. I needed them to be good because I needed scholarship offers from good universities.

'Aré had chosen not to go to university two years prior, so naturally, she had been working menial jobs to make ends meet. Then all of a sudden, she said she was moving to Ireland. I remember that conversation so vividly; we were at

Walthamstow Central trying to catch the Victoria to Peckham. She said she wanted a change of atmosphere, wanted to start afresh. What did a twenty-year-old know about starting afresh?

'I protested this because I felt it was a stupid move, and I didn't want to lose my best friend. But if you two knew your mother very well, you'd know she was an extremely stubborn person.'

Amen and Iska laughed, even though their faces were already wet with tears.

'It took a while,' Oshu continued. 'But in time, I adjusted to the move. We both did. We kept in touch as regularly as we could. By then, I had been granted a full scholarship to ICL to study computer science and management. Fast forward five years to June nineteen ninety-nine, I had just landed a role as a junior data analyst for a newly founded company called Acuris.

'I remember calling Aré to tell her the news and how excited she was for me. Apparently, she'd had news of her own… She said she was getting married. Believe me, nothing made me more elated—I was already picking out tuxedos in my head.'

Oshu uncapped one of the bottles of water on his desk and drank from it. 'She'd been dating the guy for a year. At first, I was surprised that she hadn't told me about him,' said Oshu, taking another swig of water from the bottle. 'A year was enough time to tell your brother about a serious relationship. But as she explained further, it started to make sense why she hadn't told me about him.'

'What was the matter?' said Iska, the coarseness of her voice surprising her.

'Honestly it had nothing to do with the fact that he was eight years older than her,' Oshu replied. 'Or that he was white. What put me off was that he had been previously married.'

Amen cleared her throat. 'What was so wrong with that?' she said. 'People get divorced all the time, and some go on to find new partners.'

'The key word is *divorced*,' said Oshu. 'This man and his previous wife were not divorced. As a matter of fact, it was nearly impossible for him to get a divorce, as Aré had explained it.

'Now, based on our culture, and Aré understood this fully, this was a taboo. You couldn't be married to someone who was still in another marriage, and technically, this man still belonged to someone else. I reminded her of this, and we had a heated argument about tradition and love, at which point I decided I was done with the conversation. I told her if she went on with the marriage, then I would cease communication with her.'

'So, you abandoned her,' said Amen, her voice quivering with anger. 'Your only sibling.'

Oshu's eyes were trained on the floor now. 'I was a stupid twenty-three-year-old, wrapped up in my own morality of what was right and wrong; and at the time, I was full of conviction that Aré was wrong. She was giving up our way of life—our tenets—all in the name of love with someone whom I felt didn't even have the decency to fully leave his former partner for her.'

As though previously choreographed, Iska and Amen jerked off the sofa at the same time. Anger swirled between them, shared as completely as their thoughts. 'Here I was thinking you deserve the benefit of the doubt,' said Iska. 'But Amen's right. You messed up, and we're through with you.'

'Girls, please wait,' said Ada, speaking for the first time in minutes. 'There's more to the story.'

'No!' said Amen, already heading for the door. 'We're done listening.'

Iska and Amen weren't sure how Ada was able to get to the door before them, but there she was, blocking them off. 'I can only imagine how angry you two are,' she whispered to them. 'And you're well within your rights, but you have to let him finish, please.'

'It doesn't matter, love,' said Oshu, wiping off sweat that had gathered on his forehead with his hands. 'It doesn't change anything.'

'Oh yes, it does,' said Ada, as she took Amen and Iska's hands and led them back to the sofa. 'And since it looks like you won't finish it, I will.'

Amen and Iska sat reluctantly, their muscles still tense.

'Look, girls.' Ada knelt in front of Iska and Amen. 'I know you loved your mother, and she was the world to you, but she was not without her flaws. Yes, Oshu did make mistakes, but in all fairness, he recognised them and tried to make amends.

'A few years after Aré and Patrick got married, your uncle did try to reach out to his sister. It killed him that he wasn't a part of her new life.'

'How do you know this?' Iska stuttered.

'Because I was in a relationship with your uncle by this point.' She glanced over to Oshu, who was now sitting in his chair.

'It wasn't long before he filled me in on the whole thing,' Ada continued. 'And believe me, I gave him stick for it. Just as how you feel, the whole situation rubbed me the wrong way, and I urged him to fix things.

'But Aré refused to talk to him, and at some point, changed her telephone number and correspondence... We didn't hear from your mother until—'

'August, twenty-thirteen,' said Oshu, as he walked towards Amen and Iska. 'Nikki, whom I had met once or twice in the past when visiting Aré in Ireland, paid me an unexpected visit at my office in London.'

Now Oshu was on his knees beside Ada, eyes blood red as though he had been mourning the loss of a loved one for weeks. The irony was not lost on Amen and Iska that someone as influential and powerful as Oshu looked so small and tired in front of them.

'She informed me that Aré had passed away suddenly,' Oshu continued, 'leaving behind two daughters. I swear I never knew she had you two; and as soon as I did, I asked to meet you.'

'What happened?' said Amen, still trying to maintain her anger. 'You were too busy.'

'I was ready to drop every engagement, every meeting, in a heartbeat,' Oshu replied. 'But then Nikki said I couldn't see you.'

The twins shifted uncomfortably in their seats. 'Why?' said Iska.

'She said I had to give it time,' said Oshu. 'She was convinced that neither party was ready to meet the other. She promised when the time was right, I would know.'

At certain moments in their lives, Amen and Iska were thankful they could hear each other's thoughts; how else would they have quietly deduced that it was Aunt Nikki who had thrown the card at Iska's feet a few weeks back?

'I gave her my contact to reach out whenever,' Oshu continued, his voice filled with remorse. 'So, Iska, when I received your email, Ada and I were ecstatic.

'Look, I know nothing I say now can make up for my mistakes. I was wrong, and I am willing to admit it over and over again.'

Amen shifted uncomfortably as she noticed the tears in Oshu's eyes and the tremble in his voice.

Oshu swiped a sleeve over his face, smearing tears over his cheeks. 'All I want is to do right by you.' He took a hard breath. His voice cracked. 'From the moment I saw both of you at the airport, I knew I would do and give anything to win your hearts over. You two are the spitting image of your mother, and I love you just as much as I loved her…'

Oshu was crying so much now that not even Ada, holding on to him, could stop his body from trembling violently, but she hugged him tightly all the same. 'Let it out, baby,' she said. 'Let it all out; you're free.'

Perhaps distracted by Oshu, Amen and Iska hadn't noticed that they, too, were crying.

Iska, what's the thing Mam used to say whenever we got on each other's nerves? asked Amen.

To err is human, to forgive divine...

'It's fine, Oshu,' said Amen, as she slid off the sofa to join Oshu on to the floor. 'I forgive you.'

'So do I,' Iska added, joining Amen on the floor.

Oshu wrapped his arms around them. 'Thank you, thank you.' His voice still wasn't steady.

As Iska and Amen embraced Oshu in return, each of them knew, deep in their hearts, that what they'd just told their uncle wasn't the complete truth. Had they forgiven Oshu? Yes. Would they ever forget he'd neglected Aré all those years ago? No. They weren't certain they ever would. But they were certain Oshu would stay true to his words and do everything to make up for his mistakes, and for Iska and Amen, that was a good starting point.

After a few minutes, Oshu cleared his throat to break the silence in the room. 'I'd like to add one more thing,' he said, further clearing his throat. 'I don't mean to make either of you upset, but I'm of the opinion your mother didn't die of natural causes as the police reports claim.'

Amen and Iska exchanged a quick glance on hearing this.

'I'm sorry if I've upset you, I—' said Oshu.

'—No, you didn't,' Amen interrupted.

'We never believed those reports either,' said Iska. 'You have no idea how relieved we are to hear this from someone else.'

'But what's your reasoning?' Amen asked.

Oshu climbed to his feet and wiped his eyes again—this time with a handkerchief pulled from his pocket. 'I got hold of Aré's post-mortem report a few years back.' He folded the handkerchief as he walked over to his desk. 'On reading it, I knew instantly it was rubbish.'

Oshu walked back to the sofa with an open laptop in his hand now. 'I hired the best private investigators money can buy to help me find out more,' he said, still tapping the trackpad of the computer. 'None of them could get me anything. Even your neighbours in Kilcock weren't helpful; they neither saw nor heard anything.'

Oshu spun the laptop around to face Amen and Iska, who both winced at the images they were made to look at. 'Not pretty, I know,' he said, turning the laptop screen back to himself. 'So, this is the thing with scleroderma: it is an autoimmune disease where a person's cells work against them by producing excess collagen, which may inhibit normal bodily functions.

'The first red flag I got from Aré's report was that the cause of her death was "*instantaneous* scleroderma".'

Oshu allowed some seconds of silence for the information to register. 'Based on research,' he continued, 'scleroderma is a chronic disease that happens over a person's lifetime, and not in a day or even minutes. Second, and more importantly, your mother, like me, had rapid regenerative cells—'

'—That's why you look so young,' Iska interrupted.

'Yes,' Oshu replied, allowing a little smile. 'And I'm also very healthy; hence why I highly doubt your mother had scleroderma. Even if she did, it would have taken years before making any physical manifestations.'

The more Oshu spoke about the circumstances surrounding Aré's death, the harder Iska and Amen's heart pounded; neither of them knew whether to be angry or afraid, especially now that someone else believed what they had always known in their hearts to be true.

'Where do we go from here?' said Amen.

Oshu remained silent in response to Amen's question until Ada finally gave him a gentle nod, as if encouraging him to be brave.

'There's something I want to share with you two,' said Oshu, now closing his laptop. 'But it'll have to wait till tomorrow. It's late, we've been in here for nearly two hours. You two need rest.'

'We all do,' Ada added.

Seeing the sense in Ada and Oshu's suggestion, the twins bid goodnight to the Tellas before quietly exiting the office. Although their footsteps echoed through the house as they made their way back to the room, Amen and Iska were thankful they didn't run into any of the boys. They were mentally and emotionally spent, with no desire to do anything other than crawl into bed and cry themselves to sleep.

Even though Amen and Iska were dressed in loose-fitting clothes and were in the shade, they still considered getting into the pool. As a matter of fact, they were about to follow through with this idea when Oshu finally joined them in the backyard.

'I'd get in the water myself,' said Oshu as he sat in one of the loungers. 'It's scorching today.'

'Oshu, before you start,' said Amen, nervously rubbing the palm of her right hand. 'There's something we need to tell you… It's about our trip here.'

'We thought since we've established that we're all Unix,' Iska continued. 'It's only fair to let you know that Aito and Lake are Unix as well.'

Oshu half-raised his eyebrows on hearing this.

'To be honest, our being here was only possible through Aito,' Amen added.

Oshu was even more attentive now. 'When you say "through", what exactly do you mean?' he asked.

Iska blushed. 'He teleported us here.'

'Oh wow,' said Oshu, staring at the twins in disbelief. 'I mean, I knew you two lied about how you got here; I assumed you had borrowed, maybe even stole, some money to buy your flight tickets. But this, I didn't see coming.'

'We're sorry,' said Amen.

'Sorry?' Oshu let out a big laugh. 'Don't be sorry. For a bunch of eighteen-year-olds to pull off something so daring—if anything, I'm very impressed.'

Oshu's pride in their little scheme wasn't exactly the re-action Iska and Amen had been expecting, but they were relieved he was taking it well.

'Well, this piece of information defeats the purpose of us meeting here,' said Oshu. 'I thought the boys were regular humans and was merely trying to hide the content of our conversation.'

'Which is?' said Iska, curiously.

Oshu's expression was more serious now. 'Having found nothing on Aré's death through modern means, Ada and I decided we would have to go back home and try to get more answers.'

'Where is *home*?' asked Amen cautiously.

'Dogudu,' Oshu replied. 'Technically, it's my village, but most Unix are welcome. Ada and I were going to wait till you all had left before going—'

'But you're considering changing plans now that you know we're Unix,' said Amen.

'Precisely. I know this is impromptu, but I was wondering if you two would like to visit your mother's birthplace.'

Oshu's invitation was unexpected, but Amen and Iska knew they had to accept it despite how nervous the thought of going to their mother's village made each of them feel.

'Of course!' Iska lied.

'We'd love to,' Amen added.

'Good,' said Oshu in relief. 'Because we set out on Wednesday morning.'

'Wednesday?' said Iska. 'But that's roughly two days away.'

'I know,' said Oshu, now rising to his feet. 'I'll fill you in on our itinerary later. Oh, ask your friends if they want to tag along—the more the merrier.'

Though the twins weren't quite comfortable with how quickly things were moving, they were at least glad Aito and Lake were also invited. Paranoid that Oshu might somehow retract his invitation to the boys, Amen and Iska sprinted into the house with a goal to achieve.

Aito clapped his hands in agreement right after playfully accusing Amen and Iska, and their entire family, of being the most unpredictable people he had ever met. Lake, on the other hand, had a few misgivings about going to Dogudu.

'Iska, did you tell him we're Reegs?' he asked.

'I actually forgot about that,' said Iska, her cheeks flushed with embarrassment. 'But I don't think it's a big deal, right Amen?'

'Absolutely,' said Amen. 'We can always ask him, but I'm pretty sure his stance won't change.'

Lake was still unconvinced. 'What about the fact that we're...white?' he asked.

'Mate, speak for yourself,' Aito murmured quietly.

Iska nudged Lake in the arm. 'Oh, would you stop worrying? Everything is going to be okay.'

Oshu kept to his word; immediately after dinner, he invited everyone into the ground floor living room where he discussed travel plans and the necessities everyone needed to bring along on the trip: backpacks, extra pairs of underwear, a change of clothes, and toiletries—the usual stuff. Then, he proceeded to list the things that were forbidden in Dogudu: phones, digital cameras, media players, portable video games, laptops, basically any form of electronic gadget.

'Why can't we bring any of those things with us?' said Iska, as she ran her fingers along the sides of a massive flatscreen TV, wondering why anybody would need one so big.

'Because people from Dogudu village,' said Oshu, slowly pacing the living room. 'Are what you would call averse to technology.'

'That's...odd?' said Aito.

'Well, oddities abound in Dogudu,' Oshu replied.

After disclosing a few more details about the upcoming trip, Oshu and Ada vacated the living room, leaving Amen, Iska, and the boys to themselves. Not long after, Walé, who had been quiet for most of the night, slid into the sofa next to Iska.

'So, you guys are off to Dogudu in less than forty-eight hours,' he said to Iska, making sure not to break eye contact.

'I guess so,' replied Iska.

'Ada told me I'm not allowed to come with you guys, you know,' said Walé, now scratching his right eyebrow playfully. 'As a matter of fact, she's trying to get me on the next available flight to London.'

'Oh, I didn't know that,' said Iska earnestly.

'Yeah, but I don't want to leave,' said Walé. 'I've honestly had a good time with you these past few days; I don't want it to end now.'

Iska's ears went hot. 'Neither do I… I'd really like for you to come with us,' she added after a brief pause.

As though Iska had delivered him some sort of good news with her words, Walé suddenly relaxed into a fulfilled smile.

'What?' said Iska, shaking her head in confusion.

'Nothing,' Walé replied, still smiling. 'I just needed to know if you wanted me to come along. And now that I do, I'll make sure I'm invited.'

'How?'

'Now, I don't usually pester people,' Walé admitted. 'But with Ada, I make an exception because she always gives in.'

Iska laughed. 'I think this is beyond Ada; there's Oshu to deal with.'

'Don't be so sure,' Walé said with a wink. 'Oshu rarely says no to Ada.'

It was the night before the journey to Dogudu, and from what Amen and Iska could gather, Walé's plan to tag along had spiralled into a complete mess. Although he had somehow convinced Ada to let him come, persuading Oshu was proving to be an entirely different challenge. According to Ada, who had confided in the twins earlier that day, Oshu was adamant that bringing a human to Dogudu was strictly forbidden.

Though Ada hadn't intended to burden them with the details, Iska and Amen could tell that the stress of the situation had clearly shaken her. Feeling somewhat guilty for encouraging Walé to join them in the first place, Iska had tried to come up with a solution that would satisfy everyone. But in the end, it was Amen who suggested that Ada, with their support, try speaking to Oshu one more time. Desperate and out of sorts, Ada decided to run with this idea and ambush Oshu immediately.

The first thing that caught Iska and Amen's attention as they walked into Oshu's office was the set of mechanical tools scattered all around him.

'The answer is still no,' said Oshu before the twins could even shut the door behind them.

'Oshu, why are you being so stubborn?' Ada was doing her best to keep her temper in check. 'You know he has nothing to return to if he goes back to London.'

'Well, I'd rather he be lonely than hurt,' said Oshu. 'You know Ada, I expect you, of all people, to understand my position.'

Amen cleared her throat. 'Isn't there a way around it, a compromise?'

'I'm sorry,' said Oshu, as he drilled a screw into the treadmill he was working on. 'My mind is made up.'

'Well, if he can't come, then neither can I,' said Iska defiantly. 'Or Lake, for that matter.'

'Why is that?' said Oshu, a tinge of concern in his voice.

'Because I'm a Reeg,' Iska replied. 'Lake and I both are. So, if that's the case, I guess we won't be accepted, because as far as I know, we're as ordinary as humans.'

'If she's not going, neither am I,' said Amen, crossing her arms on her chest. 'I don't go anywhere without my sister.'

'Count me out as well,' added Ada, a smirk growing on her face. 'This trip is for the twins. If they aren't interested, then what's the point?'

At first, Oshu let out a loud, frustrated sigh, but then he began to laugh, catching Iska and Amen by surprise. 'Over ten years of doing business,' he said, still laughing, 'and I'm being strong-armed by my wife and nieces.'

Amen, Iska, and Ada couldn't help but join Oshu in laughing at the situation.

'All right,' said Oshu, his expression serious again. 'Walé can come, but he's a Reeg from this moment onward... And one more thing: Ada, I don't know how you're going to pull it off, but you have to explain to him what we are, and you must make sure he promises to take our secret to his grave.'

Ada seemed nervous, but she nodded in agreement.

Knowing fully well they wouldn't be able to communicate with the outside world for a short while, Iska and Amen sent out an email to Rima explaining that their stay in Nigeria had been extended by another week. In the email, they begged Rima to cover for them a bit longer. Amen and Iska knew they were playing with fire by prolonging their absence in Howth, but they couldn't return now—not yet.

7. JOURNEY

It was only a few minutes past five in the morning, yet the house was bustling with activity. Feeling a little more excited about the trip today, Amen and Iska, who already had their bags packed, helped Lake, Aito, and Walé tidy up theirs. In fact, they were in the middle of talking Aito out of packing a pair of runners he'd recently acquired when Oshu announced that it was time to leave.

Out in the driveway, the engine of a vehicle neither Iska nor Amen had seen before was being revved up by Oshu's chauffeur. Oshu, who met them studying the glossy black van, said it was a Jet Mover: a luxurious van used for long road trips. Still fixated on the machine, Amen and Iska didn't notice their luggage had been brought out of the house and was now being loaded into the van.

'All right, people,' said Oshu, dressed in his grey top, matching cargo shorts, and hiking boots. 'We're leaving soon. I hope you've all packed according to the specifications from the other day.'

Satisfied with the collective response he received, Oshu continued, 'It's going to be a long trip, eleven hours to be precise. So, Ada took the liberty of procuring some food, which is available at any time to anyone.

'If the food isn't to your liking, or if it's completely finished before we reach our destination, we will make quick stops to get more food and allow bathroom breaks. Any questions?'

Oshu went silent for a few seconds. With no questions forthcoming, he continued his speech. 'The Jet Mover is very comfortable and one of the fastest vans out there. So, hopefully, our journey is as smooth and as fast as possible.'

After Oshu's detailed presentation, it took all of ten minutes for everyone to get settled into the Jet Mover and watch casa Tella disappear in the background.

Either Oshu had been trying to downplay the quality of the Jet Mover, or he genuinely was not aware what it was capable of, because the van had everything: multiple air-conditioners, a built-in mini-kitchen, a voice assistant, and reclinable seats with entertainment screens that slid in and out a view. But by far the most impressive thing about the Jet mover was how well it drove; the van moved so grace-fully that for long stretches of time, Iska and Amen forgot they were even on the road. The twins also found it hard to grasp the geography of Nigeria; it felt as though every acre of greenery they drove past was followed immediately by a vast expanse of shantytowns—it was both fascinating and depressing.

It wasn't long before the Jet Mover found itself stuck in a traffic jam that seemed to be kilometres long. In the thick of the jam, something caught and held Amen and Iska's at-tention: people ranging from elderly women to young boys were walking up and down the roads, carrying cartons of different products either on their heads or in their arms.

'What are these people doing?' said Amen, peering through the van's tinted windows.

'They're hawkers,' Ada replied.

'Hawkers?' Aito repeated.

'Yes,' said Oshu. 'They sell things on the roads when there's heavy traffic, like this one.'

Ada laughed at the expression on Amen and Iska's faces as they took in Oshu's explanation of what they considered to be the most bizarre thing they had ever heard.

'There's a running joke in Nigeria,' said Ada, still laugh-ing, 'that goes, you can leave your home half-naked and be fully clothed by the time you reach your destination.'

'It looks like a thankless job,' said Iska.

Oshu nodded. 'It is. This is what Ada and I are trying to eradicate. Unfortunately, this is the only means of livelihood for these people; it makes you grateful for what you do have.'

They finally made their first stop in five hours at a petrol station in a city called Benin to refuel the Jet mover. While everyone else went into the adjoining shop to buy some snacks and use the restrooms, Iska and Oshu stayed in the van.

'I was wondering,' said Iska, thankful she finally had some alone time with her uncle. 'If you're disappointed that I don't have any special abilities like Amen.'

'Really?' said Oshu, folding the map he was studying into a neat square.

'Yes, really.'

'First off, it's not your fault that you don't have abilities. You didn't even ask to be a Unix to begin with.'

'But—'

'Second,' Oshu continued, 'Aré was a Reeg as well.'

Iska's eyes widened in astonishment.

'Yes,' said Oshu. 'Your mother and I found out we were Unix at a really young age. Even though I had been scared of what I was, she made sure to always remind me that we were wonderfully made creatures.

'And so are you, Iska. Don't worry about a mundane thing like having an ability. I'll let you in on a secret: it gets pretty boring having something you can't really use for fear of scaring people shitless.'

Iska couldn't hold her laugh in. 'Thank you Oshu, for everything.'

'Cheers,' said Oshu coyly.

'So, what exactly are we going to see in Dogudu?' said Iska.

'Nirewa,' Oshu replied. 'And she's a person. More of an oracle, actually.'

Iska bit her bottom lip. 'By oracle, you mean…'

'Yes. Clairvoyance, necromancy, prophecy, all that stuff. Although, she does have her limitations.'

Iska couldn't help but feel sorry for how hard her brain had to work at times. Ever since she learnt she was a Unix, nothing in the world seemed to be just straightforward; everything was layered in ways that were at times incomprehensible to her.

'Oshu,' said Iska, as quickly as the thought crossed her mind. 'When was the last time you visited Dogudu?'

Oshu made a face like he had been expecting the question for some time. 'I haven't been there in thirty-four years.'

'Christ; that's a long time.'

'It really is.'

'How do you know the oracle lady is still alive?'

'I don't,' said Oshu matter-of-factly. 'I just hope she is. We'll find out soon enough.'

'What are you two gossiping about?' said Ada as she pranced into the van.

'Nothing,' Oshu replied, shooting Iska a wink.

About an hour and a half after resuming their journey, the rhythmic hum of the Jet Mover lulled some of its passengers to sleep. In fact, Aito, who was now snoring, had reclined his seat so far back that Walé had no choice but to move to the next available seat, which coincidentally was behind Amen, who was awake and watching the beautiful mix of green and brown landscape sweep by at a dizzying pace.

'What kind of village only lets "talented" people in?' Walé asked Amen. 'I don't get it.'

'What blows my mind,' said Amen, still looking out the window, 'is that you're still brave enough to come along even after what you've been told.'

'I wouldn't say I'm brave, if I'm being honest,' said Walé. 'But, for Iska, I think it's worth it.'

Amen finally swivelled around in her seat to look at Walé. 'You really like her that much?'

'I know we haven't had much time to talk, but your sister is an amazing person, and all I want is to explore what's there with her.'

Staring at him for more than just a few seconds, Amen

could see why Iska was attracted to Walé. Not only was he beautiful, but he also had a captivating gaze that could make anyone lose themselves in his deep-set brown eyes.

'Besides,' Walé continued, 'what would I do in England? The new academic year is still a few months away.'

'Yeah,' said Amen, suddenly remembering something she'd been curious about since she first met Walé. 'What's the story with your parents? Why can't you stay with them?'

Walé chuckled and shook his head. 'I thought Ada would have told you something about that already.'

Amen shrugged, looking confused.

'Well, my parents are divorced,' he said. 'They've been for a while now, since I was nine years old. My mum disappeared after the divorce. Haven't seen her since then.'

'Oh, I'm sorry about that,' said Amen, looking sympathetic.

'No, don't be,' Walé replied with a laugh. 'Compared to some people I know,' he continued, making a suggestive face. 'My life has been close to perfect—I was born with a silver spoon in my mouth and will probably never lack anything until the day I die—'

Amen rolled her eyes. 'Very *modest*, aren't you?'

'It's not even about that,' Walé chuckled. 'I just see life for what it is. As much as I'm grateful for my fortune, I recognise that the game is rigged, and I hate it.'

She wasn't going to let him know this, but Amen was impressed by Walé's candour. 'What happened between your parents?'

'That's a story for another day.'

'Fair enough. But Ada? What's the relationship there?'

Walé licked his lips. 'My old man and Ada are lifelong friends,' he said. 'They've known each other since they were kids. My grandparents and her parents were also friends and business partners.

'When I was born, my father asked her to be my godmother; best decision he's ever made for me.'

'She really is a wonderful person,' said Amen, glancing

over at Ada who was fast asleep. 'So do you hate your dad or something?'

Walé seemed to find Amen's questions amusing because he was laughing again. 'I don't know who's more inquisitive,' he said, 'you or your sister.'

Amen shrugged her shoulders in response.

'I don't hate him,' said Walé. 'The divorce didn't affect just him and my mum; it made our relationship as father and son really strained as well. And it hasn't come close to recovering since then.'

'I'm really—' Amen stopped herself from finishing her sentence, and Walé smiled at this.

'Anyway,' Walé continued, 'after spending one summer with Ada and Oshu in London, I realised I'd rather be with them than with someone who rarely has time for me.'

Amen turned over Walé's words in her head for a moment before finally speaking up. 'I shouldn't tell you this, and she'd probably kill me if she found out, but Iska really likes you. And it's obvious you feel the same way about her…right?' she said, observing Walé's reaction.

Walé tried to hide his smile. 'Yes, I do.'

'Good,' said Amen, her expression serious. 'Because if you hurt her, I'll show you what I can do with *my* talent.'

Walé grinned at Amen's comment just as the Jet mover came to a halt, making everyone alert.

'Are we there yet?' said Iska, peering out the window.

'No, not yet,' said Oshu. 'We're getting a connecting bus that will take us to our final destination.'

As they got out of the van, Iska and Amen realised that they were in a bus station with a single, run-down building, surrounded by buses and bustling people. Following Oshu's instructions, they retrieved their luggage from the Jet Mover's boot and carried it to the front of the dilapidated building. While Oshu and Ada frantically searched for someone to speak to, Iska and Amen looked back at the bus park, only to discover that the Jet Mover was no longer there.

Not long after, a man who appeared to be well into his seventies hobbled over with Ada and Oshu.

'Na seven of us dey go,' said Oshu, in a dialect he hadn't used before. 'You get anything wey go fit take us?

'I get one bus, but e go tight,' the old man replied.

'No wahala,' said Ada, reaching for something in her bag. 'We go manage am like that.'

'Abeg no vex,' Oshu said to the old man. 'You dey sell machetes?'

'Yes,' the old man replied, eyeing Oshu and Ada nonchalantly. 'Na one thousand naira for one. How many una want?'

'Abeg give us four,' said Oshu.

Ada handed some money to the old man, and he sauntered towards the back of the building.

'All right, guys,' said Oshu, as soon as the man disappeared out of sight. 'The bus we're getting on is going to be very uncomfortable, but on the bright side, the journey will last only an hour.'

Moments later, the old man called out to them from the bus park. As the group walked over to him, Iska rushed to catch up with Ada and asked her about the language she and Oshu had used to speak to the man.

'That's Pidgin English,' Ada explained. 'It's like the unofficial first language of Nigerians. It's sometimes used by people who don't speak fluent English to communicate with those who do.'

Iska nodded, confused and astonished.

Their new means of transportation was a far cry from the Jet Mover. The old, battered bus was missing a few windows and mirrors, had dents all over it, and one of its tires looked like it could give out at any moment. Oshu took the front passenger seat while everyone else had to come up with inventive ways to cram themselves into the cramped, worn-out interior of the bus.

The old man finally got into the driver's seat, put the key in the ignition, and brought the bus to life. In a matter of minutes, he was driving them out of the station and down a road that was flanked by lush greenery on either side.

'Una be tourists?' the old man asked, struggling to maintain his grip on the steering wheel.

'Yes,' said Oshu. 'We come from London; we dey go visit my people.'

'Na better pikin you be,' said the man. 'Where you talk say you dey go again?'

Oshu craned his neck to the right to stare at the wall of green leaves whizzing past the bus. 'Dogudu.'

Suddenly the bus screeched to a hard stop, causing everyone inside to jolt forward.

Sweat trickled down the old man's wrinkled neck as he switched off the bus's engine. 'No one goes to that village,' he said in plain English this time.

'Sir, please we need to get there,' said Oshu, his gaze bouncing between Amen and Iska. 'We can pay you extra.'

'No be about money!' the old man snapped. 'Na only mad people dey go—'

'Take us as close as you can, then,' Ada interrupted. 'And we'll find our way from there.'

The old man swallowed hard; his eyes darted from side to side, like he was contemplating leaving the bus and everyone in it altogether and making his way back home on foot. 'E go cost you another fifty thousand naira.'

Ada dug through her bag and produced two thick wads of cash. 'Na two hundred and fifty thousand naira be this,' she said, holding out the money in front of the old man. 'As close as you can get.'

While Amen and Iska were still trying to process what had just happened, the old man restarted the bus and continued the journey, his hands trembling as he steered the wheel. At first, no one noticed it, but as they drove further, the road ahead became less and less visible until they were completely enveloped in a thick fog that forced the bus to come to a stop.

'I no fit drive pass this point,' said the old man, as the

vehicle's engine hummed in silence. 'If una wan commot, do am now, abeg.'

Oshu signalled for everyone to get off the bus while Ada handed the old man his money. As soon as everyone was out with their belongings, the old man turned the rickety bus around and drove off as fast as he could.

'We'll be making the rest of the journey on foot,' said Oshu, as he untied a polythene bag, revealing the machetes he had bought from the old man earlier. Oshu handed one to each of the boys and kept the last one for himself. Then he reached into the right side-pocket of his shorts and pulled out a paper map.

'This is where we are,' said Oshu, pointing to a spot on the intricately patterned map. 'Dogudu should be here, in the middle of this forest. That means we need to head northeast.

'We need to form a line. Ada, Aito, and I will lead, while Iska and Amen will be in the middle; Lake and Walé will be at the back of the line… Is everyone okay with this?'

Satisfied with everyone's silence, Oshu picked up his backpack and made for a small opening in the thick wall of greenery. By now the sun had completely disappeared, making it much more challenging to navigate the forest. However, Ada, who was in control of the map, was still able to lead the group without so much as a torch. Pushing through thick, moist shrubs, the howls of monkeys, chirps of birds, and hisses of snakes bounced around, but it was too dark to tell if any of these creatures were hundreds of yards away or right beside them.

As they ventured deeper into the jungle, a putrid smell gradually grew stronger and stronger, eventually becoming so overwhelming that they all had to cover their noses with their arms.

Aito, who was still cutting through the foliage at the head of the line, was about to make a comment on the stench when Amen and Iska spotted something that made their blood run cold.

8. HOME

The twins froze in terror, unable to scream despite the sheer panic coursing through their veins. The creature was barely visible, blending in seamlessly with the tangled foliage that surrounded it, but its piercing yellow eyes glowed like beacons, giving away its position.

The creature took in huge gulps of air and released massive bubbles of steam as it exhaled.

'Slowly back away,' Oshu whispered to the group as he moved carefully in front of them.

Iska, Amen, and the others followed Oshu's instruction, but this only seemed to agitate the creature. Slowly pushing through trees, the creature started to reveal itself. Amen and Iska had seen silverback gorillas on their visit to the Dublin Zoo a couple of years back; although they had been majestic creatures, they had also been half the size of the one rising to its feet in front of them.

Standing on two legs, the gorilla was nearly three metres tall. As if making a statement, it slowly beat its chest with broad muscular arms that could effortlessly lift two small cars. At the same moment, something hit the ground with a loud thud behind them, and Iska and Amen managed to turn around to see Walé had passed out. Ada, somehow not paralysed by fear, wanted to help him, but the ape had its eyes locked on all of them, waiting for one person to make a false move before striking. The only person who made any movement was Oshu: he took off his backpack and shoved it at Ada, making sure not to break eye contact with the monster in front of him.

'Babe, take care of the kids no matter what,' Oshu said in a surprisingly calm whisper. 'Aito, listen to me. If this thing kills me, I want you to gather everyone and blink home. Do not hesitate.'

Aito looked like he was going to question Oshu's order before finally nodding his head. Right at that moment, Oshu fell to his knees and, with a sound like the unfastening of Velcro, transformed into a dog the size of an adult moose.

After a moment of stunned silence, Amen and Iska realised that it *wasn't* a dog at all; its black coat initially made it look like one, but it also had brown spots all around its body and an exceptionally long muscular tail with golden-brown rings near the end of it. Only when the four-legged animal glanced down at them did Amen and Iska realise what it was: the tawny tear streaks on its face were unmistakable—Oshu was a cheetah.

There was no time for this epiphany to settle because Oshu turned his big feline head back towards the gorilla in front of him and let out a menacing churr so powerful that its reverberation made Amen and Iska crumple to the ground in fear.

The gorilla, unperturbed by Oshu's goading, slapped its knuckles to the ground and, in a split second, was barrelling towards Oshu, who was already charging in the monster's direction. The impact of their collision was so powerful it rattled the earth, and for a moment, it seemed as though the gorilla had the upper hand as it wrapped its massive arms around Oshu. But suddenly, the gorilla let out a piercing scream, and Amen and Iska caught a glimpse of their uncle sinking his razor-sharp teeth into the ape's shoulder.

The initial advantage that Oshu had gained didn't last long as the gorilla swiftly prised Oshu's head from its bleeding flesh and, in one fluid motion, slapped him to the ground. Not done yet, the gorilla grabbed Oshu by the tail, hoisted him into the air, and then slammed him down onto the ground with a sickening thud that forced a heart-wrenching cry of pain out of him.

Amid the ensuing chaos, the rush of adrenaline seemed to slow down time: Ada was screaming, desperately trying to break free from Lake's grasp to reach Oshu, while Aito was pulling Walé's unconscious body closer, presumably to make it easier for him to blink everyone to safety. Iska and Amen watched in horror as Oshu lay powerless on the ground with the gorilla looming over him. Even in his animal form, Oshu had retained his kind, analytical eyes; only now the light in them was about to go out. It was clear to everyone that the end was near.

With an act of undeniable bravery, Oshu turned his head away from them and gazed up at his impending death. Amen, Iska, and the rest huddled closely, holding hands and watching solemnly as one of their own was about to be taken from them forever.

The gorilla raised its hands above its head, poised to deliver the fatal blow. There was a silence. And then, inexplicably, the beast's arms dropped to its sides. No one was certain, but it looked as though the gorilla was shrinking in size. And it wasn't just the gorilla. Oshu, too, seemed to be growing smaller, shedding fur and flesh with every shuddering breath he took. But what truly stunned everyone was when the gorilla, still in the middle of its transformation, spoke.

At first, nobody understood what the gorilla said. But then, it spoke again, and this time, everyone heard it because the once-ferocious beast was now a brawny, naked man, and what he had said earlier was Oshu's name.

'Oshu, it's really you,' the deep voice said.

Oshu, who was also in his unclad human form, looked even more confused than Amen, Iska, and the others. 'Who are you?' he said, his voice uneven and breathing laboured.

The burly man let out a deep, hearty laugh as he stepped aside and extended his hand for Oshu to take. 'Your memory was always terrible,' he said, still laughing. 'I should feel insulted, but it has been more than thirty years since we last saw you. It is me, Jimba.'

Jimba spoke with an unusual lilt. He rolled his Rs and placed distinct emphasis on his Ls and Ts. With eyes closed, it was easy to mistake his voice for a stream of water cascading down a pebbled surface—it was pure and weighty.

As soon as Oshu took Jimba's hand, he was pulled up

to his feet. This prompted Amen, Iska, and the boys to look away, while Ada reflexively started to search Oshu's backpack for fresh clothes. Perhaps overcome with every kind of emotion from nearly being trampled to death, Oshu began to laugh in spite of the tears streaming down his muddied face.

'Jimba, I remember you,' he said, holding the man's hands. 'I remember you.'

Ada, oblivious to the moment of reunion between the two men, ran to Oshu and hugged him tightly before shoving some clothes into his hand. Remembering he, too, was naked, Jimba quickly disappeared into the bushes. While he was gone, Amen walked up to Ada and Oshu and, without saying a word, embraced Oshu. A few moments later, Iska joined in with such force that it almost knocked them to the ground.

'We thought we had lost you,' said Iska.

'I can't be gotten rid of so easily,' said Oshu, doing his best to mask his pain.

Jimba re-emerged from the forest, now fully clothed in a red, sleeveless calico top paired with matching knee-length shorts. He looked even bigger up close, easily dwarfing Oshu. Ada eyed Jimba sardonically, and he didn't miss the gesture.

'Oshu, I'm sorry for earlier,' he said, weaving his long, cowry-adorned dreadlocks to the back of his head. 'I'm the protector of the Dogudu sanctuary; it was my thinking that you were an intruder.'

'No worries at all,' said Oshu, buttoning up his shirt. 'I understand your duty. One that, if I remember correctly, once rested with your father.'

'You do remember,' said Jimba proudly. 'Yes. I took over after he passed on.'

'I'm sorry to hear that,' Oshu said.

'Think nothing of it. It has been many years since he died.'

While the men continued their conversation, Amen and

Iska found themselves caught up in a private discussion of their own.

He speaks so well, thought Amen.

I know.

And the accent—the cadence of his voice. Amen continued.

I know!

But how?

I don't know!

Iska and Amen were still trying to reconcile Jimba's eloquence with their idea of how people from a village without modern day technology might sound when he interrupted them.

'Oshu, who are these people you've brought with you?' he asked.

'This is my family,' Oshu replied, wrapping one arm around Ada and the other around the twins. 'My wife, Ada; my nieces, Amen and Iska; their friends, Lake and Aito; and the boy in their arms is my godson, Walé…he seems to have lost consciousness when he saw you earlier.'

Jimba let out a disappointed chuckle.

'Everyone, as you've probably already gathered,' Oshu continued, 'this is Jimba, an old friend of mine and the current protector of Dogudu.'

'Pleasure to meet you all,' Jimba said earnestly. 'Sincerest apologies for my actions. Any family of Oshu's is family to us.'

Ada remained silent, clearly still upset from the earlier ordeal.

'Good to meet you, Jimba,' Amen and Iska said in unison.

But Jimba jerked his head slightly at the sound of his name. 'I see you two lack manners,' he said, his tone calm but firm. 'I can tell from your accent that you're from overseas, but that changes nothing. You must show respect. You call me *Uncle* Jimba.'

Jimba glared at Aito and Lake. 'The same goes for you two.'

Although Iska and Amen were confused, neither of them dared to go against Jimba's advice; his imposing physique alone compelled compliance.

'Oshu, everyone will be excited to see you,' said Jimba, before turning to Aito and Lake who were trying to heft Walé between them. 'Boys, you can give him to me.'

Jimba's strength didn't seem to be limited to his ape form. He effortlessly lifted Walé onto his shoulder and beckoned for them to follow him.

After trailing behind Jimba for half an hour along a narrow, winding path, the murky forest began to brighten. At first, Amen and Iska thought the sun was rising, but then they looked up and saw a swarm of fireflies glowing in shades of yellow, green, and red, moving in perfect synchrony. Spellbound by the choreography of lights taking place above them, Amen and Iska didn't notice that they had reached Dogudu until Jimba spoke.

'We're here,' he said, pulling their attention to the view in front of them.

Iska and Amen's eyes widened in disbelief as they took in the view of the village: rows upon rows of exquisitely crafted bamboo huts spread out in a perfect circle around a vast expanse of lush green grass.

'Is this even real life?' said Iska, still admiring the immaculately designed huts.

Jimba chuckled at the question, his voice breaking the silence of the night. 'Of course it is, and there's more, but that'll be for tomorrow. I know it's quite late, but my daughter can make something for you all to eat.'

Exhaustion rather than hunger was what everyone felt as they politely declined Jimba's offer.

'Oshu, if we had known you and your family would be visiting,' said Jimba, as he led them through a row of huts, 'proper arrangements would have been made for your accommodation.'

'We're sorry for turning up unexpectedly; I would have communicated our visit...if I could.' Oshu said the last words in a factual tone.

'It's not a problem,' said Jimba, who suddenly turned left and started up the steps of a rectangular hut. 'We'll definitely find spaces for all of you tomorrow. But I'm afraid tonight, you'll have to stay in my home.'

Oshu paused at the foot of the steps. 'Jimba, we can't intrude into your home and inconvenience you.'

'Come off that,' Jimba tried to whisper, but it was practically impossible to suppress the bass in his voice. 'The space is just enough. You might have to squeeze here and there, but it's only for one night. Besides, you're family.'

'Where will *you* sleep?' Oshu asked.

'Sleep?' said Jimba, a smirk growing on his face. 'I'm going back out there. My watch is not done until dawn.'

Jimba's home was surprisingly more spacious than it looked from the outside. The dimly lit hut was partitioned into two rooms: the parlour, which had no furniture except for a few straw stools with intricate mesh designs, and Jimba's room, which contained some of his personal belongings and a single sleeping mat in the corner. While the group put their bags away, Jimba carefully laid Walé on a spare mat he had unfolded and offered to retrieve some items to clean Walé's bruises. While he left to get the supplies, Iska and Amen inspected the finer details of Jimba's house, taking note of the tightly woven palm walls and the soft yet sturdy floors, and imagining the amount of effort that had gone into constructing it.

Upon his return, Jimba carried a calabash bowl and dry cloth in one hand and four rolled up sleeping mats in the other. 'Here,' he said, handing the bowl and cloth to Oshu. 'The water has some herbs in it; it will help with Walé's injuries and yours.'

Jimba then laid the mats in the parlour. 'Oshu and Ada can stay in my room,' he said to the group. 'The rest of you can sleep here tonight. The mats are comfortable, I promise.'

'What about your daughter?' said Amen. 'Where is she

going to sleep?'

The question reminded everyone that Jimba had mentioned something about a daughter earlier.

'Daughters,' Jimba replied with a smile. 'Both of them are asleep in the next hut. I'll make introductions tomorrow.'

'And wife?' Ada asked.

Jimba allowed a quiet smile that suggested he'd rather not answer the question.

With Jimba returning to his night watch, the group was left to sort out their sleeping arrangements. Determined to keep a watchful eye on him through the night, Ada got Oshu to help her move Walé into Jimba's room; meanwhile, Amen and Iska set their sleeping mats as close to the walls of the parlour as possible. Aito and Lake took up spots in the middle. As they watched the cloudless, star-filled sky through the skylight, Amen and Iska could hardly believe how quickly their lives had changed in just a matter of days. Drifting into unconsciousness, it was hard to shake off the feeling that they were only starting out on what was fast becoming a crazy rollercoaster ride.

The warm sunlight dancing on their faces was enough to rouse Amen and Iska from their sleep, but it was the sniggering coming from outside the hut that forced them to sit up straight. For a moment, the twins felt a surge of fear replace their confusion as they scanned the empty room, wondering where everyone was, until they saw Aito and Lake by the doorway, with unfamiliar, cherubic faces behind them.

'Grand,' said Aito. 'Finally, you're up.'

'What time is it?' said Amen, peering at the little children by the door. 'And who are they?'

'They're locals,' answered Lake. 'It's half eleven; you two have been asleep for a while.'

'After last night,' said Iska, as she got off from her sleeping mat. 'I wouldn't mind being asleep for a whole year. Where's everyone?'

'That's why we're here,' said Aito with a smile. 'Yous need to come see this.'

The children wouldn't stop following them; whenever Iska and Amen glanced behind, the kids would stop in their tracks, feigning disinterest, but they were always there, whispering in their tiny voices.

'What's with them?' said Iska as they followed the boys through a maze of huts.

'You'll get used to it,' Aito replied. 'Apparently, they've never seen foreigners before.'

'You should hear what they call us,' Lake said with a laugh.

Finally, they burst through the labyrinth of houses into an open field, and Amen and Iska's faces flushed with embarrassment at how far off the mark they had been about the village's appearance.

Just as they were about to express their amazement to the boys, someone called out to them in the distance. It was Oshu, accompanied by Ada, Walé, and Jimba.

Amen and Iska turned their heads from side to aside, mesmerised by the stunning design of the village as they walked across the clearing towards their family. Instead of a circle, the rows of huts were actually laid out in a hexagonal shape with openings in the middle of each side; meanwhile towering trees, at least ten metres tall, stood at each vertex of the hexagon, holding several arrays of huts that were connected across all six sides, like a canopy of houses suspended mid-air.

'See, I told you there was more,' said Jimba, instinctively interpreting the expression on the twins' faces.

'Nothing I've ever seen comes close to this,' said Amen in awe.

Jimba chuckled. 'We'll take that as a compliment.'

'But how do people get up there?' said Iska, pointing to

the intricate network of huts above them.

'There are tunnels,' replied Jimba, gesturing towards some translucent structures in the distance. 'They lead from the ground up.'

Amen shook her head in disbelief. *I kind of see why people here don't want modern technology,* she thought. *They don't need it.*

'There they are,' said Jimba, as two girls approached them from the north-east entrance of the village. The taller one was easily Amen and Iska's age, while the other girl was around eleven years old.

Jimba grinned with pride. 'I'd like for you all to meet my daughters, Zara and Dami.'

There was something unusual about the two girls; despite their resemblance to each other, they looked completely different in every other way.

'Welcome to Dogudu,' said the older girl with a slight nod in the direction of Oshu and Ada, completely ignoring everyone else.

Okay, she's rude, Amen thought to Iska.

'I'm Dami,' said the smaller one as she went around shaking everyone's hand. She paused abruptly when she got to Amen. 'I like your eyes,' she said before turning to face Jimba. 'Papa, have you seen her eyes?'

Dami's question to Jimba sparked a round of laughter, but Zara maintained a straight face, adding to the already odd dynamic between the sisters.

'Thank you,' said Amen, squatting to match Dami's height. 'And I love your hair.'

Dami was just about to say something back to Amen when some children on the other side of the field began calling out to her, beckoning her over.

'Please, Papa, can I go?' Dami asked, making an adorable face only a sociopath would refuse.

'All right, Sunshine, but be careful!'

It was intriguing to watch the hulking monster of last night be so fatherly.

Dami thanked Jimba, and then did what no one was expecting: she hopped into the air with one foot and never came back down. Everyone was shocked, not only because she was levitating but also because, for some strange reason, Dami being in the air made it difficult for them to lift their own feet off the ground. Finally, in one swift motion, the ebony-skinned girl zoomed away at a speed that sent blades of grass flying into the air.

Oshu stared after Dami. 'Your daughter can fly.'

'I almost wish she couldn't,' said Jimba in a tone that blatantly contradicted his words. 'I'm not fond of her flying backwards the way she just did. But yes, she's been flying for two years now.'

'Two years,' said Ada in disbelief, 'That's really young.'

'That's right,' Jimba replied. 'The children of Dogudu are exceptional, even by our generation's standards.'

'Incredible,' said Oshu.

Jimba laughed and tilted his head towards Zara. 'You should see what this one can do.'

The quiet girl gave her father a smug look.

'All right,' said Jimba. 'I'm going to get some rest. In the meantime, Zara will show you around.'

'Papa?' Zara was caught off guard.

'You will show them to their new quarters,' Jimba continued, as if he couldn't see the protest on his daughter's face. 'And to the tailors to get their measurements taken.'

'But Papa—'

'Please, Zara, don't be rude to our family,' Jimba said in a tone that ended the discussion.

'Why do we need our measurements to be taken?' said Aito.

'I mean no disrespect,' said Jimba, as he looked them over, 'but it is embarrassing for you to walk the grounds of Dogudu in those clothes. We have our own attire.'

This was true. The curious children from earlier, as well as Jimba, Dami, and Zara, all wore similar types of clothes made from the same calico fabric, albeit in different colours.

In fact, Jimba still had on the same red outfit from the previous night, while Zara was wearing a sleeveless white top cropped at the midsection with matching ankle-length trousers that had distinct lines and patterns.

'At the start of sunset, I'll take you all to meet Nirewa. For now, please enjoy the tour,' said Jimba before shaking Oshu's hands and leaving the field, leaving them with his irritable daughter.

'Shall we begin the tour with the public baths?' Zara said in a sing-song accent similar to Jimba's.

Magical. This was the one word Iska and Amen kept repeating to themselves, as they made their way through Dogudu, taking in buildings and scenery that at times seemed not to be of this world. For example, Nkọ, the village's one and only temple, built from polished pebbles and bamboo, commanded reverence simply by its presence. The small, quaint shops, tucked away in nooks and crannies along narrow streets, bustled with sellers and buyers haggling over everything from smoked tilapias to newly made aluminium lanterns. Even the shrubbery dotted all over the village was full of life, their vibrant green colours contrasting sharply against the earthy tones of Dogudu's buildings. Nearing the tailor's shop, the twins couldn't help but wonder where and how long ago the engineering expertise to create such breath-taking works of art was developed.

Zara's mood hadn't improved since they started the tour of the village, and everyone had begun to notice how aloof she was. She insisted on waiting outside the shop while they got their measurements taken.

'That one is stuck up, isn't she?' Ada whispered to Amen as they waited for Oshu to be measured.

'I wonder what her problem is,' said Amen.

'Who knows?' Ada replied. 'It's funny that Jimba scolded you and Iska for your manners when his daughter clearly needs to work on hers... I wouldn't pay her any attention, though,' Ada continued, shooting Amen a wink. 'After all, she's not the reason we're here.'

Amen smiled and nodded in agreement. She was impressed Ada had noticed, too, that Zara's animosity seemed to be directed specifically at her and Iska.

Ironically, Iska was more preoccupied with Walé at the other end of the shop. 'How's your head?' she asked Walé.

'Fine, thanks,' said Walé, feeling the mesh fibre wrapped around his forehead with his hand. 'However, what's not fine is the fact that I fainted in front of you.'

Iska stifled a laugh, not wanting to kick a man while he was down. But thankfully, Walé was also laughing.

'No, go ahead,' he said. 'It must have been funny. It's just that I'd never seen an eight-foot-tall gorilla before; I think I stopped breathing.'

'You should have seen what Oshu turned into.'

'Yeah, the lads told me. I would have found that hard to believe if not for Jimba and his flying daughter.'

'But I thought Ada told you all about Unix before the trip? Oshu told her to.'

Walé swayed his head from side to side. 'She did. But I think my rational mind tried to play it down. I thought I'd be meeting people who could jump really high or were incredibly athletic, not men transforming into animals.'

'Well, the world isn't really what it seems. In your defence, you're handling things pretty well; I remember the first time I was told. My heart wouldn't stop pounding for a week.'

'Really?' said Walé, relief filling his face. 'That makes me feel better.'

'You're adorable,' said Iska, feeling a little confident. 'I'd have kissed you if everyone wasn't here.'

Walé closed the gap between them slowly and lowered his voice. 'Maybe you should.'

'Maybe I will.' Iska leaned in, and Walé closed his eyes and puckered his lips, waiting to be kissed, but at the last moment, Iska flicked his forehead, causing both of them to chuckle.

'So, what's your thing?' Walé asked.

'What?'

'Your ability,' said Walé. 'Do you like turn into a giant eagle, or is being gorgeous your talent?'

Walé's attempt at being charming fell flat.

'That's not funny,' Iska said in an acidic tone.

'Hey, what's the matter?' said Walé, sensing the shift in Iska's mood. 'I didn't mean to be rude.'

'It's fine, you didn't do anything wrong.'

'What's up then?'

'Just that you asked what my ability is…and I don't have any.'

'You don't?'

'Yeah, it's a complicated thing,' said Iska, waving her hand in dismissal. 'I know it's weird I'm bitter about something as petty as that, but it would have meant a lot to me if I had an ability of my own.'

'I'm sorry you feel this way,' said Walé, resisting the urge to give Iska a hug. 'It must be hard for you. Is Amen the same?'

Iska stole a glance at her twin sister. 'She's a Telemin,' she said, returning her gaze to Walé. 'She can manipulate water.'

'Ah, I see.' Walé raised his eyebrows.

'I'm not jealous of her.'

'I didn't say that.'

'Yeah, not with your mouth.' Iska rolled her eyes.

Walé smiled and took Iska's hand. 'I learnt somewhere the first step to gaining control of your emotions is to recognise them for what they are.'

'What's your point?'

'Now don't bite my head off,' said Walé, allowing an earnest grin. 'But do you think a part of why you're so irritated about not having an ability is because Amen has what you want?'

'No way,' Iska replied, shaking her head rapidly. 'I mean, she's my sister—'

'And?' Walé interrupted.

'I can't be jealous of her,' said Iska, glancing over at Amen again. 'What kind of person would that make me?'

Walé was about to give Iska a response when Ada called out to him.

'Think about it,' Walé said, as he vacated the space that was now being occupied by Oshu.

'You two seem to be fond of each other,' Oshu said in a jovial yet serious tone.

'We're just friends,' said Iska, struggling to meet Oshu's eyes.

'Friends,' Oshu repeated, making sure to drown his voice in ambiguity.

Iska looked away and groped for a change of topic. When she found one, she grinned. 'So, Nirewa is alive apparently.'

'I'll be honest, I was surprised, yet not surprised when Jimba mentioned her name.'

'How do you feel about seeing her?'

'Excitement with a hint of trepidation; It has been a long time, plus the Nirewa I remember could be a bit intimidating.'

'I've been meaning to ask you something,' said Iska, now unashamed to look into Oshu's eyes. 'Last night when Ji—*Uncle* Jimba was in his Cruther form, did you really believe you had a chance against him?'

'Let's just say I knew the odds weren't in my favour,' Oshu replied.

'Then why? Why would you risk your life like that when Aito could have easily taken us back home?'

'Because all of it would have been in vain, wouldn't it? As much as we've come to Dogudu for you and your sister to know your roots, the top priority for being here is to find out what happened to someone who was extremely dear to us.

'Even though Ada would give me a good rollicking in my grave, I would have given my life in an attempt to reach our goal. After all that has happened, I owe it to Aré... Does that answer your question?'

Iska nodded, still turning Oshu's explanation over in her head.

After a quiet end to the tour, Iska, Amen, and the others arrived at the doorsteps of three dome-shaped, semi-detached huts that would be their home during their stay in Dogudu.

Zara, whose mood continued to be as sour as a grapefruit, explained the simple but strict sleeping arrangements: the boys had one hut to themselves, while Oshu and Ada would share another, and the last hut was for the girls.

To Iska and Amen's surprise, the décor inside their rounded apartment was strikingly different from Jimba's home. Here, peculiar artefacts adorned the walls of the rooms, and though the beds weren't as comfortable as the ones at Casa Tella, they were a step up from the mats the twins had slept on the previous night. Moving through the rest of the hut, Zara pointed out that the windows were fitted with retractable wooden shades to keep mosquitoes out. But the twins, eager to take a long-overdue shower, were more interested in using the bathroom they had spotted earlier. As soon as Jimba's daughter exited the hut, Amen and Iska played a quick game of rock-paper-scissors to decide who could take a shower first, with Amen coming out on top.

True to his word, Jimba arrived at the twins' hut just as the evening sunlight was starting to fade; by now, everyone was cleaned up and dressed in fresh clothes. Jimba, now dressed in cream, led them through the streets of the village filled with a myriad of noises that had been absent earlier in the day. When they finally emerged from the south entrance of the village and into the clearing, Iska and Amen were greeted by hundreds of people walking across the massive field in all directions.

'Where were all these people earlier today?' Iska screamed to be audible.

'They were at work,' Jimba replied.

'Work?' said Amen.

'Yes, we work,' said Jimba, smiling at Iska and Amen's curiosity. 'We hunt, farm, build our infrastructure, and teach. In summary, we engage daily in all activities that help our village prosper. And as long as you all are here, you will too.'

'Shite,' Aito muttered under his breath.

Iska and Amen hadn't even gotten halfway through the field when people began to stop and stare at them, whispering unintelligible words.

'What are they saying?' Iska asked, looking back at the curious faces.

'Oyibo,' Jimba replied. 'It means foreigner; they've never seen people like any of you before.'

After a few minutes, the group found themselves on the other side of the field, heading up a tunnel that rested between the north and north-western entrances of the village. The floor of the tunnel was made of bamboo strips, and the roof finished off with curved glass. Approaching the entrance of a hut, Jimba was about to knock on the door when a voice from inside spoke.

9. FESTIVAL

'Come in,' the voice said again.

Jimba took off his sandals and entered the dwelling followed by Iska, Amen, and the others. The air in the candlelit room was thick with the scents of tobacco, incense, and burning wick. To the right of the room, a figure draped in a long black dress stood motionless by a window overlooking the north side of the village.

'Everyone,' said Jimba, waving smoke away from face. 'This is the doyenne of Dogudu, Nirewa.'

Before anyone could introduce themselves, the figure sauntered into the light, revealing herself to be a middle-aged woman with a distinctive appearance. She let out a short, witch-like laugh. 'We've been expecting you.' She didn't bother to look at any of them.

Iska immediately shot a stare at Oshu, who responded with a shrug of his shoulders before approaching the woman.

'Nirewa it's me,' he said, 'Oshu Tella; do you remember me?'

'Silly question,' Nirewa replied, taking a drag of her cigarette and exhaling a plume of smoke into the air. 'I never forget a face, let alone a child I helped nurture, a child of Dogudu… You have grown into a fine young man.'

Perhaps relieved that Nirewa still remembered him after so many years, Oshu hugged the woman just as tightly as he'd embraced Jimba the night before.

'Nirewa, how's it possible?' said Oshu, leaning back to size the woman up. 'You haven't aged a day since the last time I saw you.'

'I owe it to my steady supply of tobacco,' Nirewa replied, releasing another high-pitched laugh that rang through the room.

Oshu gestured towards the group. 'Meet my family, Nirewa.'

As though realising for the first time that there were other people in the room, Nirewa hastily dusted off herself and began welcoming the group to Dogudu—her long black dress scraping the floor as she moved from person to person before suddenly halting in front of Walé.

'You're human,' she said as she studied his eyes, searching for something in them.

Everyone held their collective breath, except for Jimba, who looked confused. 'Nirewa, are you sure?' he asked, looking over at Oshu.

'Please let me explain,' said Oshu, his hands raised to his chest, but Nirewa spoke first. 'Oshu, I'm sure you still remember the reason why we don't let humans into our home.'

'Yes,' Oshu replied, his head sinking in disappointment.

'The soul of man,' said Nirewa, making her voice loud enough for everyone to hear, 'is painfully evil. All they care for is to consume and consume until they consume even themselves—like parasites eating and killing their host before looking for the next one to devour.

'If humans find a way into Dogudu, believe that they will try to control and use us for their biddings; oh, yes!'

'Never!' said Jimba, the terrifying growl from the previous night rumbling in his throat. 'I will not allow it!'

Despite the growing tension in the room, Walé managed to keep his nerves in check, even though his eyes were beginning to well up.

'He is a good boy, Nirewa,' Oshu interjected, his gaze shifting between Ada and Jimba. 'He's not like the rest of them; I can vouch for him.'

'You can vouch for him,' said Nirewa, letting out a pitiful laugh. 'My dear Oshu, you resemble a careless dog that can't tell its left from right without its master.' Before anyone could react, Nirewa took Walé's right hand and placed it on her chest. 'The only reason you and your family are still standing in my presence is because I have looked into the boy's soul, I have searched his heart… And thankfully for all parties involved, he has a good, strong one,' she said directly to Jimba, who seemed to relax a bit more on hearing this.

'Thank you,' Ada said through clenched teeth as she rushed to Walé's side and wrapped her arm around his waist as tightly as possible. But Nirewa simply smiled and tapped Walé's face.

As Nirewa lit more candles, it became apparent that her hut was not an ordinary room, but a shrine. Stacks of weathered books and scrolls heaped on top of each other lined the walls all the way to the head of the room where a slightly raised altar stood. Following Nirewa's order, Amen, Iska, and the others sat on a few mats on the floor while Nirewa perched cross-legged on the altar taking puffs of her cigarette.

'Oshu,' said Nirewa, rubbing her bald head now visible in the added light. 'As much as we're thankful for seeing you after all these years, what has brought you from your comfortable life to this old village you abandoned as a little boy?'

'I was forced to leave,' Oshu corrected with a smile. 'I won't beat around the bush. Do you remember my sister, Aré?'

Nirewa didn't respond.

'Forgive me, it's a habit,' said Oshu. 'Well, you may or may not know, but a couple of years ago, she died.'

Jimba flinched at Oshu's last words while Nirewa's countenance remained unchanged.

'Although reports said she died of natural causes,' Oshu continued. 'We believe she was murdered, and that's why I'm here with the twins. We want to see—we want to be sure.'

At first, Nirewa didn't say or do anything, she didn't even take a puff from the cigarette dangling from her darkened lips, and Iska and Amen thought she had gone into shock; but then she spoke up.

'Aré, you should have never left,' she said as tears flowed down her cheeks catching everyone by surprise. She caressed her cleanly shaved head again, as if consulting with someone or something.

'Of course, they can see,' said Nirewa, now looking Iska and Amen in the eyes. 'But they have to participate in and win the Ereto game.'

'Shit!' Oshu said, louder than he would have liked.

'What?' said Iska, speaking for the first time in minutes. 'What is the Ereto game?'

'Will you tell them?' said Nirewa, lighting another cigarette she fished from her pocket. 'Or should I?'

'By all means, do us the honours,' Oshu replied in a deflated tone.

Nirewa stood up from her seat. 'You have lost the fire in your belly, boy,' she said, releasing another cloud of smoke into the air.

Irritated by her rudeness, Iska watched Nirewa as she sauntered around the shrine lighting more candles. *I don't mean to be judgey,* she whispered into Amen's mind, *but she's strange.*

I'm still holding out on my verdict— Amen was whispering back to Iska when Nirewa suddenly shushed her.

'Come on, girls, no gossiping,' she said, forcing loud gasps out of Iska and Amen.

'What's the matter?' said Ada, out of worry.

But Nirewa didn't give Iska or Amen a chance to answer. 'Our people celebrate what we call Igboya Festival, or in plain English: *The Festival of Courage,*' she said, pacing the shrine gingerly. 'It's taking place a week and a day from today. A wonderful celebration of our people and culture; I give you my word, it's very enjoyable. However, during this festival we also have the Ereto game—'

'—The Game of Truth,' Jimba translated.

'Precisely,' said Nirewa. 'The name of the game already half explains the aim. You see, every Chi in Dogudu—'

'What's a Chi?' Aito interrupted.

Nirewa let out another eerie laugh. 'I almost forget that in the world out there they've come up with complicated nomenclature for what we are: *Slinker, Cruther, Unix,*' she said with sarcasm. 'My boy, you are a Chi, I am a Chi, so is everyone present in this room except for one.'

'Chi translates to god, Aito,' whispered Ada. 'Basically, we are all gods—'

'And we should be proud of it!' Nirewa interjected fiercely, though tears streamed down her face. 'Now, can I continue without interruption?'

The room went silent once more, and the bald, weeping woman began grinning widely, revealing brown teeth. 'Now, where was I?' she asked, rubbing her bare scalp with both hands. 'Oh yes, every Chi in Dogudu aged sixteen to twenty-five must participate in the game at least once in their life-time. Only the Chis who don't have exceptional gifts are exempt from this law.

'Even then, they still have to be involved in the game in one capacity or the other.'

Iska and Lake shifted uncomfortably where they sat.

'Nirewa, I understand the rules,' said Oshu, his voice fraught with worry. 'But the kids didn't grow up in this village, they haven't toiled. Is there no other way for—'

'Oshu,' Nirewa interjected before he could continue. 'I know you've been away for a considerable time, but please do not disrespect and disappoint me by acting like you do not remember my teachings.'

'I mean no disrespect, but the game can be dangerous—'

'—It is our tradition—'

'—But if you would—'

'—It is our rite of passage!' Nirewa's voice filled the room, her body trembling in the process. 'If you think they can't handle it, I'm afraid I have nothing else to offer you. You can pack your things and go back to your materialistic lives!'

Oshu swallowed hard but did not speak.

'I'll play the game,' said Amen, staring down at the mat she was sitting on.

'No, Amen, you don't know what this game is about,' the agitation in Oshu's voice surprised everyone. 'People have nearly lost their lives; I won't allow you.'

'It's my choice,' Amen replied, now locking her misty eyes with Oshu's. 'I want to participate in the game.'

'So do I,' Iska added.

'Me too,' said Aito.

Lake shook his head worriedly because he knew that his decision was already made for him. 'Same goes for me.'

'I know I'm not a Chi,' said Walé, making sure to catch Iska's eyes while simultaneously avoiding Ada's. 'But I'd like to participate in the game as well.'

'Haaai!' Nirewa wriggled her shoulders as if doing a dance. 'It is settled!'

'Nirewa, nothing is settled,' Oshu objected.

'It is,' countered Amen and Iska.

Oshu looked to Ada for support, but his wife returned an expression that urged him to stop resisting and consider the idea of the twins participating in the game.

'Nirewa,' said Ada, her attention squarely on the oracle. 'You mentioned that for the twins to *see*, they have to not only compete in the game but also win it. My question is: how likely is it for them to win this game?'

A few seconds passed before Nirewa responded to Ada's enquiry. 'Oh, dear,' she finally said, putting out the butt of her cigarette with the palm of her right hand.

'What does that mean?' Ada's voice was impatient.

Nirewa shook her head. 'Jimba is in a better position to explain.'

As soon as Nirewa uttered the last words, everyone looked in the towering man's direction.

Jimba let out a heavy breath before speaking. 'As Oshu rightly said, the Ereto game is dangerous; however, there are some Chis who have competed and thrived. In fact, for the past three years, one particular Chi has won the game.'

'Christ, who is this person?' Ada asked.

'Zara,' Jimba replied.

'Zara, as in your daughter?' said Ada.

'Yes,' Jimba was failing miserably at masking the pride in his voice. 'She's emerged the champion every year since her very first game three years ago. She's a fierce and relentless competitor.'

While Oshu closed his eyes and pinched the bridge of his nose as if he had just received more bad news, Ada was more positive. 'This works out perfectly,' she said. 'Zara can help train Amen and Iska; teach them—'

Jimba cut Ada off. '—Zara is competing in the game this year.'

Amen bit her bottom lip. *Just great! As if things weren't bad enough already.*

'Jimba.' Ada paused to choose her next words carefully. 'Is there a way you can appeal to Zara to opt out of this year's Ereto game? Just so Amen has a chance.'

'I'm sorry, I can't do that.' Jimba's reply was straight to the point.

'Why not? She's your daughter. Surely, she'll listen to you.'

Jimba unfolded his muscular arms and walked a few paces from where he had been stationed for most of the evening to be closer to them; his frame still as imposing as it was the first time they had met him. 'For most uninitiated Chis in this village, the game is a hassle that they can't wait to be done with,' he said. 'Zara doesn't see it that way; she takes immense pride in competing and winning the game— the girl was already training and preparing even before she was old enough to participate in it.'

'I see your point,' said Ada, 'but this is a matter of urgency.'

'Ada, don't waste your time,' Oshu chimed in. 'Zara won't back out. People of Dogudu never back down from a commitment. It is one of our tenets.'

Jimba nodded his head. 'Thank you, Oshu.'

'I see,' Ada finally conceded. 'So, what next?'

'They start training tomorrow,' said Nirewa, who was lighting another cigarette. 'There's a lot to learn before next week.'

Oshu began to rise to his feet. 'Thank you for meeting with us, Nirewa,' he said in an indifferent tone. 'It's good to see you again.'

Nirewa stood up as well. 'There's one more thing you need to know about the game.'

'What is it now?' said Oshu, as he helped Ada off the floor.

'Things have changed a lot since you and your family left the village; the rules of the game have been modified over time.'

'How do you mean?'

'Well, as we established earlier, the game can be daunting.' Jimba was the one speaking now. 'So, about two decades back, Nirewa and the Council of Elders made it possible for Chis who are competing in the game to get assistance from family members.'

'In other words,' Nirewa continued, 'Chis can work in a team with relatives to achieve their objectives, as long as the final phase of the game is completed by the participating Chi alone.'

'Why is this information relevant?' Oshu's question was almost rhetorical.

The shadows dancing on Nirewa's face made her broad smile look very beguiling. 'Just letting you know in case you want to lend the girls a helping hand. It is the least you could do, seeing as you never participated in the game yourself.'

It was obvious to everyone, especially to Oshu himself, that he was being baited; but there was something in what Nirewa said that roused him.

'Will you be assisting Zara?' The question was directed at Jimba, but Oshu was staring deep into the oracle's eyes.

'Yes, I've been at her side for two consecutive years.'

'Then it is settled; I'll help my nieces.'

The day had darkened significantly since they had entered Nirewa's shrine. Thankfully, lanterns lined either side of the tunnel, allowing Iska and Amen to locate their trainers before making their way down the tunnel and into the clearing. Interestingly, the field was still packed with villagers engaged in all sorts of activities: a group of men playing board games in one corner; another group, women this time, dancing to a song being belted out by a lady in another corner; others doing their best to make trades. Suddenly, it was obvious this was the village square where the people of Dogudu congregated after a long day of hard work—a square that seemed to be reserved for adults at this time of the day because there were no children in sight.

In the cafeteria, people sat in small circular groupings eating and talking while Jimba directed them to a space which had just been vacated by another family. As soon as they were all seated, Jimba stole to the head of the cafeteria to get their dinner. At intervals, other diners would glance in Amen and Iska's direction and mouth words to each other; this only stopped when Jimba returned with bowls of food in each of his hands. Behind him, two young ladies followed with more food, their hands steady as they carefully set the dishes on the round wooden table in the middle of the group.

The bowls were filled with different types of soup, each with its own unique look and texture. The green and yellow soup with little chunks of beef in it was called Egusi; the brown gooey soup was known as Ogbono; while in another bowl there was White Soup, a grey liquid with pieces of cooked chicken in it. Amen and Iska recognised the soups from when Aré used to cook them; they were certain Oshu, Ada, and Walé knew them as well, but the same could not be said for Aito and Lake, who both eyed the bowls curiously.

In the other plates were mounds of pounded yams—to be eaten with the soups. Without wasting any more time, the group dug into their supper. Even Aito and Lake couldn't help themselves; after all, this was their first real meal of the day, and in all honesty, they looked to be enjoying it. After half an hour, the group finished their meals, savouring the last bits of pounded yams and soups. To quench their thirst, the ladies from earlier supplied a jug of purple-coloured juice that Jimba explained was made from freshly squeezed almond fruits.

With everyone satisfied, Jimba launched into a detailed explanation of the rules and regulations of the Ereto game. But Amen and Iska struggled to maintain their focus; they felt uneasy under the constant scrutiny of other diners, whose stares seemed to be continually directed their way.

At that moment, something else caught Amen and Iska's attention: the entrance of the cafeteria was filled by the striking figure of Nirewa. As she walked the length of the hall to where the servers were stationed, Nirewa was greeted with nods and salutations. After a quick conversation with the servers, she began making her way back in Amen and Iska's direction. Just a few feet from their table, Nirewa halted and swivelled around to face the crowd.

'My wonderful people.' Nirewa's voice was as compelling as it had been in the shrine. 'You're acting as if you've never seen anything interesting in our village before. Kunlé getting into an argument with the horses was much more of a sight to behold.'

The diners erupted into hoots of laughter, with even Jimba joining in.

'Yes, I know their attire is strange-looking,' Nirewa continued, provoking another round of hearty laughter from the diners. 'And hopefully, by tomorrow they will have rid themselves of it. However, they are our people. Foreign they may be, yes; but they are our own. So, I beg you to give them the same respect we accord one another.'

At the end of Nirewa's speech, not a soul in the cafeteria uttered a word, but Amen and Iska sensed a unanimous agreement had been reached as everyone's attention returned to their tables.

Eventually, Nirewa made her way to their table, cigarette in hand. Just then, Jimba retrieved what appeared to be two small rocks from his pocket. As he struck them together near Nirewa's cigarette, little sparks flew out of the rocks, and moments later, she was taking a long drag from the thin brown stick.

'I trust you all enjoyed your meal?' Nirewa asked, her tone suggesting more of a formality than genuine concern. But before anyone could give an answer, Nirewa pointed directly at Iska and Amen. 'You two, meet me at the square at dawn.'

With that, Nirewa left the hall, leaving the twins bewildered and frightened.

The previous night would have been more pleasant if Amen and Iska hadn't been so disturbed by Nirewa's request. Instead of losing themselves to the sweet natural lullaby of Dogudu's whistling trees, the twins spent the better part of the night trying to figure out what exactly the oracle wanted with them. However, it did not matter now because, in a few minutes, they would meet with Nirewa and find out why she had summoned them so early in the morning.

Just before Amen and Iska could leave their hut for the square, a boy brought in their new clothes. There were six intricately patterned outfits, three for each of them, the boy explained. He also promised to bring them new sandals before the day was over. Knowing fully well that Nirewa would much rather prefer to see them in Dogudu's clothing, Amen and Iska quickly changed into the calico garments, with Amen opting for a yellow two-piece, and Iska slipping into grey overalls.

According to Iska's calculation it was just a few minutes past 6 a.m., but already the sun was high and bright. As they approached the empty clearing, Iska and Amen spotted a solitary figure in the distance—Nirewa was already waiting for them.

'Good morning; how did you two sleep?' Nirewa asked genuinely.

'Good, yeah, grand,' the twins answered insincerely.

'That's perfect,' said Nirewa as she began walking southward, her verdant gown brushing against the grass. 'You'll need all your strength.'

Amen and Iska exchanged a quick quizzical look before hastening their pace to catch up with Nirewa.

'I'm sorry for calling you strange yesterday,' said Iska, trying to break the awkward silence. 'I didn't mean to be rude.'

Nirewa scoffed. 'Are you genuinely remorseful or apologetic only because you got caught?'

Iska took a second to ponder the question.

'How were you able to hear our thoughts?' Amen asked.

'My dear, telepathy is supposedly one of my gifts.'

'Supposedly?' said Iska.

'Yes,' said Nirewa, who, for the first time since yesterday, wasn't holding or smoking a cigarette. 'You see, the ability is very limited. I only hear other people's thoughts occasionally, and I can't communicate with anyone through telepathy, as far as I know.'

'Oshu told me you have the ability to see into the future,' said Iska. 'I'm curious, how does that work?'

Nirewa smiled at the question, and for a second, Iska regretted asking it because she had just blatantly revealed that the oracle had been the topic of a private discussion. However, as Iska looked at Nirewa again, she realised that her smile wasn't one of scorn but rather of pride in the fact that Oshu still remembered pieces of her, even after so many years.

'If I told you I knew exactly how any of my abilities worked, I'm afraid I'd be lying to you and myself,' Nirewa finally replied. 'Sometimes I get revelations of the future in my dreams, other times in an unexpected moment; it is completely arbitrary. The most important thing one needs to know is the future is very volatile, and it changes on the slightest shift in people's whims.'

Amen, Iska, and Nirewa exited the square through the southern entrance and soon enough were walking along a clearing bordered on the right by the rear of Dogudu's dwellings and on the left by more of the village's dense green forest. A few minutes into their walk, the clearing opened up to the picturesque view of a broad lake that stretched far into a backdrop of hills and plateaus with thick vegetation.

The banks of the lake were teeming with girls occupied with various tasks. Interestingly, some of them were casting large fishing nets deep into the water. Jimba hadn't minced his words when he said everyone played a pivotal role in the sustenance of the village.

Trying to get a closer look at what each girl was up to, Amen and Iska trailed behind Nirewa, who led them to the far end of the bank where Zara was overseeing a group of girls who were diligently collecting water from the crystal-clear lake and pouring it into large basins. The sight was both mesmerising and humbling to Iska and Amen, who couldn't help but admire the girls' hard work.

It was then that Nirewa spoke, recapturing the twins' attention. 'We've not had a water Chi in Dogudu for close to a century,' she said, halting the girls' work. 'Thankfully, we have you now, Amen.'

Even with her initial shock, Amen resolved within seconds not to ask Nirewa how she knew her ability; after all, the woman worked in mysterious ways.

'It was my thinking,' Nirewa continued, feeling the water in one of the filled basins with her hand. 'That you would help my daughters reduce their workload. Fetching water from the lake can be stressful, but now you're here you can help us.'

Now everyone—including Zara, who wore an annoying smirk on her face—was watching Amen intently.

Amen cleared her throat and hesitantly spoke up. 'I

don't know if I can manipulate large bodies of water at once,' she admitted. 'Back home, I practised with very small quantities.'

A few of the girls chuckled at Amen's excuse, but Nirewa silenced them with a stern look. 'My dear, why don't you give it a try?'

Come on, you've got this. Iska tried to encourage Amen, but her little pep talk seemed to only make her sister more nervous. Despite this, Amen walked towards the lake while Nirewa instructed everyone to give her space. With both hands outstretched, Amen closed her eyes, trying to feel the density of the water. The water was light, which was good, but even with its warmth and low viscosity, Amen was struggling to move so much of it at the same time.

'I can't do it,' she said after a few attempts. 'I'm sorry, but I can't move a lot of water at once.'

Zara and the other girls burst into laughter, and Nirewa didn't bother to stop them this time. Instead, she shook her head disapprovingly. 'How disappointing.'

'It's not as easy as it looks,' said Iska, her voice low but filled with anger. 'She's worked very hard to master her ability; maybe you all need to tone down your criticism.'

'You call that mastery?' Nirewa's anger matched Iska's. 'There are Chis who can produce elements from nothing!'

'That's impossible—' Iska regretted the words as soon as she uttered them. How could she say something so naïve after all that had happened around her in the past month? Now, with Nirewa smiling, common sense told Iska she was about to be forced to eat her own words.

'Impossible,' Nirewa repeated the word with disgust. 'Zara?'

In a flash, Zara was at Nirewa's side.

'Zara, if you don't mind,' said Nirewa, 'can you show Amen and Iska the impossible?'

Zara obliged. With the palms of her hands halfway closed and facing upwards, Zara placed her right arm over her left, reversed the process, weaved her right arm in and around the left until it was extended upwards, and then pulled it down slowly.

In four swift and fluid steps, Zara had bright strings of lightning emanating from between her hands like a cat's cradle. Even though the trick came from an insufferable person, Amen and Iska couldn't deny it was impressive to watch. Finally, with the clap of her hands, Zara brought the hissing and crackling from the tiny lightning bolts to a silence.

'You see, girls,' Nirewa tapped Zara encouragingly on her shoulder. 'Impossible is fictitious.'

Amidst their anger and embarrassment, Iska and Amen were speechless.

'All right, everyone,' said Nirewa, 'let's make hay while the sun shines. Zara, please show the twins how to handle the pails.'

Just like that, Iska and Amen were left to fetch water with the other girls under the supervision of Zara. It was utter humiliation. For two straight hours, Iska and Amen were criticised for doing everything wrong: Zara complained about how poorly they handled the buckets, how slow they were, and how their shoes were soiling the water. At some point, Zara even tried to dismiss the twins, telling the other girls that they could complete their task much more efficiently without the sisters bumbling around.

'What's your problem?' said Amen, having had enough of Zara's provocation. 'Since we got here, you've been nothing but rude to us.'

Clearly not one to shy away from a confrontation, Zara marched up to Amen until only a few centimetres separated them. 'You think your uncle being from here gives you the right to raise your voice at us,' she said slowly. 'You're a foreigner, and frankly, you're not welcome here, no matter what Mama Nirewa says.'

Zara tilted her head to look past Amen. 'Same goes for you too, and your friends,' she said to Iska.

Iska, taking the bait, sauntered forward until she was

beside Amen. 'Who wants to be in this shite hole anyways?' The last words escaped her mouth too fast to catch them, but Iska was seeing nothing but red at this point. 'As soon as the game is over, we're out of here.'

Despite facing the two of them head-on, Zara was not in the least intimidated by the twins. Why would she be? She was the same height and build as Iska and Amen, although that was where the similarities ended. Even with their overt bravado, Amen and Iska knew Zara was mentally stronger than them. And they suspected Zara knew it too; otherwise, how could she remain calm despite her home being slandered?

'Oh yes,' said Zara, her gaze flickering between Amen and Iska. 'My father told me about you two competing in the game. I would have advised you to not bother, but no, I look forward to seeing you two make fools of yourselves.'

'I swear I don't give a damn about this game.' Amen spoke through clenched teeth, fighting back the tears gathering in her eyes. 'But I promise, I'll beat you.'

Zara laughed, exposing her perfect dentition. 'My little sister, Dami, is only ten years old, but if she were to compete in the game, you wouldn't stand a chance against *her,*' she said. 'For goodness' sake, you're a Chi and you couldn't even manipulate your natural element. It's laughable...and pathetic.'

Iska finally closed the last centimetre of space between herself and Zara. 'Keep talking, I'll show you pathetic,' she said in a low, intense voice.

'I dare you,' Zara whispered back.

10. TRAINING

With her blood throbbing in her ears, Iska wasn't sure if she'd heard correctly until the voice called out again.

'Iska.' The soft voice belonged to a little boy. 'Mama Nirewa wants you.'

Not comfortable turning her back on Zara while still being so close to her, Iska slowly backed away from the lightning girl whose gaze remained fixed on Amen.

'Where's Nirewa?' Iska asked the boy, hating how she couldn't squish down her annoyance.

'She's under the mango trees,' the boy replied. 'I can show you the way.'

In an attempt to avoid dealing with Zara and the other girls right after such an awkward encounter, Amen was about to join Iska when the little boy halted her in her tracks. 'No, she wants just Iska,' he said, his infantile voice mismatching with his confidence.

'Are you sure?' Iska asked.

'Yes,' said the boy. 'Mama Nirewa was very clear.'

Zara, who was already urging everyone to get back to work, called out to Amen to join in.

'I'll come back as soon as I can,' Iska said to Amen as she followed the boy. 'Just as soon as I find out what this is about...'

The boy didn't lead Iska through the same clearing she, Amen, and Nirewa had come from earlier. Instead, they took a narrow path beside the lake that led farther away from the village. As she walked along the footpath, Iska found herself constantly swatting away insects, cobwebs, and leaves from her face, trying to keep up with the boy in front of her. Fortunately, this exercise did not last long, and for her efforts, she was rewarded with a lovely view of a meadow shaded by the leaves of hundreds of surrounding mango trees.

'Repeat after me,' Nirewa's voice was loud and clear. 'Stow the boat in the bay today.'

'—Stow the boat in the bay today!—' a group of children sitting on rows of thick logs replied in a loud chorus.

'Very good—' Nirewa was saying when the little boy Iska had followed down to the meadow tugged at her dress.

'Mama, she's here,' he said.

'Thank you, Tobi.' Nirewa smiled at the little boy as he scampered to his seat amongst the other children.

Iska, unsure why she'd been summoned, was about to join the children on their log, when Nirewa suddenly stepped off the podium she was teaching from, allowing a short, light-skinned lady who had been standing to the side take her place and continue the lessons.

Nirewa waved goodbye to the kids then turned to Iska. 'Come with me.'

As with little Tobi, Iska followed Nirewa through another path completely different from the one she had just come from moments earlier; the seemingly unlimited network of routes in and around Dogudu was becoming increasingly hard for Iska to memorise.

'How were you able to learn English?' Iska asked Nirewa as they finally made their way back into the village via one of the main entrances. 'I mean, without like formal education centres.'

As soon as they made a sharp left turn, Iska recognised where she was. They had just entered the village through its northwest entrance and were now headed towards Nirewa's shrine.

'You're not the first foreigners to set foot in this village,' Nirewa replied as they reached the foot of the tunnel leading up to the shrine. 'A little over a century ago, people claiming to be missionaries and whatnot from other countries came to our lands. They tried to force the English language and other doctrines into our way of life. The former was useful for communication, so we adopted it; the rest was rubbish to us and was discarded along with the propagators.'

Not interested in learning what Nirewa meant by *discarded*, Iska steered the conversation in another direction. 'It's impressive how much of the history of the village has been preserved,' she said as they neared the shrine. 'Were these stories passed down to you from the previous generation?'

'What do you mean when you say "passed down"?' said Nirewa. 'My dear, I was alive when the foreigners came to our village; I was a little girl, about the same age as Tobi back in the meadow.'

Nirewa's reply sent shivers down Iska's spine. The quick math she did in her head indicated that the woman in front of her was over a hundred years old; the only problem was that Nirewa inarguably looked many years younger. More afraid of the oracle than before, Iska was reluctant to enter the shrine until she was commanded to.

Although the shrine still smelt faintly of tobacco and incense, the breeze coming in through the windows made the room much less stuffy. Iska, still shocked by Nirewa's age, decided to shift her focus away from this unsettling revelation and towards the confrontation she had with Zara earlier in the day.

'We really are trying our hardest,' said Iska, careful not to annoy Nirewa. 'All of this is new to us.'

Nirewa allowed a quiet laugh as she shuffled around the shrine gathering things in her arms. 'What do you want? To be applauded for your efforts?'

Iska winced at the question. 'Not even. Just some understanding.'

'Don't deceive yourself. What you and your sister want is pity.'

'Empathy, really,' Iska's voice took on a snippy tone. 'Is it such a bad thing? You don't know our story, what we've been through.'

'And you think you're the only ones who've been through a lot?' Nirewa retorted, dropping a stack of books at the altar. 'Who've lost a parent?'

Iska's brows furrowed in confusion.

'People in this village suffer as well,' Nirewa continued, 'Zara, whom I'm sure you are properly acquainted with by now, lost her mother while giving birth to her younger sister, Dami. In fact, she lost her father for some time as well. But how did she respond? Not by sulking or waiting for anyone to come pat her on the back, telling her "You've done well", but by fortifying herself mentally and emotionally. Granted, she can be harsh at times, but one doesn't build a solid backbone without antagonising a few people here and there.'

Fearing that her emotions would spill out, Iska looked anywhere but into Nirewa's eyes.

'Look, child, if you want to earn the respect of this village, you have to fight for it tooth and nail. No one is going to give it freely; as the foreigners say, "put your money where your mouth is". Now come over here so I can reveal why you were summoned in the first place.'

Iska joined Nirewa at the altar, and within seconds, she was being handed books and scrolls.

'Since your sister has shown that she clearly has a lot to learn,' said Nirewa as she sifted through dusty parchment. 'I've decided that you two need to study very hard before the day of the festival.'

'What do you mean?' said Iska.

'I'm sorry to say this, but that poor excuse for an ability your sister has is not going to take you two far in the game. The materials I have just handed you contain texts on how to harness the full potential of elemental manipulation. Read, digest, and practise every word. Until you leave this village, these are your bibles.'

Iska blinked repeatedly, as if trying to communicate something to Nirewa with her eyes rather than her mouth, but the woman in front of her was impatient.

'My dear, what is on your mind?' said Nirewa, as she fished a stick of cigarette out of a glass jar.

'You've just instructed me to study these books with Amen. I mean, I have no problem assisting her, but I can't really study them for myself.'

'And why is this?' The cloud of smoke Nirewa exhaled engulfed her curious face.

'Well, I don't have any abilities. I am one of those Chis…'

For what felt like eternity, Nirewa remained silent, puffing on her cigarette in contemplation. 'You think I am stupid for telling you to practise with your sister?' she finally said, her voice shrouded in a cloud of smoke.

'No, that's not what I meant. It's just that studying these books would mean nothing to me; I'm not gifted, not like Amen. It'd honestly be a wasted effort.'

Nirewa breathed out another cloud of smoke and murmured something to herself.

'I didn't catch that,' said Iska.

'I said comparison is the root of unhappiness. If you don't stop comparing yourself to your sister, you will never emerge from her shadow—a place you crawled into all on your own. The books will be with you; study them if you like.'

Iska gathered the books into her arms. 'Nirewa,' she said hesitantly, 'I was just curious: why does Amen *need* to win the game to see?'

'There are a number of reasons for this,' Nirewa replied. 'But the two most important are that it is a sacred rule that was created by the Council of Elders many years ago, and it proves that she is deserving. That she has what it takes: courage, judgement, and determination. These are significant virtues one must possess to relive the past or get a glimpse of the future.'

Iska's eyes flickered from side to side as she made mental notes. 'If there's only one winner of the game,' she said, 'does it mean the other Chis who participate and don't win have none of the virtues you mentioned?'

Nirewa absentmindedly rubbed her hairless head. 'You

ask smart questions, just like your mother used to. *Of course* the other Chis possess those virtues. The thing about the Ereto game is that on the outside, it appears to be a zero-sum competition where one person's gain results in others' loss.' Nirewa paused to burn some incense before continuing. 'But in reality, it is positive-sum. Having the courage to confront one's fears alone is already a victory, if and only if one truly competes and shows great valour.'

It took Iska a few seconds to comprehend Nirewa's words. 'In other words,' she said, 'everyone must give their all in the game. Even Aito can't perform poorly to give Amen an advantage.'

'Intelligent,' said Nirewa. 'Just like your mother. That's enough questions for now. You need to join up with the others for lunch.'

Upon returning to the hut to put away the books, Iska noticed Amen's wet trainers and a pair of black sandals on the floor; the boy from early in the morning had kept his promise. Following Nirewa's advice, Iska changed into the new sandals and went directly to the cafeteria instead of the lake.

Perched in the same spot as the previous evening, Amen was alone with four dishes of food in front of her. 'I had a feeling you'd be here soon, so I got something for you as well,' she said as soon as she saw Iska.

'You're the best,' Iska replied, taking a seat beside Amen. 'So, what are we having?'

'Fried yams with fish stew and some orange juice.'

'I'm starving.' Iska took a stick of the fried yam and dipped it into the bowl of stew. 'Have you seen the boys today?'

'Not at all. So, what did Nirewa want with you?' Amen asked Iska.

Amen choked on her juice several times while listening to Iska recount her day. She found it hard to believe how old Nirewa possibly was and took slight offence at how poorly her ability had been judged, even though she accepted her own demonstration had been awful.

'What happened at the lake after I left?' said Iska, now asking the questions.

'It was horrible. The other girls kept talking about us. Oh yeah, training for the game starts in a few hours, so we need to prepare for that.'

How do you feel about it? Iska whispered into Amen's head, not trusting anyone in the cafeteria.

Nervous, if I'm being honest. I don't think I'm up for this game. The pressure is too much.

Iska quickly took Amen's hand in hers. *Listen, I completely understand how you feel. Up to an hour ago, I was probably more nervous than you.*

What changed? Amen asked.

I don't know, maybe something the old lady said. But you have to play this game; and, for all intents and purposes, you must win it. You're allowed to be nervous, but you're not allowed to quit.

Are you sure about this? Amen's voice was tinged with worry.

Iska gave Amen's hand a gentle squeeze. *Yes! And before you forget; we're in this together until the very end.*

Upon seeing them for the first time in more than twelve hours, Lake, Walé, and Aito appeared a bit overworked; however, Iska and Amen had no time to ask how they had fared through the day because two people took centre stage on the training ground.

'My name is Jòla,' said the umber-skinned lady who wore her light brown hair in cornrows. 'And this is my partner, Uché. We are your trainers for the game ahead.'

'Now, some of you are familiar with how the Ereto game works,' said the hard-muscled man named Uché, 'while others are complete neophytes. It does not matter what your level of experience is. You will all be given equal training.'

'Yes,' Jòla continued. 'It doesn't matter if you've played

the game before or if this is your first time, because new twists and turns are served with each iteration of the game. This is done so no one has an unfair advantage.'

'A level playing field, if you will,' Uché chimed in. 'With that being said, let's get into things. The core of our training over the next couple of days will centre around strength training, sprinting, grappling with one another, meditation sessions, and a few other activities.'

'You see those dowatsos over there?' Jòla pointed to some mounds of granite heaped on top of each other. 'Please help yourselves to one. We'll be doing a bit of strength training before we move on to sparring.'

Following Jòla's instruction, each person grabbed a dowatso, which Iska estimated was no less than twelve kilograms.

'It is very heavy,' said a girl, who was struggling to get back in line with her ball of granite.

'That is the whole point,' Uché replied with a smile.

Jòla didn't afford any breathing space or respite. She utilised every second of the thirty minutes she had with them. Some Chis thrived, like Zara who was well into her rhythm by the second minute, while others floundered. Amen and Iska did reasonably well, but they both knew there was room from improvement.

Uché allowed the group five minutes of rest, but it was over before anyone could appreciate it. 'For the grapple session,' he said, 'everyone will have a sparring partner. I have taken the liberty of putting all of you in pairs, and I hope you will be okay with my decision.'

Uché began announcing sparring partners while a few people were still catching their breath. Lake got a boy called Bello; Aito was paired with a girl named Aisha; Walé was paired with Kunlé; Amen's partner was Chizzy, the girl who had complained earlier about the weight of her dowatso was; and Iska's partner was Zara.

'The rules are straightforward,' said Uché, beckoning Jòla over to assist him with a short demonstration. 'You must topple your opponent over, using their body weight and your wits. There will be no boxing, eye-gouging, biting, kicking—'

'Basically, like Judo!' Aito interrupted Uché.

'What is that?' said Uché.

'It's this Japanese martial art where you try to throw— ah, never mind, please carry on.' Aito was discouraged by the crowd's perplexed reaction.

'Very well,' Uché picked up from where he stopped. 'This is a best two out of three scenario, so whoever topples their opponent twice in a row automatically wins; there will be no need for a third grapple. Is this clear?'

No misgivings were offered.

'Good,' said Uché. 'Everyone, take your positions. At the count of three, you may begin.'

Iska didn't know Judo, but she knew Tai Chi. Plus, she was good at PE in secondary school. It had to count for something, right?

'One!'

She could not lose to Zara, not after what happened at the lake this morning. All those smirks. Iska couldn't show weakness in front of anybody, especially not in front of Amen, who was counting on her.

'Two!'

What did it matter though? Zara had her own internal battles; she also lost her mother when she was young, even younger than them. They were not so different after all.

'Three!'

Iska firmly grasped the back of Zara's neck with her left hand and then grabbed her right shoulder with her other hand, feeling Zara's sweaty, sinewy body quiver under her touch. As the fight progressed, Iska struggled to avoid the headlock Zara was attempting to put her in, while at the same time trying to reason with her.

'Look, I'm sorry,' she said, her voice tired and strained. 'I shouldn't have insulted your home; I didn't mean it.'

But Zara wasn't listening, and soon enough, she had

Iska in a headlock. With Iska's head firmly locked in her arms, Zara twisted her body, and Iska felt herself slide off the girl's back and hit the ground with a force that sent a shockwave of pain through her body.

'Useless,' Zara whispered as she backed away from Iska's dirt-ridden body.

Iska's heart pounded hard and fast, not only because of the sudden rush of adrenaline coursing through her body, but also because she wanted to make Zara pay for goading her—now it was personal. 'Are you ready?' she said, dusting herself off.

Zara lunged forward, but Iska was quick to calculate her moves, weaving and dodging Zara's attempts to get a hold of her.

'You don't have to be so hostile,' said Iska, still deflecting Zara's attacks while searching for weaknesses in the lightning girl's defence. 'I know what happened to your mother.'

Iska found her opening; with Zara momentarily stunned by her words, Iska dropped to one knee and rolled Zara over her shoulder, slamming her hard onto the ground.

Gasps of surprise echoed around the training ground. Amidst the action, Iska hadn't noticed more than half of the Chis had finished grappling. Now, all eyes were on her and Zara.

'One win apiece,' said Uché, laughing as he clapped his hands. 'I don't think anyone has ever seen Zara's back touch the ground.'

Whispers were flying around. Iska wanted to smile with pride for achieving what apparently had been unattainable, but the look on Zara's face wouldn't let her. The serious posture that Jimba's daughter always wore like a uniform was gone, replaced now with a look more furious than anything Iska had ever seen.

Zara rose to her feet, fists clenched, and eyes glazed over. 'I'm ready.'

Uché stood between the girls. 'This is the last round;

Iska, are you ready?'

'Yes,' Iska lied.

'Begin!'

It was as though Zara's strength and agility had tripled, as if there was a switch inside her that she had flicked on simply because she had been humiliated in front of her own people. Barely hanging on, Iska knew she would not last much longer. Her opponent was stronger, and she was smart enough to acknowledge this. But she had one more thing to do before letting go. With the last of her might, Iska pulled Zara into a tight embrace. 'I just want you to know I'm really sorry about your mother. You can talk—'

Before she could finish her sentence, Iska was hoisted into the air and slammed back-first into the hard earth. The pain was excruciating, but Iska knew it was nothing compared to what Zara was feeling. Iska had been in Zara's position before.

'Don't ever do that again,' Zara whispered through a heaving chest and teary eyes.

'That was intense,' said Uché, as Walé and Amen helped Iska to her feet. 'Unfortunately, we have no time left for meditation. That session will have to be held tomorrow after sprinting and tours.'

'Which leads us to the final agenda of the day,' Jòla chimed in. 'The old-timers know this already, but since we have new guests this season, it has to be restated.

'As most of you know, changes were made to the Ereto game, allowing Chis to work with their relatives as part of a team. *However*, what some of you might not be aware of is that it is mandatory for Chis who do not have abilities to assist those who do in succeeding in the game.'

'I don't understand,' said Amen, examining Iska's body for injuries.

'It is simple,' said Uché, studying a parchment. 'While the Chis with abilities train, those without will assist their partners in surveying the arena before the actual game. This way, even if the Chis who will be playing the game haven't seen the obstacles, they'll have an idea of what they are up against.'

I guess this is what Nirewa meant when she said Chis, who didn't have special abilities, had to participate in the game in some way, thought Amen.

While Amen dusted Iska down one last time, Uché whispered something to his partner before handing her the parchment he was reading earlier. In response, Jòla nodded her head and quickly rolled up the parchment.

'We have a little hiccup,' she said. 'There seems to be twenty-one of you competing in the game this season. That's an odd number, which means it may be a bit dicey placing you into pairs. But don't worry, we will sort it out at the end of the pairing.

'Right now, there are ten Chis with abilities, and eleven Chis without. It is customary for the Chis without abilities to do the choosing. A minute break will be given for you all to make up your minds, after which I'll call out Chis at random to pick their partners.'

Amidst the hushed whispers bouncing around, it became apparent that most Chis without abilities wanted to partner with Zara, including some Chis with abilities of their own.

'I hope you all have used your time wisely,' said Jòla, rallying everyone together. 'Let's get into things. Lake, please lead the way; who would you like to support for the game?'

Although Lake was friends with Iska and Amen, his decision to team up with Aito didn't come as a surprise to the twins; it was only logical since their bond was much stronger. Right after Lake was Chizzy, who quickly chose Zara as her partner, causing sighs of disappointment among the other Chis. One by one, Jòla called out the remaining Chis without abilities to choose their partners. As expected, none of them wanted to partner with Amen. Why would they? It made no sense to be stuck with an outsider Chi with an unknown track record. But this worked out perfectly for

Iska, as Amen was *her* preferred choice for a teammate.

'Now that everyone has their partner,' said Jòla, an unsettled expression on her face. 'We have to figure out how to fix the conundrum with our last Chi: Walé.'

Jòla and Uché discussed the problem in low voices while Walé waited awkwardly for the pair to make a decision. Finally, the two nodded in agreement.

'Right!' said Jòla. 'Rather than dragging this on by going to the Council of Elders, Uché and I have come to an agreement that Walé should decide which pairing he would like to join. Before he does, we want to give everyone the opportunity to speak against this arrangement or hold their peace.'

Although there was a drawn-out silence, no one opposed the move; after all, Walé was just another clueless foreigner who wouldn't make any meaningful impact on the game. Walé, relieved he could join his preferred team, chose to pair with Amen and Iska.

'I believe that's that,' said Uché with a smile. 'Tomorrow at dawn, the Chis with abilities will train with Jòla while the others will tour the arena with me. Thank you, everyone.'

Iska and Amen were glad to retire to their room after a long day filled with chores, confrontations, training, and more chores. Life here was so different from what they were used to back in Howth that for the first time in weeks, they longed to be surrounded by the familiar walls of Digglefield. For Amen and Iska, it was even more unbelievable to think Oshu, with all his achievements in the modern world, had originated from a village so rooted in its customs and industrious lifestyle.

'What happened between you and Zara during training?' Amen asked Iska as she climbed into bed.

'Nothing important. Just trying to gain every possible advantage for the game,' Iska replied.

'Always scheming, aren't you?'

'Always.' Iska opened one of the books Nirewa had

given her earlier in the day while tossing another book from the pile to Amen. 'This one focuses on breath and emotion control. It says here that "The foundation of strong elemental manipulation is built on one having the ability to control the rhythm of one's breath and the flow of one's emotions. As the two are intertwined, balance must exist, always. If one is angered, how can the breathing be even? And if the breathing is uneven, how is the right emotion chosen and maintained?"'

'Did you learn any of this stuff at Digglefield?' said Iska, still flipping through the pages of the book.

Amen thought about all the elemental exercises and drills Bernie and Aoife, her trainers back in Digglefield, had made her do, and how none of it compared to the training session with Jòla and Uché a few hours ago. 'Honestly, no,' she replied with a laugh. But the laugh soon died as she stared in fascination at something in her book.

Iska got out of her bed and joined Amen. 'What is it?'

Amen pointed at the graceful lines of ink. 'Look, this meditative technique here supposedly helps you search within your soul and find the casket that holds your ability. Would you like us to try it out?'

Iska's breath caught. What if she really *did* have an ability? What if she just hadn't been able to find it yet? But that rush of adrenaline died almost as quickly as it had begun. What if she found nothing? 'That sounds scary,' she said at last.

Amen shrugged. 'True, but I mean, we have to practise something.'

Following the instructions from the book, Amen and Iska dropped to their knees, closed their eyes, and bowed their heads. They felt ridiculous having to "hum right after every breath they drew", but that was what the book instructed, so they did it anyway.

'Amen, I'll be honest with you,' said Iska after several minutes of meditation, 'I don't feel anything.'

But there was no response from Amen.

'Amen, did you hear what I said?' asked Iska. Although her eyes were closed, she could hear Amen hum and wondered why she wasn't saying anything back.

Irritated that she was being ignored, Iska finally opened her eyes only to see water swirling around Amen, who seemed to be in some sort of trance.

11. STRATEGIES

Despite it being a few hours shy of noon, the sun's intense heat beamed down on Dogudu. Jòla and Uché had just concluded a briefing with all the Chis a few minutes ago. Now, Iska, Walé, Lake, and the others, led by Uché, were making their way through the village square towards the north entrance. The most Iska had seen of the northern part of Dogudu came from a glimpse through the windows in Nirewa's shrine. Even then, all she had been able to make out was a forest full of trees not too different from what was coming into focus as they neared the entrance.

For some odd reason, the wall of trees beyond the square reminded Iska of the evening they'd arrived in Dogudu—the fear in the old man's eyes as he hastily drove off; Jimba in his Cruther form; Oshu's brush with death—evoking memories she wished she didn't have. Finally out of the square, Iska was still trying to figure out if the eerie forest would feature in the game when Uché abruptly turned onto a narrow path to their right, catching her off guard. The north entrance was only just beginning to fade in the distance when a wide opening appeared in the wall of trees to the group's left-hand side.

'We're not too far from the arena now,' said Uché as they powered through the opening. A few moments later, the path they were treading opened into an empty, perfectly levelled field that stretched far in all directions.

Uché, who was touching the grass beneath his feet, caught the expression on Iska's face. 'Magnificent, isn't it?'

'Yes, but what is it?' asked Iska.

'This is the first phase of the game.' Uché's voice carried clearly over the field and anyone whose attention had drifted away looked back at him in excitement. He pointed at where they were standing. 'The competing Chis will begin the game with a race from this point,' he said, swinging his arm to a broad expanse of thick trees in the distance, 'until they reach that forest, where phase two of the game begins immediately.'

'Jesus, that's easily six hundred metres across this field,' Walé estimated. 'That's a lot of running, even for professional athletes.'

'Indeed,' said Uché. 'But the Chis don't have to run this course by themselves. This is where teammates with abilities can help.'

Iska's curiosity was piqued. 'What do you mean?'

'Well, the race is undeniably long,' Uché replied, trying to gauge the speed of a passing wind with his outstretched arm. 'And we want our Chis to have enough energy for the other phases of the game. So, for example, Zara, who unfailingly gets help from Jimba, wouldn't run this race herself.'

Lake chuckled at the intelligence of the concept. 'That way a race that would ordinarily take minutes could be run in seconds.'

'Precisely.'

Iska was still running scenarios in her head. 'What then happens to the Chis whose teammates don't have the specific ability to morph into animals?'

'I was just about to ask that,' Walé added.

'Oh,' said Uché with a smile. 'We have horses; they can choose to travel on them.'

'That's...fair?' said Iska, her black eyes still surveying the field. 'I guess this phase will be sort of easy.'

The other Chis, who had been mostly quiet, burst into laughter at Iska's statement.

'What?' she and Walé asked in unison.

Uché was also suppressing a smile. 'What has given you the impression this phase will be anything but difficult?'

The group continued the tour by heading towards the second forest Uché had pointed out earlier. Approaching the edge of the new forest, Iska and the others once again came across another wide opening, but Uché led them through it without hesitation. Perhaps it was because they were further into the woodlands, but Iska noticed that the calls of different animals now filled the air.

'I'm sorry I haven't had time for you,' Walé said to her as they followed Uché through the forest.

'It's not your fault,' Iska replied, inspecting thirty-metre-tall Iroko trees. 'We've all been busy.'

'I know, but I still feel bad—' Walé was saying when Iska suddenly stopped in her tracks, grabbed Walé's arm, and kissed him.

Two girls who caught a glimpse of Iska and Walé in the act giggled quietly.

After far too little time, she drew back. 'How do you feel now?' She'd meant the words to come out as teasing, but they ended up a bit breathless.

Walé was looking at her with stunned eyes. 'Good, but I'd feel much better if you did that again.'

Iska got herself under control and flashed him a grin. 'That's all you get, lover boy.'

'It'll do for now,' said Walé, as he wiped excess saliva off the corners of his mouth.

They walked in silence for a moment, trying to ignore the two giggling girls behind them. When the laughter finally died down, Walé asked, 'So, have you tried to resolve your feelings towards Amen?'

Iska mulled over Walé's question for a few seconds. 'Yeah, to be honest, I'm still working on that. But I'm in a better place than before.'

'Poco a poco,' Walé said with a wink. 'You're doing great. I just hope she's holding her own against those other Chis.'

'Yeah, me too,' said Iska, scratching the space between her eyebrows before retreating into her head. *Hey, you! How are things over there?*

Bloody hell! Amen was gasping for breath. *We've just been put through our paces. Now Jòla is setting up some lanes for a final eighty-metre dash.*

It was sort-of hard to hear Amen because a ringing, rushing sound had started to grow in her ears.

Walé tried to say something to Iska, but she politely hushed him. The last thing she needed was more sound. *Amen, you know that's not a problem for you. You literally still hold the girls' hundred-metre junior national record.*

Yeah, but this is different. Then I was racing other girls; now I'm racing girls and boys, and Zara... We're about to start; I'll let you know how things go later.

Iska felt a sharp pang of guilt as soon as Amen's voice faded away. Here she was, getting distracted by a boy on the equivalent of a leisurely stroll, while her sister was being tested to the limit against people who were rooting for her downfall. Iska's uselessness in readying Amen for the game was starting to annoy her, but not more than Walé's ill-thought idea to tap at her shoulder incessantly. 'What is it?' she finally snapped.

'Look to your left,' Walé replied.

Following Walé's instruction, Iska turned her head and saw the waterfall—the source of the loud ringing in her ears while she had been talking to Amen. From where they were standing, the fresh water gushing out from within the forest was just a touch away.

'Agbokim waterfalls!' Uché's voice was nearly drowned out by the roaring stream of water plummeting into the riverbed hundreds of metres below. 'After overcoming the obstacles within this forest, Chis will have to find a way across these waterfalls—' Again, Uché pointed with an outstretched arm to another broad expanse of trees just on the other side of the ravine. '—and into that forest, where phase three—the final phase of the game—immediately begins.'

Iska couldn't believe what she was hearing. 'How's anyone supposed to find a way past this?' she asked. 'A fall from this height could cause serious damage.'

Uché's lack of response gave Iska her answer.

'What obstacles are in the final phase of the game?' said

Lake, looking disconcertingly at the river below.

Uché started to motion everyone away from the water-falls. 'Unfortunately, I cannot say.'

While Amen, Iska, and Walé were seated in their usual spot in the cafeteria, Lake and Aito arrived with two large platters of palm-oil beans with tomato stew, boiled plantains, and diced pineapples, along with a bottle of milky light-brown drink known as *Kunu*. Despite all the noise around them, the ravenous teenagers ate their food in silence. In fact, it was only when they had nearly finished eating that the idea of devising a strategy for the game crossed Iska's mind.

'Amen, I'll be honest with you,' she said, as she exchanged her cup of Kunu for a bowl of water. 'We have our work cut out for us.'

'Jesus, what did you guys see in the arena?' Amen asked.

Iska took a sip of her water. 'We'll get to that in a second,' she replied. 'How did you do in the sprint?'

'I won,' said Amen, although her facial expression suggested otherwise.

'That's good news,' said Iska. 'Why aren't you happy about it?'

'Because yer wan...Zara,' Aito whispered, 'literally threw a fit.'

Iska didn't know whether to laugh or be scared. 'Shite; what happened?' she asked.

Amen gestured to Aito to carry on with the story.

'First off, *thanks* to no one for telling me this one's a bullet!' No one missed the sarcasm in Aito's voice as he pointed to Amen. Iska smothered a pitying chuckle. 'Basically, the race starts, and I think I'm doing pretty well in the first twenty-five, thirty metres. Then from out of nowhere, Zara overtakes me. In my head, I'm like "that's it, she's won the race," until Elaine Thompson over here beats Zara to the finish line.'

'Nice,' said Walé, bumping fists with Amen. 'What happened next?'

'She completely lost it.' Amen decided to complete the story herself. 'She literally started punching the ground, ripping the grass from it. I had to ask why she hated us so much, what we possibly did in our few days here to make her so angry.'

Iska leaned in. 'What did she say?'

'Her response didn't make any sense,' said Amen, trying not to make eye contact with Iska.

'Well, what was it?' Iska's patience was wearing thin.

'At first, she laughed. Then she said, and I quote, "Your sister and friends I can actually stand; it's you I have a problem with."'

'She said that?' said Iska, as she reclined into the wall behind her. 'That's very strange.'

'There's something…odd about that Zara girl,' Aito added. 'I can't quite place it yet.'

'Well, whatever it is, it's not important.' Lake's expression had never been more serious. 'What matters is that we give our best on the day of the game; so, I suggest we focus on ourselves and forget about the competition.'

'I second that,' said Amen, moving the empty platters to the side of the table to make space. 'So, what was the arena like?'

Iska, Lake, and Walé spent the next hour explaining the workings of the arena to the best of their abilities, making sure to cover all bases in the process.

'So, it's almost like an obstacle course?' Amen said at the end of their explanation.

'Yes,' Iska replied. 'A complex, multi-layered obstacle course. Thank God we have Oshu for the first leg; I really can't see any horse—I don't care how fast—outrunning a cheetah that size. Jimba, on the other hand, I'm not sure.'

Amen drummed her fingers on the table nervously. 'Aito, what about you, though?' she asked. 'I'm worried—'

Aito flung his hands up in the air. '—Ah, it's grand!

How hard can riding a horse be?'

Iska rolled her eyes. 'Honestly, compared to the waterfalls, horse riding seems like child's play. It just doesn't make any sense how anyone's supposed to cross it.'

'Well, as dangerous as the Ereto game might be, it looks like every obstacle included has been thought through; there has to be a way around the waterfalls.' Lake bent down to gather his sandals. 'We'll try to figure that out later, but for now, we have to get going because the meditation session starts soon.'

Iska and Amen clung to each other tightly as they made their way to the training ground. Even though it was their third day in the village, the twins were still amazed by how quickly the evenings in Dogudu brought cool winds to replace the scorching temperatures of the earlier hours. Fortunately, upon entering the meadow, Iska and Amen found Uché and Jòla lighting a bonfire.

'It has been a very productive day, has it not?' Jòla was ripping logs of wood apart with her bare hands and tossing them into the fire. 'Things will be calmer tonight, I hope.'

Everyone was instructed to take a seat around the bonfire, with Uché being the only exception. He stood in the middle of the circle about two feet away from the hissing flames of the bonfire.

'This meeting is more than just about meditation,' said Uché, now it was clear *he* was leading the session. 'It is about fellowship with brothers and sisters of Dogudu. A shared interest, a strongly held belief, that we are bound by more than blood or family ties; our hearts and souls beat as one, interconnected and intertwined from millennia in the past to millennia into the future.

'This is what Dogudu represents. That is why we will join our hands together and acknowledge the heroes of our future's past.'

As soon as Uché finished his speech, a melodic chorus broke out amongst the Chis. Neither of them understood the language in which the chorus was being sung, but Iska and Amen were on the verge of tears. The scale finally tipped when all of a sudden, Uché began to emit blue waves of light from his body.

Zara's past victories, a young Jimba as the champion of the Ereto game, the first elders of Dogudu. All these memories, none belonging to either of them, filled Iska and Amen's minds each time the light penetrated their motionless bodies. The last thing they saw before passing out was Uché's cocoa skin returning to normal.

'It seems Uché has the ability to project memories of the past into a person's subconscious.' Oshu's voice was as pleasant as ever. Except for the faintest loss of weight, nothing had changed about Ada and Oshu; if anything, they seemed to be glowing with health. 'Last night, he must have made you relive the most prominent events of the village's history,' Oshu added.

'But why would he do that?' said Iska, as she scooped pieces of egg sauce into her bread.

Ada crossed her arms over her chest. 'My guess would be that it's a ritual Chis have to pass through before the game to make sure all of you share a strong bond regardless of the outcome. The collective before the individual.'

'Precisely,' said Oshu, throwing a bean cake into his mouth. 'I hope they haven't been too hard on you all during training.'

'I mean, it's been a bit stressful,' Amen replied. 'But it's not as bad as any of us had thought—'

'Hey, speak for yourself,' Aito's voice was muffled by the pap and bean cake in his mouth. 'I'm shattered. Everything requires physical exertion; I swear if I was allowed to blink during most of the training, things would be so much easier.'

Aito's little tantrum was funny, but the group did their

best to stifle their laughter, not wanting to draw any attention in the crowded cafeteria.

'Well, I'm proud of all of you for doing this,' Oshu was still trying to stifle his laughter with a hand over his face. 'If it's any consolation, I've also been training, so I understand just how you feel, Aito.'

'Oh, by the way,' said Iska, deciding now was the perfect time to let the Tellas in on their strategy for the game. 'Oshu, there's something we want to talk to you—'

'—Amen and Iska,' little Tobi's familiar voice interrupted Iska. 'Mama Nirewa asked me to summon you. You'll find her in the shrine.'

But Iska and Amen hesitated to get out of their seats.

'Go,' said Oshu, reading the confused expression on the twins' faces. 'We'll have this discussion later.'

Amen and Iska assumed Tobi would be leading them to Nirewa. However, as soon as they exited the cafeteria, the little boy dashed away with his friends, leaving the twins to reluctantly make their way towards the oracle alone.

The shrine was much brighter than the last time twins had visited. Gentle winds coming in through the windows wafted in the scent of wet soil and freshly cut grass, replacing the shrine's ever-present smell of incense and tobacco.

'You sent for us,' said Amen, as Iska shut the door behind them. But Nirewa, who was sitting on her altar peeling melon seeds out of their hard shells, didn't respond.

Unsure of what to do, Iska and Amen loitered by the door until Nirewa finally cleared her throat. 'Fine morning, is it not?'

'Yes,' Amen and Iska said together, doing their best to keep the room from falling back into silence. 'Dogudu is a beautiful place,' Iska sincerely added. 'I feel like everything anyone could ever need is here.'

'Yet your mother and uncle left,' Nirewa said matter-of-factly.

'Nirewa,' said Amen, trying her best not to be apprehensive. 'What exactly made them leave the village?'

Nirewa set the tray of empty shells on the floor. 'Aré never told you the story?'

Iska and Amen shook their heads.

'Interesting,' said the oracle, getting up from her perch. 'Obviously, Oshu has not mentioned anything either... Where to start? You see, we venture out of the village every so often to purchase anything we are in urgent need of or cannot produce ourselves. As you can imagine, one needs money to make these purchases, but since we do not have that, we take valuable things of ours to trade.

'Your grandmother and grandfather...' Nirewa paused and smiled at Amen and Iska, realising from their expressions that they knew nothing about their grandparents. 'Were two of the few who used to go into town to make purchases. I do not know what they saw or who they talked to while out of the village, but for some reason, they became dissatisfied with living here.'

'Why didn't you try to stop them from leaving?' said Iska.

Nirewa beckoned Iska and Amen to take a seat. 'Because we are a community, not a cult. We *did* try to talk them out of it, but their minds were made up. They left, taking young Aré and Oshu with them.'

Imagine if they had stayed, thought Iska.

Mam would still be alive, Amen added.

'Funny how the slightest decision can completely alter one's destiny, eh?' said Nirewa, as she joined them on the mat.

'Sorry,' said Iska and Amen, remembering Nirewa could hear their thoughts. 'Old habit,' Iska added.

'Ah, don't worry about it.' Unsurprisingly, Nirewa was lighting a cigarette. 'In fact, this peculiar gift of yours might serve you two well on the day of the game. Speaking of the game, have you worked out some sort of strategy?'

Iska and Amen remained silent, not due to any reason other than confusion about why Nirewa cared about their preparation for the game.

'You don't have to tell me if you don't want to.' Nirewa reassured the twins.

'No, it's not that,' said Amen.

'We don't mind at all,' Iska added. 'We just didn't think our progress mattered to you.'

Nirewa responded by blowing a cloud of smoke into the air.

'Well, from what I saw during the tour of the arena,' said Iska, doing her best to politely bat away the smoke in her face, 'we sort of decided Oshu would help Amen go through phase one and two of the game… That's all we have.'

'That makes sense,' said Nirewa, dabbing the lit end of her cigarette. 'Cheetahs are very quick animals. But, and please correct me if I am mistaken, aren't they poor at climbing trees?'

'Yes,' said Amen, stealing a puzzled glance at Iska. 'They're built more for speed than agility. What does this have to do with the game?'

'Oh, nothing at all. Just that, personally, I have always favoured cats that are nimbler, the ones that move with lithe steps. Do you know what I mean?'

'I'm not sure that we—'

'—I understand what you mean, Nirewa.' Iska interrupted.

Amen shot a confused glance at her sister.

Nirewa let out a genuine smile. 'Good.'

'One more thing,' said Iska as Nirewa rose to her feet. 'The waterfalls—I'm not trying to make excuses, but it genuinely seems like there's no way past them.'

Nirewa sauntered back to the altar. 'If you think there's no way past Agbokim, then I'm sorry to say you didn't do a good job surveying the arena… You can excuse yourselves now; I don't want to be blamed for your lateness to training.'

Horse riding. The most Iska or Amen knew about this activity came from the equestrian magazines in the girls'

study at Digglefield. Based on the content of those magazines, the sport seemed reserved for the world's elite. Neither of the twins could have ever imagined themselves sad-
dling up horses, let alone riding them.

From what they'd heard, the fastest way to the horses
was through Dogudu's south-eastern entrance. For Iska,
Amen, and the boys, this was yet another unfamiliar zone in
the enormous village. After wandering off in the wrong direction a few times—which included walking in on what
seemed to be a private meeting between Dogudu's Council
of Elders and three veiled visitors—the twins and the boys
were finally set on the right course towards the horses.

Lake let out an astonished laugh as they neared the field
where the horses roamed. 'I have to say, these put thorough-
breds to shame.'

'We feed them nothing but the freshest fruits and fod-
der,' Jòla explained, clicking her tongue at a foal that had
just eaten an apple from her hand before it scampered off.
'They are, after all, Dogudu's prized possessions.'

As one of the larger horses trotted towards them, everyone took cautious steps backward except for Uché, Jòla,
Zara, and Kunlé, who stood their ground. Kunlé even
mouthed unintelligible words to the beast.

'Why are they so big?' asked Aito, while the rest of the
group peered at the light brown horse standing beside
Kunlé.

'They have to be,' Uché answered. 'Their size not only
helps us with our daily labour and errands but also enables
them to withstand the rigours of the game.'

Jòla cleared her throat. 'Shall we begin the session?'

'Where are the saddles and bridles for the horses?' asked
Walé, unintentionally capturing everyone's attention.

'What are these?' said Jòla.

'The seats and headgears that go on a horse,' Walé replied.

Jòla pursed her lips to stop herself from laughing. 'Walé,
we ride the horses the way they are; we don't put anything

on them.'

No, no, no—no bloody way! Amen's voice was raspy with nervousness. *What the actual hell?*

'Isn't that dangerous?' said Iska, deciding to voice Amen's concerns out loud.

'With mastery, not at all,' Uché replied. 'And that is the whole point of this training. It is important you all learn to ride Dogudu's horses before the game.'

They had missed it before, but now it dawned on Iska and Amen: Kunlé was a Surros, much like Sunail back home, except it seemed Kunlé was only able to communicate with horses, and communicate he did. At the sound of his voice, the powerful-looking creatures fell into position, like students at an assembly ground. The ease with which Kunlé spoke to the horses and they to him was nothing short of extraordinary.

'Right,' said Jòla, just as she leapt onto the back of a charcoal-grey stallion with little effort. 'These beauts can be a bit feisty sometimes, so I need you all to help each other get on their backs—'

Before Jòla could finish her sentence Zara hopped on the back of a sand-coloured horse in a gesture deliberately done to remind everyone of her athletic superiority.

'No one else try that,' said Jòla, shooting Zara a disappointed look. 'When you get on their backs, lean on their withers, and caress their necks. One more thing, please don't pull their mane, it never ends well.'

Iska began to warm to the idea of riding a horse as she watched the other Chis help each other mount their horses, but Amen remained resolute in her decision not to partake in the training.

Just give it a go, thought Iska as she and Amen feigned preparation. *Besides, I don't think Jòla or Uché will give you any other option.*

Well, they have to compromise because I don't think I can do it. Look at the size of these things!

For goodness' sake, Amen. Iska's inner voice was loud and

sharp. *What did I say to you the other day? You need this. How do you expect to race on Oshu or—*

The neighing and hopping of a disgruntled horse caught everyone by surprise; it would not let one of the boys get on its back. However, the determined boy was still attempting to get the horse under his command when Kunlé intervened.

'Leave her alone,' he said, approaching the horse. 'She doesn't want you to lead her. She already knows who she wants.'

After a brief conversation between the horse and Kunlé, the horse began to amble—to the amazement of everyone else—in the direction of Iska and Amen, who were doing their best to hide their fear. As soon as it got close enough to the twins, the snow-white horse bowed its head.

'Bei wants you two to lead her,' said Kunlé.

Well, there you go, Iska whispered to Amen, a tinge of relief in her voice. *Now you* have *to do it. Plus, look how furious yer wan is.*

On cue, Amen looked up to see a range of emotions clouding Zara's face.

Excitement filled the air in Dogudu as the villagers prepared for their upcoming festival. It was interesting to watch as everyone rushed around, making sure everything was perfect for what was the equivalent of St. Patrick's Day. Iska and Amen joined in the preparations by setting up decorations in the square. Although this wasn't as thrilling as the horse-riding session, the twins were at least grateful to have Oshu and Ada with them for company.

'Horses are very perceptive animals,' said Ada as she hung an elephant-shaped origami lantern on the branch of a tree. 'That horse's gesture meant something.'

'It's funny,' said Oshu, passing another lantern to Ada, who was sitting on his shoulders. 'Since we arrived in Dogudu, not one day has gone by without us learning about something you two were involved in.'

'For me,' said Amen, filling a mini basket with flowery vines, 'the horse thing takes the cake. As soon as we got on Bei, I wasn't scared anymore. We were supposed to be leading, but honestly, she led us.'

Ada requested the mini-basket from Amen. 'Does this mean you want to ride that horse at the game?' she asked ambiguously.

'Oh yeah, about that,' Iska finally joined in on the conversation. 'Ada, we were wondering if you could help Amen with the game.'

We were? Amen was confused. *When?*

Shut up.

Ada nudged Oshu to set her down. 'I'm happy to help in any way I can. What would you have me do?' she asked.

'Basically, we want you to take Amen through the first and second phase of the game in your Cruther form,' Iska said nervously.

'What?' Ada gasped in shock.

Iska, what's going on?

'I know nothing was decided,' Oshu said calmly. 'But I thought *I* would be the one to assist her in the game.'

Amen re-focused her thoughts on her sister. *Wasn't that the plan?*

Iska shook her head to clear her thoughts. 'Yes,' she said. 'But I surveyed the arena, and we just feel with Ada being a leopard, she can navigate the forests better.'

Amen sniggered. *So, that's what Nirewa was talking about in the shrine.*

'How do you two know that?' Oshu's tone was incredulous. 'Is this why Nirewa summoned you yesterday?'

'We used our common sense,' said Amen, deciding to back Iska up. 'I mean, the treadmills in your office, her hair. It was only a matter of time before we put it all together.'

A hint of a smile grew on Ada's shocked face.

'So, you want Ada to help you instead?' said Oshu, losing his composure for once.

'Yes,' Iska and Amen replied regretfully.

'I hope you know being a cheetah, I'm faster.'

'Please,' Ada rolled her eyes, 'the difference in our top speed isn't that much. Plus, you have to admit I *am* more agile.'

Oshu rolled his eyes.

'Look, girls I'm flattered that you want me to help,' said Ada, 'but are you sure this is what you want?'

'Yes,' Iska said without hesitation.

'If Oshu will give us his blessing,' Amen added, looking at her uncle intently.

The warm showers that began to pelt the square acted almost like a proverbial drumroll, awaiting Oshu's answer. 'I won't say I'm not disappointed,' he said, speaking over the growing rain. 'But I want what's best for you two. So, if you feel Ada is the better option, what choice do I have?'

Iska and Amen hugged Oshu before he could get another word out. 'Thank you so much!'

Ada joined in the embrace. 'I'm proud of you, babe,' she said, kissing Oshu's cheek before turning to Amen. 'I hope all your training pays off because I run nothing like a horse does.'

12. FIRE & BRIMSTONE

The days went by in a blur of training, strategies, and preparations. Before they knew it, Amen and Iska were only one day away from the festival that Nirewa, Jimba, and almost everyone else in the village had been talking about since they arrived a week ago. It was interesting how one week of intense physical training could transform the body. Fully immersed in their day-to-day activities in Dogudu, the twins hadn't even noticed any changes until the seamstresses currently taking their measurements pointed out their new musculature.

Apparently, it was customary to have specific outfits made for every Chi competing in the game, whether they had abilities or not. As the ever-diligent Uché and Jòla had explained, Chis needed to have maximum mobility of all their limbs during the game. For this reason, traditional attire would not be appropriate.

'My children, what colours would you like your uniforms to be?' an old seamstress asked.

'Blue for me,' Amen replied.

'I'll have mine in white, thank you,' Iska added politely.

Jòla and Uché had also explained that the outfits needed to be an extension of each Chi's personality, which explained the old seamstress's question.

'We're done here,' the old seamstress finally said. 'Your uniforms will come to you first thing in the morning. Good luck, my children.'

There was no need to doubt the woman's words. If there was one thing Iska and Amen had learnt during their time in Dogudu, it was that feats of nature were mundane tasks to the people here.

Amen and Iska had no time to rest as they headed off to the training ground. Although there would be no training today, Jòla and Uché had requested everyone's presence in the meadow. Power-walking the last fifty metres, the twins finally arrived at the meadow to meet Aito, Lake, Walé, and the rest of the Chis already seated.

'You're the last ones in,' said Jòla, relieved she didn't have to do a headcount.

Uché was wrestling to start the bonfire, but he glanced over his shoulder at the two girls. 'We will start shortly.' The flames finally burst to life in blistering colours of red, orange, and yellow.

'We won't take much of your time.' Jòla kicked off the session with a wide grin. 'We know you need all the rest you can get ahead of the game tomorrow.'

'Yes,' Uché chimed in. 'Jòla and I called you all here just to let you know how proud we are of each and every one of you. In addition to familiar faces, we had new entrants come into this season's training with not a lot of experience but with some courage and an abundance of eagerness to learn.'

'And for that, we say thank you,' Jòla continued. 'It goes without saying that you are all winners in our eyes.'

'Is this a clever way of consoling us?' Aito's question prompted laughter and cheers from everyone.

While the rest of the session went on, Iska couldn't help but notice Amen's irritation at everything. She frowned at all the jokes being told, refused to acknowledge the boys, and now, thinking about it, Iska realised that Amen hadn't spoken to her much throughout the day. Iska finally confirmed something was up with Amen when Uché offered to show highlights of the game he and Jòla had participated in years ago, and Amen asked to be excused even before a collective decision was reached.

'What's the matter with you?' Iska called out to Amen, who was already far away from the meadow.

'Why didn't you stay back?' said Amen.

'How could I when something is clearly eating you up?'

Amen remained silent.

'Where exactly are you off to?' asked Iska as they circled

the fringes of the vibrant village square. 'Are you pissed off because Oshu decided to help Aito in the game?'

'I really don't mind their partnership,' Amen replied honestly. 'I'm confident we did the right thing in choosing Ada. By the way, I'm headed to the lake.'

'The lake? What for?'

'Have you actually considered what we'd do if we were to find out who murdered Mam?' said Amen.

'*When* we find out,' Iska replied defiantly as they rushed past the southern entrance of the village. 'No, I haven't thought about that to be honest.'

'Well?' said Amen, swiping away a swarm of gnats from her face.

'It's a no-brainer, isn't it? The person has to answer for what they did. I'm certain Oshu will use his influence to make things happen.'

Away from the busy square, the chilly night was quiet. Amen and Iska were certain they were the only ones within a kilometre radius of the lake because in Dogudu, all types of work (except for Jimba's) ended at the beginning of sunset, which had been almost three hours ago.

'But aren't you scared?' said Amen, as she skimmed stones across the glittering lake. 'To know how the person did it, what they used, why Mam of all people?'

'I am.' Iska's voice strained with pain. 'But I'm even more scared of not getting justice for her, and that's what drives me.'

'It's what drives me too,' said Amen after a moment of silence. 'I want to show you something.'

Iska stood back as Amen quickly weaved intricate hand signs.

'I've been practising this in my head, so I hope it works,' As soon as Amen placed the palm of her right hand on the surface of the lake, the entire body of water began to ripple and stagnate continuously. 'I can feel every corner of the lake right now, it's like an extension of my body.'

Iska struggled to form her words. 'What are you doing

to the water?' she stuttered.

'Nothing,' Amen said with a laugh. 'The water's just reflecting my pulse. But I could do so much more if I wanted to.'

Amen took her hand out of the water and the whole lake went placid again.

'You're amazing,' Iska couldn't hold back her tears. 'A real goddess.'

'Hardly; I still have a lot to learn, but I couldn't have come this far without you. Look, I know you not having abilities eats you up but—'

'Forget about it,' said Iska, as she stretched her arms out for a hug. 'For the first time, I don't care anymore. It doesn't matter because I have you. *You're* my gift, and I wouldn't trade you for anything—anything in the world. I love you so much, Amen.'

'I love you too, Iska.'

The knock on the door woke both of them up, but Iska got out of bed first. She opened the door to see the same boy who had delivered their outfit a week ago holding a package in his hands.

Iska took the package off the boy and thanked him as he exited the hut. 'Amen, our battle gear is here,' she said sarcastically as she scanned the parchment-wrapped package. 'Oh, and there's a note with it.'

'What does it say?' said Amen, pulling herself up in bed while Iska perched beside her with the note open:

I made sure patterns were put on your uniforms.
The three wavy white stripes on Amen's represent flow and flexibility: the ability to adapt to any situation that may come.
The black circle on Iska's represents foundation, because if anything, be it relationships or legacies, is to stand

the test of time, it needs to be founded on solid ground.
Foundation with flexibility, you two do well to remember this.

-N.

'Really strange woman,' said Amen. 'But I'm growing fond of her.'

'Yeah, me too.' Iska closed the note. 'Sun's not out yet; do you want to sleep some more?'

'Not really.' How could she? The day had barely begun yet the village was already alive with music and felicity. It was not hard to imagine that most people didn't get any sleep out of sheer excitement.

After a few hours idling in bed, Amen and Iska decided that remaining in the hut was useless. They freshened up but opted to dress in normal village attire; since the game was not until evening, there was no need to seem overly eager. Although the sun now hung high and bright in the sky, a bank of dark clouds loomed in the corner; not that this stopped the men, women, and children who filled the village's walkways from dancing, singing, and sharing gifts with one another. Caught up in the excitement, Amen and Iska received and dished out embraces indiscriminately until they found themselves hugging the Tellas and the boys.

'This is insane!' Iska screamed into Oshu's ear.

'This is Dogudu!' he screamed back. 'Let's go to the square!'

Getting to the epicentre of the village was no easy task. The square was a mere fifty metres away, but the group had to struggle past a sea of jubilant people. Their perseverance finally paid off when they pushed through the last barrier of people and entered the open field.

Amen and Iska had never been to any carnival before, so they had no yardstick with which to measure the Igboya festival. But they were certain no party or celebration in the future would come close to what they were currently witnessing, at least not for a while, and possibly not for the remainder of their lives. Every tent had something interesting or unique to offer: face painting, dance competitions, pottery. Amen and Iska had hardly made any progress through the field when they were each handed plates with an assortment of snacks, including fried, peppery snails, mashed plantains, roasted peanuts, and other delicacies whose names they didn't know.

The group finally found a bamboo canopy to shield them from the sun while they ate and watched the festival rage on.

'What are those?' said Amen, pointing to a group of masked figures prancing their way to the centre of the square.

'Dogudu's masquerades,' replied Oshu, as he cheered on the pantomiming group. 'This is the only time in the year anyone gets to see them.'

Aito got out of his seat to get a better look. 'What are they about to do?'

'Why don't you see for yourselves?' suggested Oshu.

The masquerades moved to the beats drummed by a group of men. On one beat, the masquerades jerked their bodies once; twice on two beats; and began to gyrate in complex lines and circles on multiple beats. The crowd loved it; they whistled and cheered the performance nonstop, with some children even trying to imitate the choreography from where they stood. All of a sudden, the costumed group stopped their act. Each of the five masked people pulled out a piece of fabric from their heavily yarned garments and formed a circle on the ground with them.

'Oh, this is the best part,' said Oshu as he rose to his feet.

'What's going to happen—' Aito began to ask when another tube-like masquerade shot out of the circle on the ground and rose swiftly into the air like a sky-dancer, swaying and rocking to the continuous pounding of drums. At intervals, the iridescent serpentine creature would reduce its height to barely one metre and then abruptly stretch twenty metres into air.

'Is there some air mechanism controlling this thing?' Iska asked.

'If only it were that simple,' Oshu replied with a laugh. 'Not to scare any of you, but apparently the spirits of dead villagers are controlling that masquerade. From the stories I learnt as a child, there are techniques used to bring them around during the time of the festival, and they use this medium to celebrate with the living. Right now, those spirits are dancing.'

The masquerades finally ended their performance and exited the square, making way for other acts to take centre stage. Amen and Iska no longer found the festival amusing, and this had nothing to do with the current crop of performers. Before their eyes, the day had aged significantly, which meant at any moment they would need to begin preparations for the game. During an earlier performance, they had caught a glimpse of Zara; she came to watch the act but disappeared not long after. Obviously, she was used to all of this; for her, the game was her only priority, her life.

As though reading Iska and Amen's minds, the mood of the village suddenly shifted. Everything and everyone went quiet as Nirewa, accompanied by the matriarchs and patriarchs of Dogudu, marched into the square.

'The time has come—' Nirewa's voice echoed through the field. '—for our combatants to take the ultimate oath! Come fire and brimstone, they will never cower in fear. Through will and mettle, they will uphold the values that our great village is built on. So let them go and don their armour while we make our way to *hokuan* to receive them.'

'You all need to go get ready.' Oshu's voice was urgent. 'Now! We'll be waiting for you in the northern forest.'

As Amen and Iska were leaving the square, a solemn, unrecognisable chant broke out amongst the villagers.

Amen's unsteady hands couldn't undo the strings on the

package containing their outfits, so she passed it over to Iska who immediately ripped through the parchment. There was no time to admire the level of artistry and detail put into the uniforms, although Amen and Iska did notice the designs Nirewa had spoken about in her note were embroidered on the backside of their diamond mesh leotard crop tops.

'The tights are padded,' said Iska, as she put on the matching bottom half of her outfit.

'Yeah.' Amen felt her chest. 'The tops as well. I guess it's for protection.'

Just before they left the hut, the twins opted to both wear their hair in pigtail braids to show solidarity.

The overcast that had been threatening all day had finally engulfed the sun, leaving the weather reflecting the tension that was no doubt building for everyone. How ironic it was that the square, which had been teeming with life barely an hour ago, was now deserted? From all indications, the game held as much significance as the festival itself.

Since Amen didn't know the way to the arena, Iska took the lead. Upon exiting the north entrance, they spotted the boys about twenty paces ahead but refrained from calling out to them. All three could easily pass as professional athletes; their uniforms—Aito in his orange skin-tight vest and matching shorts; Lake in the same outfit but in black; and Walé in a white neck-to-ankle unitard—accentuated the muscles they too had packed on. Like Iska and Amen, the boys' feet were also bare.

'—Eweiya jaku weya idam! Eweiya jaku weya idam! Eweiya jaku weya idam!—' The chants grew louder as Amen and Iska approached the waiting crowd. About fifty metres away, Zara, whose scarlet-coloured uniform was identical to the twins', was exchanging sign language with a towering gorilla. Remarkably, the horses selected to take part in the race did not flinch at the sight of Jimba; but then again, Dogudu's horses were majestic in their own right.

Another four-legged animal stood away from the

crowd, far from the racing lanes. The last time Oshu had transformed into a cheetah, Iska and Amen hadn't been able to fully appreciate his beauty because it had been dark and they'd been terrified. But now, bathed in daylight, Oshu was as hypnotic as he was frightening. Everything about him, from the tawny splotches on his black coat to the intensity of his gaze, seemed to beckon the twins closer. Yet, as they neared, the muscles in his chest and forelegs quivered and his long, powerful tail flicked left, then right. In that moment, their uncle was indistinguishable from a predator.

And beside the predator stood his mate, still in human form.

'Ada, please don't tell me you changed your mind,' said Iska, doing her best to mask the nerves in her voice.

'And miss all the fun?' Ada grinned as she pulled out the bands in her hair. 'No way; I was waiting for you two.'

As soon as Ada finished her sentence, Oshu let out a sharp hiss.

'He says I'm a show-off,' Ada said with a laugh. 'Oh yes, and so what?'

Suddenly, Ada started walking towards an Iroko tree. Before either of the twins could ask where she was going, she leapt onto the trunk of the giant tree and began climbing it like a spider. Within seconds, she was gone, disappearing into the tree's branches and leaves without a trace.

'Where do you think she went?' Amen asked as she and Iska scanned the tangled branches overhead, trying to spot their aunt.

'I don't know, but she needs to—'

'—We're about to start the game,' Aito's voice briefly drew the twins' attention. 'Uché said to call—Mother of God!'

Iska and Amen whipped their heads around to follow Aito's line of sight. And there Ada was, devoid of her human body; restored now by the flesh and fur of a golden leopard easily the size of Dogudu's horses. The twins watched as Ada crawled down the trunk of the Iroko with a deftness that reminded them why they had chosen her instead of Oshu as their teammate.

'Oshu, don't shred me to bits,' said Aito, taking cover beside Amen and Iska, 'but your wife is gorgeous!'

Aito spoke no word of a lie. Ada was just as mesmerising as Oshu, and truthfully more intimidating—even her purr was louder, deeper, more compelling than his.

Remembering why he came to them in the first place, Aito jerked his head in the direction of the crowd. 'Girls, the game's about to start. We need to go. And Amen, good luck out there, we're all rooting for you.'

The villagers, whose continued chants had reduced to just above a whisper, gave way for the competing Chis to get into the race lanes. Amen tried to control her breathing, but her pounding heart made it difficult to stay calm.

You're on lane five. Iska whispered into Amen's head.

But Amen already knew this. In fact, she was aware of the position of every Chi: Kunlé was in the first lane; Aminat was in the second; Zara, already on Jimba's back, occupied the third lane; Mazino was in the fourth; Doreyin was in the sixth lane; Aito had been assigned to the seventh; while Oinem, Kaffy, and Yinda in the eighth, ninth, and tenth lanes, rounded things up.

Through the training sessions, Amen and Iska had come to know the other Chis a little better. It turned out that most of them were not actually hostile; they were just shy, which was a normal reaction given the fact that they had spent their whole lives never encountering anyone outside of their own people. In one week, Amen and Iska had learnt to appreciate their humour, their stories, their warmth, as well as their strength, valour, and determination. There was no denying that each racer was as formidable as the next, and this was what troubled Amen the most.

Before Amen could think about the advantages of being in one of the two middle lanes, Ada brushed the right side of her body with her massive head; it was time. The giant feline crouched low enough for Amen to get on her back—

the race had not yet begun, but already Amen was beginning to understand what Ada meant when she'd said she didn't move like a horse. For one, Ada did not have humped withers like horses. Secondly, the slope of her neck was closer to a horizontal line than to the natural diagonal shape a horse's neck had. All of this simply meant that balancing on Ada's back while she ran at full speed would be precarious. But Aito, riding a cheetah, would be in an even worse spot. Thankfully, Amen had received a brief lecture from Ada on how to hang on and stay on her back. For example, she was under no circumstance allowed to raise her head while Ada was at her top speed; she was, however, allowed to wrap her arms as tightly as she could around Ada's neck; and finally, she could, albeit gently, clutch Ada's sides with her legs. If Amen followed these three rules, she would be fine, but it was easier said than done.

'Chis, on your marks!' Uché's voice boomed from behind them. 'Get set! Go!'

Amen reflexively shut her eyes as soon as Ada lurched forward. Something in her was determined not to see how things were unfolding—perhaps it was adrenaline or fear. Whatever the reason, it had to be set aside; the time to back out was over. Now was the moment for nothing but bravery.

The grass beneath them swept by at a nauseating pace, an indication that Ada was covering good ground. But upon slightly tilting her head, Amen noted that the Chis to her left flank were not far off. Interestingly, Zara and her father were lagging behind—Jimba clearly couldn't match the speed of the horses.

Keeping her head low and tucked in, Amen turned to the right side. The horses on this side were also holding their own, but it was the black cheetah each of them was trying (and hopelessly failing) to catch up to. In fairness, everyone was struggling to keep up with Oshu and Aito, who were no less than fifty metres ahead.

Amen was still watching the lean cat eat up more ground

with each coil and uncoil of its body when the first speck of dirt hit her in the eyes. There was no time to react; more mud and grass splattered around as Doreyin and her horse crashed into the earth. There was something underneath the grasses catching at their legs. Ada, who also noticed this, began to run in zigzags instead of a straight line. They might have been slower for it, but Ada's insistence on running capriciously paid dividends when a vine-like plant sprung out of the soil and latched onto the legs of the horse Mazino was riding on, sending them tumbling to the ground.

Another loud scream about fifteen metres to the left, and Amen caught a glimpse of a dozen giant tendrils subduing Aminat and her horse. Further up the field, Kunlé and his horse disappeared into the forest—the second phase of the game. Amen blinked wildly to try and rid her eyes of the dirt even as she scanned the field. There was no sign of Aito and Oshu at the forest's edge, but Kaffy and her horse appeared to be safe as they reached the threshold of the woodlands when yet another group of relentless vines burst out of the ground fast enough to entrap them in its unyielding tentacles. Perhaps not wanting the same fate to befall them, Ada's muscles shuddered as she increased her pace. Amen was just about done tightening her grip when the leopard lunged a good ten metres across the field and crashed headlong into the thorny bushes of the forest.

The only thing worse than the blood seeping out of various cuts and scrapes on Amen's body was her own sweat stinging the wounds. However, there was no chance of stopping to examine herself; the game was still on.

I'm in the second phase of the game, Amen reported.

Thank goodness! Iska replied with genuine relief. *We couldn't see much from here. How was it?*

Let's just hope whatever is in here isn't as bad as what happened on the field… Got to go.

Amen wished she could maintain a direct line of communication with Iska, but after what she'd just seen, she needed to stay very alert. So far, nothing had crept out from under the soil to attack them. However, Ada didn't want to leave anything to chance, so she heaved herself up a grand Iroko tree and used the outstretched branches of neighbouring trees to travel forward.

The forest's surroundings were quiet—too quiet, in fact. This, coupled with the fact that they were enveloped in darkness, left Amen at the brink of an emotional breakdown. Thankfully, Ada was nocturnal; her eyes were perfectly suited to navigate these kinds of conditions.

As they navigated their way through the forest, Amen marvelled at how much Ada had done for her in a short span of minutes. There was no doubt about it—if she didn't have Ada as her partner, she most likely would have been out of the game by now. Compelled to express gratitude, Amen leaned close to the leopard's ear and whispered, 'Thank you.'

Ada wriggled her head, a gesture that could be interpreted as "Don't mention it" or, more realistically, "We're not out of the woods just yet". The latter interpretation seemed more appropriate to Amen.

Still trying to figure out the aim of this phase of the game, Amen almost missed the fact that she could now see the entire forest clearly. The reason for this was the thousands of fireflies zipping around. Amen wondered to herself whether it was a coincidence or by design that these fiery insects were always in the right place at the right time.

It was no surprise that the light in the forest had a green tone to it; besides the green leaves that blotted out the sky above, almost all the trees were covered in green algae while the ground beneath them was carpeted in moss. The forest was also beginning to show signs of life: bushbabies cowered in the shadows, chittering birds flitted from tree to tree, and vervets howled in the distance; but there was still no sign of the remaining Chis.

Realising that Ada needed a break from carrying her, Amen decided to walk alongside the massive cat instead—after all, the tree branches were strong and wide enough to accommodate them both. As she walked beside Ada, Amen couldn't help but be in awe of her size and magnificence. She was still running her hand through Ada's shimmering fur, feeling its warmth and softness, when suddenly, the bark of a nearby tree revealed a pair of eyes and hands.

13. NIGHTMARE

Startled, Amen flinched and lost her footing, falling back-first onto another tree branch a level below. She struggled to catch her breath as another figure, also camouflaged like the trunk of a tree, emerged out of nowhere and lunged towards her.

Fight or flight? Amen didn't know her surroundings well enough to flee. Plus, even if she could outrun this masked person, how could she be sure there weren't more of them around? Fight.

She pushed her attacker backwards with her legs and scrambled to her feet just in time to defend against the next wave of attacks. Like clockwork, all of Jòla and Uché's teachings flooded Amen's mind as she weaved and dodged the man's attempts to grab her. But she'd only had one week of training, and she wasn't *quite* fast enough. The man finally seized her wrist, but Amen quickly countered his next move, clenched *his* wrist, twisted his arm to his back, and yanked it up until he winced in pain. Refusing to surrender, the man attempted to grab Amen with his free hand until she shoved him so hard that he lost his footing and tumbled several feet to the ground below.

Amen stood at the edge of an outstretched branch and peered down at the stranger who lay motionless, long enough for her to begin to worry she had killed him. Suddenly, he flinched, wriggled his head, and looked up at her with a sinister grin. While Amen tried to anticipate the man's next move, someone grabbed her from behind. She tried to fight off her new assailant, but two more camouflaged men appeared out of nowhere and subdued her, taking hold of her ankles.

Amen desperately tried to scream for help, to call out to

Ada, but a big, calloused hand clasped over her mouth prevented her from doing so. She considered using her ability to free herself, but her hands and feet were bound tightly. This was it; the game was over. Tears streamed down Amen's face as the possibility of never getting justice for Aré loomed.

Iska, they have me! They won't let me go! Amen screamed as the camouflaged men carried her away, when suddenly, her body slammed into the tree. Dazed from being dropped, Amen blinked repeatedly to clear her vision. As everything came into focus, she saw Ada swatting one of the camouflaged men off the tree before returning to her to lick off the sticky weed binding her limbs together.

Who has you, Amen?! What's out there? demanded Iska, but Amen didn't have time to explain herself—a score of men were advancing quickly towards her and Ada. Just like at the start of the game, Ada crouched low for Amen to get on her back, and as soon as she did, the leopard took off in the north direction. Although they were not nearly as fast as Ada, the men continued to chase after her. At first, Amen thought her eyes were playing tricks on her, but Ada jumping from one branch to another confirmed what she'd suspected all along: there were more of these camouflaged men popping out of different trees, and they all looked identical, almost like they were...

'Clones!' Aito screamed from the ground several metres below. He was still riding on Oshu, who was struggling with the forest's uneven terrain. 'Don't let them get a hold of you!'

It seemed Aito and Oshu had first-hand experience of what the camouflaged men could do.

'How do you know they're clones?' Amen's strained voice shocked her.

'I fought—some of them—off!' Aito was barely audible with all the running. 'Saw them—split bodies—before my eyes!'

As though sensing imminent danger, Ada hastened her

strides, leaving Aito and Oshu in her wake. The leopard's intuition was not far off; seconds later, one of the clones jumped from a branch directly overhead, landing on Ada's back just behind Amen. Ada, still running, tried to shake the clone off, but he stayed latched on and was now aiming his hands at Amen's hips. If he got a hold of her, that was it. Amen was sure there would be no miraculous intervention from Ada this time around.

Amen blindly aimed a kick at the clone; she missed with the first attempt but connected solidly with his chest on the second kick. The clone winced in pain, but Amen's jab wasn't powerful enough to knock him off Ada's back. Just as the clone began tugging at her back with his hands, the first droplet of water hit Amen's forehead, followed by another. Suddenly, a flurry of showers whipped her in the face. For the first time throughout the game, Amen had leverage. With a twitch of her head, she sent pellets of water directly into the face of the clone, increasing the intensity of each hit until he loosened his grip on her back.

Amen continued to fight off the clone behind her when another clone, positioned about twenty metres ahead, crouched down in an attempt to stop Ada in her tracks.

Big mistake.

Ada charged forward and plucked up the man with her teeth, flinging him over her head and causing him to crash into the clone already on her back. But as they tumbled over, one of the clones snatched at Amen's ankle, peeling away at the skin on her leg with his tight grip. Before the clone could do more damage, Amen conjured a ball of water with her foot and blasted it hard into his head.

As soon as Amen steadied herself on Ada's back, the deafening roar of an ape reverberated through the forest. Unfortunately for her, Zara and her father seemed to still be in the game.

Unnoticed by Amen, the onslaught from the clones had stopped. She looked around for any sign of Aito and her uncle, but the deluge from the unrelenting rain had reduced the visibility of the forest. Amen wondered if they had been caught by the clones, and this left her with mixed feelings: on one hand, Aito being out of the game meant she had one less competitor to worry about, but on the other hand, she wanted him to be safe. No victory was worth the well-being of her friend.

Ada had slowed her pace to a trot; she was clearly tired. However, when Amen tried to get off her back, she growled in resistance. Just as Amen was about to protest the leopard's stubbornness, the sound of water rushing with disconcerting rage filled her ears. A quick glance around revealed the water flowing beneath them. Iska hadn't exaggerated how intimidating Agbokim was. However, she had failed to give the best layout of the waterfalls. Iska had only focused on how the water flowed into the riverbed from the tail end of the forest that Amen was currently in, but she hadn't mentioned that water also cascaded down the mouth of the forest on the other side of the ravine. This new and improved information made the already complicated task of finding a way across the waterfalls exponentially harder.

'Ada, I need to get off so I can see better,' Amen said confidently.

Reluctantly, Ada crouched down so her belly brushed the dirt.

Amen crept unsteadily to the edge of an outstretched branch that overlooked Agbokim. The gap between the two forests stretched endlessly to either side. There was no chance of jumping across the ravine; it was too wide, even for Ada. While Amen was trying to think of a solution to the seemingly insurmountable problem in front of her, the leaves of a tree a few metres below rustled. Upon closer inspection, Amen saw that Aito and Oshu had successfully made it past the clones, although it seemed Oshu was struggling to maintain his balance on the tree branch he was standing on.

Aito wasted no time; he leaned over the edge of another branch to scan the ravine for an opening. Finding one, he returned to Oshu and whispered something into the cheetah's ear, then suddenly burst into a full sprint towards Agbokim. When he reached the tip of the branch, Aito jumped into the air and disappeared with a blink.

Amen wasn't even afforded time to react to Aito's wit; there was another rustling of leaves about ten metres to her left. This time, it was Jimba and Zara, both of whom looked worse for wear. But what did it matter? They were still in the game. Zara's urgency meant she discarded surveying the waterfalls altogether. A quick sign language between the girl and her father, and in seconds, Amen watched as Jimba threw Zara across the ravine into the other forest.

Just like that, Aito and Zara had made their way into the final phase of the game, leaving Amen, who had gotten to Agbokim before either of them, to weigh the impending consequences of her misfortune. She had no way across. Deflated and dejected, Amen had almost forgotten Ada was still beside her. The leopard gave her a nudge with her massive head.

'It's over, Ada,' said Amen, still on her knees. 'We've done our best.'

Ada purred and jerked her head to the sky, and that's when Amen saw what the big cat was trying to show her: vines. Vines that ran along the branches directly above them to the branches on the other side of the forest. But the problem was only half solved; Amen still needed to climb to the higher levels of the tree before painstakingly edging her way across any one of the vines that dangled precariously over the waterfalls. She was about to explain this to Ada when the leopard sprang high into the air and snatched one of the vines with her razor-sharp teeth on the way back down—problem solved.

Once more, Ada's indomitable spirit had shone through, but this was not the right time for Amen to show gratitude. Fear rocked her body as she took a hold of the slippery vine, but this feeling was not compelling enough to thwart her from what she was about to do next. Holding the vine as tight as possible in both hands, Amen took a few steps back, drew in a deep breath, and then sprinted towards the end of the branch.

"Don't you dare look down!" Amen frantically commanded herself as cold air swooshed past her ears. The vine sent her crashing into a bank of moist soil, narrowly missing the fast-moving stream beside her. Not bothering to check for any bodily damage, she lifted herself off the dirt and began sprinting down the only available path. Whizzing past encroaching shrubs, Amen tried to remember who else she could encounter. Aminat, Kaffy, Doreyin, and Mazino had been eliminated in the first phase. She wasn't sure of Oinem, Kunlé, and Yinda's fate but assumed they were still in the game. Armed with this information, Amen dug the balls of her feet deeper into the earth, propelling herself even harder.

Although the rain, which had quietly eased off for the better part of the last ten minutes, was now pouring with more intensity, it did nothing to slow Amen down. Determined to catch up to the voices not too far ahead of her, Amen pressed forward despite the severe cramping in her calves. Just when she thought she had finally caught up to her opponents, Amen slipped into a pit of what seemed to be mud. However, the harder she tried to wriggle herself free, the deeper she sank into it. It was then that Amen realised she was stuck in quicksand, and the voices she had heard were actually groans belonging to Aito and Zara, who were also struggling to get out of the bog.

Amen drew in deep breaths to stop herself from panicking. Her feet were touching the earth underneath all the water and sand, so at least she would not be sinking any deeper. Other than that, everything else was bad: she was exhausted, her mind was bruised and battered, and her opponents were farther along in the pit.

Amen, where are you? Iska's worried voice was a pleasant distraction.

I'm in phase three of the game, but before you say anything, I'm stuck. We all are: me, Zara, and Aito.

I'm just glad you're alive! Some of the others were hurt really bad. Are you close to the end of the game?

This was a valid question that Amen hadn't thought to ask herself amidst all the action. Now, as she took in her surroundings, the one thing that stood out besides the hundreds of bamboo trees encircling them was a luminous red ribbon, held up by two poles, at the end of a muddy fifty-metre-long track that lay beyond the patch of quicksand.

I think I am. Iska, the last part of this game is a race.

What are you waiting for then? You know you're faster.

I told you, I'm stuck! Amen's frustrations were beginning to spill out.

What exactly is it that you're stuck in?

Quicksand! It's hard for me to move my legs.

Amen, you— Amen could hear Iska sniggering, *you do know it's raining, right?*

Thanks. Amen said after a few seconds of silence. She shook her head in disappointment as she made intricate signs using both her hands. What would it take to start believing in herself more? As soon as she wove the last sign together, Amen began pulling large amounts of rain from the wailing heavens into the quicksand around her. The result of her experiment was positive: she could move her legs. She pulled harder, this time focusing the raindrops directly in front of her, and a narrow path began to form steadily.

Amen's legs tingled with excruciating pain, but she continued to trudge through the quicksand. Within seconds, she had left Aito behind and was closing fast on Zara, who was just about pulling herself free from the quicksand. Renewed energy coursed through Amen's body, not only because there was a fair chance she could win the game, but also because Aito was cheering her on, verbally pushing her towards the finish line, towards victory.

Amen emerged from the quicksand just half a second after Zara did and began to run as fast as she could. From experience, she knew being even a millisecond behind your opponent in a race like this one could be very costly. It was what separated losers from winners, and it was the reason Amen was giving everything she had to close the five-metre gap between herself and Zara.

Amen's lungs burned as she pushed her worn out body to overtake Zara, who had to be equally exhausted. Approaching the forty-metre mark, she was certain Jimba's daughter was falling behind. Still, Amen ran even harder, putting a reasonable distance between herself and the girl. She was not going to fail; there was too much at stake, too many people counting on her: Iska, Ada, Oshu...Mam. Glinting in the darkness, the red ribbon was more pronounced than ever. Amen was only a few strides away from breaking through it. The game was nearly over; in fact, it seemed the ceremony had already begun. There was a growing body of light right behind Amen, most likely Iska and the others running with their torches to congratulate her. Their cheers were so loud.

Amen couldn't help it; she glanced behind her to catch a glimpse of the jubilant crowd, but something else unfolded slowly before her eyes. Nobody was coming to congratulate her; the lights and even the sounds she had heard were coming from one source: Zara. Before Amen could draw in her next breath, Zara, whose right index finger was already held out in the rain, transformed into a streak of lightning and zipped across the track just in time to cross the finish line before her.

They both crashed into the damp earth in a heap, Zara on her back and Amen on her belly, her face buried in the dirt, just the way she wanted. She was perfectly content with living out the rest of her life like this. The lump in her throat was unbearable, and it hurt to dig her fingers and toes into the ground. But she did not stop; could not stop. All the training, all those lessons, and it was all for nothing. Someone was trying to lift her out of the dirt, but Amen didn't want to move; she resisted.

'Please get up.' The voice belonged to Zara, and she was on her knees right in front of Amen.

Amen tried to look anywhere else except into Zara's eyes, but she couldn't stop staring at the girl who had taken to loathing her since the day she arrived in the village; the girl whom she had dreamt about every night since the first time she laid eyes on her; the girl she had so desperately wanted to prove a point to. The girl who now gently placed her hands on Amen's hips as she eased herself onto her knees.

For the first time, Amen understood clearly what Aito had meant when he said Zara was odd, yet she knew Jimba's daughter was the farthest thing from that. Or, better still, if Zara was odd, so too was she, because she wanted to kiss Zara just as much as she knew Zara wanted to kiss her, and it was about to happen. Their lips were within millimetres of connecting when the real lights and the real cheers flooded in from all around the forest towards both of them.

Within seconds, Zara was lifted into the air by different pairs of hands in celebration, while Iska—accompanied by the Tellas and the boys—helped Amen to her feet.

'I'm sorry.' Amen couldn't stem the tears flowing from her eyes. 'I let you guys down; I'm so sorry.'

'Stop apologising!' said Iska, hugging Amen as tightly as she could. 'You did your best.'

'Yes,' said Oshu, joining the twins in embrace. 'You, who knew nothing about this world a little over a week ago, gave it your all to the end. We couldn't be prouder of you, Amen. Believe it or not, everyone in this village respects you. They respect all of you.'

Amen freed herself from Iska and Oshu's arms; she knew who she wanted to talk to next. Ada stood there; arms already wide open as if she could read Amen's mind.

'Forgive me,' said Amen, collapsing into Ada's arms. 'After everything you did—'

'—I don't care what anyone says,' Ada interrupted Amen, kissing her forehead. 'You're a winner to me. That's all that matters. Now, let's get out of the rain and get you cleaned up.'

The night's dinner was held out in the square, as the festival technically was not over yet. The new tents which had been erected in and around the square to block out the unceasing rain were illuminated by lanterns and candles that hovered enchantingly over rows of stools and tables, girding the grand stage. Calling the purpose of this gathering "dinner" was an understatement; it was a feast.

A host of performers took to the stage as food and drinks were served around. Amen, who had no appetite, stuck to guzzling down cups of water while the rest of the family helped themselves to a wide selection of meals. Although she tried her best not to, Amen replayed the scenes of the game in her head, particularly what had transpired between her and Zara, while her eyes roamed the square for any sign of the lightning girl.

Amen didn't need to look for long, because Zara finally came into view. She strode towards the twins with determination, and Amen held her breath as she reached their table. Amen felt a sudden thirst but decided against reaching for her cup, as that would require lifting her head and risk meeting Zara's eyes—something she wasn't entirely sure she wanted to do.

'Congratulations on your win today, Zara,' Oshu said courteously. 'You're a formidable lady.'

'Thank you,' Zara replied indifferently. 'My opponents were equally formidable.'

Moved by Zara's words, Amen finally looked up to see the girl's eyes squarely on her. Even with all the cuts and scrapes around her face, Zara had never looked more beautiful.

'My father asked me to summon you all,' Zara continued. 'He says it's urgent.'

Within seconds, they were all out of the lively square and trying to keep up with Zara, who hastily made her way through Dogudu's walkways. They finally arrived at Jimba's hut, and Zara knocked on the front door three times before it was opened just wide enough for each person to squeeze through. Although Jimba's parlour was filled with the familiar smell of incense, it was the lit candles that gave the hut its ominous aura.

'Thank you, Zara,' Jimba said from the right-hand side of the room where he was standing. In response, his daughter nodded her head and exited the hut quietly.

Amen stared after the lightning girl as she shut the door behind her. She wasn't sure what it meant, but she didn't like the way the knots in her stomach tightened whenever she was in Zara's orbit. Though her feet remained rooted inside the hut, her soul had already chased after Zara and cornered her. *How were you able to transform into lightning? If you hate me so much, then why did want to kiss me? How do you really feel about me?*

Without asking permission, these questions had taken up space in Amen's mind. Worse still, they were shoving aside the questions about Aré's death; each one demanding to be unpacked first.

'I hope there are no issues, Jimba?' said Oshu. 'Why did you send for us?'

'I was the one who sent for you.' Nirewa emerged from Jimba's room with a determined expression on her face. 'And we don't have much time. I know I said Amen and Iska could see only if they won the game, but their character throughout the preparations and the game itself deserves a chance.'

Jimba, who had disappeared into his room moments earlier, returned with a large stainless steel basin filled to the brim with water and placed it in the centre of the parlour.

'I usually need the council's approval to perform this ritual,' said Nirewa, running her right hand along the surface of the water. 'But I can bend the rules tonight, provided we act fast.'

Oshu was about to say something, but Nirewa silenced him with a stern look. 'Don't thank me just yet,' she said. 'This ritual can be fickle. Sometimes it works, other times it doesn't. It depends on the desire of the participant.'

'Nirewa, we're desperate.' Iska couldn't keep her silence any longer.

'Yes,' Amen added. 'The ritual will work; we want nothing more than to seek answers.'

'In that case, let us begin,' Nirewa whispered. 'Everyone, take a seat around the basin.'

As soon as the last person was seated, Nirewa began to dance and mutter mysterious incantations. Before they could all fully appreciate the grace and balance with which the oracle circled the basin, she pulled a small knife from the pocket of her dress and sliced the palm of her left hand, directing the blood that seeped out of it into the basin of water.

'I have done my part,' said Nirewa as she took a strip of cloth from Jimba to bind her bleeding hand. 'Now it is time for the girls to do theirs.'

'Which is?' Ada asked immediately.

Nirewa knelt beside the basin and swirled the water until it turned red. 'They have to dip their heads into the water and inhale it.' she said.

Jesus, thought Iska.

'Are you having second thoughts?' Nirewa's face held no emotion.

'No, we're not,' said Amen, her voice as steely as her face. 'I'll go first.'

Already on her knees, Amen crawled to the basin and peered into the crimson water.

'You can close your eyes, but make sure you breathe in the water,' said Nirewa. 'It will hurt only for a brief moment.'

For a few seconds, a deafening silence filled the room,

and it felt as though the entire village had paused its celebration to witness this forbidden moment. Not wanting to prolong the ritual, Amen held her breath and dunked her head into the water. Her natural reflexes rebelled, but she managed to inhale just enough of the liquid to feel a sharp pain pierce her brain.

Iska, who repeated the process soon after her sister, quickly returned to her seat while struggling to prevent the red liquid running down her face from dripping onto her white dress.

'Nirewa, what happens next?' Oshu's anxious voice filled the quiet room.

'We wait. Any moment from now, they should begin to have visions.'

But nothing happened. There were no visions, no recollections, no prophecy—nothing. A few more minutes passed before it became evident to everyone in the room that the ritual hadn't been successful.

'We can try again.' Iska tried to steady her trembling voice. 'Maybe if we—'

'Once is always enough, Iska,' Jimba said solemnly. 'I know you're eager, but submerging your head into that water again won't change anything. I know this because I was once in your shoes.'

'Jimba, there's no need to—'

'It's fine, Mama,' Jimba politely interrupted Nirewa. 'I've long made peace with my past. You see, when my wife died, I fell into a depression that could have easily ended my own life. I was lost and hopeless, neglecting my duties, my people, and my daughters.

'Nirewa pitied my plight and decided to help me find peace of mind by performing this same ritual, just so I could talk to my sweet Kyellu one more time. Just like tonight, it didn't work for me. I performed the ritual over and over again, each time with no results. Each time, I grew more frustrated, as you are now. But, you see, the failure of those rituals freed me.'

'How?' Amen's voice was barely audible.

'It helped me realise that Kyellu had moved on, and she needed me to do the same. Sometimes the departed don't want to be disturbed, no matter how much we miss them. I know this is painful for both of you, but you can see this as a sign that your mother is at peace and that she wants you two to move on.' Jimba explained.

As heartbreaking as Jimba's words were, Amen and Iska didn't need anyone to tell them everything he had just said was most likely true. That didn't make it any less bitter. Jimba whisking away the basin was the final confirmation that they would never get the chance to see what truly happened to Aré, to help identify her killer, to find some sort of closure.

They didn't blame Oshu or Nirewa—or anyone, for that matter—for the false hope they had been fed, but Iska and Amen no longer wanted to be around any of them. It had been a difficult day in every sense of the word. All the twins wanted, as they retreated to their room, was to go to bed and try, if only for a few hours, to numb their pain.

On any other night, the celebration raging in the square would have been far too loud to allow either of them to fall asleep. But tonight, the noise travelling through the village did nothing to stop Iska and Amen from slipping into a deep slumber.

The repeated click of boot heels on the wooden floor was the only sound resonating through the silence, and it bothered Amen. Who was the stranger disrupting the serenity of this room? A room that bore a disconcerting resemblance to the hallway of their old house at Sixty-Nine Fenton Green Street, Kilcock. Amen was mere inches away from touching the familiar pastel cream wall to her left, to find out if it was real or a figment of her imagination, when the footsteps she had heard earlier drew near once again.

Amen's first instinct was to hide, but fear froze her muscles as the faceless figure came into view. Trying to appear bolder than she really felt, Amen quickly decided that she would confront the stranger by demanding to know their identity and their reason for being in what appeared to be her family home. But before she could utter a word, the figure abruptly turned on their heel and headed towards the kitchen.

Puzzled and afraid, Amen reluctantly followed the mysterious person dressed in dark clothing. She watched the figure, who moved with the grace of a woman, systematically rummage through their cupboards and pantry. Unsatisfied with her search, the stranger exited the kitchen, with Amen trailing closely behind.

The moment they entered the living room, all the questions plaguing Amen were instantly answered. As she had suspected earlier, the events unfolding before her eyes were not real life but neither were they a dream. It was easier to sum this place up as the intersection of both: a trance. Amen had slipped into the trance Nirewa had attempted to put her and Iska into.

But she didn't want to be here, watching her mother beg for mercy while this faceless intruder drained the life from her with each touch. Amen desperately tried to make it stop, to push the faceless woman off Aré, but she couldn't get close enough to change what had already happened so many years ago.

'—Thank you for finding me—'

A deep, frightening voice echoed all around Amen.

'—Thank you—' it repeated, as a pair of hands forcefully tugged at her shoulders from behind. Just as she was being strangled, Amen jolted upright in her bed and turned to her left to see Iska panting heavily and staring wide-eyed.

14. ENGLAND

'And in your dream, Iska, what happened?' asked Ada as she picked up withered leaves and empty calabash gourds from the ground. The sun had barely reached its peak in the sky, yet more than half of the village was already out, cleaning up the mess left behind after the festival.

'You mean nightmare,' Iska corrected. 'I don't know how I ended up there, but I found myself on a cliff overlooking the sea. At first, the weather was warm and bright. Then, suddenly, everything changed. A storm came out of nowhere and brought this freezing cold with it…

'As if that wasn't bad enough, I noticed three dark-suited figures approaching me from a distance. At first they were walking, then they started running. It seemed like they were out to hurt me, so I ran in the opposite direction. I tried to scream for help, but my voice was gone, as if I was in a vacuum—'

'—That's exactly how I felt too.' Even now, Amen couldn't stop her hands from trembling.

'What happened next?' said Oshu, fully engrossed in Amen and Iska's story.

'The three figures were closing in on me,' Iska continued. 'So, I ran into some woods to try to lose them, but that didn't work. I could still hear them trailing after me; they weren't far behind. Just as I was trying to decide which way to go next, I was tackled to the ground by one of the strangers. The others were nearby when the one who had me pinned to the ground whispered something into my ear; that's when I woke up to see Amen drenched in sweat…'

Iska had almost forgotten they were in the middle of a chore and fell silent as other villagers passed by with their baskets of dirt.

'I'll be honest,' said Oshu once they were alone again.

'I'm struggling to find a meaning behind your dreams.'

'Iska,' said Lake. 'In your dream, on the cliff, was there a tower nearby?'

'No,' Iska replied, still searching her memory. 'I don't think I saw any. Why?'

'Oh, nothing. The only cliff I know of in Ireland is the Cliffs of Moher; I thought maybe that was where you were… You never said what the stranger whispered to you.'

'Oh yeah, I nearly forgot about that,' said Iska. 'It sounded like a woman, and I think she whispered a name; something Bailey—Rupert Bailey! That was the name she said to me before I woke up.'

'Well, I give up,' said Oshu, as he raked the last pieces of litter scattered around. 'We might have to go to Nirewa and see if she can help us understand these messages—'

'I know who Rupert Bailey is,' Walé said abruptly. 'It took me a minute to remember, but as soon as Iska mentioned the name, I was sure I knew it. He's the Senior Professor of Humanities at the University of Nottingham.'

'How do you know this?' Ada asked sceptically. 'And why are you so sure he's the same person mentioned in Iska's dream?'

'This is going to sound bizarre,' Walé began. 'But last semester, we had him over at Durham to give a seminar to first-year humanities students on the evolution of the human race through the ages. Before he began his talk, he made a statement about how he had searched all the English names in circulation in the world, and he was the only one with the name "Rupert Bailey" in that combination. It was sort of a weird brag about how seriously he took his work.'

'It doesn't seem like much, but it's good enough for me,' Oshu said after a few seconds of silence. 'We've gotten our first lead. Now, we just need to decide when we want to follow it.'

Iska jumped to her feet. 'I'm ready to go.'

'What about you, Amen?' asked Oshu. 'Are you ready?'

Her response should have been straightforward, but

Amen found herself struggling to speak. 'I… I guess so.'

Oshu's eyes narrowed with curiosity. 'You don't seem sure; is everything okay?'

'Yes,' Amen replied. 'I'm ready whenever you are.'

But Iska was not at all convinced by Amen's response. *Hey, what's wrong?*

Nothing, I'm fine.

'All right, it's settled then,' said Oshu. 'Unless anyone has reservations, we'll leave Dogudu before end of the day. I suggest we meet up at the square in an hour and then go tell Nirewa we're leaving. It's only right.'

Between finishing up with their chores and taking a much-needed shower, the next hour passed by quickly. Amen and Iska found themselves in the square, waiting for the others. It was remarkable how tidy the field looked, considering its state just a few hours ago. It was also no surprise the village was quiet; Sundays in Dogudu were reserved for lounging. Besides, after the previous day's festivities and the morning clean-up, it made sense that most of the villagers were in-doors, catching up on some much-needed rest.

Apart from a few children playing around, the square was so empty that Iska and Amen easily spotted Oshu, Ada, and the boys finally approaching from a distance.

'What took you guys so long?' Iska said jokingly, though there was a hint of seriousness in her voice.

'Have either of you packed your bags?' Ada replied with a smile.

Iska smacked her forehead. 'Oh my gosh,' she said em-barrassedly. 'I didn't know we were supposed to do that now. Can we—'

'Don't worry about it,' said Oshu. 'You can pack after we see Nirewa.'

Walking through one of Dogudu's numerous pathways to Nirewa's shrine, Amen and Iska were filled with a bitter-sweet feeling as they passed by a mother breastfeeding her baby at the steps of their hut, a group of elderly men playing board games, and a woman captivating a bunch of kids with her stories.

I can't believe we've been in Dogudu for just a week, thought Iska.

I know, right? Feels like we've lived here a lifetime. It might have been tough at times, but I've actually enjoyed my time here.

Is that why you're reluctant to leave?

…*Yes,* Amen lied.

Despite all the window shades being fully drawn back, the shrine remained poorly lit—thanks largely to the thick, dark clouds that had slowly crept over the village in the past hour. Trying not to trip over anything as she fumbled about the gloomy room for a spot to stand, Iska was certain that if any person other than Nirewa inhabited it, they would have lit some candles to fight off the growing darkness. But since the oracle owned this space and was anything but normal, she was perfectly content with sifting through a basket of bean seeds in the dark while Iska, Amen, and the others bumbled around the shrine like a bunch of idiots.

The oracle began before anyone could speak. 'You two were able to see after all.'

Oshu's lips parted as if to ask the question that was on everyone's mind, but he thought better of it and remained quiet.

'And now you have come to tell me you are leaving.' Nirewa added.

It was hard to tell if Nirewa's words were a product of visions she'd had or simply common sense.

Oshu finally found his voice. 'We just want to thank you for everything—'

'Save all the gratitude, Oshu,' said Nirewa teasingly. 'You are speaking as if you are a guest, whereas you all are family. Family that will always be welcome home any time.'

Moved by Nirewa's statement, Oshu refrained from speaking but nodded in understanding. Throughout their stay in Dogudu, Oshu had carried himself with such poise that it was easy to forget how emotional it must have been for him to return here after so many years.

'And as for you two,' said Nirewa, finally picking herself off the altar and walking over to Iska and Amen. 'What can I say? You were deserving. I just hope that both of you can maintain and build on the courage you displayed during your time here... You'll need it. And remember that darkness will always vanish whenever light approaches.'

'Thank you,' said Amen and Iska quietly while Nirewa allowed a tiny smile.

With nothing more to be said, Iska, Amen, and the rest of the family quietly exited Nirewa's shrine. The sound of rain drumming hard on the roof of the tunnel signalled that they would have to hurry to their huts.

Despite how fast they had run, Iska and Amen were soaked by the time they reached their room, but they had no time to change clothes. Since they hadn't brought much with them to begin with, it only took the twins a few minutes to put away their belongings. They scanned the room one last time to make sure they weren't leaving anything behind; once they confirmed this, they left to meet up with the others in Ada and Oshu's hut. However, upon arriving at The Tellas' accommodation, Amen and Iska were shocked to see Zara, along with her little sister, Dami, and Jimba waiting for them.

'There they are,' Jimba's voice was audible despite the steady crash of thunder all through the village. 'Were you going to leave without saying goodbye?'

Amen and Iska let out an awkward laugh. 'How did you know?' said Iska.

'Have you forgotten I'm the protector of this village?' Jimba said with a wink. 'No one comes in or goes out without my knowledge. Now stop asking questions and come give your favourite uncle a hug.'

Even as Amen embraced Jimba, her gaze remained partially fixed on Zara, who reciprocated the gesture. Among all the emotions that flooded Amen, the most intense was anger; anger at not having an extra day to ask Zara questions, or to share that kiss. It was frustrating, almost tragically ironic, that the things she desired the most always seemed to be within reach but just out of her grasp. It had happened when Aré died, during the race, and now with Zara. These simple things, so close, yet *always so far away*.

What? thought Iska.

Nothing! Amen replied immediately. *Sorry, I was thinking out loud.*

Dami's voice quivered with sadness. 'I'll miss you all.' she said.

'Come on, Dami,' said Iska, cupping the little girl's chin. 'We'll visit soon, I promise. And next time, you better be ready because we won't let you beat us in a game of *isiso*.'

Dami giggled. 'I might go easy on yous next time.'

'Looks like someone is picking up new words,' said Jimba, lifting Dami off the floor before turning his gaze to his older daughter. 'Zara, do you have anything to add?'

Zara couldn't conceal her disappointment at being put on the spot. At this point, it was well known that the lightning girl was not much of a talker, but she had no choice now. 'We hope to see you soon.' she said sincerely and decisively.

'We won't take up anymore of your time,' said Jimba as he and the girls approached the front door. 'We wish you all a safe journey back home.'

The last Iska and Amen saw of the trio was Zara opening a wooden umbrella while Dami sat securely in Jimba's arms, just before the door finally closed behind them.

'Wait!' said Iska, as though having an epiphany. 'Isn't Jimba coming back to show us the way out of the village?'

'He's not,' said Ada, picking up her rucksack. 'Because we're not leaving the same way we came.'

Oshu nodded at the boys before the twins could ask any more questions. 'Remember what I told you, Aito?'

'We're blinking?' Amen's voice held a hint of worry.

'Of course, we're blinking!' Aito chuckled. 'And yes, I

remember, Oshu. You said to blink us to the living room on the first floor.'

'Grand,' Iska muttered sarcastically as she tightened the straps on her backpack.

'It can't be that bad.' Walé chimed in. 'I'm actually looking forward to it.'

'Until your first trip,' Lake retorted. 'Then you never want anything to do with it again.'

'All right, that's enough,' said Oshu, extending his arms out. 'Everyone, form a circle and hold hands. Aito, take your time visualising the room, and blink whenever you're ready.'

Despite the rain rumbling on, an uncomfortable silence filled the room as they anxiously waited for Aito to teleport them home. Even the grip with which Walé held Iska's hand showed that his earlier excitement at moving through space had vanished. Just as Iska was about to reassure Walé that he would be fine, they were suddenly plunged into a pool of water. As they resurfaced, their surroundings came into focus: the white building, the neatly trimmed hedges, the loungers—it was undeniable. They were back home in Lagos but not in the living room.

'Sorry,' said Aito, fighting the urge to laugh. 'I couldn't help myself; I've missed this pool.'

Although Aito's little prank was amusing, it didn't stop Oshu from cautioning him about the potential problems that blinking in front of the household staff could have caused. Luckily, nobody was home except for Roxie, who excitedly pounced on Ada. Aside from the footprints they were leaving on the floor, the house was as immaculate as the day they had left it. For the second time in one day, Iska and Amen were completely drenched. However, since they didn't have any immediate plans, they headed to their room to change into dry clothes.

'Did you notice the way Zara was looking at you in the hut?' asked Iska, tossing her wet clothes into the laundry hamper.

'Really?' Amen replied, making sure to mask her dishonesty. 'I didn't catch that.'

'It was weird.' Iska pulled on her tank top. 'It was as if she was trying to tell you something with her eyes. And it's not the first time she's done that. Last night, when she came to get us from the square, she gave you that same look. Did anything happen between you two during the race?'

Amen pretended to struggle with the neck of her dress to avoid making eye contact with Iska. 'Nothing I can remember.'

'Are you sure? You know you can tell me anything, Amen. I'm here for you.'

'I know you are,' Amen replied, her voice full of reassurance. 'There's nothing to tell.'

'If you say so. I'm probably just reading too much into it. Almost everything anyone does or says in Dogudu is cryptic. Like, what did Nirewa's speech about darkness and light mean?'

'That, I picked up on.' Amen admitted, taking a seat beside Iska on the edge of the bed.

'Do you think it has anything to do with Mam's killer?'

Amen pondered the question for a moment. 'I couldn't tell you, to be honest; could've been just some advice for all we know.'

'I hope it was,' Iska murmured absentmindedly. 'There was something about the way she said it that left me feeling uneasy—'

'Sorry to be a bother.' Walé's voice followed his quick knock on the door. 'But Ada and Oshu want you two downstairs.'

The gentle waft of music through the ceiling speakers served as a quick reminder to Amen and Iska that they were no longer in Dogudu. Not a single mat, wooden stool, or clay pot was in sight; it was as if that part of the world had never existed, yet it was undeniably real.

'I know we're all starving,' said Ada as Amen and Iska

approached the dining room. 'So, I took the liberty of ordering us a few things.'

'You call this "a few things"?' Iska eyed the boxes of food and snacks spread across the dining table.

'Come on, don't make me feel bad,' Ada replied, lowering the volume of the music with her watch. 'It's just three boxes of pizza; two southern fried chicken kebabs; two packs of bacon garlic cheese chips; a few double beef cheeseburgers for anyone who wants something different; and some milkshakes and iced teas. It really isn't that much considering the boys we have in—'

'Don't start without me!' Aito's voice echoed from across the hallway. 'Just let me get dressed; I'll be there soon!' The muffled sound of a door closing echoed through the house.

'Well, you heard the young man,' Oshu said with a chuckle from where he was sitting.

True to his word, Aito entered the dining room a few seconds later, with Lake and Walé joining shortly after. Ada's prediction about the takeaway being sufficient proved accurate. Barely fifteen minutes had passed since they sat down to eat, yet half of the food on the table had already disappeared. It wasn't only the boys who devoured most of the food; Amen and Iska had also underestimated their hunger as they eagerly opened the third box of pizza.

'Now that we're all fed,' said Oshu, resting his chin on his interlocked hands. 'Let's discuss the next steps we need to take in figuring out Professor Bailey's involvement in Aré's murder. And Walé, you were right about him being the only person with that name combination in the world. I ran multiple searches through a database management application, and only his name came up each time. Ada also did some digging and found out that he's currently in Nottingham, so we need to act quickly—'

'How—But when—' said Amen, interrupting Oshu.

'We only just got back a little over an hour ago,' Iska voiced Amen's thoughts. 'When did you manage to do all of this?'

Ada and Oshu politely ignored Iska's question, responding with a smile.

'I know we just got back from Dogudu,' Oshu continued. 'But Ada and I think it would be best if we leave for London by Tuesday. That way, we can get a head start on tracking down the professor.'

'The question, as always,' said Ada, looking directly at Amen and Iska. 'Is whether you two are up for it.'

'I mean, we've come this far,' Iska replied without hesitation. 'There's no point in slowing down now.'

'As long as the boys are okay with it,' Amen added thoughtfully.

Lake looked up from the milkshake he'd been slurping. 'I'm ready to go.'

'So am I,' Walé added.

'Same here,' Aito chimed in. 'Oshu, whenever you're ready, show me photos of where we're going. I promise no more pranks.'

Oshu chuckled. 'You're fine, Aito. You don't have to worry about blinking us to England; Zikora will take us there.'

'Who's Zikora?' Iska asked, her mouth full of pizza.

'Our private jet,' Ada answered with a wink. 'You'll love her.'

'That reminds me,' said Oshu, completely oblivious to the incredulity on Amen, Iska, and Aito's faces. 'I'll need some details from the four of you. You'll need travel documents.'

The entire morning had felt like déjà vu with all the prepping and packing. In fact, Amen and Iska would have been convinced they were returning to Dogudu if they had seen the Jet Mover in the driveway. Instead, they were on their way to the airport to catch their 6 p.m. flight out of Lagos. Although most of the drive to the airport had been a blur for Iska and Amen, the realisation that they would be boarding an airplane for the first time in their lives suddenly made them very alert. As they drove through the tunnel leading to the airport's departure building, the twins found themselves preferring the idea of blinking to getting on a plane. But it was too late to back out; the convoy had come to a stop, and through the car windows, Iska and Amen could see Oshu's security guards opening the doors.

It didn't matter that it was a Tuesday evening; Murtala Muhammed airport was bustling with people going in various directions, much like the first time Iska and Amen had blinked there. Fortunately, they didn't have to navigate through the crowd themselves. The security guards formed a human force field around them, swiftly guiding them through the airport. Within minutes, Amen, Iska, and the others reached the customs area, where they underwent a thorough frisking to check for contraband. Next, they boarded a shuttle bus that took them on a ten-minute drive from the departure building to a magnificent airplane, standing alone on the tarmac—Zikora was even more impressive than Walé had described it the day before.

'Leave them,' Oshu said to Iska and Amen when they tried to grab their bags. 'The aircraft crew will stow them into the cargo hold; come with me.'

Beside the steps leading up to the entrance of the white jet, a stewardess and steward stood with beaming smiles. 'Good evening, Mr and Mrs Tella. Welcome back on board!' they greeted, their voices rising above the purring engines of the jet. As soon as they stepped through the aircraft's door, Amen and Iska's fears momentarily dissipated. Everything about the interior of the plane was designed to cater to the human desire for convenience, from the matt-finished oak desks and drawers to the sleek white leather seats.

'So, girls,' said Ada, settling herself onto a black and white chequered couch positioned to the left of the main cabin. 'What do you think of Zikora?'

'She's gorgeous!' Amen and Iska said in unison as they scrutinised the touchscreens embedded in the cabin's wall panels.

'Of course, she is,' Ada laughed. 'I designed her myself.'

'I didn't know you were an interior decorator,' said Amen as she toggled a digital switch that changed one of the cabin's windows from curtain dark to completely transparent.

'An expensive one at that,' Oshu appeared out of nowhere with two glasses of champagne in his hands. 'The invoice her company sent to me when Zikora was finished cost a fortune.'

'You'd think he wasn't a multimillionaire,' said Ada, rolling her eyes as she took one of the glasses from Oshu.

'I wouldn't have become one if I were a spendthrift.' Oshu quickly retorted.

Ada opened her mouth, then closed it. A smile full of humour grew on her lips. 'I was going to say comfort doesn't come cheap, but Dogudu has shown us otherwise, hasn't it?'

'Cheers to that.' Oshu clinked glasses with Ada.

'Girls!' Aito called from deep within the cabin, interrupting Iska and Amen's laughter at the banter between Ada and Oshu. 'Yous need to come see this!'

But before the twins could join Aito, a uniformed man, who was undoubtedly one of Zikora's pilots for the evening, entered the cabin. 'Good evening, Mr and Mrs Tella,' he said with the assurance of someone who had done this many times before. 'Zikora will be taking off in five minutes. Captain Obiora would like for everyone to take their seats and strap in. Estimated time of arrival at Heathrow airport is midnight.'

'Thank you, Captain Robert,' said Oshu, eliciting a courteous smile from the co-pilot as he exited the cabin. 'Aito, whatever you want to show the girls will have to wait until we're airborne. For now, please tell the boys to come get seated.'

All of a sudden, the anxiety returned. Amen and Iska strapped themselves into their seats but wished they had more belts to fasten. In contrast, everyone else, including Aito and Lake, seemed relaxed, which not only made Iska and Amen scared but also self-conscious. Ada, seated nearby, kept casting reassuring glances their way, conveying her support through her eyes. However, despite their appreciation, Ada's gesture did little to calm Amen and Iska as Zikora surged forward, picking up speed on the runway. Initially, there was a low rumble, followed by vibrations that reverberated through the cabin; then, the aircraft began its gradual ascent.

After a few ear pops and Zikora soaring silently through the sky, Iska and Amen began to feel somewhat at ease. Moments earlier, a chime had signalled that passengers were free to move about the cabin, and to the twins' surprise, the steward and stewardess from earlier reappeared, offering drinks, food, and various other items. A few hours into the flight, Iska felt confident enough to explore the plane and see what Aito had wanted to show her earlier. On the other hand, Amen was determined to remain seated. However, just as Iska and the others disappeared towards the back of the plane, Ada took the seat opposite Amen.

'I give you my word,' said Ada. 'The plane isn't going to fall out of the sky; you're perfectly safe.'

'I believe you,' said Amen, glancing at the dark skies through the window. 'It's just interesting watching the earth go by from this view. Besides, I know it's either a bar or something fancy that's back there.'

Ada chuckled. 'To be honest, it's just rooms to sleep in. But aren't you curious to see what they look like?'

'Not really.'

'Alrighty then,' said Ada, lifting herself off the chair. 'I just wanted to make sure—'

'There is one thing I'm curious about though,' said Amen, fighting the smile growing at the corners of her mouth.

Ada fell back into her seat. 'What would that be?'

'It's silly—'

'No, go on,' Ada encouraged in a teasing tone. 'You can't stop now.'

'I just wonder if your kids, when you have them, will be Cruthers like you and Oshu, or if they'll have different abilities.'

Ada mulled over the question for a moment before responding. 'As you know, having Unix for parents doesn't guarantee a child any abilities. That being said, it would be nice to have children who end up with me or Oshu's talents. It would also be nice if I could actually have them.'

Just as Amen gasped at Ada's statement, Iska walked back into the main cabin. However, upon seeing Ada in her seat, engaged in what seemed like a serious conversation with Amen, Iska decided to join Oshu where he was seated.

'What do you think?' Oshu asked, tapping at a tablet in his left hand.

Iska scanned the cabin one more time. 'It looks like a spaceship back there. I don't think I can ever get used to this.'

Oshu finally looked away from his tablet. 'You will, soon enough,' he said matter-of-factly.

Not wanting Oshu's response to make her feel embarrassed, Iska chose to change the subject. 'I know you said my mam cut you out of her life, but it's hard to believe that was the only reason you stayed away. You could have easily come to Ireland to see her, couldn't you?'

'Yes, I could have.' Oshu slid his tablet into a special pocket sewn onto the wall and looked back up at Iska.

'Then why didn't you?'

Sighing, Oshu leaned back in his chair. 'It would be easy to put all the blame on my ego or arrogance, but mostly it was blind ambition. I was so consumed with my start-up at the time that everything in my life took a backseat. On more than one occasion, I nearly lost Ada too.

'But you know what? Your mother's passing was a wakeup call for me. Suddenly, none of it mattered as much—the money, the wealth. What good was any of it if it couldn't be used to make more time for the ones we care for the most? Shortly after Nikki's visit, I stepped down from my role as CEO of the company and decided I was going to use every resource I had accumulated to help people in need, and spend more time with my happy place.'

While Iska was still processing Oshu's words, another question arose in her mind. 'When Aunt Nikki told you about our mam's death, did she mention anything about our dad?' she asked. But just as Oshu was about to respond, the airplane encountered some turbulence.

15. BOOK OF CLANS

Within seconds, the stewardess was scrambling around the cabin, trying to get everyone seated and strapped in. According to her, the plane had just entered an unexpected storm, and the pilots were working hard to get out of it.

Amidst the turbulence, numerous questions raced through Iska's mind but none was as crucial as the one she had just asked her uncle. 'What were you going to say?' she inquired, her eyes fixed on Oshu, who was intently observing the skies.

'I'm sorry,' said Oshu, finally tearing his gaze away from the window. 'It just doesn't seem like we're in a storm. Anyway, yes, Nikki did mention your father, but only after I pressed for information. Unfortunately, the details she provided weren't particularly useful.'

Despite Zikora continuing to shudder and surge forward, Iska persisted with her questions. 'What did she tell you about him?' she asked.

'Only that he left your mother just before you and your sister were born. She said she hadn't known him well because he was hardly ever around. Anyway, after Nikki's visit, I tried to search for him, but he seemed to have disappeared without a trace.'

'Why didn't you tell us earlier?' said Iska, her voice a mix of curiosity and frustration.

'What difference would it have made?' said Oshu, returning his gaze to the skies as the pressure on Zikora intensified. 'I was right about him, though. I'm sorry, but I always had this gut feeling he was a coward, unwilling to take responsibility for anything. I mean, what kind of man abandons his unborn children? I hope he continues to hide under his little rock because if I find him—'

Iska couldn't tell whether Oshu had stopped talking because the seatbelt signs had turned off or because her eyes had filled with tears.

The worst of the turbulence appeared to have passed as the aircraft slowly steadied itself, while the captain announced over the intercom that they would be arriving in London in half an hour.

Before long, the lights from Heathrow Airport flickered past as Zikora smoothly glided along the runway, eventually coming to a stop near one of the airport's hangars away from where the commercial aircraft were being prepared for departure. As Iska and Amen disembarked from Zikora, their luggage was already being loaded into the boots of three cars. Meanwhile, a couple of customs officers and the pilots were engaged in conversation at the base of the passenger steps. It turned out the officers were there, at the Tellas' request, to inspect their travel documents away from the airport crowd. Once the inspection was completed, the family hurried to the cars because despite it being summer, the night was overly chilly.

The streets of London at 1 a.m. on a Wednesday mirrored the atmosphere inside Amen and Iska's car: lethargic and silent. After a thirty-minute drive through a series of tunnels and roundabouts, the convoy of cars came to a halt in front of a white stuccoed townhouse nestled in a row of similar-looking houses. Unbeknownst to Iska and Amen, exhaustion had given way to amazement as they ventured deeper into the house; the blend of Victorian architecture with modern furnishing left them pondering whether Ada had also been involved in the design of their Belgravia home.

'I'll give you all a proper tour later in the day.' Oshu's voice echoed from the main living room. 'Right now, we all need to get some rest.'

Although the two velvet bathrobes resting on the king-sized canopy bed instantly caught Iska and Amen's attention, it was the decor of their new room that left them open-mouthed. Of all the rooms they had slept in, this one, with its symmetrically spaced furniture, rococo art pieces, and hypnotic lighting, was easily the most elegant.

At the very end of the room, their belongings had been neatly arranged on a seat underneath a window that over-looked the estate. The fatigue from earlier had returned, but Amen and Iska figured a quick shower would help, even if it meant sifting through their bags for pyjamas to sleep in.

'What's that?' said Amen, pointing to the block of parchment Iska was pulling out of her backpack.

'Oh, it's the scrolls and books Nirewa gave to us in Dogudu,' Iska replied.

Amen palmed her forehead. 'Leave it to my sister to steal the sacred teachings of a village.'

'Hey, I didn't steal it,' said Iska, setting the package aside. 'I'm borrowing it. Besides, Nirewa never said anything about giving it back.'

'Why do you even want this stuff?' said Amen.

'Really?' Iska frowned.

'You know that's not what I meant.'

'Mhmm, I'm sure that's not what you meant,' said Iska sarcastically. 'First off, you should be thanking me. There's still so much you can learn from these; I brought them spe-cifically for you. And yes, I'll read them as well; just because I don't have abilities doesn't mean I can't know more about what we are.'

'Iska,' Amen said after an awkward silence. 'Thank you, I—'

Iska rolled her eyes, but she couldn't stop her small smile as she headed towards the bathroom. 'Yeah, yeah. I know you didn't mean it like that.'

Amen and Iska were awakened by the sound of the inter-com in their room. Since Amen was closer to it, she reached for the receiver.

'We're about to have brunch,' said the voice on the other end of the line. 'Please come downstairs; the kitchen is the third room to the right along the hallway.'

As usual, Iska and Amen were running late, finding the rest of the family already seated around an ornate dining table.

'What time is it?' said Iska, pulling out one of the two empty chairs from under the table.

'It's half-past one,' Ada replied.

'Oh my gosh, we're sorry,' said Amen, helping herself to some slices of pancake. 'We overslept—'

'You're fine,' said Oshu. 'You all deserved a good sleep-in, and you have the chance to get even more rest because there's good news.'

'And some bad news,' Ada added almost immediately. 'Which do you want to hear first?'

I'm too nervous, thought Amen. *Please choose.*

'The good news,' said Iska, trying her best to conceal her own nervousness.

'Good choice,' said Ada, setting her glass of orange juice on the table. 'So, we were able to contact the University of Nottingham, and as we speak, Professor Bailey is on the grounds.'

Amen and Iska would have felt elated if they didn't have to brace themselves for the not-so-pleasant news that was about to follow.

'But when we reached out to him,' said Oshu, 'he declined to have a meeting with us, now or in the future.'

This new piece of information rendered the previous one inconsequential. What was the point of the professor being in England if he could not grant them an audience?

'But did you try—'

'He was adamant, Iska,' Ada interrupted. 'At the end of the day, he's entitled to do as he pleases, and there's nothing we can do about it. Having said that, Oshu and I will work hard to make something happen, so lift your heads up. Finish your food and get as much rest as you can; or better yet, I'll arrange for all of you to be taken around town. After all, this is your first time in London; honestly, it will help.'

But it didn't help. In fact, nothing did. Not the trip to the London Eye, nor visiting Madame Tussauds, nor the walk around Trafalgar Square. If anything, Amen and Iska's anxiety only heightened as the minutes ticked away. Now, on their way back to the house, they hoped for something positive from Oshu and Ada—anything other than that would completely devastate them.

Iska and Amen arrived back at the house to meet the Tellas in the living room, working away at their laptops and tablets while a record player in the corner filled the room with soothing jazz music.

'How was your—' Oshu began, but Iska interrupted him before he could finish his sentence.

'—Any new info about the professor?'

'Please take a seat, all of you,' Oshu said with a slight smile, waving everyone into the room.

'I'm sorry, Oshu,' said Iska, realising her forwardness. She knew, better than anyone, that her uncle and his wife's willingness to help was an act of kindness, not an obligation. 'We've just been worried all day.'

'I understand how you feel,' Oshu replied. 'In fact, it's because of this understanding that Ada and I were able to secure a meeting with the professor for both of you.'

Amen and Iska wouldn't have believed Oshu's words if Ada wasn't beaming with joy.

'You guys are just the best,' Amen said with relief.

'Thank you,' Iska added gratefully.

'Don't thank us just yet,' Ada chimed in. 'There's a slight snag. The meeting is scheduled for twelve p.m. tomorrow, but Oshu and I can't come with you. Unfortunately, some pressing issues came up at the last minute, and we can't back out of it.'

Oshu stood up from his seat and walked over to a shelf where he picked up a white envelope. 'We're really sorry we can't come along, but I believe you two are capable of taking this trip,' he said. 'And you won't be alone. Now, anyone except for Walé can opt out; but I bought train tickets for the boys as well, just in case they decide they want to accompany you on the trip. Ada has also booked a couple of rooms at the Jurys Inn in Nottingham, and there's an Airbnb option if you prefer that instead.'

'We're in,' said Aito, while Lake went over to Oshu to collect the tickets.

Iska and Amen had long accepted that they would never fully understand why Lake and Aito were so supportive, but they felt nothing but gratitude for these boys who consistently stood by their side, no matter the circumstance.

'Why don't I have a choice?' said Walé, hopelessly failing at pretending that he was not pleased to get more time with Iska.

'Because, as I learnt from Ada a few hours ago,' said Oshu as he returned to his seat. 'You took a tour of the university when you were checking out colleges last summer, you know the grounds to an extent; you'll be their guide.'

Walé's silence after Oshu's explanation showed he was happy with the arrangement, prompting Ada to stand up from her chair. 'Now that that's all sorted out, can we get started on dinner?'

'I have a question,' said Amen, also getting up from her seat. 'What do we say to the professor when we meet him?'

Amen's question had the unintended effect of keeping everyone quiet until Oshu finally cleared his throat. 'I know this isn't of much help, but the right questions will come to you at the right moment. Trust me.'

They had to wake up early the next morning to catch their 8 a.m. train from St. Pancras railway station. Fortunately, the light traffic had allowed Amen, Iska, and the boys to reach their carriage on time and squeeze in a quick nap. Now, an hour into the journey, Amen and Iska still couldn't help but admire their private carriage. Their most vivid memory of being on a train was the sombre ride from Kilcock to Howth following Aré's death. It had been a cold and depressing journey, and the dilapidated state of that carriage had been nothing like the one that was now slowing to a stop at Nottingham station.

'There's not much time left,' said Walé as soon as they disembarked the train. 'We have about forty-five minutes to get to the professor's office. He's known for not tolerating lateness; let's not give him a reason to call off the meeting.'

The meeting getting cancelled was not an option for Iska and Amen, not after everything they had been through; the race was on. Finding a taxi was relatively straightforward, but getting to the college grounds proved to be an obstacle. Of all the days for a marathon to take place in Nottingham, it had to be the day they were racing against time. After twenty-five minutes in the cab, Amen, Iska, and the boys had made some progress. But heavy traffic, coupled with a crowd of marathon spectators blocking the south entrance of the university, meant they needed a miracle to get through.

'What do we do now?' said Iska, already considering the option of getting out of the taxi and making a run for it.

'I can get us in,' whispered Aito. 'At least close enough to that lake beyond the entrance.'

'Are you insane?' said Amen, 'There are people—'

'Time's running out,' Walé interrupted. 'Unless you want us to spend all day here, Aito's suggestion is our best and only option.'

'What about...' Amen nodded her head towards the taxi driver.

'We need to distract him,' Lake said through clenched teeth.

'I have an idea,' said Iska, as she searched her pocket for something. 'Everyone, grab your bags and hold hands; Aito, you know what to do.'

'Really crazy traffic today, isn't it?' Iska said to the taxi driver as she casually placed two fifty-pound notes on the car's dashboard.

'I know!' the taxi driver replied enthusiastically. 'It's because of the Robin Hood Marathon; I dread this time of the year, even though the race is for a good cause.'

'I guess so, but why are those runners going in that direction?' said Iska, pointing to the taxi driver's right-hand side. As soon as the taxi driver turned his head, Iska, Amen, and the boys found themselves by the bank of the lake that Aito had pointed out earlier, gasping for air. With only a few confused faces peering at them, Iska, Amen, and the boys were fortunate to not have raised any suspicions as they frantically made their way into the university.

With ten minutes remaining, they decided to forgo the college's maps and instead asked random strangers for the location of Professor Bailey's office. Fortunately, one passer-by knew and explained that it was in the western block of a building called the Trent Building, which was approximately eight minutes away.

Perplexed heads turned towards Iska and Amen as they sprinted along the banks of the lake in a bid to reach the building. But with only three and a half minutes left, they didn't have time to care what people thought. Finally inside the building, Iska, Amen and the boys raced up a flight of stairs and hurried through a hallway, confident that they had found the professor's office. However, upon opening the front door, they were greeted by an empty lecture room. Realising they had mistaken the blocks, Amen and Iska, and the boys sprinted in the opposite direction, finally stopping in front of what they hoped was the right office.

Upon opening the door, they found themselves face to face with a middle-aged man, sporting a head full of long, silvery hair. He was settling into his seat behind a desk cluttered with stacks of papers, a telephone, and a name plate that read: *Professor R. Bailey*. 'You'd think the people who wanted to meet so badly would arrive on time,' the man said with a hint of annoyance.

'With all due respect, Professor,' said Walé, clearly irritated by the man's statement. 'Finding your office would have been easier if proper directions were provided. Besides, we are on time.'

Walé was correct. They had managed to make it to the professor's office, albeit with only a few seconds left on the clock.

'Well, you have my undivided attention for the next thirty minutes; what is it that you want?' said Professor Bailey.

Perhaps due to the exertion of their recent sprint or the professor's intimidating demeanour, neither Iska nor Amen knew exactly how to proceed—Oshu's prediction wasn't unfolding as expected.

'Do—Do you know anything about Aré Tella?' Iska finally asked.

'What?' said Professor Bailey, genuinely confused.

'Or her death?' Amen added.

'Her death,' Professor Bailey repeated, letting out a sardonic laugh. 'So, you mean to tell me you impudent kids had—God knows who—buy out my entire department, not to mention my precious time, to ask me questions about some insignificant person I have never heard of.'

'Who happens to be our mother,' Iska added defensively.

'I couldn't care less if she was your guardian angel,' said Professor Bailey, his voice getting more aggressive with each word. 'You spoilt, deluded children thought it best to waste precious resources monopolising my time! I should have all of you thrown out of my office, and you know what? I will.'

But just as Professor Bailey began punching the dial pad of the telephone on his desk, Aito blinked right beside him and disconnected the line. 'I'm sorry, Professor, but we've come a long way to talk to you. The least you can do is answer our questions.'

Although Aito's gesture was appreciated, he had just broken Aunt Nikki's rule for the second time in one day. Only this time, they were all still in front of the human, whose reaction to seeing a teenager teleport in front of him did not match their expectations.

'I didn't know you all were Unix,' said Professor Bailey in a shaky but calm voice.

'Yes, we are,' said Amen, not wanting their newfound leverage to slip away. 'Are you one of us?'

'No, no,' said Professor Bailey, still eyeing Aito. 'I've just had encounters with a few others like you. In fact, it is my past encounter with one Unix in particular that's made me averse to meetings.'

'Let's start from there,' Lake said unexpectedly. 'Who was that and what did they want from you?'

'I—I'm afraid I can't divulge that information.'

'Professor,' said Amen as casually weaved intricate patterns in the air with both her hands. 'Do you know what my ability is?'

Amen, what are you—

Shh!

'I can manipulate the elements,' Amen continued.

'You're a Telemin?' said Professor Bailey.

'That's correct, Professor,' Amen replied. 'Why don't you take a look out your window.'

Just as the professor was getting out of his seat, an animated crowd right outside the Trent building could be heard reacting to some sort of spectacle. Out of curiosity, Aito, Lake, Iska, and Walé joined Professor Bailey by the window to see what all the commotion was about. And there it was, ripples spreading repeatedly across the university's lake.

'Are you the one doing that?' said Professor Bailey, his gaze alternating between the lake and Amen.

'Yes,' Amen replied, bringing the lake to a rest. 'Now imagine what I could do to you with the bottles of water behind your desk.'

The others couldn't tell if Amen was bluffing, but they all moved away from the professor as a precaution.

'I usually don't respond well to threats,' said Professor Bailey. 'But after what Mr Cormac did to me, I'd rather not take my chances. He made me swear not to tell any other soul, or he would come for me. However, at this rate I don't think it matters anymore; we're all doomed anyway.'

'What did he make you swear not to tell?' said Iska, not understanding what the professor was going on about.

'That he obtained the Book of Clans from me.'

'What's that?' Aito asked.

'A codex,' Lake chimed in. 'That supposedly contains all the information regarding the most powerful Unix clans all across Europe from hundreds of years ago.'

'Chap, how do you know this stuff?' said Aito.

'You really should listen to Marius when he's speaking,' Lake replied before returning his attention to the professor. 'But I thought the book was a myth? That was what we were told.'

'Oh, I assure you,' said Professor Bailey, walking over to a large bookshelf at the end of his office. 'It is not a myth.'

He returned to his desk with an old-looking piece of cloth, which he unfolded to reveal labyrinthine drawings. 'My great-grandfather and his forefathers, all the way back to the High Middle Ages, or the twelfth century as it is commonly known today, recorded, compiled, and watched over the Book of Clans. Although they were never gifted themselves, they mingled with your kind long enough to be allowed to make the codex, which was entrusted to me by my late father.'

Aito tutted. 'Professor, I'm sorry to say this but your father would be rolling in his grave if he knew what you did to the book.'

'I didn't have a choice.'

'Professor,' said Lake, still analysing the drawings in the cloth. 'Why, exactly, did this man want the book?'

'I don't know, but I can tell you he didn't take it so he could do a bit of light reading. Look, Mr Cormac is a very dangerous man who will stop at nothing to get what he wants. If you take self-preservation seriously, I suggest you stop looking for him.'

'We weren't,' said Iska, a disappointed frown etched on

her face. 'Thank you for your time, Professor Bailey.'

For obvious reasons, the atmosphere in the car as they drove to their Airbnb was heavy with silence and disappointment. Iska and Amen had journeyed all the way to Nottingham in search of answers, and while they had stumbled upon new information, it brought them no closer to figuring out what really happened to their mother.

Still wallowing in despair by evening, Amen and Iska barely touched the chicken tikka masala Walé had ordered for them, choosing to sit in silence and stare into space instead. Perhaps moved to cheer them up or simply put off by the twins' self-pity, Aito suggested watching a movie. At first, his suggestion was met with indifference, but after some pleading and coaxing, Aito was able to gather everyone in front of the TV; everyone except for Iska, who insisted she wanted to be by herself. In fact, she had only just gotten into bed when someone knocked on her bedroom door.

'Didn't mean to disturb,' it was Walé. 'Just wanted to remind you our train's at eleven a.m. tomorrow.'

'Thanks; you do know you can come in, right?'

'I know,' said Walé, walking into the room. 'I'm just trying to give you some space. How are you holding up?'

'I don't know; confused,' said Iska, sitting upright. 'Disappointed, exhausted...'

Walé joined Iska on the bed. 'It's okay to feel those things. You know, I only went on the trip to Dogudu because I wanted to spend more time with you; entirely selfish interest. But after seeing all that you and Amen have been through just to get a glimpse of what happened to your mother, the bravery alone to do that, I'm rooting for you. I hope Oshu can help. I hope we can *all* help find who murdered your mum. Both of you deserve that closure, you really do.'

'It's funny you mentioned the word selfish,' said Iska, snuggling herself under Walé's right arm. 'Most of the time, that's how I feel. There are people—friends of mine back home—who are in the same position as Amen and me; I don't think they've done half the things we have just to feel somehow closer to our mam. Sometimes I feel we should just let it go and move on.'

'Hey, you don't know what your friends do. People process things differently. Just because you're looking for answers doesn't make you selfish. Don't apologise for going after what you want.'

Iska wanted to say something to thank Walé for supporting them, for being by her side. Instead, she leaned in for a kiss, and thankfully, this gesture was reciprocated by Walé.

'Speaking of going after wants,' said Walé as he pulled away from Iska. 'I have a request to make.'

'Oh, you wish!' Iska said with a laugh.

'No, no, not that,' Walé was laughing too. 'I was just wondering, why does it have to end this summer? I mean, if we both like each other—'

'Will you get to the point?' Iska said jokingly, but with a hint of seriousness.

'Okay, okay. I would like for you to come to Durham University. They have a good computer science programme; it's a good city, and you'll be closer to me. I mean, you don't have to do it, I'll understand. You probably have your own plans—'

'Shut up, Walé,' Iska said for the third time, this time placing her finger on his lips. 'What's the food in Durham like?'

Iska could tell from Walé's expression that he hadn't expected her to respond the way she did; neither had she, in all fairness.

'It's no jollof rice,' said Walé, trying to contain his excitement. 'But I promise you'll love the fish and chips. Thank you—'

'Hey, relax, I haven't said yes yet. My mind's about seventy-five percent made up; I just have to speak to Amen about it.'

'Speak to me about what?' said Amen as she walked into the room.

'Oh, just this trip Walé has planned for next summer,' Iska lied, suddenly worried her sister might have overheard her conversation with Walé.

'Walé, you take "planning ahead" to the next level,' said Amen, as she took a seat at the end of Iska's bed. 'I didn't mean to bother yous; I just couldn't concentrate on the film Aito put on. Leave it to him to make us watch kids fight to the death for their survival—'

Walé burst out laughing before Amen could even finish her sentence. 'Hey, *The Hunger Games* is a classic.'

'*No*, it's barbaric,' Amen retorted. 'Anyways, that's not why I'm here. I just used the tablet our hosts left us to check my email inbox, and I haven't received any messages from Rima. I think it's time to head back home, Iska. We've been gone for too long; I'm starting to get worried.'

'Why the panic, though?' said Iska. 'You don't know, maybe she sent *me* an email.'

'That's the thing,' said Amen, twiddling her thumbs nervously. 'I do know; I'm sorry, I was worried, so I checked your inbox as well. There was nothing.'

'Oh, damn,' said Iska, as she got out of bed. 'That's bad.'

'Hence my panic,' said Amen. 'There is a bit of good news, though.'

'What is it?' Iska asked.

'You got an offer from Trinity College.'

16. TWO SETS OF TWO

Iska struggled to focus on the ongoing conversation. Between having to make up her mind about whether she wanted to go to Trinity College or Durham University and mustering the courage to share this decision with Walé and Amen, she had missed a good deal of what the Tellas were saying to all of them.

'Are you sure there's no way around all of this?' asked Oshu. 'I'm willing to speak with whoever is in charge.'

There was also the pressing issue of Iska, Amen, and the boys having to leave for Digglefield as soon as possible.

'No, there isn't,' Amen replied, shielding her eyes from the glare of the setting sun. 'We were never given permission to leave, let alone to be away for this long. If Rima couldn't get through to us, there's a high chance either Aunt Nikki or Marius knows what's going on.'

'Which means we could all be in big trouble,' said Aito, who was sitting precariously on a balcony railing.

'As much as we'd like for you all to stay a little longer,' Ada said as she packed away her laptop. 'I understand your situation. Look, regardless of the dead end with the professor, we'll continue searching for connections to your mother's killer, and we'll stay in constant communication. What time do you all plan to leave?'

Amen glanced at the others for confirmation. 'In a few hours.'

'That's perfect,' said Ada. 'The mobile phones I just ordered for you will be here in an hour.'

Neither of them wanted to admit it, but preparing to leave for Howth was more upsetting than Amen and Iska had anticipated. During the weeks spent with Oshu, Ada, and Walé, the twins had formed a strong bond with the family.

Leaving them so abruptly, although the smart thing to do, felt like a punch to the gut.

'Fun fact,' said Aito in an attempt to lighten the mood as they gathered in the kitchen. 'Did yous know we left Digglefield on a Friday? How weird is it that we're returning on a Friday a month later?'

Rather than making Amen and Iska laugh, Aito's remark only made them worry about what sort of trouble they might be in back at Digglefield. They had been in Nigeria for a month, and in that time, Rima had emailed them twice. The first time was on the day the twins had arrived in Nigeria, asking if they'd made it there in one piece. The second time was a few days before Amen and Iska set out for Dogudu; in that message, Rima had confessed to being jealous she wasn't at the fundraiser, but more importantly, reassured the twins she'd share the latest happenings in Digglefield. But she hadn't done that, and the harder Iska and Amen tried to figure out why, the more anxious they grew.

'I hope that when we meet again, it will be under better circumstances,' said Oshu as he handed each of them their new phones. 'I installed an encrypted messaging application on all of them; please reach out to myself or Ada if any of you ever need anything.'

Amen and Iska didn't need anyone to tell them that this was Oshu's way of saying goodbye. It was brief and straight to the point, as if he were confident that they would see each other again soon.

'To say having you all over was a blessing would be an understatement,' said Ada, embracing each of them in a hug. 'I already have ideas of what we could do together when we see you all again. For now, take care of yourselves.'

Walé, sitting silently, nodded his head in agreement. He had already said goodbye to his favourite person within the group, so all he offered was a peace sign and a click of his tongue.

'Okay then, let's do this,' said Aito, extending both of his arms out. Holding on to one another, Amen and Iska were still trying to steady themselves for the blink when tiny icy pellets suddenly began to rain down on them.

Digglefield's rooftop terrace was almost unrecognisable. Swirling rain and hail obscured the view. True to form, the Irish weather was playing by its own rules even during summertime. Fortunately, the storm provided the perfect cover for Amen, Iska, and the boys to enter the halls of Digglefield undetected. Moving as quietly as possible, all four of them descended from the rooftop to an empty atrium where they said their farewells and went their separate ways.

As Amen and Iska hurried across Digglefield's east block and into the girls' dormitory, they were relieved to find no other girls or minders in sight. It was understandable why most of the building seemed deserted, though. During storms like this, it was normal for most girls to gather in the study or common room.

But as Iska and Amen approached their room, they could hear voices coming from within it, though it was difficult to discern to whom they belonged. Soaked from the rain and fearful of being discovered, the twins cautiously reached for the doorknob, hoping to find only Senait and Rima in the room. To their dismay, they were instead greeted by two faces that sent a chilling wave of fear through their bodies. Two *familiar* faces. Two *impossibly* familiar faces.

Terrified and in disbelief, Iska and Amen instinctively tried to retreat from the room, but someone behind them forcefully pushed them back inside. It was Rima and Senait.

'What the hell is going on?' said Amen, still attempting to break free from Senait. 'Is this some kind of dream?'

'It's not a dream!' Rima responded, gripping Iska tightly. 'But yous need to calm down or else you'll cause a scene.'

'I can't calm down,' said Iska, pointing at the two girls sitting nonchalantly in her bed like they owned it. 'Not until I know who they are.'

'They're you.' Senait spoke softly.

'Well, technically, they're clones of you,' Rima corrected.

'What—How?'

Senait released her hold on Amen. 'I created them a few weeks ago, after Rima told me what you two were up to. By the way, thanks for not telling me.'

'How is this even possible?' said Iska, staring at her silent doppelgänger in disbelief. 'I thought Reegs didn't have any abilities.'

'Turns out I'm a full Unix,' said Senait. 'Shortly after yous left, my abilities kicked in.'

'But Marius—'

'Said he'd never seen anything like it; called me a late bloomer. Even Nikki was confused when I told her.'

'Aunt Nikki is back?' Amen and Iska said in unison.

'Yes, she returned a few days ago,' said Rima. 'But I suggest yous wait until tomorrow before you go see her; it's kinda late now, you know?'

'Senait,' said Amen as she warily set her backpack on the floor. 'I don't mean to be ungrateful, but can you please make them go away?'

Although they had been away from Digglefield for only a month, the multitude of experiences they had accumulated during that time made it feel as though Iska and Amen had been gone for years. Everything, from the shower handles in the bathroom to the mattresses on their bunk beds, appeared altered. Even Rima and Senait, who kept the twins awake all night with questions about their trip, seemed slightly different. However, according to Senait and Rima, not much had changed during Amen and Iska's absence, except for Senait also creating replicas of Aito and Lake to cover for them in training, and people receiving college offers.

Surprisingly, Amen and Iska were happy to be back in their daily routine. Life at Digglefield might not have been as grand as at the Tellas' or as magical as Dogudu, but it was still their home, and they had missed their friends. The storm from the previous night had subsided, and a warm glow now enveloped the castle. After finishing breakfast, Amen and Iska decided to visit Aunt Nikki, who, according to one of the minders, was in her office.

When the twins arrived at Aunt Nikki's office, the door was ajar, and their guardian was seated behind her desk, busy with paperwork.

Is she ever not working? thought Iska as she and Amen entered the room.

'Are you two going on a date or something?' Aunt Nikki asked the twins even before they could shut the door behind them. She was staring them dead in the eyes, but her hands moved across her desk at mind-boggling speed. It was all very disorienting.

What is she on about? thought Amen, clearly confused.

'Why do you ask?' said Iska.

'I mean, you two were much paler yesterday; you've obviously put some fake tan on.'

Iska and Amen had nearly forgotten that Aunt Nikki had been interacting with their clones since her return from Romania.

'Oh, yeah,' said Iska, suddenly realising that visiting Aunt Nikki might not have been the best idea. 'Just trying to look alive, you know? It's summer, after all.'

'Fair point,' said Aunt Nikki. 'I might just do the same. Do you have any tanning products left?'

'Yeah, we do,' Amen replied, attempting to change the subject. 'We'll bring them to you later. So, how are you?'

'Good?' said Aunt Nikki, finally setting her pen aside. 'I'm surprised you're asking me this now. I thought you two were pissed off at me, considering how you've been avoiding me since I got back. Are you okay?'

Jesus, Iska whispered. *How clueless are Senait's clones?*

'Yeah, we're grand!' Amen replied. 'It was probably just mood swings.'

'Yeah, you know; period and all,' Iska added nervously. 'Definitely feeling better now.'

'I'm glad you are,' said Aunt Nikki, returning her gaze

to the heap of files in front of her. 'You should have said something, I was getting worried… So, any plans for today?'

'Not really,' Iska replied. 'Maybe some practise with Marius out in the garden and then a walk out to the pier.'

'Sounds like a solid plan,' Aunt Nikki said after a brief pause. 'And Amen, how do you feel about the conversation we had before I left for Romania?'

'Grand, yeah,' said Amen, already reaching for the door. 'I'm over it now. Sorry Aunt Nikki, Iska and I have to meet up with Senait and Rima; it's urgent.'

'Talk to you later,' Iska added, hoping Aunt Nikki was buying the lies.

Amen and Iska bolted out of Aunt Nikki's office before she could ask them any more questions. It felt strange having to keep their recent escapades a secret from her; for as long as the twins could remember, even before Aré's death, they had always shared everything with her. But this time was different; neither of them wanted to risk getting on Aunt Nikki's bad side or, even worse, triggering a panic attack by telling her what they had been up to in the past month. Motivated to never be found out by Aunt Nikki, Iska and Amen were in the midst of working out their alibis for the past month when Amen received a text.

'It's Aito,' she said, tucking her phone back into the pocket of her hoodie. 'He's outside with Lake. They're going down to the village and were wondering if we wanted to come along.'

'Why not?' said Iska. 'We do have to get fake tan, thanks to you.'

If they hadn't arrived just in time to witness it for themselves, Amen and Iska would have sworn there hadn't been a storm in Howth. Except for the damp lawn, the sunny skies showed no signs that there had been a clash of water, wind, and lightning only a few hours ago. Just outside Digglefield's main entrance, Lake and Aito were waiting patiently as kids, much paler than them, whizzed past. Now, Amen and Iska understood why Aunt Nikki had so easily concluded they had darkened their skin. With the way all four of them looked, anyone could claim they had just returned from a trip to Marbella, and their counterargument would barely hold any weight.

'I'm guessing yous made it back to your building without getting caught?' said Iska, as she gave each of the boys a hug.

'Of course,' said Aito, reaching out to Amen for an embrace. 'Have you no faith in us?'

'Something weird happened, though,' Lake said seriously. 'The lad we paid to cover for us said he kept seeing us around Digglefield a week or so after we left, but whenever he tried to talk to us, we ignored him.'

'Yeah, sorry about that,' Amen said with a laugh.

Aito's eyes widened. 'Wait, yous know something about this?'

'It's a long story,' said Iska, already a couple of paces ahead of them. 'We'll tell you about it on the way to the village.'

Every summer without fail, Howth became home to thousands of tourists from all over the world who came for the food, the cliff hikes, and all of the recreational activities the charming town had to offer. This summer was no different. As Iska, Amen, and the boys manoeuvred their way through a sea of people, the twins recounted the story of how Senait had discovered her ability and saved them from getting caught.

'Rima says it's why she didn't bother emailing us while we were away.' Amen stuffed the last of her churros in her mouth. 'Senait's clones were doing a good job of standing in for us, so she kinda went with the flow of things. I just wish she would have at least given us a heads-up.'

'Jesus,' said Aito as he collected his hot dog and soft drink from a food kiosk server. 'I wish I had an ability like that.'

'Really?' said Iska as they resumed their walk towards Howth pier. 'You'd give up your ability to blink just for that?'

Aito finished chewing and swallowing before responding. 'When did I say that? Let me rephrase: I'd like to have an ability like that in addition to being able to blink.'

'Aren't you a greedy bastard?' Amen chimed in.

'I know, right?' Iska laughed. 'At least you have an ability; you should be grateful.'

'Yeah, yeah, I am,' said Aito, taking a sip of his drink. 'You know what, though? It feels weird being back at Digglefield. It hasn't even been a day, but I already miss Oshu, Ada, and Walé. I even miss the crazy old lady back in Dogudu. Plus, everyone's getting ready to leave for college. Oh, and I almost forgot—I got an email from a big construction company based in Cork; I was offered a place on their apprenticeship programme.'

'Congratulations!' said Iska and Amen, nearly smothering Aito with their hugs.

'All right, all right, get off me,' said Aito, playfully pushing Amen and Iska away. 'Lake has also decided to accept the scholarship offer from the college in the US; can someone please talk him out of it?'

Lake rubbed his forehead. 'Mate, thanks for putting me on the spot.'

'Are you sure, Lake?' said Amen.

'Yeah, my mind's made up,' Lake replied. 'I mean, I love Ireland, and I've had the best summer since I moved here, but home is home, you know? Besides, the career opportunities there are better if football doesn't work out.'

'So, you'd rather play in the MLS?' said Aito jokingly but with a hint of disgust.

'As opposed to the Irish Premier League? Yes,' Lake replied with a smile.

'Traitor,' Aito muttered.

Lost in their conversation, Iska, Amen, and the boys didn't realise they had reached the top of the pier.

'Lake, you know we support you no matter what you decide,' said Amen, gazing at a lighthouse in the distance.

'Just make sure to stay in touch and visit.'

'Yeah, Lake,' Iska added nervously. 'I completely understand where your head is at; I'm in a similar position myself. I mean, I have a chance to go to Durham University in England, and I think I'm going to take it. They have a good Comp-Sci programme—'

'You mean a good Walé programme,' Amen interrupted. 'I can't believe you, Iska; when were you going to tell me about this?'

'Girls, I don't mean to butt in,' said Lake, surveying their surroundings. 'But this seems kinda personal; maybe save it for later?'

'No, we'll talk about it right here,' Iska said defiantly. 'What do you care? Aren't you the one who wants to move to Dingle?'

'I can't believe you're using that against me,' said Amen, the sides of her temple throbbing. 'We've been over this. You know why I need to move there. Besides, wasn't the plan for me to find a college closer to you before you went ahead to play detective?'

A good number of people in and around the pier were starting to glance over at Amen and Iska squabbling, but neither of them was prepared to yield their stance.

'As if you're not thankful for where that got us?' said Iska. 'If I had listened to you, we would never have known we had family in Nigeria.'

'Yeah,' said Amen, shaking her head. 'A family you're ready to leave your actual family for—a family you literally met just a month ago. You know what? I'm done with this; do whatever you want.'

The walk back home was awkward, to the extent that Lake and Aito were cautious not to say or do anything that might trigger another argument. Meanwhile, Iska and Amen were now clear-headed enough to acknowledge that they each shouldn't have flared up in front of so many people, but they were still too angry to want to talk to each other, so their feud persisted throughout the rest of the day.

Back in their room, each sister explained her side of the story to Rima and Senait in an attempt to win them over. However, like Aito and Lake, the girls chose not to take sides. Instead, they encouraged Amen and Iska to work things out between themselves. But it wasn't that easy. The truth was that both Iska and Amen were convinced they were right and the other was wrong. Changing their positions, even for the sake of peace, would mean relinquishing that conviction; this was something neither of them was prepared to do as they retired to their beds for the night.

Hundreds of metres beneath her, the waves crashing against the rocky shores shimmered brilliantly under the sunlight. Yet, the shivers rocking Iska's body hinted at her being in a dream. That was the only cogent explanation for why there was a disconcerting chill working its way towards her core, even though the sun above was shining intensely.

It took Iska a few seconds to get her mind going, but it was all starting to make sense: the sea, the rocks, the grass beneath her feet. She had been here before; it was on this cliff that she was chased relentlessly by three strangers. Yes, there was no mistaking it, all the details from that memory were the same as now, expect for…

'Oh Jesus! Have you come here to annoy me too?' said a familiar voice that startled Iska, causing her to make a one-eighty-degree turn.

'Amen, what are you doing here?' Iska asked in surprise.

'I should be asking you,' said Amen, bracing herself for warmth. 'You're in *my* dream.'

'No,' said Iska, shaking her head as if trying to remember something. 'This is my dream. This is the cliff I told you guys about in Dogudu, remember?'

'You're both wrong,' said a male voice from no particular source. 'Sorry for the confusion, but the two of you are in my dream.'

I know this voice, thought Amen, as she moved closer to Iska. *It's the same one I heard when I was in that trance.*

'That's correct,' the voice replied, stunning Iska and Amen. 'I'm glad you didn't forget.'

'How can you hear us?' said Amen, struggling to contain her fright.

The voice let out an intimidating laugh. 'You're in my dream, remember?'

'Who are you?' said Iska, gripping Amen's hand tightly. 'Why are you doing this?'

'You're the stubborn one,' said the voice, as the bright, cold atmosphere around the cliff began to mix and stir and slowly transform into a boiling darkness. 'Who I am isn't relevant for now. However, I must say I am impressed with the tenacity in both of you. The efforts you're making to find your mother's killer, talking to Rupert—'

'You leave the professor alone!' said Iska, sweat dripping down her face. 'He did nothing—'

'—You should at least stay silent when I'm talking,' the voice interrupted Iska. 'Courtesy only demands. This is why your mother's pathetic life was slowly drained out of her body: she didn't know when to shut up.'

'You know nothing about our mother.' Iska tried to keep her voice steady, but it came out breathless. The growing heat seemed to drain her of energy.

'I beg to differ,' the voice replied with a sneer. 'I know all about you, Amen and Iska. And I suspect soon enough, you will know more about me too. But for now, let's end our meeting here.'

As soon as the voice finished speaking, Amen and Iska were plunged into a darkness that robbed them of all their senses, leaving them paralysed and desolate for what seemed like eternity.

Amen and Iska were eventually awakened by the gentle rays of a dawning morning. By then, they didn't need anyone to tell them that whoever or whatever had made contact with them was hostile. Their muddled minds had already worked that out. What they truly wanted to know was why, even hours after the nightmare, they couldn't shake off the angst and dejection they had felt when they were being addressed on the cliff. What had that thing done to leave them so shell-shocked?

'Hey, we've been looking for both of you,' said Rima as she and Senait approached the dining table where Amen and Iska were sitting. 'Why do yous look so lifeless?'

'Ah, nothing,' Iska and Amen replied simultaneously, eager to avoid recounting what happened.

'Just all the travelling is starting to catch up, you know?' Iska added.

'What I would give to have your problems,' said Rima sarcastically, as she took a seat on the opposite side of the table. 'Well, we come bearing news that might bring yous back to life!'

'What is it?' said Amen, failing to conceal her indifference.

'Calm down, Ms Grumpy,' said Senait, still standing behind the last empty chair at the table. 'It's obvious yous have forgotten, but Debs is in two weeks—'

Iska buried her head in her hands. 'Oh my gosh, Brady!'

'Yeah, him.' Rima rolled her eyes. 'Anyways, we were wondering if yous wanted to come dress shopping?'

'But it's Sunday,' said Amen.

'So?' Rima replied. 'Shops are open; plus, this is the perfect time to go before all the good dresses are gone.'

Do you want to go? thought Amen.

'Come on, it'll make yous feel better,' Senait added.

Yeah, I don't mind, Iska answered, drumming her fingers on the table. *Anything to stop feeling like this.*

Because it was Sunday, the girls only needed one bus ride to reach Bachelors Walk in Dublin city. Surprisingly, the town was bustling with people moving purposefully in different directions. Unsurprisingly, many teenagers were among the crowd, also looking to take advantage of the calm before the storm that was the Debs shopping season. Fortunately for Iska and Amen, Rima and Senait knew which stores they wanted to visit and in what order. All they had to do was follow along and try on outfits. But even after leaving the third store, Iska and Amen struggled to match Senait and Rima's level of excitement, and it had nothing to do with the dresses.

Despite the twins' desire to be fully present in the moment, the lingering effects of last night's dream continued to erode their enthusiasm. They feared that if they didn't step aside and give Rima and Senait some space, their day might be ruined as well. To prevent this from happening, Amen and Iska patiently waited until they were well into the fourth store before informing the girls that they were hungry and needed to find something to eat.

'Would yous like us to tag along?' said Rima, her eyes fixed on a turquoise off-the-shoulder gown.

'You're grand,' Amen replied. 'Yous keep on shopping. We'll meet you at the Spire in an hour.'

'Are yous sure?' said Senait, her question more out of politeness than genuine concern.

'You girls do your thing!' said Iska, already walking backward towards the shop's exit. 'We'll see yous in an hour.'

Amen and Iska's reason for parting ways with Senait and Rima turned out to be more than just an excuse as they walked down a street that was growing increasingly crowded. With their stomachs grumbling, both girls decided to satisfy their hunger at a Burger King on O'Connell Street. Their decision was quickly rewarded when, less than twenty minutes later, they each received a Whopper Burger meal from an old classmate working behind the counter.

I still don't get it, thought Amen as she and Iska settled at a table overlooking the intersection of O'Connell and Henry Street. Despite each sister's reluctance to apologise for the argument yesterday, the dream had brought about a temporary truce between them as they tried to make sense of their current situation. *How did he know our names and what we've been up to? Are there Unix with all-knowing abilities?*

'There might be,' said Iska, taking a huge bite out of her burger. *Marius never mentioned anything about omniscient Unix.* 'But then again, you can't rely on Marius to know everything. Honestly, what concerns me more is what this stranger wants with us.'

Amen mulled over Iska's words as she munched on some chips. 'Do you have your phone with you?' she finally asked.

'Yeah.' Iska rummaged through her bag until she found her device. 'Why do you ask?'

'Oshu said we could reach out for anything. I think we should tell him and Ada about the dream; they might be able to help. Can you shoot him a message?'

After a few swipes and taps on her phone, Iska repositioned her chair closer to Amen. 'I just did, in the group chat I created. I added the lads as well.'

Amen glanced up at the ceiling with barely restrained exasperation. 'Why?'

'Stop rolling your eyes,' Iska responded. 'Not everything is about Walé. Aito and Lake have been with us throughout all of this; it's only fair they know—Oshu just replied.'

'What did he say?'

Instead of explaining, Iska centred the phone so Amen could read the message along with her:

Oshu: Although the vagueness of these visions is starting to irritate me, one thing is clear: whoever it was that put you in that dream is no ordinary Unix. Being able to manipulate other people's subconscious is a trick reserved only for the few.

Aito: It's obviously that Cormac fella the prof told us about. How else would the person know we were at the

Uni? Pretty sure the prof snitched on us.

Lake: But what does a man who stole a sacred book want with Iska and Amen? And how does he know about their mom? It makes no sense.

Ada: Oshu, I think you should tell them.

Iska: Tell us what?

Oshu: One of my private investigators confirmed to me yesterday that on the day your mother died, one of your neighbours did see two strangers going into your house. According to the informant, it was raining heavily on that day so the figures were hard to make out, but they swore the strangers were a man and a woman. This person in your dream could have been one of the strangers, although the facts are still not airtight.

...
...

Iska: Oshu, do you think that our father could be behind all of this?
Behind our mam's death?

Oshu: As sadistic as it sounds, I've seen a lot in my lifetime to know that you can't rule out any possibility.
There could have been a motive; Aré might have fallen out with him, and that's why he left so suddenly before you two were born. Maybe he came back to get revenge.

Ada: I don't know, Oshu. Why all the charade then?
Why taunt your own family? We shouldn't be so quick to judge; I mean, we don't know if he's even alive.

Iska and Amen exchanged glances, their lips tight with stress and fear, until Amen motioned for her sister to hand over the phone.

> Iska: Is there a way we can find this out? (This is Amen speaking; I left my phone at home).

Iska glanced at the text and nodded silently. Then, with Amen still holding the phone, they watched the little dots dance as someone typed.

…

…

Oshu: As I said to your sister, I've searched and am still searching for your dad. But I've just had an idea on how you can find out more about the stranger in your dream. It seems the night both of you were put in that trance, a link was formed between you and someone out there, someone who happens to have telling information on you. Fortunately, communication is almost always multidirectional, so if they could reach you, it is (in theory) possible for you two to reach back.

Ada: Oshu, don't tell me you're suggesting the girls try to talk to someone who is clearly dangerous. Are you even serious right now?

Oshu: What other choice do they have? I'd rather they do something than let whoever is orchestrating these visions cause more damage. I just need them to squeeze some info out of the person; I'll handle the rest. Sometimes the best defence is offence.

Lake: With all due respect, Oshu, I think this a very bad idea; we haven't a clue what this person is capable of. Amen and Iska could get seriously hurt.

Amen and Iska exchanged glances. After how they'd been

feeling all day, it would be far better to *do* something than let whoever had trapped them in that dream get them again and again.

Iska: There's a high chance we could get hurt either way.
Amen and I want to hear the rest of the plan.

Lake: Girls, I could never claim to know what you're going through, but maybe you should think things through, or at least find another alternative.

Ada: I agree.

Walé: So do I.

Iska: We understand your concerns, but just as you said Lake you have no idea how this feels.
You may think we're being rash, and you're probably right.
But at this point, we're willing to do whatever it takes to never experience anything like last night again.
Besides, Oshu says he has it under control.

Oshu: Yes, I do. Your safety is my utmost concern; that is why all you have to do is try to make contact and ask questions. I don't expect it to be so easy, so if you two can get any useful information, that's good. If not, then we'll explore other options.

...

Iska: Right. What do we have to do?

For the next half an hour, Amen and Iska received instructions on how to return to a place they had hoped never to find themselves in again. While some of Oshu's directions made sense, most of them lacked any consistency. By the time the conversation ended, Amen and Iska were fairly certain the plan wasn't going to work.

Back at the Spire, the twins had to wait nearly an hour longer for Rima and Senait, who appeared to be putting their summer job earnings to good use, as they eventually arrived with several shopping bags. Although Amen and Iska were tempted to scold them for their tardiness, they knew that Rima and Senait weren't responsible for their current dissatisfaction. That achievement belonged to someone else, someone beyond their reach. Instead, they chose to focus on the positive by expressing their delight that the girls had found outfits and asking if they were pleased with their choices.

It turned out they were, because Senait and Rima couldn't stop raving about how lovely their dresses, shoes, and accessories were throughout the drive back to Howth. Amen and Iska found the whole thing amusing because, although they were used to Rima having these kinds of reactions to acquiring anything new, they had never seen Senait behave this way before. Who knew secondary school balls could bring out different sides of people?

'It's too bad yous couldn't find any decent dresses,' said Senait as all four girls walked the final stretch of road leading to Digglefield. 'We can go to town again on Wednesday; Rima and I will be free.'

With Amen quietly shuffling her feet through the gravel-ridden ground, Iska immediately knew she was on response duty. 'Yeah, yeah,' she stuttered. 'Wednesday is cool. Although, there's still a bit of time left—if we're being honest.'

'You would think that,' Rima said with a chuckle, 'until you get to town and realise the only shop that has any dresses left is Carraig Donn.'

This statement squeezed a laugh out of the girls, including Amen.

'I'm telling yous,' Rima continued in an ominous tone. 'The girls at school are out for blood this year. So, my friends, every second is precious.'

'Noted, O' wise one,' Iska replied as they closed in on Digglefield's black gates. 'I actually can't wait to see what the other girls in Digglefield wear on that day.'

'Forget the girls,' said Amen, who was finally in the mood to talk. 'I want to see what Marius wears. He's usually the chaperone for the Debs, isn't he?'

'Well yeah, but he won't be this year,' said Senait, as she swung open the gate reserved for pedestrians. 'Seeing as he's away, and—'

'Wait, what?' the edge in Amen's voice startled not just the girls, but Iska as well. Now she was trying to interpret the expression on Amen's face.

'How long has Marius been away?' Amen asked worriedly.

'About two weeks now,' said Rima. 'Why, what's—'

'Shite!' Amen interrupted, and Iska finally understood why Amen was getting worked up. But before she could say anything, two pairs of feet came into view.

'We've been looking for both of you,' said Anya and Olive, minders from the girls' dormitory. 'Nikki wants you in her office right away.'

Anya and Olive didn't specify by name which two of the four girls Aunt Nikki wanted to see, but they didn't have to; Iska and Amen (and even Rima and Senait) knew this was about them.

17. CIPHER

The air in Aunt Nikki's office almost always smelt of coffee, a testament to how much she loved her caffeinated beverage and how much of a workaholic she was. However, this time there was another aroma in the air. It was tangy and intense, and it was coming from only one source: Aunt Nikki herself. She was so angry that when Iska squinted her eyes, she could almost see steam emanating from the matron's body.

'How stupid do you girls think I am?' said Aunt Nikki, trying but failing to smoothen the tremble in her voice.

Amen and Iska knew Aunt Nikki's question was rhetorical, but the manner in which she asked it compelled them to think twice about giving a thoughtful answer. The problem, however, was they did not have one.

'Nikki, I can explain, it was my fault—'

'I don't want to hear it!' Aunt Nikki interrupted. It was only when Aunt Nikki shushed Aito that Iska and Amen realised he and Lake were in the office as well. In fact, they had been there the whole time; Amen and Iska had just been too blinded by fear to notice.

'The four of you really thought you could sneak out,' Aunt Nikki continued, pacing the room in a blur. 'Out of Digglefield, out of the country! To see a complete stranger, and I wouldn't find out?'

How did she find out we left the country? Amen whispered into Iska's head.

No idea, Iska whispered back before speaking up. 'Aunt Nikki, you have every right to be angry. Maybe... maybe we took things too far by going to Nigeria to see Oshu, but you left us his card. Surely you wanted us to contact him?'

Aunt Nikki stopped dead in her tracks, as if she had run into a brick wall. 'I can assure you, I did no such thing,' she said with a confidence that promptly sent a thousand questions sprouting in Amen and Iska's minds. 'Is that the excuse you've cooked up for how you were able to get your hands on something that was clearly not meant for you?'

Another question neither of the girls could answer.

'And here I was,' said Aunt Nikki, her voice as sharp as a razor blade, as she resumed pacing the room. 'Thinking both of you would be focused on getting into college, instead you were globetrotting. Have you two even gotten offers from any of the colleges you applied to?'

The growing silence in the room indicated that this could be yet another question that would go unanswered, but then Amen spoke. 'I got an email from Sacred Heart University in Dingle a few days ago. I was offered a place in their fashion programme.'

Grand, thought Iska, visibly as shocked as everyone else in the room. *And you didn't think to tell me?*

I didn't think it was any of your business, Amen shot back.

'Well,' said Aunt Nikki, relief eating away at some of her anger. 'Congratulations are in order. What about you, Iska?'

Another brief silence followed before Iska spoke up. 'Since the cat's out of the bag, I got an offer from Trinity College; but I think now's the time to let you know I've decided to go to a college in England instead. I've already sent in my application, and Walé is assisting me with the remaining process.'

'Who is Walé?' said Aunt Nikki, realising she was the only one in the room unaware of this new development. 'You know what, don't even answer that. I have a lot on my plate right now with the new children coming in—I need to get them settled. Once I'm done with them, we'll revisit this topic. Until then, all of you are grounded. You're not allowed to leave the confines of Digglefield for a week.'

'Jesus, Aunt Nikki,' said Iska, the only one bold enough to speak up. 'Debs is in two weeks. We need to—'

'Need I remind you,' Aunt Nikki interrupted, her anger resurging. 'This punishment is subject to extension at my discretion. If I were you, I *wouldn't* push it.'

With these last words, it was clear to the twins that there was no room for negotiation. Exiting Aunt Nikki's office one after the other, Amen, Iska, and the boys all understood, without needing to exchange a single word, that despite her anger, Aunt Nikki's punishment was lenient. To Amen and Iska, it was obvious why.

Not wanting to risk further trouble, Iska and Amen headed straight to their room where Rima and Senait appeared to have been anxiously waiting for them. After some consolation from the girls, Iska and Amen faced a barrage of questions. However, similar to their experience in Aunt Nikki's office, neither of them had any answers to offer. In fact, figuring out who told on them or how Aunt Nikki had discovered their absence was the least of Iska and Amen's concerns; at the moment, all they felt was an overwhelming urge to yell at each other.

As they brushed their teeth, changed into their pyjamas, and settled into bed, more questions were directed at Iska and Amen. However, by this point, they had completely tuned out Rima, Senait, and their curiosity. All the twins desired was for the day, the problems, and the fights to be over. While Amen attempted to achieve this by forcing herself to sleep, Iska chose to read a few of the scrolls she had brought with her from Dogudu.

Unbeknownst to Amen, Iska had worked her way through several pages of a dossier that covered elemental control and pacing. However, there was one paragraph she couldn't quite grasp, and she found herself repeatedly reading the words in it as if trapped in a time loop. Frustrated, Iska peeled her eyes from the dossier, breaking her focus for the first time since she had started reading it. To her surprise, she wasn't in her bed in Digglefield, but in a room on an island, judging by the view through its solitary window. Sensing that this was yet another unwelcome dream, Iska began examining the old room for any clues about where she was when suddenly the creak of a floorboard startled her. Iska spun around just in time to see a familiar figure emerging from the room's doorway: Amen was also here.

'I can't believe it's happening again,' Amen whispered while she scanned the room. 'Any idea where we are?'

Before Iska could respond, Amen pointed behind her. *Who's that?*' she asked.

Iska turned around once again and saw a figure—a woman, judging by the visible parts of her body—rocking in a chair. Just moments ago, Iska had believed she was the only one on this strange, tiny island, but now, she was in a room accompanied by Amen and a stranger cradling a baby in her arms. Although they were aware that all of this was happening in their subconscious, the twins couldn't help but wonder if the woman, whose gaze was fixed on the baby, was also aware of their presence. Without hesitation, Iska exchanged a quick glance with Amen before cautiously approaching the woman.

'You know, I'm a lot like both of you,' said the woman, causing Iska and Amen to flinch in fear. Although the woman's lips moved while she spoke, her voice was eerily similar to that of the stranger who had taunted the twins the night before. 'I didn't have a father growing up. Like you, I was raised solely by my mother.'

Iska skittered back into Amen and they both retreated as far away from the woman and the baby as they could. Iska and Amen were unsure how to interpret this revelation or why the stranger chose to disclose it. Nevertheless, they were grateful for any form of conversation. Oshu had emphasised the importance of engaging the stranger to gather their own information. However, with adrenaline coursing through their veins, Iska and Amen were finding it hard to remember any of Oshu's instructions.

'If you can empathise with our situation,' said Iska, mustering the courage to ask whatever she could. 'Why then did you take our mother from us?'

'Have you ever heard the saying,' said the woman as she rocked in the chair, tenderly stroking the child's forehead.

'"An eye for an eye makes the world blind"? Personally, I find that saying to be rubbish. You see, I subscribe to a different philosophy—I believe in vengeance, in its beauty and necessity. It provides an opportunity to rectify the wrongs in your life, even if this means ruthlessly punishing those who have wronged you.'

'What did our mother ever do to make you—make you—' Amen struggled to voice her question, feeling as though the words were searing hot coals in her throat. Yet, she knew she had to release them before they scorched through her. 'Take her life?'

Unlike Iska's question, Amen's query was met with silence. As seconds ticked away and the room's golden hue faded to sombre grey, it seemed that the orchestrator of the dream had departed, leaving Amen and Iska to grapple with their own unanswered questions.

'Do you like riddles?' the woman finally said, her uncanny baritone resonating in the air.

The randomness of the question caused a moment of confusion for Amen and Iska, who exchanged glances with each other.

'Yes,' Iska finally replied.

'Our mam used to tell us loads when she was alive,' Amen added, eager to keep the conversation going.

'Wonderful.' A ray of sunlight highlighted the contours of the woman's face, her fiery hair, and her emerald eyes. It felt unjust for such a beautiful person to be manipulated for such sinister purposes. 'Because I have a good riddle for you. One that will have you not just searching your minds for an answer, but also your hearts. The stakes are high, so getting it wrong comes with consequences.'

What does the last part mean? Amen asked, knowing fully well that there was a possibility the woman could hear her thoughts.

And indeed, she could. 'It means that while you may have missed the opportunity to save one of your parents, there is still a chance to save the other.'

Upon hearing these words, Iska and Amen had their second most crucial question in life answered. Their father was alive, and this stranger possessed knowledge of his whereabouts. Amidst all the uncertainty and fear, they finally discovered a glimmer of hope, a flicker of optimism to cling to. However, a sudden thought shattered Iska's excitement as quickly as it had arisen—what if it was all a lie, a ploy to expose and exploit their vulnerability?

'Cormac,' she said, remembering one of Oshu's tactics: *speak the name with confidence and carefully observe the stranger's reaction.* 'You don't have to go through with this. We may never know what happened between you and our mother. But if you really do have our father, please—please let him go. In return, we'll move on with our lives and accept things as they are.'

'Two scores of men plus eleven beasts,' the woman began. There was no twitch of the lips, no change in the pitch of her voice, no stutter—nothing. Not a single gesture gave Iska any hint that this person was the same dangerous individual who had stolen a sacred book about Unix. 'Trudge along the coast of an island to the left below, trying to find the rising fire. Little do they know, the flame they seek extinguishes itself at the feet of a dozen women, three heads removed, who tell tales of Hesperus, the Greek god.'

Amen repeated the last few words of the statement to herself, attempting to establish a connection between each of them and understand their relevance to her and Iska. 'This isn't a riddle,' she finally said. 'It's a cipher. How are we supposed to decode it?'

'That's a good question,' said the woman, rising from the chair for the first time; the baby now absent—as if it had never been there. The woman's white dress brushed against the floor as she walked towards the window, obstructing most of the incoming light. 'But it's one you must answer for yourselves if you ever want to see your father alive. So, I suggest you get started figuring out the cipher. Time is of the essence. One more thing: if you involve anyone else in our little game I will kill Patrick first, and then I'll come for both of you.'

Amen and Iska had received a few threats in the past, but never one that endangered their lives. The convergence of this threat and the realisation that their father's survival depended on their ability to decipher a cryptic message left the twins feeling more than just anxious. To make matters even worse, they were now constantly being monitored by Aunt Nikki. All of this left Iska and Amen with no respite or means of escape from the nightmare their once-promising summer had swiftly turned into.

But what about that line "plus eleven beasts"? Amen lay in her bed, her gaze fixed on the palms of her hands. Her fingers were twitching a lot lately. Whether this was stressed-induced or somehow connected to her ability, she wasn't sure. *Could it have something to do with Cruthers? Specifically, animal shapeshifters like Ada or Jimba?*

I don't know, thought Iska, tapping incessantly at her phone before finally tossing it to the far corner of her bed. *I've searched for wordplays, anagrams, famous riddles—everything. There's nothing useful on the internet; the cipher makes no sense!*

Upon hearing Iska's words, Amen swallowed hard to soothe the ache in her throat. She held back her thoughts, knowing that voicing them would only make her sister panic even more. But the fact was clear as day: if Iska, the most intelligent person she knew, couldn't decipher the meaning behind the stranger's words, all hope of rescuing their father was lost.

Ada and Oshu may be the only ones who can help us, Iska continued. *But we can't even let them know.*

In one fluid motion, Amen leapt off her bed, landed gently on her feet, and nestled into an empty space in Iska's bed. *Look, there's no need to work yourself up,* she whispered into Iska's head, even though they were only half a metre apart. *I know it seems impossible now, but we'll figure this thing out together.* The lie rolled effortlessly out of Amen's mind.

Iska drew imaginary patterns on her bedsheet with her left index finger—something she did whenever she was nervous. *And how do you know this?*

I just know, Amen replied, extending her leg to gently stroke Iska's knee. *Trust me—*

Before Amen could finish her sentence, Rima burst into the room, followed by Senait. 'You do realise you were only told not to leave Digglefield, right?' she said. 'No one said anything about not eating.'

Engrossed in their search for answers to an insurmountable mystery, Amen and Iska had lost track of time as the morning slipped away. Though they hadn't planned to skip breakfast, neither of them felt particularly hungry, and they doubted their appetites would return anytime soon.

'We'll join for lunch,' Iska said unconvincingly as she rose from her bed and headed towards the wardrobe tucked in the corner of their room.

'Look, there's no need to be so hard on yourselves,' Senait reassured the twins. 'The days will go by quickly, and we're here to help with anything, right Rima?'

'Yeah. In fact, we bumped into Nikki on our way back here, and Senait and I sort of pleaded with her to shorten your punishment. I won't lie, she's still very upset, but she said she'll think about it.'

Suddenly, Amen sat upright in Iska's bed. Something about Senait and Rima's words had sparked an idea in her mind. 'You guys are the best,' she said, her misty-white eyes gleaming as she crafted her next words. 'Actually, our uncle has given us this brain-teaser challenge for a prize, but it's incredibly difficult. I—we were hoping yous could assist us in solving it.'

Senait and Rima paused, considering the request, but before either of them could respond, Iska's backpack crashed to the floor with a resounding thud.

Are you out of your mind? Iska mind-shouted. *What the hell are you doing? Do you want to get us killed? Did you forget the instructions we were given?*

I haven't forgotten, but I've never seen you struggle to find a solution to any problem before, Amen replied earnestly. *We need help. Remember what Mam used to say? "Two heads are better than one." Maybe right now, four heads are better than two.*

So what? Iska picked up her backpack and shoved it back into the wardrobe. *You're willing to risk their lives, along with ours and Dad's, just because you think they might have the answer?*

Not exactly. I have a plan—

'I swear, one of these days I'm going to smash yous up—' Rima half-jokingly threatened, '—if yous keep doing that thing. Did you even hear what we said?'

'What?' Amen and Iska said simultaneously.

'We're in,' Senait responded with a smile. 'As long as you share the prize with us.'

Of course, there was no tangible prize, not unless being the first people to crack the world's most nonsensical statement was considered a reward in and of itself. Yet, Amen had made up her mind to give Rima and Senait whatever they desired if they could help uncover the answers that would ensure the safety of her family. While allowing herself to entertain the idea of her friends being the key to preserving her father's life, Amen was also determined not to put them in harm's way. She explained the *brain-teaser* to Senait and Rima in the study, carefully omitting certain words and altering the structure of the cipher until it was slightly different from the original, while still preserving its core message.

'Now that's a mouthful,' said Rima, already halfway out of her seat. 'It's a good thing we're here,' she continued, scanning the shelves of books in the study. 'There should be something in the Greek mythology section. Senait, care to join me?'

Senait didn't hesitate to get out of her chair, and within seconds, both girls were at the other end of the room, sifting through stacks of books. Not that Amen had never known or noticed, but years of doing homework, studying, and occasionally playing computer games in the study had made her oblivious to how well-stocked it was with a multitude of books spanning different years and genres. Aunt Nikki always insisted that Digglefield, regardless of the circumstances, catered to the minds of its occupants. Now, Amen hoped that Aunt Nikki's determination to maintain a comprehensive collection of texts would prove helpful in their hour of need.

I have a bad feeling about this, thought Iska, as she opened the laptop in front on her. *I don't want anyone getting hurt because of us.*

I promise, no one is going to get hurt. Amen's confidence surprised her, especially as she didn't entirely believe her own words. *But this might just be our best shot at figuring out what the hell is going on; just go with the flow. I'm going to join the girls and see what I can find.*

Iska watched as Amen walked towards the girls, her strides purposeful and a little *too* confident. But perhaps that was precisely what the situation called for: a blend of self-assuredness, optimism, and teamwork. Amen was right; up until this point, Iska had never encountered a problem she couldn't solve. Finding solutions to difficult problems had been second nature to her, as effortless as breathing. Yet, this cipher presented an entirely different challenge, and as much as she worried about their safety, Iska couldn't deny that Rima and Senait were clever enough to make a positive difference in their efforts to figure the darn thing out. With this realisation, Iska swiftly made up her mind: instead of opposing the girls' involvement, she would facilitate it; she would assist them to the best of her abilities.

However, as the day progressed, it became clear to Iska that this was easier said than done. The girls had read every available book on Greek mythology, meticulously scanned through articles about Earth's islands, and inputted various combinations and permutations of the cipher into search engines. Yet, their efforts yielded no results. In fact, it seemed that the more they searched, the less they found. Aito and Lake's incessant text messages only added to the complexity of the situation, but Amen and Iska chose not to respond—as much as they wanted to tell the boys everything, they recognised that there were already enough lives at risk.

'Your uncle really wants yous to work for that prize, doesn't he?' said Rima, sliding a textbook to the centre of their study desk where other unhelpful books had accumulated. 'I'll be honest with yous, this brain-teaser thing is way harder than I thought it'd be. And Senait and I have about an hour to get to work...' Rima paused, cautious not to come across as rude, but the message was clear, nonetheless. 'We can pick up where we left off when we get back,' she continued. 'Although, I think yous also need a break, right Senait?'

'Absolutely,' said Senait, who looked mentally exhausted. 'I think yous should call it a day. There's always tomorrow.'

Yes, to the girls, there was always tomorrow. But to Iska and Amen, every minute that passed was precious time wasted in the race to save their father's life. If only the girls could see things this way, if only they could understand the magnitude of the task at hand, a task much more pressing than a job or rest. But they couldn't, and who could blame them? In their minds, this was all just a game they had grown disinterested in.

Frustrated as they were with the situation, Amen and Iska could still hardly deny that the girls were right. Forcing themselves to remain in the study, though it seemed like the right thing to do, was counterproductive. They were exhausted and hungry, and the answers they sought were not in here—at least not today. If the exercise in code-cracking had revealed anything, it was that a collective effort was their best bet at achieving any tangible result. It only made sense to take Senait and Rima's advice and regroup.

Over the next few days, this was exactly what the girls did to the point where it became a routine: shower, breakfast, then research; lunch, then more research; and then, for

Iska, a bit of light reading after dinner. On the days when Senait and Rima had to work, Amen and Iska took it upon themselves to tackle the cipher. In between all of this, they appealed to Aunt Nikki (whenever they ran into her) to shorten their punishment, but their pleas went unanswered. As the weekend approached, it felt as though they had been in lockdown for years, rather than just a couple of days.

Throughout the week, Aito and Lake had sent a good number of texts, no doubt concerned about how they were coping with the punishment. But Amen and Iska neither responded nor reached out to them, not until Sunday night at least. Just an hour before midnight, Iska had created a group chat for all four of them and simply asked the boys to meet on the rooftop terrace at noon the next day. She had provided no further explanation for the request, not even when Amen questioned her.

However, as they now made their way through the castle towards the rendezvous point with Rima and Senait in tow, Amen demanded to know what Iska had planned.

Just give it a few minutes, thought Iska, as she led the way up the winding atrium stairs towards the terrace. *Everything will make sense, I promise.*

As soon as they walked through the rooftop door, the girls instinctively shielded their eyes. The sunlight beaming down on them was much brighter than the windows in Digglefield had let on, but unfortunately, it wasn't nearly as warm as they would have liked. Between protecting her eyes from the glaring sun and bracing herself against chilly gusts of wind, Iska spotted Lake and Aito at the far right-hand corner of the roof engrossed in an intense conversation while looking in the direction of Dublin Bay.

'When are you two ever not fighting?' said Iska, playfully slapping both boys on the back of their heads.

'I was just telling this eejit,' said Aito, as he hugged Iska and then Amen, 'that with enough concentration, I think I can blink to the past, just like Marius said.'

'No one encourage him, please,' said Lake as he shook

hands with Rima and Senait. 'I'm the one he's going to come crying to if he gets hurt. I don't want that responsibility.'

'You wish you were that special,' said Aito, cupping his hands to his mouth for warmth. 'So, why did yous ask to meet here, and why haven't you been returning our texts?'

While Iska contemplated how to respond to Aito's question, she surveyed the terrace, noting that Rima, Senait, and Amen were eagerly awaiting her answer with expectant eyes. Pleased that the rest of the terrace was mostly empty— there were two other girls up there with them, but they were engaged in a conversation at the opposite end—Iska stretched out both her hands.

'You guys hold hands,' she said.

'Iska, are you serious—'

'Just trust me,' Iska said through clenched teeth, and everyone obliged, albeit confusedly.

'Now what?' said Aito after a few awkward seconds.

But Iska neither responded nor opened her eyes. She seemed to be concentrating hard on something—a piece of information? A memory? Amen wasn't sure, but she was about to find out. *Iska, what's wrong with you? Why are you being weird—*

'Aaah!' Aito screamed in fear as he hastily let go of Lake's and Senait's hands. 'What the hell was that?'

'What?' said Amen.

'I just heard you speak,' Aito replied. 'But like, in my head!'

Amen smiled sheepishly at the others, hoping they weren't taking Aito seriously. 'Chap, what are you talking about?'

'I heard your voice as well,' said Senait; she was shaken but a lot more composed than Aito.

'So did I,' said Lake.

'Me too,' Rima added.

'Have yous lost your mind?' said Amen, determined to sow doubt in the minds of friends. 'Iska, did you hear anything?'

Amen anticipated her sister's support, but Iska merely met each person's gaze in turn and silently encouraged them to join hands once more, which they reluctantly did.

I didn't think this would work, Iska's inner voice reverberated in their heads like music wafting through headphones. *The essay I read on this mass-telepathy thing said it had been successful only a few times. I figured we'd give it a try.*

Iska paused, expecting the others to speak, but after a few seconds of silence, it was obvious they either didn't know how to, or shock had rendered them speechless. *It's as easy as talking to yourself or thinking, but this time try to vocalise your words.*

I'm—I'm so—Jesus, this is strange. Aito was doing his best to gather his thoughts. *I'm glad you finally got your ability, Iska. I never stopped believing—*

What are you on about? Iska cut Aito short. *This isn't my ability. Amen and I have always been able to do this. This is how we communicate in private. It is—was our secret.*

Then why are you sharing it with us? Senait's soft, sweet voice echoed in their minds.

Because Amen and I really need your help. Iska proceeded to tell them about the dreams, the cipher, how she'd discovered this new trick, and why she felt it was necessary to try it with them.

It's obvious we can't figure this thing out ourselves, Iska continued. *But we also don't want anyone getting hurt because of us. I thought this would be the safest way to work together without being found out...assuming, yous want to do this.*

Why would you say that? thought Senait.

Because we're risking everything by doing this, Amen responded, her first contribution since they began the telepathy exercise. *If this person is responsible for our mam's death, it means they've killed before; it's not hard to imagine they can do it again... It's better you know what you're getting involved in.*

What about both of you? Lake's voice had a steely edge to it. *Have you considered how dangerous what you're doing is? This could be a sick game by some crazy Unix out there. Look, wouldn't it be better to just tell Nikki—*

No! the twins thought in unison.

Lake, Iska continued, the dread in her thoughts unmistakable. *I know you're looking out for us, but I need you to promise, right here and now, that under no circumstance will you tell anyone else about this.*

The whole conversation might have been happening in their minds, but at the moment, all eyes were fixed on Lake, awaiting his response.

I promise, he eventually replied, although his displeasure was evident on his face.

Good, thought Iska. *The same goes for everyone else. One more thing: Amen and I would be saddened if any of yous decide not to help us, but trust me when I say we won't hold it against any of—*

Before Iska could finish her speech, Rima clicked her tongue in disapproval. *I'm offended you would even say that. First off, I'll pretend like I didn't just witness yous forget that Senait and I are also your sisters, which means we're family. Second, what good is family if they don't support you? Look, your dad is my dad, and I'll do anything to help him.*

Same goes for me, Senait added almost immediately.

It took all of Iska and Amen's willpower not to smile with joy as they turned their gaze towards Aito, who had been uncharacteristically quiet.

Yous know I'm in till the end. His lips widened into a smile. *Too many sacrifices have already been made. Let's try to get to the finish line. Oh, and for the record, Lake is in as well. He knows the story: he's helping! Even if I have to beat him into it, right buddy?*

Lake chuckled at Aito's last words, but his expression remained sour. He seemed to have so many reasons why cracking the cipher was a bad idea. It was almost as if he knew something no one else did but either lacked the courage to say it or refused to do so altogether. *Right,* he finally admitted. *I'll help, even though I still think we're making the wrong move.*

Now Amen and Iska smiled unabashedly. While they had meant it when they said they wouldn't hold it against their friends for not wanting to be part of the rescue effort, it was gratifying to know that they were willing to help.

I do have one thing to say, though, Lake continued. *If the cipher is as difficult as you girls say it is, then we have to leave Digglefield to find more clues.*

18. THE OLD LIBRARY

Over the next couple of days Amen, Iska, and the others meticulously implemented Lake's suggestion by visiting every library and bookshop in and around Howth, searching for any kind of book or document they hoped would be useful in decoding the cipher. Although they were no longer grounded, Amen and Iska remained overly cautious about the places they visited. They didn't want to risk getting on Aunt Nikki's bad side again, or worse, falling into a trap set by the stranger from their dreams.

Another cause for concern was the weather. In the days since their meeting at the rooftop, the weather in Howth had quietly but quickly taken a turn for the worse. Initially, there were sporadic showers here and there. However, on Tuesday, strong winds arrived, and by Wednesday, the entire country was engulfed in a storm. Weather forecasters had predicted that it would subside the following day. But now, on Thursday, with the thunderclaps rattling the village, it was evident that Mother Nature had other plans.

Although they had been fortunate enough to gather sufficient research materials before the storm hit Howth, Iska, Amen, and the boys found themselves confined to their respective dormitories due to the constant rainfall. Fortunately, they had their phones, which they used exclusively and with caution to communicate and collaborate in their efforts to decipher the cipher.

'Could the "scores of men and beasts" part have anything to do with someone's age?' Aito asked Iska from the other end of a video call. 'Because I came across a passage in the bible from the Book of Psalms, chapter ninety verse ten. It makes a reference to age and ageing.'

'I don't think so,' Iska replied, passing the phone to Rima before getting out of her bed. 'I've read that passage before, and I doubt that part of the brain-teaser has anything to do with age or years.'

'But what if—'

'Aito, it can't be that straightforward!' Iska interrupted, her voice carrying an unexpected sharpness that surprised the girls. 'Those words are unique; they were created with a specific context in mind. This is a problem that requires critical and creative thinking.'

'Will we revisit the other theory then? You know, the one to do with the days of the week?' Senait asked.

'Did you not listen to anything I just said?' Iska retorted.

'Whoa, whoa!' said Rima, the tone of her voice matching Iska's. 'What's with the attitude?'

'Yeah, Iska,' Amen chimed in, placing the book she was holding on her crossed legs. 'You're being a bit aggressive; we're all trying to figure this thing out. We'll have a breakthrough eventually.'

'That's the thing, though.' Iska's eyes welled up with tears. 'We're running out of time. Guys, I'm sorry for my behaviour, but it just feels like we'll never crack this brain-teaser in time. It seems like for every forward step we take, we slide back five steps. We've gathered every document, book, and dossier we could find, but still, nothing. I feel like we're failing...'

Iska desperately wanted to finish her sentence, but the lump in her throat prevented her from doing so. The tears she had been holding back began streaming down her cheeks and lips, and every attempt to wipe her eyes clean only seemed to make them produce more of the warm, salty liquid.

'Listen, Iska,' Rima spoke up, still holding the phone in her hand so that the boys could see almost everyone. 'I understand your frustration. You know why? Because we all feel the same way; but you have to realise we're giving it our all. If you know any other way we can move faster, let us know. But don't lose your cool or take your frustrations out on us.'

Iska closed her eyes to avoid making eye contact with the girls. 'I don't know any other way. We've searched practically everywhere we can, both physically and online. I don't know what else to do.'

The gentle hum of a laptop, which the girls had smuggled into their room a few days earlier, combined with the raindrops pelting their window, created the only sounds that fought off the silence accompanying Iska's words. For the first time since they began their research, it seemed as though none of them knew what to say.

'I know one place we haven't looked.' Lake's muffled voice came through Iska's phone. 'It's a long shot, but it wouldn't hurt to try...'

'Where, chap?' said Aito, as the girls huddled around the phone like flies to decaying matter, with Iska (still wiping away her tears and sniffing) joining in last.

'Again, I say it's a long shot,' Lake responded, centring his face on the screen. 'Because there are millions of books in there, and we would have to—'

Aito sighed. '—Lake, would you just say the name already?'

For a brief moment, Lake looked sideways at where half of Aito's face was visible in the video call. The force of his glare made it look almost as though Lake was contemplating punching Aito in the face. But after a long, charged moment, Lake blew out his breath and turned back to the camera. 'Do any of you know the Old Library?'

While the other girls, including Aito, shook their heads in confusion, Iska nodded. 'I've heard of it. Is it the same one in Trinity College?' she said.

'Yes, that's the one,' Lake replied. 'It's the number one legal deposit in Ireland, which means it's home to every book ever published in the country, including the Book of Kells. But as I was saying before Aito interrupted, it would be difficult to pinpoint the specific texts that could help us solve our...brain-teaser.'

'Assuming the right texts are even in this library,' Iska

added quietly.

'Still, there's no harm in trying,' said Rima. 'I mean, we sort of have a base to build on already. We may not know exactly what we're looking for, but something tells me we aren't far off; the only problem is we're in the middle of a storm and there's no way to get to the College.'

Aito let out a deep sigh. 'I'll be honest, I'm a little disappointed.'

'Aito, can you do it?' Amen asked immediately, cutting off Rima from asking a question they all knew would be answered in a few seconds.

'Is that a trick question?' Aito replied, grinning ear to ear. 'All I need is photos.'

'Oh,' said Rima, the realisation suddenly dawning on her. 'Oh! I forgot you could do that! That's brilliant! I'm absolutely coming along.'

'So am I,' Senait chimed in.

'Guys, I love the enthusiasm,' said Amen. 'But we need at least one person to stay back and be on the lookout.'

'Why have one person?' Senait closed her eyes and bowed her head. 'When we could have four?'

Suddenly, accompanied by what sounded like the crack of a whip, a fully formed, identical clone of Iska appeared in the room. Before the girls could even react, Iska's clone was joined by another clone, then another, until there were four clones staring silently at their real counterparts.

'I seriously don't think I can ever get used to this,' said Amen as she eyed her clone warily.

'You just wait till I figure out how to give them a full range of emotions,' Senait replied with a laugh.

'Right,' said Iska, drumming her fingers repeatedly on the keyboard of the laptop. 'Aito, I've just emailed you a couple of photos in addition to whatever yous find ahead of tomorrow—'

'Tomorrow?' Aito interrupted, already scanning through the pictures on his phone. 'I thought we were going tonight?'

'Are you crazy?' said Amen, exchanging a look of incredulity with the other girls. 'We can't go tonight.'

'Why not?' Aito replied, exchanging a confused look with Lake.

'Because we haven't planned things out,' said Amen, scanning the room for a consensus while the girls covertly avoided her eyes. 'Plus, Aunt Nikki is addressing the senior girls tonight at ten p.m.'

'Yeah, right after she talks to the senior boys at half-nine,' Aito retorted. 'I'd say it's about the Debs. Look, it's perfect, we'll leave after lights out. And as for making plans, we can do that right now.'

Although Amen was determined not to acknowledge it, Aito's argument was compelling. In fact, his case was so solid she now looked to Iska for a counterargument, but her sister's expression said it all—she was on his side.

'Amen, listen,' said Iska. 'I understand where you're coming from, but you need to remember how important time is in all this; Aito is right: we have to move fast. Please come on board with this one.'

Without even shifting her gaze, Amen could tell all eyes were trained on her, nervously waiting for her to confirm whether she was in or out.

'Like I have a choice,' she finally said, forcing sighs of relief from the others.

'You never did,' said Aito with a triumphant grin. 'Now we've established I'm right, what's the plan?'

Amen may not have succeeded in convincing Iska and the others to postpone their trip to Trinity College, but she could at least take pride in being right that there would be a few logistical challenges to overcome before getting there. It had taken them the entire evening and numerous absurd iterations to come up with a reasonable plan to get into the library. Yet, as she and the girls headed to the common room for the meeting with Aunt Nikki, not one of them fully grasped the finer details of their hastily prepared road map.

'Wait, I forget,' whispered Rima, as the four girls searched for a spot to perch in a room full of chattering girls. 'Where did we say we would rendezvous again?'

'We decided on the cuckoo's nest.' Senait whispered back.

Rima nervously waved at a girl trying to get her attention from across the room. 'Is that the codename for the bathroom or atrium?' she asked.

'The bathroom,' Iska replied through gritted teeth. 'Look, if yous want to go over the details of the plan one more time, feel free. But you need to stop talking right now; Aunt Nikki is here.'

Iska had not minced her words. Their matron was in the room. Aunt Nikki might have possessed the superhuman ability to move at breath-taking speed, but it was her more mundane ability to command attention in virtually every space she walked into that made her so revered at Digglefield.

'Thank you all for meeting with me,' said Aunt Nikki, as she settled against the empty ping-pong table resting just a few feet from Iska and Amen. 'As you know, your Debs is coming up in a few days…'

Aito's guess was right after all. At the top of the agenda for this gathering was their school ball, or rather, the lack of it. Iska was certain Aunt Nikki had called the meeting to inform them that the Debs would be cancelled, and who could blame her? The bright, unrelenting lights flashing in the murky skies were a clear indication that the storm was not going away anytime soon. While bidding a final farewell to their classmates with whom they had shared a few memorable years would have been nice, ensuring they didn't get swept away by a flood or struck by lightning was undeniably a much higher priority for Aunt Nikki.

Although she was already mourning the Debs, Iska was well aware that she had more pressing desires than wearing a ball gown. While she watched Aunt Nikki carry on with her speech, Iska gently took Senait's hand in hers.

Hey, she whispered into Senait's head. *Get hold of Rima and have her do the same with Amen.*

Senait followed Iska's instructions and casually leaned into Rima, who in turn slumped her head against Amen's shoulder, creating the appearance that all four girls were passively listening to Aunt Nikki when, in reality, they were about to have a meeting of their own.

But just as they all connected, Aunt Nikki said, '…as such, the venue has been moved. We shall have your school Debs here!'

A rustle of excitement moved through the grouping of senior girls.

Did yous hear that? thought Rima a little too enthusiastically, causing the girls to wince at the sharpness of her inner voice. *We're having Debs here, in Digglefield!*

Yeah, Rima, we did, Senait replied, rolling her eyes. *I'll be honest though, I thought Nikki was about to tell us Debs had been cancelled.*

So did I, Iska chimed in. *But that's not why we're here.*

Why are we here then? thought Amen, her eyes still fixed on Aunt Nikki, unlike Senait and Rima, whose heads swayed left and right clumsily.

Because I want us to go over the plan one more time. We have one shot at this, and as you've just heard Aunt Nikki say, we'll be prepping for the ball in the next couple of days. So, if anything, the importance of our trip tonight just quadrupled; we can't mess it up. Iska allowed a pause for her words to sink in before she continued. *Right after the meeting, we'll meet up in the bathroom— not the atrium and* definitely *not the rooftop. Then Senait will create clones of us who'll go to the bedroom to act as decoys while we wait for Aito to come get us right after lights out. Any questions?*

I have one, thought Rima. *I know Aito blinks and all, but how will he find his way to the girls' bathroom? In the dark, no less.*

I already sent him a few photos of the bathroom. Iska replied confidently.

That's not creepy at all.

Amen's sarcasm stung Iska, mainly because she knew it was wrong to give the boys access to such a private part of the girls' dormitory. But, with minders patrolling every inch of Digglefield and the boys potentially running into other girls in either their bedroom or the girls' common room, the bathroom was truthfully the most ideal place to meet them without being seen.

Any other questions? said Iska.

What happens when we're caught? Amen's voice held no humour.

Jesus, not this again, thought Iska, her vexed sidelong glance finding its target. *Why do you always have to be so negative?*

And why do you have to always be so impulsive? Amen's last word ended with a sharp whistle that cut through the girls' heads like a knife slicing effortlessly through butter.

You two need to simmer down right now, thought Senait. *Nikki is nearly done with the meeting, which means we need to leave soon.*

Aunt Nikki, who was now slipping her little notepad into the back pocket of her jeans, cleared her throat. 'You all know the standards we hold ourselves to in this house,' she said. 'Don't let it waver on Sunday; but please, above all else, have fun because you all deserve it. Have a good night.'

Trailing behind a group of girls, Amen and Iska were just about to exit the common room when Aunt Nikki called out to them, causing Senait and Rima, who were waiting by the doorway, to each palm their forehead in panic.

'I thought I might have a quick word with both of you,' said Aunt Nikki as she approached them. With the two minders who had accompanied her also leaving, the common room was now empty. 'Um, how are you two keeping?'

'Good,' said Iska and Amen, the latter trying to recall if she had ever seen Aunt Nikki act so awkwardly.

'Good, good,' said Aunt Nikki as she rubbed the palm of her hands along the sides of her jeans before tucking them into the back pockets. 'Look, you two understand why you were grounded, right?'

'We do,' Amen and Iska replied in unison. This was not the time to express their opinions on whether or not they deserved to be punished. The focus now was on carrying out their plan, and the longer this conversation continued, the less time they had to do so. 'Aunt Nikki, we need to go get ready for bed,' Iska added.

'Yes, yes, I know,' said Aunt Nikki, her eyes desperately searching for something in the common room to focus on. They had missed it earlier, but it was now clear to Amen and Iska that Aunt Nikki had kept them behind for a reason—an important one given the timing. It was even more apparent that she wasn't exactly sure how to express what she needed to say, but she pressed on stubbornly. 'Believe me when I say that I completely understand why you two did what you did. You have so many questions, and while I may not have all the answers, I can still provide you with some, which I intend to do starting now...'

Suddenly, it seemed as though whatever Aunt Nikki had to say to Amen and Iska was more significant than any book the Old Library held. But as Amen waited intently for Aunt Nikki's next words, the phone in her back pocket began to vibrate.

'Aunt Nikki,' she said, doing her best to muffle the vibration of her phone with her hands. 'As much as Iska and I appreciate you wanting to share more with us, is it okay if we do this another time? It's just that it's really late, and as you've made clear, the next few days are going to be busy.'

Iska, realising what Amen was trying to do, yawned exaggeratedly.

'Yes,' said Aunt Nikki, clearing her throat. 'Yes, I suppose you're right. In that case, we'll make out time to have a chat after your Debs. How's that sound?'

'Grand!' said the twins. They were already halfway out of the common room.

As Amen and Iska sprinted up the stairs, the pendulum clock on the first landing informed them that they had just a little over seven minutes to gather everything they needed from the bedroom before reaching the rendezvous point in time for lights out. Upon entering the room, they were greeted by four girls who were as familiar with the environment as the people who actually lived in it.

'Senait must have gone ahead to create the clones while they were waiting for us,' said Iska, quickly grabbing a pair of trainers. 'We have to hurry.'

The hallway leading to the bathroom was mostly empty, with only a few girls on their way back to their rooms. With barely a minute left on the clock, Amen and Iska took advantage of the situation and moved in an awkward walk-run hybrid, reaching the bathroom just in time for the building to be plunged into complete darkness.

'I'm just after shitting myself thinking you-know-who found out our plan,' whispered Rima, panic evident in her voice. 'What took yous so long?'

Before the twins could offer an explanation, a strong scent filled the air.

'What's that smell?' said Senait, her soft voice echoing off the bathroom's tiled walls.

'That would be me,' said a voice that startled Rima, causing her to let out a squeal.

'Aito, you made it,' said Iska, while Amen pointed the brightened screen of her phone at him for reassurance.

'Why did you douse yourself in cologne?' said Rima.

'I thought I'd smell nice,' Aito replied.

'Yes, that makes sense,' said Rima, fighting the urge to sneeze. 'Because we're going to a disco, as opposed to a library.'

Aito, unsure of what to say, looked at Lake, who shook his head and said, 'Chap, I told you.'

'How Aito smells is the least of our worries,' said Iska, glancing over her shoulder towards the bathroom entrance. 'We have to leave, right now.'

Sensing the urgency in Iska's voice, the teenagers quickly formed a circle, reminiscent of the one they had assumed the day they left Dogudu. This time, however, it was

Senait and Rima who were about to experience the disorienting effect of a blink. Seeing Rima's trembling hand, Iska felt compelled to say something to calm her down, but Aito beat her to it.

'It's not so bad, I promise,' he said, squeezing Rima's hand a little tighter in his. 'I'll try to make our landing as smooth as possible.'

'Speaking of landings,' Amen whispered suddenly. 'Why didn't we hear yous blink in here earlier?'

'I thought no one noticed.' Aito's grin stood out even in the darkness. 'It's something I've been working on recently: controlling the impact of my landings—'

'I don't mean to be rude,' Iska interrupted. 'But why don't you give us a practical demonstration?'

'Oh,' said Aito, 'You mean like this…'

Iska wasn't sure if Aito had finished his sentence. Between struggling to catch her breath and finding her footing, she couldn't recall the past few seconds of her life. What she knew for certain was they were no longer in Digglefield because their bathroom didn't have towering bookshelves that spanned the entire building.

So, this is what the Old Library looks like, Iska thought to herself. However, it was Rima who voiced these words while Aito steadied her arm.

'That's a lot of books,' Amen whispered as she peered down at the ground floor. 'There's no way we can go through all of them; it'll take forever.'

'That's why we'll be here tomorrow night and the night after.' Iska was already scanning the spines of books that were easily older than all their years combined.

'Is no one worried that someone else might be in the building?' whispered Senait. 'Security, perhaps.'

'We're good.' Aito unzipped the large compartment of his backpack, revealing sweets, crisps, chocolate, and soft drinks. 'I already went around the building; it's as empty as the last bus to Limerick.'

'What's with the snacks?' said Rima.

'Since we're going to be here for most of the night—'
Aito tore open a pack of fizzy strawberry belts. '—I figured
if we had the munchies, at least we'd eat stuff that gave us a
burst of energy.'

Aito's reasoning made a lot of sense, and for most of
the night, the snacks kept Iska, Amen, and the others going
as they searched through the library, getting their hands on
whatever reading material they could find: magazines, jour-
nals, newspapers, scriptures—nothing was too old, too sacred, or too controversial to be read. However, by the early
hours of the morning, not even sweets could keep them
fully awake or focused. Slowly the conversation around the
desk shifted away from the cipher. Apparently, Ada and
Oshu were back in Lagos for a fundraising function they
were hosting, although they were still carrying out their own
investigations. Meanwhile, Walé had stayed back in London
to unwind for the remainder of his holidays. Senait and
Rima also shared with the group that they had each received
an offer from National College of Ireland. Senait was going
to study Early Childhood Education and Care, while Rima
opted for a BA in Journalism.

'Congratulations,' was the only word Amen and Iska
could muster as they were lulled to sleep by the heavy drumming of rain on the roof of the Old library.

'All right,' said Lake, his eyes half-closed from tiredness.
'We need to get back home. It's quarter to five, and we have
to be up at seven a.m. to set up decorations in the atrium.
One hour of sleep would make a lot of difference.'

Lake's tone was somewhat fatherly, but there were no
protests. If anything, each one of them, including Amen and
Iska, was thankful he'd made the call. With fatigued limbs
and groggy heads, the teenagers cleaned up after themselves
and stuffed their backpacks with as many books as they
could, with the promise of returning them later on. Although he needed no reminder, Aito made sure to blink the
girls into the bathroom with his newfound technique before
abruptly teleporting off, presumably to get Lake from the

library and head back home. Back in the room, Senait's clones would have easily passed for sleeping humans if their eyes hadn't been gleaming in the receding moonlight.

Lake had been wrong: one hour of sleep did nothing but make the girls crave even more rest. In fact, it was a struggle to get out of bed, and even more difficult to start decorating the atrium. But by noon, the progress they had made in sprucing up the space gave Iska and Amen a surge of energy. Since the theme for this year's Debs was *The Oscars after-party*, hundreds of silver and white balloons were inflated with helium and allowed to float gracefully across the hall. A group of boys had set up numerous rounded tables and draped them elegantly in sheer chrome tablecloths while another group adorned them with elaborate centrepieces of roses, hydrangeas, and lilies. A set of girls marked a designated space for professional photos, and set up the bar—although no one was entirely sure *who* was in charge of finding the beverages to stock it with. Lastly, a stage was set up where students would be presented with faux Oscars awards in recognition of their achievements in school.

In just a few hours of decorating, the atrium had already transformed into a glamorous red-carpet event, thanks to Aunt Nikki and her excellent coordination skills. But while Iska and Amen were fascinated by the preparation process, the cipher weighed heavily on their minds. Since they couldn't freely enter or exit the atrium while everyone else was diligently working, they devised a simple plan: take full advantage of their breaks to do some research, then meet up with the others after lights out and head off to the library.

The plan had worked flawlessly on the first attempt, and even on the second try the following day. However, there was one significant drawback: the cipher remained unsolvable. Nevertheless, as Iska watched Senait and Rima trying on their ball gowns with the Debs just a few hours away, she was nearly convinced that she had discovered a break-through.

'I can't believe you got these from Nigeria,' said Rima as she caressed the blue and white dresses hanging off the side of Amen and Iska's bunk bed. 'If they weren't bespoke, I would have swapped dresses with yous.'

'Which one would you have picked though?' Senait was fiddling with her earring.

'Both,' Rima replied. 'Either one, I don't mind. They're both stunning.'

'Well, now's a good time to be content with what you have 'cause Amen and Iska will be wearing them pretty soon.'

'Yeah, about that,' said Iska, her head bowed where she sat. 'I want to go to the Old Library; I feel like I'm finally starting to piece the puzzle together, but I need to look up something first.'

'Fair enough?' said Rima, shooting Senait and Amen a confused look. 'We'll do it after the ball.'

'No, I have to go now.'

'I knew it,' said Senait. 'I've been watching you all after-noon; I knew your mind was somewhere else.'

'But—but you can't go now,' said Rima. 'The ball starts in less than two hours.'

'I'm ready to go to the library,' Senait said matter-of-factly.

'You know I'll come too,' said Rima, a whisper of dis-appointment in her voice. 'I just thought—'

'No, no,' said Iska. 'Yous can stay. I'll convince Aito to take me. I won't be gone for long, I promise. I'll be back before the party starts.'

'Well, I appreciate you asking for my opinion,' Amen chimed in sarcastically. 'But I'm coming along.'

Iska was about to say something, but her tongue went numb at the glare Amen shot at her.

'Are yous sure?' said Rima, the look of guilt growing on her face.

'Yeah, you're grand,' said Iska, already tapping away at her phone. 'I just sent Aito a text; if he agrees to blink us to the library, I'll leave my phone with yous, just in case…'

Aito wasted no time replying to Iska's text and unsurprisingly agreed to blink Iska and Amen, but on one condition: he and Lake would stay with them in the library. As much as Iska appreciated the gesture, she really didn't want to be a distraction to anyone's evening. However, after a few back-and-forth text messages failed to convince the boys, she had to concede defeat.

With the bathroom full of senior girls either doing their hair, applying makeup, or taking showers, and the atrium bustling with event planners and supervisors, the rooftop terrace seemed to be the only logical place for Amen and Iska to meet Lake and Aito. Fortunately, all four of them were wearing tracksuits and hoodies because the terrace was being pounded by heavy rain. Racing against time and trying to avoid getting soaked, Aito quickly blinked them to the library.

'What is it you're looking for?' asked Lake.

Iska frantically scanned through the books in the theology aisle. 'I'm not exactly sure.' She pulled a few hardbacks from a shelf and flipped rapidly through the pages of one. 'But I admit that I was wrong for dismissing Aito and Senait's theories the other day. There seem to be religious and temporal themes within the brain-teaser; I just need a few minutes to read and think.'

A few minutes quickly turned into an hour as Aito, Amen, and Lake waited for Iska to make a breakthrough, to make sense of all the scribblings she had made on a piece of paper, to provide them with something concrete to work with.

'I know how important this is.' Aito's voice filled the silent hall. 'But the ball starts in thirty minutes. Iska, is there no way this can wait until tomorrow?'

Iska raised her head slightly, as if about to give Aito an

answer, but then buried it even deeper into the book she was reading, prompting a sigh from Aito.

Amen glared at him. 'What's your problem?'

'Are you serious?' Aito replied, his voice laced with frustration. 'Don't do that; don't act like this past week we haven't made ourselves available whenever you needed us. How many times do you get to experience a ball?'

'Then leave!' Amen's words echoed through the library. 'No one asked yous to stay in the first place.'

'Guys!' said Iska, interrupting what was quickly turning into an argument. 'I think I've cracked it.'

19. REUNION

Before anyone could react, Iska put a finger to her lips and then stretched out both of her hands. Understanding what her gesture meant, Amen, Iska, and the boys took hold of each other's hands, forming a circle at the table.

What do you mean you've cracked it? Aito was the first to speak. *You've figured out the cipher?*

Yes, Iska replied. *Some of it, at least. I still don't understand the core of the message, but it seems to be a map of some sort.*

I'm not sure I understand you, thought Amen while the boys nodded in agreement.

I'll explain, starting with the first paragraph of the cipher, thought Iska. *If I remember correctly, it says, "Two scores of men plus eleven beasts search for the rising fire." What's the hottest thing you can think of that floats?*

For a few seconds, three pairs of eyes shifted from side to side, pondering the question. Then Amen tilted her head slightly. *The sun?*

Correct! Iska was relieved she didn't have to provide the answer. *And where does the sun rise?*

The east, Lake responded immediately.

Correct again, thought Iska, aware she was probably beginning to sound like a schoolteacher. *And of the four cardinal points—the four main compass directions—what lies left of the rising sun? I'll answer this one: north.*

Iska expected gasps of realisation or understanding, but instead, she received puzzled stares. *Don't you get it? The word "north" is related to the Old High German word "nord", and both of these words are descendants of the word "ner", which in modern-day English means "left" or "below". Two scores of men plus eleven beasts trudge along the coast of an island to the left below, trying to find the rising fire—*

Oh my God, Amen gasped.

Iska didn't need to say more; the expression on their faces told her everything.

I mean, I always knew you were smart, but the way your mind works… Aito was too impressed to finish his sentence.

What about the other parts of the cipher? Lake's expression was more serious now. *Did you find any other clues?*

Yes, thought Iska. *The second part of the cipher is much like the first. The men and beasts search for a fire that extinguishes at the feet of a dozen women, three heads removed, who tell tales of Hesperus, the Greek god. This book—* She tapped on one of the books she had been reading earlier, *—contains Greek mythology, and in their stories, Hesperus, the son of dawn goddess Eos, goes by many other names, such as "Evening star", "Supper", and the most important to this puzzle, "West".*

Why is "West" the most important name? Amen was trying really hard to make sense of all the information, but it hadn't quite clicked.

Because that's where the sun sets, and according to the cipher, "fire", which we've established is a metaphor for the sun, extinguishes at the feet of the women who tell tales of Hesperus. Get it?

They all nodded in response. *It makes a lot of sense now,* Aito added.

But if "left below" and "Hesperus" represent north and west, what does the part about the men, beasts, and women mean? What role do they play in all of this? thought Amen.

Iska let out a long breath. *That's the part I'm struggling with. Like I said earlier, I think it has something to do with a map—*

Coordinates, thought Lake, his eyes scanning the library in search of something. *It's not a map, it's coordinates to a location.*

All eyes darted to Lake.

How do you know this? Amen asked.

It's actually straightforward, Lake replied with a disappointed smile etched on his face as he finally connected the dots. *But easy to miss if you don't know what you're looking for. The cipher uses non-numerical quantifiers. Elementary stuff, you know? A brace means two; a dozen—twelve; a gross—twelve dozen; a score—*

Twenty, Iska interrupted.

Precisely, thought Lake. *Going by this logic, "two scores of men" means forty men, plus eleven beasts. That's fifty-one entities on an island in the north. While a dozen women, three heads removed, leaves us with nine women who tell tales in the west. Fifty-one degrees north and nine degrees west.*

For a long moment, they all just looked at one another as they each contemplated Lake's explanation.

We have to find a map or atlas, said Iska, breaking the silence in their heads.

On it, Aito replied before blinking off, while Amen fished her phone from her pocket and began typing away. In seconds, Aito was back with a massive book that was opened to a page listing the coordinates of prominent locations in Ireland and its surrounding territories.

'It says here,' he said, placing his finger on a spot in the atlas where the coordinates were inscribed, 'that "this is the location of Fastnet Lighthouse, which is built on Fastnet Rock, also known as Ireland's Teardrop".'

'It checks out.' Amen placed her phone on the table right beside the atlas for everyone to see. 'It's an islet just off the coast of County Cork. That's where our father is being held hostage—in a lighthouse on a miniature island.'

'We don't know that for sure,' said Lake.

'Yes, we do,' Iska replied defiantly. 'At this point, all the evidence points to Fastnet Rock, and—and I think we should go there, now.'

'Whoa!' Aito was already shaking his head.

'Have you lost your mind?' Lake's face showed more emotion than it ever had since Iska and Amen met him. 'You can't seriously be considering this. Do you want to get yourself killed?'

'She's right,' Amen chimed in. 'We have to. No one knows what he's been through or what he's going through right now, as we speak. There's no way I can go back to Digglefield knowing what I know now; I just can't—'

'—And that's fine,' said Aito, moving around the desk

to hold Amen's hand. 'But let's talk to someone who's in a better position to help, perhaps Nikki—'

'—No!' Iska didn't bother to wipe away the tears wetting her cheeks. 'No one else can be involved in this; the instruction was clear. We already took a gamble involving—' Iska caught herself mid-sentence. 'This is something we need to do by ourselves.'

Lake clasped his trembling hands around his head. 'But you two don't even know who or what is out there. A psychopath; a murderer? Who happens to be a Unix as well. Think this through, I'm begging you!'

'There's nothing to beg for,' said Iska, wiping her face with the sleeve of her shirt. 'Our minds are made up.'

Amen picked up her vibrating phone with her free hand. 'Lake, if it makes you feel any better, I'm a Unix as well; so is Aito, together we—'

'Oh no, no, no,' said Lake. 'There's no "we" because I'm playing no part in walking us into what is clearly a trap.'

'And that's fine,' said Iska, frustrated with Lake's behaviour. 'You're entitled to your opinion, and we respect that; you have to do what's best for you.'

'What about me?' said Aito.

'Yes Aito,' said Amen, looking at their interlocked hands. 'What about you?'

The silence amongst all four of them seemed to last for an eternity before Aito finally shook his head. 'I mean Lake is right, that this is extremely dangerous… But then again, when has anything dangerous ever stopped me?'

While Amen and Iska let out sighs of relief, Aito's words seemed to disappoint Lake, a disappointment that quickly turned into fury. 'I know you're prone to making harebrained decisions—' The impudence in Lake's voice seemed to shock even Aito. '—but this is a new low for you. The least you can do is get me the hell out of here, so I have an alibi.'

'You know, Lake,' Iska voice was surprisingly calm. I really can't believe you're doing this to us; you're letting us down when we need you the most. But I don't even hold it against you—you have to look after number one, right?'

Iska was hoping for a response from Lake, but he simply ignored her and began packing his bag.

'By the way, you remember in Dogudu when you asked me if I had seen a tower on the cliff in my trance?' Iska continued. 'I had said no because there wasn't… or I hadn't just noticed. But the second time I was on that cliff, I saw it—the tower. It was there, right at the edge of the cliff, beige and circular, kind of like the Martello on Ireland's Eye but cleaner.'

Iska wasn't exactly sure what she thought giving Lake this piece of information would do, but the bewilderment on his face and the tremor of unease travelling through his body was not what she was expecting.

'You all right, buddy?' said Aito, quickly by Lake's side. He, too, had noticed the disturbed look on his friend's face.

'I've changed my mind,' said Lake, his face growing paler by the second. 'I'm coming with you guys.'

'What? How come?' The library was quiet enough for everyone to hear Aito's question, yet Lake completely ignored it, choosing instead to resume stuffing his backpack, but at a much faster pace this time.

How did you know saying that would get him to change his mind? thought Amen, still eyeing Lake suspiciously.

I didn't, Iska replied. 'Lake what's going on? Just a few seconds ago you were hell-bent on having nothing to do with this. What changed your mind? What does the tower mean?'

'I—I can't explain,' said Lake, tapping rapidly on his phone before pocketing it. His countenance had changed again—this time from fear to an expressionless state. 'At least not right now.'

'Okay? So, you don't think what we're doing is dangerous anymore?'

'No, I do. And I still don't want you to go, but since I have no chance of convincing you otherwise… I just want to help.'

It made no sense, Lake's sudden turnaround. Iska knew there was more to it than what he was letting on. She wanted to press further, but she was also conscious of the fact that every second spent interrogating him left more time for her father to be tortured by the hands of his captor. 'Fine,' she finally said.

Although very strange, Lake's newfound willingness to join the group was welcome; so much so that everyone tried to match his pace as they made preparations to leave the library. Aito had looked up a good number of pictures of Fastnet lighthouse from every imaginable angle. In the day-time, the lonely island was a sight to behold, with its jagged rocks protruding from the ocean, giving it a welcoming feel—a stark contrast to the gloomy aura it assumed by night. Although they wished their circumstances were dif-ferent, Iska, Amen, and the boys knew from the dark, cloudy skies and unyielding storm that an unforgiving expe-rience awaited them on the island.

But before embarking on the unnerving trip to the light-house, there was the issue of the ball to address. 'I missed a few calls from Senait and Rima,' said Amen, as she scrolled through her phone. 'They also sent some messages. They say that the party has just started and the crowd's growing. What should I say to them?'

'They're going to hate us for this,' said Iska. 'But tell them we'll be in the library a bit longer; tell them we're close to the answer.'

'What if people get suspicious?'

'Tell Senait to make clones of us wearing our dress,' Iska replied, zipping up her jacket. She turned her gaze to Lake and Aito. 'And clones of them too.'

'What will the boys wear?' said Amen, prompting a mo-ment of silence until Aito cleared his throat.

'Yous give me a few seconds,' he said before teleporting away. True to his word, Aito reappeared in the library no more than five seconds later. 'I stashed our tuxedos in the girls' bathroom, under the sink closest to the entrance. Problem solved.'

'Aito, you really do make hare-brained decisions.' A faint smile crossed Iska's worried face.

With all the excuses sorted, Iska, Aito, and Lake watched as Amen exchanged text messages with the girls until she finally clicked her phone off. 'They're not happy, but they'll do it. They want us back soon.'

Soon. The word served as a reminder to Iska and Amen that there was a real possibility that neither of them would ever return from this journey. Compared to moments ago when their adrenaline was surging and their confidence soaring, Lake's suggestion to proceed cautiously was beginning to sound wise. But it was too late to turn back now; Aito had finished analysing the pictures, and with his arms outstretched, he was ready to go. Exchanging one last glance, Amen and Iska took hold of Aito and Lake's hands...

'Where are we?' Amen could barely hear herself over the loud whistling wind and the hard drumming of rain against her jacket's hood.

'On a helipad!' screamed Aito, somehow managing to catch the question. He pointed towards the island's lighthouse with urgency. 'We need to get in there!'

It seemed unwise to enter a building where they could potentially be ambushed by anything, but with the wind threatening to sweep Amen and Iska into the ocean, they had no other choice.

Finding a way into the lighthouse proved to be another challenge altogether. After circling the rocky island for several minutes, stumbling and slipping along the way, the teenagers finally discovered what appeared to be an entrance. Pushing past the stained-green steel door, Amen, Iska, and the boys were immediately greeted by the strong smell of petrol, accompanied by the distant hum of a generator somewhere within the building. As they climbed from the ground floor using a spiral staircase attached to the wall, they were met with the musty odour of mould. Under different circumstances, the nauseating smell of petrol would have prevailed over the smell of mould, but the decaying state of the lighthouse meant that the musty fumes lingered on.

Upon reaching the first floor, the teenagers found a single room with its door wide open. In the centre of the room stood a tall white rectangular box with an array of thick, multicoloured cords extending from its base and running both inside and outside the room.

'This is the generator that powers the lighthouse,' said Lake, his voice barely audible over the humming machine. 'I'm no expert, but a generator should constantly be attended to when it's running.'

Lake's words hinted that something was already awry; that they were possibly being lured into a trap. However, instead of pausing to reflect on the unmistakable dangers posed by an unmanned generator in a lighthouse situated in the middle of the sea, Iska proceeded up the stairs, with the others briefly following suit.

The second floor differed from the first in several ways. Instead of a single room, it had two separate rooms. Unlike the first floor, which housed a generator, the rooms on the second floor contained wooden bunk beds and wardrobes. But despite the distinctions between the two floors, there was one significant similarity: the second floor was completely empty as well. This same emptiness greeted Iska, Amen, and the boys as they climbed the stairs to the third floor and then the fourth floor, where they found a kitchen.

Upon entering a dining room on the fifth floor and finding it empty, the teenagers' nerves were stretched to breaking point. Nothing made sense; the entire building was empty, yet an undeniable feeling of something or someone lurking in the shadows hung in the air, intensifying Amen and Iska's unease. Just as they were about to leave the dining room and begin their descent down the tower, a faint hum floated down from above. It was delicate and melodic, distinct from any of the mechanical sounds they had heard on their way up.

'I thought this was the topmost floor?' Amen whispered, her eyes darting around in confusion.

'So did I,' Iska replied, her gaze fixed on the ceiling. 'But now I think about it... the room with the lamp should be the last floor.'

Aito, closest to the doorway, briefly peered outside the dining room. 'There are no other stairs out there,' he said.

A moment of silence passed as Iska, Amen, and the boys contemplated the possibility of another way up. Then, without a word being exchanged, they each began scouring the dining room for any signs of an entrance.

'Guys,' Aito whispered, beckoning Iska, Amen, and Lake to join him. 'I found something.'

'What is it?' said Iska, her eyes fixed perplexedly on the sophisticated wall panelling in front of them.

'Don't yous see it?' Aito responded, tracing an invisible line along the wall's surface. 'I think it's a hidden entrance.'

Still unable to see anything, Iska was about to question Aito's sanity when the flashlight from Lake's phone illuminated a narrow groove etched deep into the wall. So subtle and inconspicuous, yet now strikingly prominent in the light, the groove ran along the length of the light green panel on two sides, forming what seemed to be a sizeable door.

'Anyone know how to open it?' said Aito while he scanned the corners of the wall.

'From my experience,' Lake whispered, 'hidden doors usually have a pressure point. If we can find that, the wall should give way.'

Without hesitation, all four of them began to feel the wall, running their hands along its engravings, hoping to discover a hidden pressure point. Meanwhile, the humming continued overhead. At this point, there was no doubt that the melodic yet ominous sound was coming from a human; the question was: to whom did it belong?

Click, Click. The wall finally let out a soft sigh and swung open, revealing a two-metre-tall ladder bolted to a brick wall. Directly above them was a steel mesh flooring, serving as another level. Iska and Amen stared at the ladder with concern, their minds willing to climb up to the next level, but their bodies paralysed by fear. Sensing their hesitation, Lake decided to take charge.

'Wait here,' he whispered as he moved silently towards the ladder. He turned around and signalled with his hands that he would go up to check if the coast was clear.

Amen and Iska tried to protest, but Lake's hands and feet were already in motion, working their way up the rungs of the ladder. When Lake reached the sixth floor, he peered down through the opening above the topmost rung and gave them a thumbs-up.

Feeling a little less afraid, Iska, Amen, and Aito climbed up the ladder to join Lake. Up there, they found him staring at a door painted the same light green as the wall panel below. Unlike the panel, this door had a knob with a reptilian appearance. However, it was not the knob's design or its blacker-than-black colour that drew Amen and Iska closer to it. It was the song being sung by a melodious voice on the other side of the door.

Iska's hand was about to encircle the doorknob when Amen's thoughts startled her. *Whatever or whoever we see in there, we stick to the plan.*

The plan. For a brief moment, Iska closed her eyes, allowing the plan they had hatched up just before leaving the library to resurface in her memory. When her eyes reopened, she took hold of the knob, twisted it, and pushed the door open.

'—Row, row, row your boat, gently down the stream. Merrily, merrily, merrily, merrily, life is but a dream—'

Now it made sense why the song was so recognisable. During their preschool years, Amen and Iska had to sing it during morning assemblies. However, their school recitation was never quite as good as Aré's version, not only because she had tweaked the lyrics to make it more interesting but also because singing it with her on Saturday mornings while pretending to help with chores had become sort of a ritual for Amen and Iska. But as they grew older, they cared less and less about the song; by the time Aré's funeral came around, it had been long forgotten. Nursery rhymes were meant for children.

This then raised the question: why was a red-headed man sitting on a mattress without any bedding or bed frame singing it?

'You know,' the man said, his head still bowed, face still obscured, a large jute bag wriggling on the floor beside his feet. 'I'm not at all surprised you involved other people; I knew I'd be foolish to believe you'd take my words seriously. Why do you think I have this bag beside me? Why do you think—'

'Now, Aito!' screamed Iska.

The plan Iska and Amen had concocted was simple: they would find and identify their father, free him, and then Aito would blink them all out of the lighthouse as quickly as possible to avoid any confrontation. Everything seemed to be on track as Aito teleported right in front of the red-headed man, grabbed the jute bag, and teleported back to where they stood. Amen and Iska kept their eyes fixed on the man, whose head was still bowed, but they could hear Aito pulling apart the strings that bound the tip of the jute bag.

'Oh, did I forget to mention,' the man finally said. 'I am a twin myself.'

The crunch was swift but loud enough to startle Amen, Lake, and Iska, who turned around to see Aito unconscious, blood trickling down his nose. The perpetrator of this act was another red-headed man who had emerged from the jute bag and was now dragging Aito out of the room by his feet. Determined to save Aito, Lake was about to make a move towards the man when he suddenly pulled out a pistol from a holster under his shirt and aimed it at Lake. However, instead of cowering in fear, astonishment filled Lake's face.

'Finn?' he said, stumbling backwards until he bumped into Iska and Amen, whose gazes shifted between the stranger in the bed and his twin with the gun. 'Finnian, is it really you?'

'How do you know that name?' said the man on the bed, his raised head revealing a sickly pale face. His deep emerald eyes now studied their faces, absorbing the information they provided.

Lake's lips hadn't even parted when the man began to laugh, his deep voice reminiscent of the stranger from Iska and Amen's dreams. *Click*. Amen and Iska turned around to find that Aito and the man with the gun were no longer in the room.

'For your own good, don't bother going after them,' said the man, who was now on his feet. 'I'll be candid with you; your friend is as good as dead. If you try to escape this room to…save him…a similar fate awaits you.'

'Why are you doing this?' Amen's voice trembled with fear and anger, yet the words managed to find their way out of her mouth. 'What do you want from us?'

'Why am I doing this?' said the man, a mocking laugh hovering on the edge of his words. 'Good question. Dad, why don't you help them out with this one?'

Dad? Iska and Amen's eyes darted around the golden-lit room, searching for another human, a reference point for the question. But there was no one in sight. The twins did the next best thing and followed the man's gaze, which fell squarely on Lake.

'I'm sorry.' Lake's eyes were filled with tears, his forehead creased with worry. His trembling lips barely able to form the words. 'Finnian—'

'Don't call me that!' The disgust in the man's voice lingered in the room, though he swiftly regained his composure. 'For the rest of your wretched existence, if you must address me, it is Cormac.'

Instantly, the mention of the name sparked a memory in Amen and Iska's minds. This was the man who had stolen the Book of Clans, the maniacal individual Professor Rupert Bailey had warned them to avoid if they valued their safety. And yet, here they were, confined in a room with him, wondering what possible connection he could have to Lake.

'Since a cat's got your friend's tongue,' said Cormac, his eyes piercing holes in Amen and Iska. 'I'll answer your question. But before I do, allow me to give some context—I hope you aren't in a hurry?'

As if Iska and Amen had any choice.

'Many years ago, a boy was born into a noble Irish family. He had a beautiful, powerful mother and a regal father who were destined to oversee vast Irish lands for many years, eventually passing the baton to the boy when he came of age. The ultimate cliché story, right? Some might say it's very pedestrian—boring and predictable. However, there are others who would call it tradition, and I agree with the latter camp. Sometimes, predictability is necessary. Unfortunately, this was not the case for the boy's father, who decided he wanted nothing to with tradition and abandoned his wife and young son—'

'—That's not true—'

'—Keep shut, you old fool!' Cormac's words carried a sting. 'You had your chance to speak. You've had years to speak! But you remained silent; I suggest you continue to do so.'

Lake obediently complied with the command, mostly out of distraction. The expression on his face hinted at a person whose mind had wandered millions of miles away from the unfolding scenes before him.

'Where was I?' said Cormac, shifting slightly from the spot where he had been standing since he got to his feet. 'So, the boy who once had great things destined for him was left without a father and a grieving mother. For years, the boy hated his estranged father, but not nearly as much as he hated himself. For years, he blamed himself, cursed himself, hurt himself! For making his father run away.'

Telling this story seemed to fill Cormac with heat, as within seconds he had unbuttoned his flannel shirt and was now rolling up the sleeves of his undershirt. Under different circumstances, his behaviour wouldn't have been out of the ordinary, except that the room was freezing cold.

'But it gets even worse,' Cormac continued. 'While the boy struggled to make sense of his reality, everyone in his kingdom neglected him. It did not matter that he was heir to a formidable empire; he was shunned. "The disturbed, broken prince," they all called him, except for one person: his mother. After climbing her way out of the pits of despair, she rescued the boy from the clutches of his demons. It was not easy, but she moulded him, shaped his confidence, and provided him with everything he needed to thrive. And thrive he did. I'm sure by now you have an idea where this story is heading?'

Despite their attentiveness to Cormac's story, neither Amen nor Iska could claim to understand why he was sharing all of this. It wasn't for lack of trying on their part, though. Between not knowing whether Aito was still alive and Lake's near catatonic state, the twins were struggling to prevent their own minds from unravelling.

'Of course, you don't,' Cormac shook his head in disappointment. 'Don't worry, I'll help you two along. Very quickly, the boy became a man filled with drive, ambition, and the respect of everyone in the kingdom. The once timid prince was now a brilliant king. But this king still yearned for his father, so he set out to find him. Years of searching proved fruitless, until seven years ago when the king discovered that his father had fallen in love with a commoner and, to make matters worse, had fathered children with her. She had given him twin girls.'

Suddenly struck by an epiphany, Amen and Iska began to see everything fall into place, thanks not only to Cormac's story but also to all the clues that had been littered around them their whole lives; clues that had been hiding in plain sight. It was all like a jigsaw puzzle, with the missing pieces finally fitting together to reveal a deeply sorrowful and disturbing picture.

'I know the look on your faces,' Cormac scoffed. 'I had the same look when I discovered that my own father, a former dignitary, had procreated with a lowlife and effectively made me related to mongrels.'

'Our mother is not a lowlife!' said Iska, her expression a mix of fear and anger.

'Oh, I beg to differ. How else do you explain what has happened to your pitiful father? Just look at him,' Cormac pointed to Lake, who was crouched on the floor, still lost in his own world. 'Once a noble man, he allowed himself to be seduced by your mother, and now he's running around pretending to be a teenager. You cannot convince me that your mother was not a lowlife. She certainly begged like one when I ended her insignificant life.'

Cormac's final words were enough to trigger Iska's charge towards him, and he appeared all too eager to have her within arm's reach. With a powerful punch, he struck Iska in the face, causing her to collapse to the floor in an unconscious heap.

A feeling of déjà vu washed over Amen as she watched Iska lay motionless on the floor, curled up like a foetus, just as she had been the day Maeve, the bully, knocked her out all those years ago. At that time, Amen had felt powerless, unable to intervene.

This time was different.

In the left corner of the room, there was a well—a hidden feature of the lighthouse that had gone unnoticed by everyone except Amen; she had sensed the presence of water within it from the moment they entered the building.

Drawing from the depths of the well, Amen unleashed a forceful jet of water towards Cormac in an attempt to subdue him. However, upon impact, instead of engulfing him, the water transformed into billowing steam, shrouding the lamp above. It was then that Amen saw the flames emanating from Cormac's hands. They were devouring her wall of water and steadily advancing towards her.

Amen fought to keep the fire at bay, but its intensity was overwhelming. The flames licked at the tips of her fingers, threatening to engulf her. With her stamina quickly depleting, the threat of Amen being completely incinerated was about to become a grim reality when an invisible force swept Cormac off his feet and slammed him into the floor with a bone-crushing thud. At first, Amen thought Lake had regained his senses and fought off Cormac, but after wiping sweat and tears from her eyes, she realised it was Iska who had subdued him.

'Are you okay?' said Iska, extending a hand to help Amen to her feet.

How did you do that? thought Amen, still too weak to speak.

Before Iska could provide an answer, a sinister cackle echoed from where Cormac lay. 'This is perfect,' he said, rising to his feet, blood gushing from a gash in his forehead. 'I missed my first opportunity to get rid of both of you; I won't make the same mistake this time.'

What followed next was a spectacle the twins were all too familiar with: limbs elongating into sinewy appendages, flesh peeling away from bone. Cormac was undergoing a transformation, but unlike Oshu, Ada, and Jimba, he wasn't morphing into an ordinary animal. No, this creature lacked hair or fur. Instead, it possessed black scales, webbed wings, claws that punctured the floor, and a mouth radiating a vivid orange glow—this was a dragon.

Amen and Iska stood in awe of the majestic beast before them. Yet, their astonishment quickly transformed into fear as Iska swiftly conjured a barrier of air, which Amen reinforced with a layer of water, to intercept an incoming fireball. Hard as they tried to stave off Cormac's attack, he seemed to possess an endless supply of flames, and Amen and Iska quickly realised that their makeshift shield wouldn't hold much longer. Cormac had taken Aré's life, and now he was on the brink of taking theirs. Yet, as each sister looked into the other's eyes, there was no trace of fear. Deep within their hearts, they knew that they were about to be reunited with their mother.

With their eyes closed and muscles relaxed, Amen and Iska let down their wall of water and air, ready to be consumed by a fire they hoped would grant them a swift and painless death. However, instead of being engulfed in scorching flames, they were greeted by a biting cold. Iska and Amen cautiously opened their eyes, each of them wondering whether they were already dead, only to witness a sight that truly astonished them. Before them stood a light green, serpentine creature, exhaling icy breath from its mouth. The target of its frosty assault was Cormac.

In an instant, the room began to fill with water as fire clashed with ice.

'Where's Lake?' screamed Amen. She struggled to keep herself and Iska from being submerged in the rising pool. But Lake was nowhere to be seen.

Then, realisation struck the twins. Lake hadn't been washed away; he had transformed into the green Oilliphéist, and it appeared he was defending them against Cormac, despite Cormac gaining the upper hand.

In a blur of motion, Cormac abruptly stopped his fiery assault and willingly took a full blast of ice to his chest. Surprisingly, this self-sabotaging act allowed him to close the distance between himself and Lake. With swiftness and precision, he sank his teeth into Lake's scaly neck, mercilessly tearing away a huge chunk of flesh.

'No!' screamed Iska and Amen in unison as Lake collapsed to the floor, writhing in pain.

With Lake out of the way, Cormac redirected his attention to the twins. Despite his injuries, he staggered towards them, his fiery gaze fierce and unwavering. Uncertain of their next move, Iska raised her hands, preparing to mount a last defence; but Cormac let out a guttural sound that sent shivers down their spines.

'You two don't understand,' he said, leaving Iska and Amen stunned. 'My conviction is resolute; you die tonight.'

Cormac was on the verge of unleashing the inferno brewing in his throat upon the twins when something powerful tugged him from behind. It was Lake, sinking his sharp teeth into Cormac's fin and forcefully dragging him towards the opposite end of the room. Cormac tried to resist, but his attempts to break free of Lake's grip were in vain. Then, to the horror of Iska and Amen, Lake shattered the wall behind him, wreathed his long, muscular body around Cormac, and hurled both himself and Cormac out of the lighthouse and into the depths of the dark sea.

For seconds, Iska and Amen stood frozen in place, their gaze fixed on the gaping hole in the wall. They wondered whether everything that had happened in the past ten minutes was real or merely an illusion; whether Lake, or even Cormac, would show his face again. But nothing happened.

Exercising caution, they waded through the pool of water until they reached the shattered wall. The winds howled and rain poured heavily, but there was no sign of life. Suddenly, something forcefully crashed through the front door of the room.

Neither Amen nor Iska could recall ever feeling such relief upon seeing Aunt Nikki, and to make things even better, she had a conscious but weakened Aito leaning on her.

'How did you find us?' said Iska as she and Amen rushed into Aunt Nikki's open arms for shelter.

'I'll explain everything.' Aunt Nikki planted a kiss on each of their heads. 'But we need to get out of here now.'

'But Lake is out there,' said Amen, unable to stop sobbing.

'We can't leave him,' Iska added, her voice quivering with pain.

'Girls, listen to me.' Aunt Nikki's face hardened. 'Whatever has fallen into that water is never coming back out; we need to leave. Aito, can you manage it?'

Aito, bruised and bloodied, managed a quick nod, and in an instant, they were gone.

Even with autumn well under way, the gravestones in Kilcock cemetery remained free of dead leaves. As Iska and Amen placed wreaths on their parents' graves, they couldn't help but wonder if this was a sign from them—a sign that Lake, Patrick, or Dad, depending on who knew him, was in a better place; a sign that they didn't need to mourn because he had willingly sacrificed his life to save theirs. Whatever the case, it bothered Amen and Iska that such an act of heroism couldn't be properly honoured, especially in Digglefield, where he was known and possibly loved by so many.

Lake had suddenly flown to the United States to fulfil his scholarship offer. That was the story circulating through the halls of Digglefield. But among the few who knew the truth, one of them refused to attend the funeral today, not only because the person whose death they were acknowledging had lied to him for years, but also because amidst all the lies, Lake had become his best friend, his family, his brother. Aito simply couldn't bear it.

If the occasion was too overwhelming for Aito, it didn't seem to faze Aunt Nikki, who spoke a few words before concluding the gathering to avoid arousing suspicion. Just as Amen and Iska were preparing to leave with Rima and Senait, Aunt Nikki called out to them.

'How are you two holding up?' she asked as the three of them walked along the asphalt path towards the main entrance of the cemetery, where their taxi was parked. 'I'm sorry I haven't been available. It's been a strange three weeks, with organising your father's—I mean, Lake's funeral and seeing some of your peers off to college.'

But we already know this, thought Amen, pretending to

ponder Aunt Nikki's words. *Why is she bringing it up?*

Because she has something more important to say to us, Iska replied.

'Look girls,' said Aunt Nikki, stopping in her tracks.

There it is.

'I don't know if you've made the connection already, but that night in the lighthouse, I was only able to reach all of you because of Lake. If he hadn't sent me a text before you guys left the library, this place might have become a permanent home for more than one of us. The point I'm trying to make is that your father, despite making a lot of mistakes, was a good man. Everything he did from the day you two were born was to keep you safe.'

Perhaps the weight of losing another person in her life was too heavy, because Aunt Nikki was now shedding more tears than Amen and Iska had ever seen. 'He made me promise to give you this.' She reached into the inner pocket of her coat and pulled out a medium-sized manila envelope. 'He said everything you needed to know was in it.'

Iska accepted the envelope. 'Please stay,' she said to Aunt Nikki, who was about to walk away. If anyone had earned the right to know the contents of the envelope, it was her. As Iska opened the envelope, she couldn't help but notice how light it felt considering its supposed importance. She peeled back the flap and pulled out a piece of paper, holding it up for everyone to see:

TO MY BELOVED ISKA AND AMEN,

If you are reading this, there is a possibility that I am no longer alive. While this may sound grim, please understand that it is a blessing that I have lived long enough to even write this letter. I am grateful to have watched you two grow, albeit from the shadows, into two amazing and strong ladies who are capable of achieving whatever you set your hearts to. Your mother would have been just as proud as I am, if not more proud.

I wish she were here; we all wish she were here. She had a remarkable way of making things right, of making anyone she crossed paths with feel seen and heard. That's why I fell in love with her. She understood every aspect of me; my past, my plights, my vices, my strengths, and my weaknesses.

She saw my complexities yet still accepted my proposal and bore two beautiful angels; our pride and joy. You both became the redemption of my present and the moral compass for my future. I swore I would protect both of you with every ounce of my being; I would be the father you needed and wanted at any moment at every stage of your lives. But unfortunately, my past caught up to me, forcing me to break those promises.

I never intended to hurt your mother, I never meant to hurt either of you. Words fail to express how deeply sorry I am for the pain I have caused. Time and again, I wish I had made different decisions in my life, maybe things would have been less messy. But then again, I realise that if things had been perfect, I may not have had the privilege of being your father. Instead of dwelling in regret, I decided after your mother's passing to stay as close as possible to both of you, to protect you from an unknown danger that lurked in the shadows. But I was determined to uncover the source of this danger, so much so that I involved you two by giving you your uncle's contact. Little did I know this would introduce us to a whole new world; the world of your mother.

I understand that your uncle hates me, and rightfully so. Yet, after spending time with him and his wonderful wife, Ada, I find solace in knowing they will take care of you. Everyone will take care of you; Aito, Nikki, Walé. Do you know why? Because both of you are good and pure.

My angels, I wish we had more time to truly know each other. However, I sense that my time here is coming to an end, and yours is just beginning. It saddens me that I will not see you two go on to do wonderful things in life, but I am at peace knowing that I will be reunited with your mother.

Always remember how immensely proud we are of you both.

Yours sincerely,
Dad

By the time Amen and Iska finished reading the letter, the top half of it was soaked with their tears. In fact, Iska might not have noticed the additional item in the envelope had her tears not left an outline on it. Her fingers searched within the envelope until they retrieved a photograph of her and Amen as babies, cradled in Aré's arms, with Patrick standing beside her, all of them smiling. More tears streamed down the twins' faces as they took in the photograph, each wondering why their lives had unfolded the way they did.

Even more frustratingly, Lake's letter had left Amen and Iska with a multitude of unanswered questions. However, a quick glance at Aunt Nikki and the expression on her face made it clear that she had no more answers or explanations to offer.

'If there's one thing I've learnt from this ordeal,' said Aunt Nikki as she resumed walking, 'it's that it is never too late to tell the people you care about how you truly feel.'

Their faces still moist with tears, Iska and Amen followed her, each of them reflecting on Aunt Nikki's words.

You know, Amen, thought Iska, wiping tears from the corners of her eyes. *Aunt Nikki is right. You can talk to me, I'm always here for you... Is there anything you want to tell me?*

Amen bit her bottom lip, unable to evade Iska's gaze, her sister's face slightly blurred because of the tears in her eyes. *No, not really.*

That's fine, thought Iska as they neared their taxi. *I'll wait until you're ready...*

SEABREEZE

ABOUT THE AUTHOR

Michael Enearu is a Nigerian-Irish author whose literary journey has taken him from the bustling streets of Lagos to the serene landscapes of Ireland. Growing up in Lagos, a city teeming with energy and culture, Enearu developed a deep appreciation for storytelling from an early age. Inspired by the rich oral traditions of his homeland, he began crafting his own tales, drawing upon the vibrant tapestry of Nigerian life for inspiration.

After completing his education, Enearu made the bold decision to embark on a new chapter of his life in Ireland. Immersing himself in the country's rich literary tradition and drawing inspiration from its lush countryside and ancient folklore, Enearu found a new muse for his writing.

Enearu's debut novel "SeaBreeze" is a captivating work of science fiction that seamlessly blends elements of Nigerian and Irish folklore. Set in a world where the boundaries between the natural and the artificial have blurred, "Sea-Breeze" follows the journey of young protagonists as they navigate a world on the brink of transformation.